Stealing Arthur

Stealing Arthur

A NOVEL BY

Joel Perry

BEAR BONES BOOKS

Stealing Arthur
Copyright © 2015 Joel Perry.

All rights reserved. No part of this work may be reproduced or utilized in any form or by any means, electronic or mechanical, including photocopying, microfilm, and recording, or by any information storage and retrieval system, without permission in writing from the publisher.

Published in 2015 by Bear Bones Books,
an imprint of Lethe Press, Inc.
118 Heritage Avenue • Maple Shade, NJ 08052-3018
www.lethepressbooks.com • lethepress@aol.com
www.BearBonesBooks.com • bearsoup@gmail.com

ISBN: 978-1-59021-586-9
Cover art and design by Staven Andersen
Book design by Peachboy Distillery & Designs

This book, in whole and in part, is a work of fiction and is a work of parody, as defined by the Fair Use Doctrine. Names, characters, places, and incidents either are the products of the author's imagination or are used fictitiously, and any resemblance to actual persons living or dead, businesses, corporations, brands, establishments, agencies, clubs, organizations, events, motion pictures, television or radio programs, songs, musical acts, media, websites, buildings, or locales is entirely coincidental.

    Library of Congress Cataloging-in-Publication Data

Perry, Joel.
  Chasing Arthur : a novel / by Joel Perry.
     pages cm
  ISBN 978-1-59021-586-9 (pbk. : alk. paper)
  1. Motion pictures--Awards--Fiction. 2. Los Angeles (Calif.)--Fiction. I. Title.
  PS3616.E792965C47 2015
  813'.6--dc23
                       2014047076

AS ALWAYS,
FOR MY FRED

Part One

Wednesday, March 8th, 2000

Michael Foster Fowler sipped another poison and made a sour face. He was in the paint department of the Hollywood Home Depot on Sunset tasting turpentines, varnishes, and stripping gels. He found them all unsatisfactory.

He wiped his mouth and moved to another section of the store, around and past a short, black man as fat as Marlon Brando with dreadlocks carrying a bottle of lethal looking weed killer. *Weed killer,* thought Fowler raising a thick eyebrow. He hadn't considered that. Fowler located the Ortho Weed-B-Gone, but he couldn't bring himself to try it. The giant colorful flowers on the stand-up display, the far-too-bright yellow sun, the happy smiling bumblebees, no, it was just too cheerful to endure.

He wandered farther down the aisle to another family of bottled death. He found a much more appropriately grim jug of Ortho-Klor Termite & Carpenter Ant Killer. The safety seal wasn't coming off. "It's insecticide," he growled, "it's *supposed* to be unsafe." Why, then, were they making it so hard to get at? It didn't make any sense — until, with a pang, he remembered something his mother had always told him: "God in His wisdom gave you to me because He knew you were too stupid for other mothers." With a sigh, he put the Ortho-Klor back on the shelf. This product was intended to poison people smarter than he.

In another aisle he found products for unclogging drains. Sampling them he found the lye crystals too dry and Liquid Plumr burned. He picked up a bottle of Drāno Max Gel.

The label described a witch's brew of highly aggressive acids designed to bubble and fizz through a long list of biological elements, foodstuffs, meat, proteins, lipids, basically all the things of which Michael Foster Fowler himself was made. Chemicals that would reach into his guts to destroy all that he knew was unholy, disgusting, and vile within him. He wondered if Drāno Max Gel came in cherry or mint.

Michael Foster Fowler left the Home Depot with two half-gallon jugs of Drāno Max Gel. He tossed the bag into the back of his rusty green '87 convertible and gazed west toward the setting sun. By this time tomorrow he would be dead. He would be dead and condemned to eternity in the fiery lake thrice-over. Once, for killing himself; twice, for his unclean thoughts and disgusting desires; and thrice, for what his mother would have called a wasted life. He remembered many things she had said to him over and over, like, "You're thirty-five, if you can't find a woman and give me a grandchild, at least make an impact. Cure cancer, do something important, but find a purpose so you don't embarrass God." Well, he couldn't cure cancer because, after all, she'd told him he was too stupid. Instead, she had died of it three years ago. Tomorrow he would be dead, too.

Dead and burning in hell for the sins of unnatural lust and suicide. But at least he'd be free of his mother. "Please, God," he said to the sun, "don't let her be in hell."

At midnight, Michael Foster Fowler poured the viscous Drāno Max Gel into jelly glasses he had lined up along the edge of the moldy sink in his tiny kitchen. The plan was to force himself to drink as many glasses as he could, as quickly as possible, dropping each one in the sink as he finished it, grabbing the next. He took a deep breath.

It was a somber moment. It needed something to drown out the bickering neighbors, the blaring TV from the family of ten upstairs, and the street people rummaging through the dumpster in the alley behind his building. He turned on the radio.

News. That wouldn't do. He switched stations. Advertisements, no. More news, something about the Arthur Awards. Rap, no. Country, no. Arthurs had been stolen. *There's gotta be a classical station, something serious,* he thought. Ads, ads, traffic, Arthurs. Some awful boy band, a stock-market report, sports, Spanish ads . . .

". . . stolen from a loading dock in Downey, California . . ."

Flaming Satan, he thought, *don't they play music on the radio anymore?*

". . . with the Arthur Awards ceremony just days away . . ."

Classical music! No, it's a car ad, blast it. Followed by some overweening deejay gushing over —

". . . the Arthurs! Hey, all Hollywood's on pins and needles, I hear Tom Hanks called the Institute of Motion Picture Artists and Technicians and said, 'Hollywood, we have a problem!'" The deejay yucked like a moron. "My, oh, my, fifty-five little gold men stolen," the deejay clucked. "Talk about *Gone With the Wind,* huh? Somebody over at World Deliveries musta had their *Eyes Wide Shut,* har-har-har!" It nauseated Fowler that this man should be getting paid to be on the air — but the subject hooked him. "Love the security over there in Downey. Hollywood's highest honor, and they let somebody who has no business near the things just walk off with fifty-five of 'em. I mean, Anna Paquin did that a few years back, but she only got away with one. Gotta wonder what the rest of the world thinks of this, huh? I mean, how embarrassing can ya get?"

Michael Foster Fowler's heart pounded, his head throbbed. Sparkling colored lights danced at the edges of his vision. It was a Message. It was Truth, smiting him like Balaam smote the ass in the presence of the angel. It was more than he could have hoped for only moments prior. It was *Purpose*!

All he had to do was consider the evidence: that afternoon he had been at a Home Depot — in *Hollywood.* While there he'd seen a man who looked exactly like Marlon Brando — a two-time *Arthur winner.* And hadn't he heard *Entertainment Tonight* wish The Monkees' Mickey Dolenz a happy birthday that very evening? — a happy *fifty-fifth* birthday? Michael Foster Fowler was shaking in the presence of the Almighty — who, he realized, had sent him twelve months of part-time detective experience as a mall security guard to prepare him for this. He steadied himself against the kitchen counter, weeping at how God had chosen him at this moment in his life for this task: *rescue these icons.*

He straightened up and saw the six glasses of Drāno Max Gel. One by one he poured them down the sink. He now had a part to play in God's Plan, a role in the universe, a sacred duty. And probably the fastest-draining sink in east Hollywood. Michael Foster Fowler had more than a purpose, he had a quest — *find those little golden naked men.*

And woe unto any who would stand in his way.

Thom pushed his grocery cart down a dimly lit alley on the edge of Hollywood. He was far too thin, off his meds, and crusted in filth from life on the street. His rusty cart overflowed with rags, blankets, and plastic bags of odds and ends he had scrounged from trashcans and dumpsters. Thom knew exactly what was in each bag. In the three large trash bags he knew he had 161 redeemable soda cans: fifty-one regular Coke, twenty-one Diet Coke, three Diet Caffeine-Free Coke, fifty-three regular Pepsi, fourteen Diet Pepsi, nine 7-Up, three Diet 7-Up, and two each of Mountain Dew, Orange Crush, Diet Dr. Pepper, plus one Sprite. Nobody drinks Sprite anymore. He pushed the unwieldy cart with one hand and pulled at his bedraggled beard with the other.

In the street lights' sputtering 3:00 A.M. glow, Thom saw a pile of white boxes nestled next to a tree on the other side of a chain link fence. He noticed a hole in the fence and slipped through. There were fourteen boxes, eighteen inches square, wrapped together in packing plastic on a wooden pallet. Thom pulled at the plastic until he freed one. With some difficulty Thom opened it to find four smaller boxes inside, packed so tightly that he couldn't get them out. Fourteen big boxes with four little boxes each. "Fifty-six little ones," Thom murmured. He tossed that larger box aside. He picked up another box, the weight inside shifted. It was also lighter and easier to open. Inside there were only three boxes in this one, loose, so he could dump them out on the ground. Thom adjusted his math. "Fifty-five. If all the rest of you are full," he told the stack of white boxes.

Using a penknife, he cut one of the smaller boxes open. He methodically peeled back the cardboard to discover two halves of Styrofoam, bound together with strapping tape. He beat it against the tree until the Styrofoam cracked. What he found made him shove it away in horror.

It was an idol worshipped by millions. A symbol of so much that was wrong with this world. Greed, obsession, money-lust, distraction, fame, arrogance, inhumanity. And here were boxes and boxes of them.

Eventually the shouting, competing voices in his head subsided so he could think. Thom picked up the golden graven image. He also grabbed the other two unopened boxes and put all three statuettes in the larger box. He folded the flaps and lobbed it over the fence, then thrust himself through the hole in the chain link.

They were despicable, evil idols. But a guy's gotta eat.

Thursday, March 9th

In the bright morning sun, Thom pushed his grocery cart forty-three blocks to a small, dark, shingled bungalow in Little Armenia behind Hollywood Boulevard. All the windows were covered with bars and one had a broken neon sign of a hand with the word "Palmist" beside it. He climbed the seven stairs to the porch and rang the bell.

A heavy dark woman in a paisley caftan opened the inside door, leaving the barred safety door on the outside closed. She raised a single eyebrow. "You again?"

"I have some things," Thom said. "Golden. Bad things but golden."

Madame Sylvia looked him up and down. "When did you last eat food?"

"Thursday."

She smiled. This would be easy. "Show me these things."

Thom unwrapped three heavy golden items from a blanket. Her pupils dilated. She counted to ten, then asked calmly, "How much?"

"I need seventy-five bucks. I can get meds at the center and a room for seventy-five bucks."

"Will they feed you?"

"I don't know. Sometimes."

"Wait here." She went into her cramped kitchen filled with plants that would never grow in the windowless light. She made a sandwich of two pieces of white bread, and a single slice of bologna. She put the sandwich on a Star Wars paper plate from the 99¢ Store and brought them into the living room where she did her readings. She set the food on a rickety table just inside the front door and told him, "I give you twenty."

"But I really need seventy-five bucks," Thom said too loudly. "Seventy-five!"

From behind the barred door she held up a twenty-dollar bill. "I only have this," she said. "But I will throw in this," and she produced the sandwich for him to see, holding it at his eye level behind the safety door. Thom's mouth opened. "How hungry are you now?" she asked. "Think."

Thom began moving agitatedly side to side. "I need more!"

"We all need more. We get what we get, then we die. Take the money and the food."

Thom looked down and closed his eyes. In a voice as broken as his shoes, he softly murmured, "Okay."

Eric Burgess walked down the long dark jetway tube into the light of his new life in Los Angeles. Carried along in the human flow, Eric realized his worn black slacks and white button-down

Oxford shirt that had been fine for weekend trips into Saint Louis from his home in Rosebud, Missouri, clearly would not do here.

Eric fought the crowd at the baggage carousel and then staggered outside to get a cab driven by a man who yelled at him in animated bursts, but not in English. Eric gave him a slip of paper with the only address he had in L.A.

There was a party going on in the charming little indigo blue house where the cab driver let him out. Eric double checked the address, Westbourne Drive in West Hollywood. He picked up his suitcase with everything he owned inside, and knocked on the door.

A tall, redheaded man opened the door. In a blinding burst of light, he took Eric's picture. While Eric tried to blink away the novas burned into his retinas, the man looked at Eric from his head to his feet. "My God, it's a homeless Mormon."

"Eric!" shouted a familiar voice, "you're here!" Eric's best high-school gal-pal, Suze, pushed the redhead to one side, "He's not homeless, Patrick, he's staying here."

"Not on the sofa, he's not," Patrick said letting the camera dangle from the rainbow-colored lanyard around his neck. "I didn't drink half a bottle of Grey Goose to stagger back to my place."

"You might want to ease up," Suze warned him, "unless you want to be sick like New Year's." Suze pulled Eric inside, hugging him. "Oh, it's so good to see you! You're going to love it here! Guy threw a party so you could meet everybody; it's so L.A. There he is — Guy!" she called out to a tall, heavyset thirty-nine-year-old man in black Gap wear, goatee, and Gitano sunglasses. "He's here! Guy Lanner, this is my bestest-best friend ever from back home, Eric Burgess."

"Suze has told me so much about you I'm sick of you already," he said heartily. "Have an appletini." Guy thrust a cartoon-sized martini glass with three slices of red apple floating in the pale green booze at him. "Welcome to the City of Angels, honey," he said guiding Eric into the svelte crowd. "Come, eat something. God knows nobody else will, and if they do they won't keep it down. Here, try this." Guy popped a stick of something hammy in

Eric's mouth. "Prosciutto wrapped around a breadstick, it's what everyone's serving but not eating this month. Your room is down the hall on the left. Mingle, mix, network. Suze, he's all yours. I gotta make sure nobody's purging in my koi pond."

As soon as Suze showed him his new room, he shut the door and spat out his prosciutto breadstick. "You told me he was normal," he blurted to her, "not some fruity, middle-aged party bear with a house full of freaks."

"This is L.A., Eric, we're all freaks."

"I am not a freak."

"Excuse me, but as the only homo in Rosebud, you clinched that title a while back so get off your high horse." Suze tipped Eric's mega-martini toward his mouth. He took a grudging gulp. "You're just jetlagged. Tomorrow you'll come by the agency, we'll find out your skills and you'll be a working freak in no time."

Eric stowed his suitcase in the closet sullenly and they rejoined the party. Patrick was even more sloshed than before. "No more for you," Suze said removing the drink from his wobbly hand. "How are you feeling, Patrick?"

"A little woozy, but I simply had to drink. Everyone is yammering about those goddam Arthurs. They drove me to it."

"Isn't it terrible?" asked a short muscular African-American man in nerd-chic Moschino flannel and dark orange Serengeti glasses. "Mark Sparks, *E! Entertainment News*. So who do you think stole them?"

"Oh, God, I can't escape the damn things," moaned Patrick. His long arm rescued his drink from Suze. "Calgon, take me away!" he slurred as he drained it.

"What Arthurs?" asked Eric.

"Oh, my God, it's only the biggest story ever," huffed Sparks as Guy came over with a fistful of prosciutto sticks. "Several boxes of Arthur awards were stolen off a loading dock today. It's the biggest award theft since Marisa Tomei."

Patrick pushed Guy's armful of prosciutto away. "Please, Guy," he said, "spare me your pungent pork. I'm not feeling very well."

Sparks was still going at Eric. "How can you be in this town and not know we're missing fifty-five Arthurs? I mean, where have you been?"

"On a plane," Eric said.

"Well, thank God you're back," Sparks said looking him over with a wrinkled nose and condescension. "Wherever you were was turning you into Lance fucking Bass."

That was enough. Guy reached over and took Patrick's camera that was hanging around his neck. He stuck it in Sparks's face and snapped a flash photo. "Just wanted to have a picture of an asshole," Guy said to a blinking Sparks.

"Who the fuck do you think you people are?" bellowed Sparks as he fought for his vision to return.

"This is my new good friend Eric. And this is Patrick, he vomits on people I don't like. I am Guy Lanner and this is my house you're leaving."

"Fuck you."

Guy turned to his clammy friend. "Sorry, Patrick, but . . ." He waved the ripe prosciutto sticks under Patrick's nose. Instant nausea produced a spectacular result, all over Mark Sparks.

Friday, March 10th

The next morning at a few minutes to nine, Eric dressed and tiptoed out of his bedroom. Guy was snoring loudly in the next room. Patrick was sleeping off his drunk on the sofa bed in the living room, naked and almost as white as the sheet he was under. Eric left the house for his appointment with Suze at Star Temps on Wilshire at the edge of Beverly Hills.

When he arrived, Suze hugged him and said, "Now, let's see what we can do with you."

Among other things, Eric discovered he couldn't work a computer, type, file, take dictation, or operate a switchboard. After two hours of testing he stood and declared, "This was a huge mistake. I'm going home."

"Okay, sweetie," Suze sighed. "I'll give you a ride."

"I'm not talking about Guy's place. I mean home to Rosebud."

"Oh come on, have faith," she said putting her arm around him. "Let me work on it, okay?"

When he got back to the house Patrick and Guy were up. Eric found them out back on the sundeck reading the paper and eating their way through pastries from Michel Richard's. From the kitchen window he watched Patrick try unsuccessfully to fend off Guy's orange cat.

"Here, Pussy," Guy said at last. "Leave the hung-over homo alone." He glanced at the entertainment headlines. "Do you realize there are three articles about those stolen Arthurs in this one section?"

Patrick swallowed a piece of almond brioche. "I say we round up Shelly Duvall, Melanie Griffith, Keanu Reeves, Laura Dern, Demi Moore, and Steven Segal and torture them with hot pincers until they crack."

"Why?" asked Guy. "You think they took the Arthurs?"

"No, I just think it's a good idea in general."

Eric joined them on the deck. Guy sat up with a smile, "Hey, how'd it go?"

"Awful," he sulked, plopping himself down on a step. "All I am is an incompetent screwup."

"Oh, you're not a screwup," Guy said soothingly, tousling Eric's blond hair. "Although we still haven't figured out what you did with the remote last night that's got the TV stuck on Spanish."

"I've been a camp lifeguard and trail leader, helped put out forest fires and built levees." Eric stood as he listed his resume items on his fingers. "I can hang drywall, put in a window, replace a floor, shingle a roof, insulate an attic, and re-plumb a bathroom."

"God, he's a butch little twinkie," said Patrick in admiration, "I think I'm getting a hard-on."

"I know CPR," Eric continued in growing intensity. "I know first aid. I can work a hay baler or combine. I can mow, plow, seed, spread manure, and do anything else there is to be done with a tractor, but I can't get a job here because I can't type!"

At the end of Eric's outburst there was a sudden silence. Guy remembered something from earlier in the morning.

"I don't suppose now would be a good time to tell you your mother called?"

Sunday, March 12th

"Late, late, always the fucking late. Ugh." Madame Sylvia unfolded her metal table at her spot at the Fairfax High flea market. She pulled the first statue out of her cardboard box. She set it on the table where it gleamed in the sunlight.

Instantly she heard a man say, "That's it!" She spun in fear of cops, then relaxed. *Only two homo queers,* she thought. They always knew the good stuff. Best to watch my step, though.

"Ah, you like the fake. It is a very good fake, no? But it is a fake, you understand. Very fake."

The heavyset man with the goatee declared, "I love it. How much?"

"A hundred dollars," Madame Sylvia said.

"Get outta town! Twenty."

"Are you insane?" the tall, thin, redheaded homo queer said. "It's worth five bucks tops."

"Five dollars? No, no, no. Seventy-five," Madame Sylvia countered. After several minutes of haggling Madame Sylvia sold her non-fake fake for fifty bucks.

"It's a very good copy, feel the heft." Guy shoved it in Patrick's hands. "Besides, it's for Eric, he could use a nice gift right now." He turned back to the woman. "Can you take a check?" Madame Sylvia made a face like sniffing shit. "It's local. I'm on Westbourne in West Hollywood, just west of here." He showed her the address on his check. "See? West, West, and just west," he added jokingly.

"Cash only."

Guy sighed. "Patrick, how much do you have on you?"

As soon as they had gone, Madame Sylvia pulled out the other two that she had. She set them in the sun and instantly had two more customers. Each grabbed a statuette and examined the bottom. The man gasped. The other customer struggled to keep her face blank, but her eyes were far too wide to carry it off.

"How much for the pair?" the light-skinned black woman whispered urgently.

"I'll double it," said the Asian man, maneuvering to shield the shiny awards from the view of others.

"They're mine," the women growled at the man. She turned to Madame Sylvia, "I saw them first."

"Two hundred dollars," Madam Sylvia said, looking from one to the other. "Apiece."

"No, no," the Asian man said adamantly. "Two hundred for both. Cash." He knew exactly what he was looking at. "No questions asked."

"I won't ask any questions, either," Sarah said, rummaging in her purse. "Like anyone would believe this," she muttered. "And, look, I'll give you two-hundred-twenty." She held up her billfold with a wad of twenties in one hand, and two rolls of quarters in the other. It was all she had, plus now she wouldn't be able to do laundry.

Madame Sylvia smiled and shrugged at the Asian man. "I take her money."

Sarah laughed, "Yes! Can you put them in a bag?"

"Make that two bags," Hiro said with an edge to his voice. "Because I now have a description of someone receiving stolen goods . . ." He scrutinized Sarah's driver's license in her open billfold. ". . . Ms. Sarah Utley."

She snapped it shut. Sarah glared at him. "Look, you," she whispered, "we all know there's fifty-five floating around somewhere. Maybe she has another you could buy."

"I do not know what you are speaking about," said Madame Sylvia quickly. "But these are all I have left."

"If you are wise, I think you will sell me one of those," Hiro said softy, but firmly. "One hundred and ten dollars would be half," he said holding the cash in front of Sara's nose.

Sarah glared at him. Gritting her teeth, she angrily snatched his money and jammed it in her pocket. At least she could do laundry. "Fine. Two bags."

⭐

When Guy and Patrick returned, Eric was watching *Grease 2* on HBO in Spanish.

"For the love of Dios, there will be no Adrian Zmed in my house," declared Guy. "I just had it fumigated." He zapped the TV off before Eric could protest. "Besides, we have a true Hollywood event about to happen live, right here."

"What's up with you two?" Eric asked suspiciously.

"From beautiful Boys Town, U.S.A., we bring you the 72nd Institute of Motion Picture Artists and Technicians Awards," intoned Guy in announcer-speak. "The nominees for worst experience coming to Los Angeles are Rodney King! Robert Kennedy! And Sharon Tate! And the Arthur goes to," Guy paused for dramatic effect, then produced the golden award, "Eric Burgess! — for his starring role in *To Live and Be Unemployed in Los Angeles*."

Eric stood there in surprise. "For real?" was all he could say.

"Well, it's certainly not for *Working Girl*," said Patrick.

"Wow," Eric said, taking the heavy fifteen-inch statue. His eyes brimmed with tears. "You like me. You really like me."

The phone rang and Guy headed for the kitchen to get it. "Just do me a favor," he said over his shoulder as he went. "If you hate the thing, don't tell me. My ex-wife used to do that to me all the time."

"Ex-wife?" Eric mouthed to Patrick.

"I wouldn't go there," Patrick whispered back, "that's all blood over the dam."

"I love it, Guy," Eric called out. "Maybe it'll be lucky for me."

Guy came back with the cordless receiver in his hand. "It's for you, it's Suze."

Eric took the phone. "Hey, Suze, what's up?"

"How about a job?" she giggled.

"I'll take it. What is it?"

"How would you like to be Madonna's assistant's assistant?"

Monday, March 13th

Hiro drove into the PrattswaterfordDouglas parking garage in downtown L.A., and gave his sleek navy blue BMW to the valet. In his briefcase were his usual items. Files, forms, industry periodicals, but nestled among them in a thick foam pad was his newly purchased authentic Institute Award.

Hiro strode into the lobby and boarded a crowded elevator. He smiled. None of them had so much as seen an actual Award in person. Wait, no, there was Finkelstein in the corner. Hiro, Finkelstein, and Balch had for the last six years been the PrattswaterfordDouglas vice presidents trotted out as the official Accountants of the Arthur Balloting during the Awards telecast. It was the thrilling highlight of Hiro's year. Both he and Noel, his spouse of thirteen years, were Arthur-obsessed. He couldn't wait to show this one to Noel when he returned from vacation and surprise him with it.

Even if it was stolen. Even if his grandmother had always told him stolen things were terribly unlucky. But that was all Yokohama superstition. An old wives' tale that had no place in a new country and a new century.

On the forty-ninth floor Hiro seated himself behind his wide mahogany desk in his corner office and opened his briefcase so no one could see. He removed the business section and other papers. He took out his bento-box lunch of sushi and set it on the desk. Then he opened the special foam compartment in his briefcase.

There, shining for him alone, was his secret stolen trophy. He opened the bottom right desk drawer and laid it down, hidden from everyone's view but his. It lay there in the open drawer, so beautiful. So precious and rare. So his.

The phone rang. "Yamamoto."

"Hey, Hiro, Bob Davies."

"Hello, Bob," Hiro said. "Um, everything on schedule for the big night?" he tried to laugh nonchalantly.

"What a pain in the ass, huh? You'd think the cops could find at least a few of 'em. By now God knows where they are."

"Yes, it's a shame," Hiro said glancing at the one in his drawer. "Unlucky."

"Tell me about it. Had to rush order a whole new batch from D.L. Paul & Co. in Chicago. Anyway, the wife and I were thinking if you're not busy, why don't you and Noel come on over for dinner on Saturday?"

"Noel's on vacation, doesn't get back for another couple of weeks, but tell Betty I will come and also that I look forward to it."

"Wouldn't be too sure of that. She just finished another damn course at Sur la Table. Japanese cuisine. Think she wants to see if she can pull it off on a native. Say 7:30 on Saturday?"

"I will be there." Hiro hung up, smiling. He liked Bob and Betty Davies. Bob was part of the Arthur brotherhood who, like himself, helped shepherd the Awards to their ultimate recipients. He hoped Betty would be more successful at Japanese cooking than she had been with Indian. Or Thai. Or Vietnamese . . .

His lunch!

The tekka-maki and uni needed to be in the refrigerator immediately. He leapt up from his chair, seized the bento box and headed toward the door — only to trip over the open lower drawer with his contraband Arthur on horizontal display. He crashed to the floor spilling his lunch, splintering the drawer, and banging his head on the floor. Hard. His assistant rushed to the doorway.

"I am fine, Jenean," he told her, though he felt blood trickling down the side of his right leg. Oh, this was unlucky. Whatever happened he did not want her coming to him and seeing his illicit treasure in the broken drawer behind him. "Go get me a Band-Aid from the first-aid kit, Jenean. It's in the breakroom, please."

"But you're bleeding," she said pointing.

"What?" He lifted his head. He saw blood on the carpet. He felt his eyebrow. It was numb and wet. "Ice, then. Get me some ice." Jenean moved to help him. "No!" he roared. "Ice! Go! Get ice now!" Jenean ran out, her hand over her mouth. "And Extra-Strength Tylenol," he shouted after her. "Ohhh," he moaned. This was most unlucky.

"Is not my problem you are unlucky," the large Greek man told Roger Davies, pinning him against Roger's Lexus in the USC parking lot. "Is my job to make you face responsibilities, okay?" Nicholas was a good foot and a half taller, at least a foot wider at the shoulders than Roger, about ten years older, and a lot more experienced in beating the shit out of people. Not to mention following and surprising them on their way to class. "I make a deal with you," Nicholas grinned. "You give me five hundred, okay, and we talk next week about the rest."

"I'll get your five hundred, Jesus!"

Nicholas eased up on Roger's arm. "See, I knew we make a deal. Free enterprise. Very American. Three o'clock here, tomorrow." He smiled and smacked Roger's face much too hard for a friendly pat. "I like you, okay. Maybe next week I only ask for a thousand." He walked away whistling.

Roger leaned against his navy Lexus, shaking, trying to calm down. His gambling debt was only something like seven thousand, maybe ten. It's not like he couldn't come up with it, although it would be difficult keeping it away from his parents. He glanced at his watch, 10:32, half an hour until class. He had just enough time.

He entered USC's Harris Hall. *I shouldn't be doing this*, he thought, but he knew it would calm him. He casually walked to the ground floor men's room at the south end of the building and entered. The far stall door was closed. Roger took the stall next to it. He took his pants down and sat, keeping his eye on the black Puma shoe visible in the other stall. After roughly thirty seconds it tapped, very deliberately, twice. Roger's dick began to swell as he tapped his foot in reply.

When he was done Roger had to run all the way to the Lucas Building. He wanted to brush his teeth. He wanted to take a bath in bleach. He really wanted to stop doing this degrading shit.

He got to class just as Dr. Utley began. Sweating, he flopped in a seat and concentrated on regaining his breath. He was in luck. She was going to show Chaplin's *The Gold Rush*.

The room went dark and the movie began. Sometime during the teetering cabin sequence, Roger noticed that Dr. Utley had moved to the back near where he was seated. She sure didn't look like a professor, not with that figure. How long had it been since he'd had sex? Real sex. With a woman. He couldn't remember for sure. Certainly time to try it again and hope for better results. When the class was over he made his way to Dr. Utley.

His teacher smiled at him. "And what did you think of *The Gold Rush*?"

"It's mythic."

"Oh, there's a word. How is it 'mythic'?"

"He abandons everything to pursue worldly gold, but his humanity won't allow him to have it. Ironically, though, his humanity leads him to find ultimate riches in the human connection, if only fleetingly. Plus it's fuckin' funny." His teacher laughed. This is working, he thought. "Would you like to get some coffee?"

She shook her head. "I don't even know your name."

"It's Roger," he said, giving her his best smile, and his card.

"Well, Roger, the teacher-student thing isn't exactly approved of."

"I'm not asking for a 'thing,' just coffee. Maybe a movie."

"Some other time, I think," she said pleasantly. She gathered her things and left.

It felt good. It was exciting to hit on his teacher. And a woman this time. She hadn't given his card back, either. He felt confident he'd nail her by the end of the term.

He could just bet on it.

Guy dropped off Eric at Madonna's hidden estate in tony Los Feliz below Griffith Park. Once past the gate, he was escorted to a back door by a handsome if grim-faced eastern European guard barely restraining a barking black and brown Doberman. Shaking, he rang the bell on the large, secluded Spanish-styled house. Before he had withdrawn his finger, the door was yanked open by a young but severe looking, olive-skinned woman in a perfectly tailored charcoal Chanel business suit. She glared at the noisy dog.

"Stop it!" Instantly the dog was silent. She then looked Eric over with disdain. "You looked taller on the closed circuit. Inside!" With a start, he obeyed. The door was closed and Eric found himself in a small business suite on the lower level of the grand house. The woman stood behind her exquisite French Empire desk. "I am," she said imperiously, "Gwyneth. I am Ms. Ciccone's Assistant's Assistant."

"Oh, um, I think there might be a mistake," Eric corrected politely, "I was told I was to be the Assistant's Assistant."

"You were erroneously informed. You are being considered for the Assistant's Assistant's Assistant. And you will never correct me again, got that? Say 'yes, Gwyneth.'" As Eric did, she pulled out a pager and pressed several numbers.

"Wow," he breathed in awe. "Were you just telling Madonna I'm here?"

"First, it is Ms. Ciccone. Second, no. And third, you will never meet her. In fact it's part of my job to prevent that."

A tall, beautiful African-American woman appeared at the door and crossed her arms in annoyance. "You rang?"

"This is Lee. She is also being considered for an Assistant's Assistant's Assistant. Don't get chummy, we're still running a background check on her."

"Did you do one on me?" Eric asked.

With a smirk Gwyneth picked up a paper on her desk and read. "You have fifty-six dollars in your savings account back in Rosebud, Missouri, graduated fourteenth in a high school class of forty-three students, two years junior college, registered Independent, and worked at BSI Construction in Saint Louis until you were caught fellating the foreman's son."

"My God," Eric said, bright red. "How much more could you possibly know?"

"You come when you're fucked and you curve to the right." She set the paper down. "We're very thorough."

Eric was mortified and speechless. The black woman chuckled. "Don't let her get to you, kid. Hers curves to the left."

Gwyneth glared and then said loudly, "Be so good as to show Mr. Burgess the areas accessible to the lesser help."

"Follow me, bottom boy," Lee smiled and led the way out. Eric hurried to keep up with her. She took him through rooms of storage racks of old tour costumes, props, never-worn clothes, and odd gifts.

"Is this a Dolce & Gabbana sling?" Eric asked amazed.

Lee shrugged. "People send this girl all kinds of crap. Our job is to organize and categorize it. So far I'm to the letter B."

Eric couldn't believe his good luck. "So much left to do," he whispered in joy.

"No it's all done," Lee said. Eric looked confused and crestfallen. "I just filed it all under B for Bullshit." She cocked her head back and laughed. Eric frowned, but couldn't help laughing, too. Lee shook her head at him. "You are one gullible cracker!"

Eric pointed at a small stand with a rectangular glass cover. "What's that?"

"Empty," Lee replied, indicating the small plaque on the base.

Eric craned forward to read aloud, "Institute Award for Best Actress 1996 — *Evita*?" and raised his eyebrows.

Lee nodded, saying, "That's why it's empty, honey. Wouldn't have wanted to be around the day they announced the nominations that year, huh?"

"No way. Can you say 'snubbed'?"

"Oh, please. Can you say 'overweening whack bitch'? Wouldn't surprise me if she's behind that batch of Arthurs that disappeared."

By lunch they had bonded. As they ate alone in the austere servants' hall, Lee told how she'd come from a small town in Georgia. "I knew I had to leave when I told my family I was a lesbian and they got mad 'cause they thought it meant I was no longer a Democrat." They both laughed.

As they munched their gourmet sandwiches Eric mused, "I just thought I'd actually get to see Madonna, you know? Have a little glamour. I was really hoping for some excitement here. Pretty naïve, huh?"

"Read the trades, honey, she's not even in town."

"Like that would matter," he snorted. "We're stuck down here."

"Maybe," Lee said archly, "maybe not." She scooted her chair over right next to his. "Would you like to sneak upstairs? See where she lives?"

"Oh, my God, yes! How?"

"Gwyneth doesn't know I swiped this little ol' security card," Lee said, sliding it across the table to him. "Just don't get caught upstairs. And if you do, girlfriend, you did not get this from me."

By mid-afternoon, Eric could wait no longer. He touched the magnetic card to the pad by the door at the top of the stairs. It made a tiny beep and the lock clicked open. With his heart thumping loudly in his chest, he pushed the door open and entered the realm of his idol.

He stepped into an enormous dining area with a massive table and chairs that belonged in a castle. He took two steps onto the thick peach-colored carpet when he heard the whir. Looking to his right he saw a state of the art surveillance camera in the ceiling corner aimed directly at him. An electronic alarm sounded.

"Oh, shit!" Out the window he saw two guards running toward the house, one with the insanely barking dog. He ran back to the door but it had locked behind him. He fled in the other direction, through a large gilded room with a wall of recording equipment, a grand piano, and a six-foot gleaming steel cage hanging from the ceiling. *What the fuck is that about?* Eric thought as he raced into the grand foyer where he tried to escape through the front door. It had an indecipherable electronic lock. Behind him he heard the guards and snarling Doberman entering back in the dining room.

Over hidden speakers came Gwyneth's hard voice, "He's at the front door."

He saw stairs and took them, three at a time, up to the actual living area.

"Upstairs, you morons, get him!"

He ran past a nursery, the nanny's room, other closed and locked doors and, at the end of the hall, into a master bedroom as big as a store. He stopped with a shock as he realized where he was. He had entered the holy of holies: Madonna's bedroom. A golden bed the size of a barge seemed to float in the center and by it was an elaborate nightstand with a huge assortment of lube and condoms plus a copy of *The Cat in the Hat*.

What the hell is she teaching that kid? he thought fleetingly, but there were guards thumping down the hall toward him. Leaping over a Soloflex machine, he ran to the other side of the room to a door covered with elaborate Oriental carvings. It opened onto a dazzling gold-and-black marble bathroom that looked like an empty harem. He slammed the intricately worked door shut and locked it just as the dog got there. "Keep that dog off the door, you oafs, it's from Bali!" Gwen demanded over the speakers. "I'll be right there."

Eric had only a short time to think. He ditched Lee's illicit security card by stuffing it into the air conditioning vent and sat on the golden throne wondering how he had gone from sitting on a tractor in Missouri five days ago to sitting slumped on Madonna's crapper. Then — he noticed a hair. One delicate, short, erratically curled hair on the floor.

Eric's jaw dropped. It could only be from Her. He picked up the blonde pubic hair with reverence. At least he would have a memento. He wrapped it in a square of scented pink toilet tissue and smiled sadly. Gwyneth was now outside instructing the guards, threatening to fire them if they damaged the door. Huddled in a corner he thought, *Maybe I can just stay here forever.*

Then he noticed the screws turning on the door hinges.

"Wait for the blasted light!" Michael Foster Fowler shouted at Eric, who'd walked right into the street in front of him on Los Feliz. Eric was still in a daze from being literally thrown off Madonna's property. He jumped back on the curb as the rusted green convertible roared past, the engine burning oil.

Eric supposed he'd catch a bus home, but other than that he had no idea what to do. He saw a sign a block away: House of Pies. Comfort food, he thought. And right now he could use a lot of comfort.

Half a mile away on Los Feliz, Michael Foster Fowler was still muttering about the little blond twink who'd practically stepped in front of him. "You'd think the cops would do something about menaces like that," he sneered, swerving in and out of traffic. *Not that the cops in this town do jack spit anyway,* he thought. *There's fifty-five Arthur statues missing and they don't care. Nobody cares. Except me.*

That was why he was careening toward an address on Wilshire Boulevard in Beverly Hills. After several days of bullying the secretaries at the Institute of Motion Picture Artists and Technicians he'd finally weaseled an appointment with a VP.

Bob Davies, VP of Promotions at the Institute was exactly what IMPAT wanted in a fringe-of-industry executive. He was white, wealthy enough, married, and well preserved for a man in his fifties. He was holding the phone away from his ear as his eighty-five-year-old elderly shut-in and royal-pain-in-the-ass aunt was cursing at him. It didn't matter what he had or hadn't done, nothing was ever enough. "Margaret," he said, not that it stopped her streaming invective, "you're going to give yourself an aneurysm." *If only,* he thought. Since Bob Davies was her only living relative, she was now a bitter, angry millstone around his neck. *God,* he thought, *aren't old people supposed to die?*

His vintage old-fashioned intercom buzzed. "Mr. Davies, that man I told you about is here," his secretary informed him. "Do you want him to wait or, ahem, should I get him some tea?"

"Tea" was the code for "or should I call Security," but he covered the phone and buzzed back, "Send him in. After my aunt, how bad could he be?" He uncovered the phone. "Margaret, I have to go now, I'll try to get somebody for you, okay?"

"I don't want somebody, you callous turd, I want you, I want you here, I want —"

He hung up as an obvious lunatic entered his office. He steeled himself, stood, and offered his hand to shake.

"Arthurs are missing, Mr. Davies!" Michael Foster Fowler boomed, ignoring Davies's hand. He pounded on the desk for emphasis saying, "They! Must! Be! Found!"

Davies stared at this loon, wishing he had had that emergency button installed under his desk. "Yes, well, we're working with the police —"

"The police," Michael Foster Fowler hissed, "are worried about petty crimes like shootings and murders! You need somebody dedicated to finding these precious symbols, even at the cost of human life!" Fowler railed alarmingly. "That's why you need me. Somebody with almost a year's hard experience as a mall security guard. Somebody familiar with rituals of self-denial and discipline to focus the mind. Did you know I haven't been intimate with anyone in over forty-three weeks? Not even with myself!"

"I think I'd like some tea," Davies said reaching for the intercom. "I'm just going to have the girl bring us some tea, okay? Doris, I'd like you to quickly order me some —"

Fowler slammed his hand down on the intercom. Davies recoiled in fear. "You don't need tea!" Fowler thundered. "You need me! Whoever took these statues must be brought to divine justice, and when I find them —" he said as his eyes involuntarily rolled up to a vengeful God, "ohhhh, the cops will have plenty to deal with then."

Shit, Davies thought, *crazy and dangerous*. He decided to tell the psycho anything he wanted to hear as long as it got him the hell out of his office. "Sounds like a plan, then. Why don't you get started on your search? Like, right away started."

"You mean it?"

"Absolutely. The sooner you're out on the street, Mr. Fowler, the better I'll feel."

Michael Foster Fowler drew himself up. He had his mission! He smiled with a sudden calm resolve that gave Davies the creeps. Fowler strode to the door with angry purpose, then suddenly stopped and turned. "There's just one more thing," he said as he fixed Davies with a steely glare. He slowly reached into his jacket pocket.

"Oh, Jesus, God, no!" said Davies cringing, certain he was a dead man.

Fowler pulled out a parking stub. "Do you validate?"

Half an hour later, Davies was driving east on Melrose. After a day like this he needed to calm down before going home to his wife in Toluca Lake.

"I'd like a room, please," he said at the window of Flex bathhouse.

"You're in room #108," the handsome Mexican in the ribbed Flex tank top behind the glass said. He slid a towel and room key to Davies through the slot at the side of the window. "Check out is one A.M."

Davies smiled. He liked 'em young and muscular. He preferred blond, but dark and Latino looked damn good, too. "What's your name?"

"Rudy," the young man said with a deliciously Hispanic lilt.

"You know where I am, Rudy," he said flashing his room key.

Rudy buzzed the door for the gentleman. "Sorry, I'm getting off now."

"Me, too, with any luck," Davies said as he entered.

Rudy Diaz got his cap and jacket, punched his Flex timecard, and ran to catch the #11 Melrose bus just as it drove up. Breathing heavily, he leaned against the pole by the driver as the bus lurched away from the curb. He quickly scanned the other passengers. Near the back of the bus in the seats that face the center, there was a beautiful blond blue-eyed Anglo boy about his age looking at him.

Eric immediately looked away. When he glanced back, the man was still looking. Eric lowered his eyes in embarrassment.

Rudy walked brazenly to Eric's seat and stood in the aisle blatantly cruising him. Eric turned bright red, his crotch responded, too. Rudy smiled, took the seat next to him, and casually allowed his leg to press against Eric's. Rudy dropped his cap on the floor in front of him, then reached down between Eric's legs to get it. Eric gasped. As Rudy sat up he gave Eric a quick grope. Eric's heart was thumping, the cherry pie á la mode he'd recently eaten at the House of Pies gurgled in his stomach. This had never happened in Rosebud, and certainly not by someone as exotically handsome as this. The man kept staring at him, his beautiful face so close he could feel his breath. Eric trembled not knowing how to handle it.

The bus slowed at Van Ness by Paramount Studios. Rudy rose and stood directly in front of Eric. "This is my stop," he said, his straining crotch directly in front of Eric's face. The side doors opened and Rudy hopped down to the sidewalk. There he turned to face Eric.

Fuck, thought Eric, *what should I do?* The doors closed.

"Wait!" Eric shouted to the driver. He forced the reluctant doors open and practically fell off the bus. It pulled back into traffic leaving Eric on the curb in a diesel cloud, making him even more dizzy. "What the hell am I doing?" Eric mumbled as he began to follow Rudy down what felt like a decidedly iffy neighborhood. *This is insane,* he thought, *I shouldn't be here.* The man turned in front of a tiny Hollywood bungalow, strode to the front door, opened it and walked inside — leaving the door open.

What do I do now? Eric asked himself.

He peered inside the house from the sidewalk. The interior was dimly lit and appeared mostly empty. *If I go in there,* Eric said to himself, *that guy could beat the shit out of me. He could murder me. What am I doing?*

Rudy walked into the afternoon light at the open door. He was totally naked and startlingly, utterly beautiful. He showed a sparsely hairy chest, muscular thighs, and a thick, fully hard, uncut dick that curved upward. The man smiled. Eric melted.

Tuesday, March 14th

At daybreak, Eric hopped off the #11 bus and fairly skipped up Westbourne singing "A Boy Like That" from *West Side Story*, laughing. As soon as Eric stepped inside he heard Guy's deep growling basso demanding, "Where the hell have you been?"

"Oh, I'm sorry. Are you pissed at me?"

"Am I pissed?" Guy said, gathering his full-length Beverly Hills Hotel robe around his bear body, rising from the couch where he'd spent a fitful night. "Yes! I'm pissed I spent all night worrying about you. I'm pissed that I got a backache while you obviously got laid. And I'm pissed that — wait a minute." Guy abruptly stopped. "You're glowing. What the hell is that about?"

"Oh, Guy, I met the most handsome, funny, smartest, most sexy man alive!"

Guy looked at him in disgust. "Oh, Jesus, he's in love." He turned and shuffled toward the kitchen. "I'm gonna need coffee for this."

Over Yukon Blend, Eric told him all about how he met Rudy after getting fired from Madonna's mansion.

"You're getting it on with a bathhouse attendant?" Guy shook his head. "That is so *Honcho*. Hey, think you could get a job there?" Eric gave him a dirty look. "Well, it's not like you have anything to show from your Madonna gig."

"Actually, I do," Eric said proudly. He removed the folded pink toilet paper from his pocket, carefully opening it. "I got this while I was holed up in her private john."

"What the hell am I looking at?"

"It's one of her pubic hairs."

"What? This is a diva pube?" Guy narrowed his eyes. "Are you sure this is from Madonna?"

"Well, it's not from Lourdes. And everybody else there had dark hair."

Guy picked up the delicate package reverently. "This, Eric, could be your salary for a month."

"What do you mean?"

"I'm going to put this adorable little cunt hair on eBay. Guy patted Eric on the shoulder happily. "Congratulations, I think you just made rent."

Tuesday, March 14th

Roger Davies leaned against his Lexus calculating what he could sell. Or borrow. Or steal.

"Fuck!"

Earlier that morning he had met and paid Nicholas the five hundred dollars, and agreed to come up with another seven-hundred-fifty next week. Then Nicholas suckered him into betting on the Spurs–Hawks game that had just cost him another fifteen hundred.

"God damn it, when do I get a fucking break?"

He peeled out of the parking lot, driving nowhere at high speeds while he worked out what he was going to do next. The problem was he had that damn need again. *Okay,* he thought, *I'll just get that over with so I can fucking think.*

He stopped at Circus of Books in Silver Lake to grab a free copy of *Frontiers*. He turned to the personals thinking, *One call, one price, one fuck and it's over.* He opened his cell phone and punched in the number of the guy with the ad in the upper left corner.

"Hello," a professionally sexy voice answered.

"Hi, uh, is this —" Roger had to glance back at the ad, "— Frank 'B.C.' Powers?"

"Yeah, what's up?"

"I saw your ad in *Frontiers*, how much are you?"

"What are you, a cop?"
"No, I . . . Look, how do I do this? This is new to me."
"You looking for a friend? Tonight?"
"Yeah."
"Well, tonight's really bad. I got a death in the family."
"Oh. Uh, sorry." What the hell kind of hustler was this?
"Yeah, I gotta take care of some stuff." There was a pause and Roger thought the guy had hung up. Then he heard, "You wanna meet tomorrow?"

No, damn it, he wanted to blow his wad right now and get it out of his system, but the death thing threw him. How nice did he have to be to a hustler? "Sure, okay, yeah."

"Meet me at Numbers at 10:00 tomorrow night. I'll need your number so I can confirm."

And Roger gave it to him, making a date he no longer wanted.

"Big Ed" DeLello sauntered into his room in his parents' house in Las Vegas and dropped his bag by his bed. He checked his wallet to make sure he had Noel's card. Just looking at the card was making his dick grow.

He threw his massive frame on the bed, looking up at the cottage cheese ceiling, smiling. Big Ed replayed his weekend time at INNdulge, one of the many all-male resorts in Palm Springs. First night there, he met the hottest Filipino guy he'd ever seen, and they spent the rest of Big Ed's four days in his suite. Asian men made him hard 24/7. And this guy, Noel, was every bit able to keep up with a horny, six-foot-nine, two-hundred-seventy pound, twenty-nine-year-old Italian goombah.

In between their room-wrecking sexcapades, they talked movies. It was rare for Big Ed to find someone as into movies as he was, so filled with knowledge of actors, awards, and arcane motion picture history. It made their discussions almost as fun as the fucking. Almost.

He clicked his computer on to kill time by surfing eBay. If there was one thing Big Ed loved as much as hot Asian men, it was celebrity gossip and memorabilia. His room was chock full of American cinema posters, promotional items, movie props, and other tchotchkes, and even some genuinely valuable memorabilia, all of which he had found on eBay.

And he'd found something else intriguing on eBay. He had just submitted his second bid on what was purported to be one of Madonna's pubic hairs when his father barged into his room.

"Eddie, I got a job I need you to do."

"Aw, c'mon, Pop, I just got back."

"Yeah, back under my roof which means you do what I say." His father had grown doughy with age, but he was still one of Vegas's most feared and respected men. "What the fuck is that?" he demanded pointing at the computer screen.

Big Ed switched screens guiltily, "Nothing. eBay."

"What, you don't have enough shit in here? Jeez, it looks like a girl's room." He took a breath for a trademark sigh. "Okay, end of discussion. You're going out to Cactus Lounge and beating the shit out of a guy name of Tony Bett, you got that?"

"Pop, don't make me do this."

"I got no choice. Vinnie fucked it up. Asshole roughed up some other Tony some other place, now he's gotta lie low. This cocksucker Bett don't want to put my machines in the lounge, I need someone to explain it to him. That someone is you."

"Pop —"

"I'm not asking you to kill him, just break an arm or two, huh? Can you do that? Am I asking so fucking much here? Can you do that for your father?"

"All right, all right," Big Ed said petulantly. "Fine."

His father shook his head and left his son's room, muttering, "Jesus, Mary, and Joseph, it's like pullin' teeth." From down the hall, he shouted, "And be back by eight, your grandmother's making her lasagna."

Big Ed shut down the computer. This aggravation is exactly why he hated living at home. Maybe he should move out. Out of the house and away from Vegas. There was a wise guy named

Petey who used to work for his father until he got caught bottoming for a bellman at the Belaggio. *Disonore.* Petey was in West Hollywood now. Big Ed changed out of his nice shirt and pants. Didn't want to get blood on those. He put on an old blue Puma running suit. He'd give Petey a call later.

Big Ed was so over this strong-arm stuff, anyway. There had to be a better way to make money. Something with more class, glamour, and style. He slipped two sets of brass knuckles into the zippered pockets in his running jacket and noticed his hands. His fingernails were a mess.

That's what he'd do. After he beat this guy so bad he'd be in the ICU for a week, he'd treat himself to a nice, calming manicure and an old movie. He'd found a rare copy of the old classic *The Ring of Truth* in Palm Springs, starring one of his favorites, Margaret Atherton, and was looking forward to watching it. He grabbed his car keys, kissed his nònna in the kitchen, and drove off to do a little family business.

Wednesday, March 15th

Eric found Guy at the breakfast table reading the paper. "Has Suze called?"

"No, Tractor Boy. Apparently all superstars have their menial positions filled. But your mother called. Twice."

"I'll call her later." Guy shot him a look. "I will! Just later, okay?" Eric plopped himself down at the table with a cup of Italian Roast. "Besides, with no job maybe I should just go back to Missouri."

"Maybe you should just give it a day or two. The early bidding on Madonna's little material curl is already up to fifty-five dollars. We have high hopes for it."

The phone rang and Eric grabbed it. It was Suze, excited about a two-day assignment for Eric at Sotheby's auction house starting as soon as he could get there.

That evening Roger met his hustler, Frank "B.C." Powers, at Numbers on Santa Monica Boulevard. Numbers was L.A.'s premiere hustler bar. Large booths, large drinks, and large prices for the cocktails, the food, and the men. But one gets what one pays for. Roger found himself exceedingly uncomfortable in a gay bar.

"Is it me, or does everyone here know you?" Roger asked.

Frank gave him a smile that added to his discomfort. It somehow managed to be both self-effacing and dazzling. "They've seen me around."

Roger had had that feeling earlier himself. He narrowed his eyes. "Where would I have seen you?"

"Film. Internet. Parties. Around."

Roger remembered where he'd seen that face. Cover of a porn video at Circus of Books. The rest of the picture came into focus. Frank "B.C." Powers. B.C. for "beer can." He shifted uneasily on his barstool, looking around at so many young and beautiful men smiling so charmingly at so many rich old men. "Can we get out of here?"

"Rest! I need rest," Roger panted after the third time he had come. He rolled off the dresser and collapsed on the sheepskin rug.

"Just want you to get your money's worth," Frank said standing over him with a wide grin.

Roger looked up at Frank's sweat-soaked body. God, he was beautiful, even if he was a man. "Come here." Frank obeyed, bending down to take Roger's cock in his mouth, but Roger pulled him up to his chest. "No, just lie here."

Their breathing synchronized. Naturally. Quiet. Nice. Roger was so relaxed he didn't notice his thumb absently stroking Frank's neck. "Did you, I mean, were you able to take care of things yesterday? You mentioned a death?"

Frank heaved a sigh. "Oh, that. My family's kinda messed up. Brother-in-law was killed in some shoot-out in Pomona so I had to go out there and take care of my sister. Trina's her name." Frank remembered she had looked so small, so lost. When he hugged her, she was trembling. Suddenly Frank was crying. The unexpected intimacy shocked Roger, and for that brief instant banished the fright he carried in his heart. Instinctively Roger held him tight. "No, don't," Frank said pulling free. "Aw, shit, I'm sorry." He wiped his face roughly and turned away, sitting with his back to Roger.

Roger sat up and touched Frank's shoulder. It was cool and damp now. Part of him wanted to run away, but another better part told him to put his arms around Frank's neck. So he did.

At last Frank said, "Thank you." Then he pulled Roger's arms away and stood up. "It's getting late."

"Okay." Roger noticed the alarm by the bed read 4:06 A.M. "So how much do I, you know."

"Three hundred," Frank said, barely glancing up. "Just leave it there."

Thursday, March 16th

Eric loved his new temp assignment at Sotheby's of matching auction catalog photos to the actual items. He was sorry it would only last until the auction on Friday. The auction highlight was a collection of vintage movie memorabilia, including the Institute Award given to Luise Rainer as best actress for *The Good Earth* in 1937. That night, Guy and Patrick were unwillingly regaled with the minutia of tomorrow's auction items all dinner long.

"And there's costumes from Joan Blondell and Bette Davis in *Three on a Match*! My boss, Leda, let me touch a collar Bette Davis wore. Bette Davis!"

"Speaking of useless, if famous castoffs," interjected Guy in an effort to change the tired subject, "did I tell you that hair from Madonna's muffin is up to seven-hundred-eighty dollars?" Eric had been so jazzed about his job that he'd forgotten about their own auction on eBay.

Patrick raised his glass in a toast, "God bless people with too much money and no lives." He drank deeply, then muttered, "Which would include me — except for that money part."

The challenge with doing porn was maintaining stamina. Frank, drenched in sweat, glanced at the clock off-camera. It was now 5:41 and he'd been ass-fucking this cute Arab boy in different positions since 2:20 for a scene that would be maybe fifteen minutes on the DVD.

"I have an appointment tonight," he reminded the director without breaking rhythm. "A new one."

Iconic porn director Cha-Cha LaBouche didn't even glance from his monitor showing the closeup shot. "I know, darling, but I need just a bit more. Can you take it all the way out, and slam it in a few times?"

Frank complied without a thought. His mind returned to the beautiful blond kid he'd had last night. How could he have charged him half for that much time? Bad business. Unprofessional. There were other things to consider.

His sister, for one. Trina was a wreck. Well rid of that worthless redneck husband, but still a mess. And given his crappy salary and benefits, they couldn't afford the dialysis she needed. *Well, that's what big brothers are for, right?* he thought. Besides, it wasn't like it'd be forever. He had an appointment at Cedars-Sinai tomorrow for a kidney compatibility test. Oops, no, wood-kill, don't think about that.

"Very good, Frank," Chi-Chi said. "Whenever you're ready."

Frank tried but nothing was happening. He pounded the man in hard thrusts, grunting loudly, trying to make himself cum. He was so close but the climax just wasn't coming. Concentrate, he told himself. Stop thinking about the kid last night and fucking shoot. That damned kid. Roger. Sweet face. Smooth white belly, line of hair going down from his chest to his pubes. Beautiful balls, silky skin, delicate odor, perfect ass. Perfect ass. Oh, yeah.

Perfect ass. He pulled out, whipped off the condom and jizzed all over the back of the man bent over the bed.

On his way to his car Frank called Roger on his cell phone. "Hello?"

"Frank Powers here. Look, I know this is — oh, what the hell. You wanna get together again?"

"I, I mean, no, I, I can't afford it."

Neither could Frank, really, but he continued anyway. "No, no, I'm just talking dinner." He winced at what he was about to say. "On me."

There was a long silence. Then, "Why are you calling me?"

That was a damned good question, and Frank couldn't think of a lie. "You . . . were nice to me."

"And so you want to take me to dinner?"

He was right. This was stupid. "I'm sorry, I don't know what I was thinking. This, I shouldn't, just forget I called."

"Wait!" There was breathing on the other end. "Oh, man, this is weird," Roger whispered, followed by more silence. "Okay. Okay, sure, dinner, why not."

Frank arrived at his car hating the feeling he had, this nervousness in the pit of his stomach. Or was it excitement? Or both? He got in, started the motor, and headed out to Malibu for this new client, a record producer who was taking him to dinner. For dessert he wanted Frank to shit in his mouth. Whatever pays the rent.

Frank made a mental note to enforce his standard no-kissing policy up front.

Friday, March 17th

Eric could feel the electricity of the auction permeate the building. His new temp boss, Leda, a faded Argentine beauty, had taken a liking to him. She invited him down to the auction room, and when he saw the genuine Arthur statuette, he stopped in awe.

Leda smiled. "Would you like to hold it?" she asked.

"Oh, could I?" asked Eric. "Please, I've never seen a real Arthur, not in person. I never imagined I'd get to touch one." Leda gave him a pair of cotton gloves and let Eric pick it up. He looked disappointed. "I guess I thought it'd weigh more or something. I have a fake one at home but it feels just the same."

"Your fake doesn't have this," Leda said turning it upside down and pointing to a special mark on the bottom. "This symbol is only on statuettes manufactured by D.L. Paul & Co. of Chicago. It's how you know it's an authentic Arthur."

Ten minutes later Eric grabbed the payphone off the lobby. "Guy, I need you to do me a favor. Go get that Arthur you guys gave me Sunday." He breathlessly waited for Guy to retrieve it. "Turn it over and look on the bottom. Is there a mark stamped in it, like a trademark kind of off to one side? Describe it to me." As Eric listened to Guy he slid down the wall to the floor in disbelief. "Guy, I don't know how to tell you this, but that's not a reproduction. You're holding a real Arthur." Guy screamed so loudly over the phone that the lobby receptionist looked over. "No, I'm not shitting you. What? How much? Well, the one we had here just sold for more than half a million!" Guy screamed again and the receptionist glared disapprovingly at the blond young man lying on the floor who could not stop laughing.

Leda signed Eric's time sheet, letting him off an hour early with pay. He put it in the mail to Star Temps and got on the bus to Flex to tell his new boyfriend Rudy about owning a real Institute Award. With transfers, it took him an hour to get there but he was so high on excitement he didn't care. He didn't even mind when Rudy told him he had to work another hour before he got off. Rudy buzzed him in free and told him to enjoy himself.

This was Eric's first time in a bathhouse. Ordinarily he'd have been trembling in fear of this dark house of sex, but he was still riding on his Arthur elation, feeling invincible. He stripped and tossed his clothes in a locker per Rudy's instructions and wrapped his towel around his waist.

In one room he saw a very fit older man lying on the bed casually stroking himself. What made Eric stop short, though, was that the man looked almost exactly like Coach Ewing, Eric's twelfth-grade gym teacher back in Rosebud, one of his hottest fantasies. Athletic looking, fiftyish, balding, impressive even at half-mast.

"Come on in," Bob Davies said.

Eric hesitated. Rudy had told him to have a good time, so it wasn't really cheating. And here was his chance at fulfilling a seven-year fantasy. He entered.

This slender blond young man strongly reminded Bob Davies of his stepson, the one with the golden treasure trail all the way down from his chest. He smiled darkly. The most potent fantasies are the most taboo. "You remind me of someone I know named Roger."

"My name's Eric."

"Would you mind terribly if I call you Roger?"

"Not at all . . . Coach," Eric said as he entered. He started to shut the door.

"Leave it open, Roger," his fantasy gym teacher said, "I like a crowd."

Rudy was heading down the hallway to clean up Room 35 when he saw half a dozen guys watching something going on in Room 29. Naturally he had to look.

He saw his boyfriend with his legs in the air getting it from that hardbody older guy who always came on to him when he checked in. Damn it looked hot. And the blissed-out expression on Eric's sweaty face was too good to miss. Rudy opened his pants and pushed his way through the men, joining these two so fast that Bob didn't have a chance to shoo him away like the others. With a shock, Bob realized who this was. *Oh, God,* he thought, his stepson and the hunky bathhouse employee. With a yell he filled his condom. Eric felt the spasms and shot so hard he hit Rudy's shirt. Rudy pulled out of Eric's mouth and began beating off. That's when the manager arrived.

"What the fuck are you doing, Diaz?" he shouted at a moment Rudy was unable to stop. The manager barged in and grabbed Rudy by his Flex T-shirt. "You are fired! No fucking with the customers, you asshole." He turned to Eric and Bob, "Both of you, out! Get your shit and get the fuck out."

Eric, Rudy, and Bob Davies found themselves in the parking lot. Eric was dazed, Rudy was outraged, but Bob was clammy and pale. He collapsed to his knees. "I can't breathe!" He clutched at his chest.

"Should we call 911?" Eric asked.

"No! God, no!" Bob winced in pain. "No one can know about this!" He fumbled in his pocket. "Here are my keys," he managed in between short breaths. "The red Benz. Get me to Cedars-Sinai!"

At the hospital, Rudy bailed. "I don't have a green card, Eric," he said as they pulled into the Emergency entrance. "I can't get mixed up in this. I'll see you later, chulo." He kissed Eric, opened the door, and was gone.

Eric got Bob inside and into the hands of medical technicians who slapped him on a gurney and rolled him away. Eric leaned against a wall to catch his breath. Moments later, he saw a man who took that breath away. He was shorter than Eric imagined from his porn, but there was no mistaking that face. Pausing a moment to smile at Eric in that devastatingly sexy way, was Frank "B.C." Powers himself. He winked at Eric, deliberately adjusted his crotch, and walked on out the door.

Stunned, Eric plopped down on an uncomfortable sofa. When he remembered to breathe he thought, *Way too much goes on here!*

Ninety minutes later Bob came walking out like a man with a new lease on life. It had been only a panic attack, but Bob hugged Eric with an enthusiasm shipwreck survivors usually reserve for their rescuers. "Let me drive you home, Roger."

"My name's Eric."

"Eric. What a beautiful name, Eric," Bob said with great sincerity. He looked out at the smoggy sky and sterile parking building. "What a beautiful, beautiful world."

On the short drive from Cedars-Sinai to Westbourne, Bob asked if there was anything he could do for his "guardian angel." Eric shook his head saying he was new in town, had been working through Star Temps, and just wanted a job. When they pulled up in front of Guy's house, Bob winked and said he'd see what he could do.

⋆

After a full afternoon of medical tests exploring the possibility of donating a kidney to his sister, Frank was more than glad to be leaving Cedars-Sinai. He drove to Mark's Restaurant on the edge of West Hollywood. Roger was at the bar polishing off a cosmopolitan. Frank smiled, happy to see him.

"Hi," he said. "I hope this isn't too weird."

"Actually, it is, but I've had two of these," Roger told him, holding up his large empty glass. "That helps."

"Let's get some food in you."

On the way to the table middle-aged and older patrons nodded at Frank and gave Roger knowing smiles, making him most uncomfortable. Once they were seated Roger immediately asked, "Why did you want to see me?"

Frank wanted to say, "Because I can't stop thinking about you. Because I didn't know how fucking lonely I was until I met you and you held me and you took that away." But he choked that back and instead said, "You were fun."

"'Fun?'"

"Not many people are fun, in my line. And nice."

"And 'nice'?"

Frank shifted uneasily. "When I, you know."

"Cried?" Roger watched Frank nod. "All right, so I'm fun and I'm nice."

"Okay!" Frank said in exasperation, "and you're hot."

Roger frowned. "Well, I'm a student with no money, especially after what you charged. Anyway, I have other debts, so you're wasting your time."

"Will you get over the money? Is it so hard to believe that maybe I thought you were worth seeing again? Besides, if you don't trust me, why did you come?"

Shame burned in Roger because he had feelings for another man. He looked down at his lap and mumbled, "I liked you."

That quivering feeling Frank hated in his stomach came back, only being here now with Roger, he didn't mind it so much. "How so?"

Roger didn't look up. "You weren't what I expected."

"You mean for a hustler?"

"I mean ever." Roger couldn't tell him he was soft but firm, and smooth, and warm, and tasted good, and felt like strength, and looked like confidence, and brimmed with easy masculinity, everything Roger felt he lacked in himself. And with all that, Frank was still vulnerable. He decided to risk being vulnerable himself. "And I didn't think I'd see you again. That's why when I was in Circus of Books yesterday morning, I bought the newest video."

It was one of the sweetest things anyone had ever said to Frank. "You bought *Saved By the Balls* because of me?"

Roger nodded and Frank beamed. He knew this was going to mean saying no to high-paying clients so he could see Roger, it meant reshuffling his regulars who were not going to be happy about it. Oh, yes, this was going to be very bad for business but at that moment he didn't care.

Hypnotized by that awesome smile, Roger was able to set aside his conflicting fears and enjoy his dinner with Frank.

After dessert, Frank noticed the time. "I gotta get to Numbers," he explained, "but this was great. Thanks for taking a chance."

The abruptness was startling. "You have to work tonight?"

"Business is business," he shrugged. "Can I see you again?"

The old anxieties returned and Roger was unable to answer. He knew he was supposed to be dating women and this was a man. A man who fucked other men for a living. "I don't know, Frank, I —"

"Call me Dave."

"What?"

"Dave Cohen, it's my real name. I go by Frank Powers for work. I'd like you to call me Dave."

This had been nowhere on Roger's radar. His thoughts whirled. This was insane. This was a man. But as Roger looked in Frank's eyes, Dave's eyes, one thing was clear: he needed to see this man again. "Tomorrow night?"

"Saturdays are really bad for me. Make it Sunday night? Say 6:00 at the French Market? I should be up by then." In a daze, Roger nodded. Dave smiled. He stood and came around the table to Roger, and kissed him. Full on the lips. Jaws dropped all over Mark's Restaurant. As all of his clients knew, Frank Powers never kissed.

"See ya Sunday, Roger."

"See ya . . . Dave."

Saturday, March 18th

Betty Davies opened the door and exclaimed, "Oh, my God, Hiro, what happened to your head?" She stared at the stitches over Hiro's left eye, a souvenir from falling over his drawerful of Arthur at work.

"Just some bad luck." He air-kissed her so as not to disturb her makeup and hair which was every bit as professionally decorated and sterile as her Toluca Lake home.

"Well, come in, come in. I'm so sorry Noel couldn't make it. Bob tells me he's on vacation?"

"Yes, we like to give each other a week or two apart. He's in Mexico. Sportfishing."

"How exciting! May I take your briefcase?"

"No. Thank you." He held out an imported bottle of premium sake. "I hope this is proper, in honor of tonight's cuisine."

"Oh, how lovely," she said taking it.

Bob Davies entered from the study and shook his hand heartily. "Did you hear Madonna got an Arthur? Luise Rainer's. Over half a million at the Sotheby's auction yesterday."

"I heard about it on *E!*," Betty said. "Is that why you were late last night, Bob?"

"No!" Bob said too quickly, trying not to sound like someone who'd had a panic attack after being thrown out of a bathhouse twenty-four hours earlier. "I, uh, had to see someone in the hospital. Cocktails anyone?" He led the way swiftly to the bar in the den and poured himself a soothing double Scotch. "Hiro?"

"Diet Coke for me."

He poured Hiro his Diet Coke. "So. Madonna. At least she didn't steal it, huh? With any luck maybe now she'll stick to music and leave movies alone," Bob said, followed by a deep swig of his drink. "God knows what she's gonna do with it. Probably have sex with it in her next video."

Hiro raised an eyebrow. Sex? He hadn't thought of that. He glanced down at his briefcase by his chair. The very idea was appalling, disgusting. Intriguing. His hosts were staring at him. He recovered with a start. "This is not the first theft, you know," he said to break the uncomfortable silence. "In fact, at the awards ceremony in the Biltmore Hotel in 1937, Miriam Hopkins won Best Supporting Actress for *Away We Go*. She had stayed home because she was ill. A man went up to the podium, accepted it for her, and walked out with it. He was never seen again and the statue was never found."

"Yes," Betty said. "That was the night Bob's aunt Margaret lost Best Actress to Luise Rainer."

"Margaret . . . Atherton?" Hiro asked in awe. "You are related to Margaret Atherton, the famous actress?"

"Yeeessss," Bob sneered under his breath. He knocked back more Scotch.

"I had no idea my friends had such illustrious relations."

"Yeah, it's a big freaking honor."

"Bob," his wife said with a warning.

"Sorry," Bob answered into his drink. In the other room the telephone rang. "I just hope they find whoever took this batch of Arthurs and string 'em up," Bob said. "You wouldn't believe the pain in the ass this has been for me. Did you know yesterday I had a full-on nutcase in my office? Spouting some nonsense about recovering icons and a Mission from God."

Their housekeeper, Bernice, stuck her head into the den. "Mr. Davies, it's Ms. Atherton."

"Thank you, Bernice," Bob said blackly, getting up. "I'll take it in the study." He apologized to his guest and family and left the room.

Miserable ancient bitch. Why couldn't he simply pay someone to be her "companion" and keep her out of his thinning hair? Some naïve, unsuspecting chump kid to dump her on and... hey! The kid he'd fucked yesterday afternoon at the bathhouse! Sweet, dependable, drove to the hospital, even waited. And he said he needed a job. What was it, Star something? Star Temps. *Yeah*, he thought, *to babysit a star.*

For the first time in years Bob Davies actually smiled as he picked up the phone to listen to his aunt rant. "Hello, Margaret. What's up your ass now?"

Sunday, March 19th

Michael Foster Fowler had searched flea markets in Downey, where the Arthurs had been stolen, and *mercados* all around L.A. County. Now he sized up vendors at the Sunday morning flea market at Fairfax High, wondering who might be sleazy enough to sell stolen Arthurs. An old foreign woman in a paisley caftan was selling trashy videos, but she had movie reel tins, a clapboard, and several obviously fake six-inch Institute awards. Could this be a sign from God? He asked her about the plastic Arthurs.

"Two dollar. Each."

"Do you have anything nicer?" he asked meaningfully. The woman stared at him. He leaned in closer. "A lot nicer?"

She narrowed her eyes at him. "I only have replicas."

"Of course. Very nice replicas. Maybe fifty-five very nice replicas?"

The woman shook her head. "I had one or two. Sold for fifty bucks," she told him. "I remember nothing else. My memory, at my age, grows cloudy," she added, holding her hand out. Fowler gritted his teeth and put a twenty in her hand. "Oh, yessssss. Sold one to homo queer. He was heavy, with goatee, and skinny tall friend. Tried to write check. Lived near here. "

"Where?"

"West, he said. 'West, west, and west.' Maybe West Hollywood with other homo queers. You homo queer? I have Jeff Stryker poster."

"No!"

"You sure? You have look."

"I do not! Liar!" He sputtered as he pointed at her. "Cursed shall you be in the city, and cursed shall you be in the field! Cursed shall be your basket and your kneading bowl and, and your ugly caftan and stupid ugly table full of ugly stuff!" He stormed away in fury. He was frustrated that after a week this was his only lead. And what the hell is west, west, and west? But it hardly surprised him that some faggot would buy it. Of course — west. It had to be West Hollywood.

It was right after lunch when Hiro set the Arthur on the floor near the lube. He took all of his clothes off except for his socks. Squatting, he positioned himself over the lubricated statuette. He watched himself in the full-length mirror on the closet door. He felt the statue's head touch his anus. Cold. But exciting. The very idea was unthinkable. Perverse. Thrilling. His touch warmed the metal.

He took the head into him with no trouble at all. He eased himself down onto the shoulders, allowing them to warm up. Bouncing slightly, ever lower, he felt the shoulders spread his asshole. Filling, but still no problem. He hadn't been a size queen all his adult life for nothing. He shifted his weight to see himself better in the mirror. This was a piece of cake. He had taken it past the laurel wreath the golden man was holding, down to the hips. He was slowly going up, and then down, from the hips to the head, and back down, and back up, a marvelous sensation feeling all the smooth bumps.

He shifted his weight again. Damn, he thought with a wince, wrong way. Try it this way, a little more, come on. The sock on his right foot slipped on the hardwood floor and Hiro fell onto the Arthur, all the way down to the base. The pain was blinding and he blacked out.

It was mid-afternoon when Hiro came to, lying on his bedroom floor. *Oh, God,* he thought, *what have I done to myself?* Without moving from the floor, he carefully, gingerly removed the Arthur from his rectum. He looked at his hand and saw there was blood on it. *Oh, this is very bad luck.* Slowly he pulled himself up to a semi-seated position, favoring his anus by leaning on one hip. There was a little more blood on the floor. A little smear. Some shit. And there was that deep dull ache in his bowels.

This was too mortifyingly embarrassing to go to a hospital. He lay back down on the floor trying to decide what to do. If he truly ruptured something, he could die. Right here, alone, with his lover hundreds of miles away in Mexico. He was frightened. What if he did die? The pain in his gut, the mess on the floor, it could happen. *If I am going to die,* he thought, *what would I like to do before I go?* He reached up on the nightstand and pulled down a pad and a pencil. He did what any good accountant would do.

He made a list.

Roger Davies met Dave at the French Market, a glorified neighborhood diner, for their second official date.

Roger overcompensated for his nervousness by being too hearty and making half-assed jokes. Dave was just happy to tune out and simply watch Roger's mouth move. He noticed Roger had become silent. Dave decided to wait it out.

At last Roger blurted, "I don't know if I can do this."

"Why not?"

"For one thing, I'm not gay." Dave choked on his Cobb salad. "Well, I'm not. I date women. I'm seeing my film professor. Female film professor."

"Really? And how many dates have you had with your female film professor?"

"None of your business."

"That's not very many. You know, I never went to college but maybe you should stop seeing your film professor and start seeing a therapist."

That was exactly what Roger had been thinking lately. Especially having these feelings for Dave. Just being near him made him feel safe. Accepted. Sexy. And right. But Dave was a man so the feelings had to be wrong. "I'll see who I want to see."

"That's fair," Dave said, looking almost as vulnerable as he had the other night. "But will you see me, too? Will you see me again? Because I really want to see you. Will you agree to that? Will you see me again?"

"I'm not ready for this. I'm confused."

"Well, I'm not. You suck cock. Straight boys don't do that. And you take it up the ass, greedy for more. And God help me, but all I want to do is fuck you. And hold you. And feel you hold me. And talk to you. Because, Jesus, I feel good when I do. And I don't know what to do about it except try to see you more." His mouth was dry. He took a gulp of water and looked around the restaurant. Then, "Have you ever seen me bottom?"

"What?"

"Bottom, play catcher, take it up the ass."

"I only have the one video."

"Trust me, you haven't and you won't. And I want to. For you."

Roger boggled. "Is this you being romantic? Because you really need to rent some movies to see how it's done." Dave stood and planted a big sloppy kiss on him. It tasted like garlic bread and melted him like the butter. Roger reached for Dave's head and held it there until he had to come up for air. "Okay," Roger breathed at last, "it's not *Breakfast at Tiffany's*, but it'll do."

"Think of it as *The Lady and the Tramp*," Dave smiled, sitting back down. "So can we be a thing?"

"A thing? You mean like boyfriends?"

"Don't call it that. Don't jinx it. Not yet. What do you think?"

Roger thought this man was the damnedest piece of work he'd ever met. "Sure. We can be a thing." He raised his iced tea. "To thing-dom."

"To thing-dom come."

⭐

Guy and Patrick returned to Guy's on Westbourne after shopping at the Beverly Center. "I could be wrong," Patrick said as they entered the house, "but it sounds like you're infested with rutting wildebeests."

"Tell me about it," Guy said heading down the hall. "It's like this every time Rudy gets off work early." He pounded on the closed door to Eric's room. "Your mother and I are home," he shouted, "and the neighbors are complaining." Instantly the noises stopped.

"Sorry!" Soon more subdued rhythmic noises were coming from the room.

Guy joined Patrick in the den. "I have got to get laid. Soon. It may be time to go back to the sex club. You want to come with me sometime?"

"Thanks," Patrick said. admiring the new jacket he'd bought at Bloomingdale's, "but if I want crabs I'll go to Red Lobster."

About an hour later, Eric came into the den, freshly showered and dressed. "Sorry about that," he said sheepishly."

"Oh, please," Guy said, polishing some of his recent estate sale purchases, "I should be so lucky. Hey, Tractor Boy, do you mind if we go out for dinner instead of eating here? I don't have the right pasta and I can't face improvising. It'll be my treat."

"Sure."

"Good, because I already called Suze and she's bringing a friend."

Patrick was flipping through an old issue of *Wallpaper*. "Your mother called while you were indisposed."

"Shit!" exclaimed Eric. "When?"

"Around the time you and your friend were shouting '¡Sí!' 'Yes!' '¡Sí!' 'Yes!' I knocked on your door but you seemed otherwise engaged."

"Oh, my God, did she hear that?"

"She did ask what was going on."

"Jesus, what did you tell her?"

"That you were being drilled in Spanish." He flipped another page and looked up. "Why are you covering your face with your hands?"

"Because she doesn't know I'm gay!"

Guy dropped a pewter paperweight. "You have got to be kidding." Without removing his hands from his face, Eric shook his head and sank into a chair. "No offence, Eric, but look at you. Does the rest of Missouri pluck their eyebrows? How many other people do you think exfoliate in Brownstar?"

"Rosebud."

"Whatever!" Guy threw up his hands in resignation. "You have got to tell her."

"I'll try to call her tomorrow," Eric said evasively. He was relieved to have Rudy join them.

"You have a *gato*?" Rudy asked. "I saw a little bed for him."

"Her," said Guy. "And I don't know where she is. Her name is Pussy and she disappeared four days ago. I'm getting worried, she's never been gone this long before."

Rudy sympathized and told him about his cat Toro. By the time Suze arrived, they had bonded over tales of feline affection. Suze arrived with Lee as her guest, who recognized Patrick immediately.

"Hey, boss," she said.

Eric was confused. "Boss? I thought you were temping for Madonna?"

"*Somebody* got me in a little trouble there," Lee said pointedly. "So now I'm at the mortuary."

"Wait, you have a mortuary?" Eric asked Patrick.

"Surely you didn't think I was paying him to hang around here," Guy said.

"Although you should," Patrick said. "God knows I improve the décor."

"How do you think I got the job order?" Suze said, kissing Patrick on the cheek.

Guy introduced Rudy to everyone, then herded them all outside to the cars.

At Rugby Drive, Guy and his entourage passed a rusty green convertible lumbering slowly in the other direction. Inside, Michael Foster Fowler was seething as he prowled the neighborhood. He had one slim lead and even that couldn't be easy, oh, no. There were three accursed streets in West Hollywood with 'West' in their names: West Knoll, Westmount, and Westbourne. At least they were all together, a block apart from each other running parallel between Santa Monica and Melrose. Those statues had to be here somewhere on one of these streets.

He punched himself in the thigh, hard, for about the fiftieth time for not asking the woman at the flea market for more information. But it wasn't his fault. She practically called him an abomination and he'd lost it. Now he was stuck here, wading through the sin-filled streets of West Hollywood. With all the men. The men who go to the gym and parade their near nakedness. Their hard bodies giving him those upsetting, wicked, lustful thoughts again. He violently shook his head to stop himself from thinking like this. To dispel his unclean thoughts he turned on the car radio, loud.

"— amazing news story about the missing Arthurs," blared the radio DJ. "A junk dealer found them, apparently in a dumpster, believe it or not, in Thai Town. So the stolen Arthurs have been found in time for the next week's Institute Awards ceremony. Police are questioning junk dealer Eddie Bowl —" Fowler smacked the radio off.

No!

It couldn't be. Some junk dealer found them? His Arthurs? In a dumpster? "No, no, no, no, no, no, NOOOO!" he moaned to streetlights that were as uncaring and silent as God.

Monday, March 20th

Shaking, Roger handed twelve-thousand dollars over to Nicholas.

"Roger," Nicholas said sadly, putting his arm around Roger's neck. "Do you know why I am annoyed with you?"

"I'm three hundred bucks short?" Roger stammered.

"Yes, my friend." With sudden terrifying strength, Nicholas slammed Roger's head into the fender of his Lexus, denting the car above the front wheel. Nicholas shoved him to the ground. "That was to get your attention, okay? Two thousand in two weeks. If not," and here Nicholas shrugged sadly, "something breaks." Nicholas turned and left Roger who still lay stunned on his back in the USC parking lot.

The silence that followed the big Greek's sudden assault was eerie. Roger sat up and tenderly checked his head for blood. None this time. He looked at his dented car.

His cell phone rang, scaring him so badly he gave a yell. He answered angrily.

"What!"

"Goodness, Roger, what kind of way is that to answer the phone?"

"Sorry, mother, it's been a bad morning."

"Well, I hope it improves because I want you to be home tonight for dinner, honey. And in a better mood. Your sister's bringing her boyfriend to meet us."

"Ugh, God!"

"No excuses. And be home early enough to make yourself presentable. Okay, sweetie? Roger?"

"Yes!" He ended the call with a furious stab at the End button. *Fuck dinner*, he thought, *where am I going to get two grand in two weeks?* His sister Janice was so good with money. So goody goddamn good with everything. Maybe he should hit her up for some of it while she was home with her boyfriend. Maybe this was good timing after all.

※

Eric shuffled into the kitchen where he found Guy perusing the garage sales in the paper. "What's for breakfast?"

"Pastry from Canter's," Guy said without looking up. He gestured toward the counter. "It's in the pink box. Which reminds me, have you seen Pussy this morning?"

"No. Not for a week. I put cat food out last night for her, though, just in case."

"I'm sure the raccoons thank you." Guy looked up. "After breakfast, would you help me look for her?"

Eric agreed as the phone rang. It was Suze.

"How cool is this?" she bubbled excitedly. "You were requested specially! Your new assignment is with a Margaret Atherton. Apparently she's this old movie star. You start as soon as you can get there. Just go and do whatever she wants, sort of like a houseboy."

"What do you mean I was requested?"

"This Atherton woman is Bob Davies's aunt. He's the one that called, asking specifically for 'Eric,' which I finally figured out was you. He's some VP at the Institute of Motion Picture Artists and Whatever. How do you know him?"

Eric smiled remembering the scene at Flex. "As a bottom."

"Wow," Suze replied, impressed. "That's networking!"

※

Around 3:30 Guy dropped Eric at Margaret Atherton's house on Hillcrest in Trousdale Estates above Sunset. It was a long, low, gray clapboard home with dark green trim and manicured juniper hedges all around. As he walked up the meticulous flagstone drive, Eric noticed a van from *E!* parked out front. At the dark entryway he rang the bell and waited over a minute, wondering if the star knew he was out there. Nervously, he rang the bell again. The door opened imperiously. There stood a large, tall, and muscular thirty-something Asian man wearing nurse's scrubs and a lot of attitude.

"I'm from Star Temps," Eric offered with an unsure smile. "I was assigned to Ms. Atherton. Bob Davies asked for me?"

The man looked him over and shook his head. "Honey, what did you do to deserve this?" He stepped aside for Eric to enter. "Come on in." He led Eric down a dark hallway lined with old black-and-white movie stills and hand-tinted studio photos. "Miss Thing is holding court today," he told Eric. "It's some cockamamie *E!* interview, so she's on her best behavior."

"I thought she was retired," Eric said. "Is she making another picture?"

"It's for the obituary, honey."

"She's dying?"

He snorted. "We should be so lucky. Okay, I have to announce you, so what's your name?"

"Eric. Eric Burgess," he said holding out his hand.

The man looked at it, but pointedly did not take it. "My name is Ming. I'm her nurse."

"Hi. Uh, Ming as in the famous vases, right?"

"No. As in 'The Merciless' so don't piss me off. Now get your bubble butt in there," and he pushed Eric into the spacious living room.

There the ancient Margaret Atherton dominated the room like a 1930s movie queen. She was swathed in overdone vintage late '60s pink finery, Dame Edna blue hair, and far too much pancake and blush. Thin and wiry in her wheelchair under the portable television lights, she looked on this intrusion with such frozen, arctic resentment that Eric shuddered. The longhaired cameraman turned around to see what could cause such peremptory cold disdain, as did an annoyed Mark Sparks of *E! Entertainment News*.

"Cut!" said Sparks, scowling.

Ming paid him no mind. "Eric Burgess, Margaret Atherton. Margaret Atherton, raw meat. A present from your nephew."

The actress gave a sudden, star-powered smile and was instantly charming in her hospitality. "Oh, it's lovely to meet such a fine looking young man," she said clasping his hand warmly for her interviewer's benefit. Then, with an edge: "Sit." She turned her fawning attention back to the camera. "Where were we?" Mark Sparks was staring at Eric, thinking he looked vaguely familiar. "Mr. Sparks?"

"Sorry. Um, the Institute Awards, 1937," he prompted.

"Oh," she frowned, "that." Sparks motioned for the cameraman to roll. "Yes, I was nominated for my role in *The Ring of Truth*, but it went to my dear and cherished friend Luise Rainer. I never got an Institute Award. This was her second. But I never resented her winning back-to-back Arthurs. It will be a terrible shame when she finally dies."

The interview concluded with shots of Margaret showing off the shelves of other awards and honors she had garnered over her career. The equipment was packed up and Mark Sparks was all smiles as he graciously thanked the actress for her time and generous hospitality. Actually, he loathed every second of this. His boss, Madison, had assigned him to do interviews with a laundry list of expected-to-drop-dead stars of yesteryear. It was a menial chore and there was no aspect of it he didn't resent. He was only too happy to be out of that Atherton woman's three-thousand square foot crypt.

The moment the front door closed behind Sparks and his cameraman, Margaret Atherton let loose. "The nerve of those bastards!" she yelled down the dim hall. "Fucking vultures can't wait till I'm dead. Sending that queer-ass monkey boy and his shit-for-brains camera moron into my house." She wheeled to a front window. "Fuck you!" she shouted at the departing van, using both hands to give the finger through the sheer drapes. Eric was in shock.

"My, my," said an unruffled Ming, "Mary Poppins gets PMS."

"Up yours, you faggot slant."

Ming shrugged. "If I recall, you accepted their request for an interview."

"Shut up and turn on my show!"

"Yessa, massa." Ming strolled to the old stereo/tuner and flicked on the radio.

Dr. Laura's shrill, judgmental voice filled the room like an overflowing toilet, but Margaret was too distracted to listen. She slammed her fist against her chair. "That cunt Luise Rainer. That was my goddam award!"

Ming flipped through a magazine. "You know this isn't good for your blood pressure."

"Fuck my blood pressure! You'd love it if I died, wouldn't you, you homo gook?"

"I'm chilling a bottle of champagne for the occasion," Ming called out over the Dr. Laura blather. "But until someone finally does drop a house on you, you really ought to calm down and have some lunch."

Margaret glowered at him in fury. Nothing was more maddening than not getting a rise out of a servant. Then she saw Eric cowering in a corner. Here was a person she hadn't abused. Yet. She rolled her chair over to him. "Don't just stand there with your thumb up your butt!" she railed. "Get your pansy ass in that kitchen and rustle me up some grub." As she wheeled out of the room, she barked over her shoulder, "And turn that Dr. Laura bitch off. She's too damn soft and namby-pamby."

Ming tossed the magazine on the credenza and smiled at Eric. "Welcome to your new job."

Bob Davies drove to his home in Toluca Lake. Tonight he would have a normal family around a normal table meeting his daughter, Janice's, normal boyfriend for dinner.

Janice met her father at the door with a kiss and a drink. "Hi, Daddy," she said like a '50s sitcom. "Come in, I want you to meet Elliott." Janice's boyfriend was an absurdly good-looking young man with black hair that hung in perfect waves. He had beautiful skin, hazel eyes, shaped eyebrows, and a jock's physique. He looked like a poster boy for privilege, and Bob Davies approved in spades.

Roger came down from upstairs to check out his sister's date. He noticed Elliott's fitted Lucky Brand jeans and a white button-down Oxford shirt under a rich burgundy Hermès sweater that matched his crisp new Nikes. Roger smirked as his gaydar registered off the scale.

"You must be Roger," Elliot said standing just a little too close. "Janice has told me so much about you, I feel like I know you."

Was he flirting? "Uh, don't believe everything you hear."

"I don't believe I've ever seen shoes like that, Elliott," said his stepfather.

"You haven't, Sir, and you won't," Elliott smiled. "You have to get 'em from the Nike Website. Special online order only. They let you design a pair any way you want. I got blue and burgundy because those are Janice's favorite colors. And look, on the heel, my initials E.S."

"I'll have to look into that," Bob said admiringly. "Tell me more about them after dinner?"

"It's a promise, sir."

Janice had convinced her mother to let Bernice cook, so the lamb chops, baby potatoes, and broccoli vinaigrette were delicious. Roger, though, was unable to eat any of it. He was too distracted by what he needed to ask his sister. And he could swear Elliott, who was absurdly attractive, kept giving him the eye.

After dessert and coffee, Janice went up to her old room. Roger fidgeted in his chair, eating nothing. When his stepdad and Elliott started talking college sports, he could stand it no longer. He excused himself, went upstairs, and confronted his sister.

Janice squealed in alarm. "You need how much money?"

"Two thousand, just to tide me over." Janice was frowning at him. "Oh, come on, it's not like I'm asking for ten." He knew, though, that day would come. "It's just two thousand, I know you can afford it."

"Yes, but that's not the point, is it? You haven't even told me what it's for so it must be something bad or wrong or something. Are you on drugs?"

"No!"

"Well, that's what I'd expect a person on drugs to say."

"I am not on drugs, okay? I just need a little cash here."

"No. Whatever it is, you're ashamed of it, and I'm not going to be an enabler."

Roger shook with rage. "Your boyfriend's gay!"

Janice rolled her eyes. "No, he's not. He gets that all the time, but he's not gay. Trust me. And if I do say so, that was pretty pathetic."

"Yeah, and you're a lot of help, Dr. fucking Phil." Roger stormed into his room, grabbed his keys, and charged out of the house.

Downstairs, Bob heard his stepchildren bickering and frowned. To cover, Bob suggested they all move into the den. "Tell me, Elliott, where you got such distinctive shoes?"

"Just go to www.nike.com and click on CUSTOM and you can design whatever kind you want."

"They sure look comfortable. Is it available in any size?"

"I don't know, sir. I know they're available in size elevens 'cause that's what these are."

"That's what Bob wears!" said Betty, pouring a highball.

"Would you like to try them on, Mr. Davies?"

"Oh, no, no. I just think they're very stylish. Very cool."

Elliott already had them off his feet. "Go ahead, Mr. D. They really are very comfortable."

"Well . . ." They were a good fit on Bob, snug yet accommodating. And then the phone rang. Bob was immediately sorry he answered it.

"It's terrible what they're doing!" his aunt railed on the other end. "These queers you hired, they're touching my things and abusing me. They're physically abusing me!"

"Oh, for God's sake, Margaret," Bob snarled at her.

"It's true! I have bruises! If you gave a damn about family you'd come put a stop to it." Bob was trying hard not to engage in this, so he let her sentence just hang there. In the silence, she guessed this tack wasn't working. She turned on a dime to play the pity card. "Oh, please come and send them away," she whined. "Make them stop. I don't have long to live."

"Ha," Bob said. "From your mouth to God's ears!"

"You get out here before I report you for elder abuse," she snapped and hung up.

"Fine!" Bob yelled at the silent phone before slamming it down. He snatched up his car keys.

"Honey, where are you going?" Betty asked, trailing after him down the hall.

"Where do you think?" he growled without looking back.

Bob Davies's red Mercedes roared up the driveway on Hillcrest a bit past 8:00 that night. He killed the engine and got out, slamming the door shut. He angrily walked to the front door. How many fucking times had he put up with these calls at all hours? Using his key, he entered to find his Aunt Margaret perched in her wheelchair, arms crossed, waiting for him imperiously by the fireplace.

"Took you long enough to get here."

"Don't," Bob warned her in a low voice. "Don't you even start that crap with me. Jesus, Margaret, what is your problem?"

"I've been abused! This candy-ass faggot you hired on top of that queer gook you call a nurse," she spat, indicating Eric and Ming over on the sidelines, "both of them are calling me names and they're touching my things!"

"I am sorry you have to hear that from her," Bob said apologizing to Ming.

Ming shrugged. "I heard worse this morning when she didn't quite make it to the toilet," he said, knowing it would mortify the old battle-ax.

After going through twelve nurses in seven months for this shrill harpy, Bob was so grateful to have one that stayed that he didn't care if this one was taking dumps on her dresser. As for that kid — Eric, was it? — who was currently cowering behind a leather wingback chair, he was more likely on the receiving end of lord-knows-what kind of abuse from her. God, he was cute. He flashed on fucking him just three days ago while — *Focus*, he thought, *focus!* He looked at his aunt.

"You know what, Margaret?" Bob said with finality. "I am never coming back." Margaret's hand fluttered to her throat. She looked hurt, wounded. Bob snorted. "Oh, you can't be serious. Do you really think anybody buys your shit anymore?"

"I only want my family around me," she almost whispered.

"Then you shoulda thought about that before you drove us all away." He moved directly in front of her chair. "Get this. Next time I'm ever in a room with you, one of us is gonna be in a coffin. You're an ungrateful, paranoid, bitter, soul-sucking God-damned millstone around my neck, and I have more than done my duty by you."

Margaret gathered all her angry strength to rise from her wheelchair. She stood there teetering, and she summoned a voice as cold as a blue iceberg. "I will thank you to leave my house this instant."

"Done!" Bob Davies turned on his rubber heel and walked out, not bothering to shut the door behind him.

At a little past 9:00, Roger parked his dented Lexus behind a Koo-Koo-Roo Chicken restaurant near the corner of Ventura and Laurel Canyon. After being rebuffed by his sister, he had driven aimlessly, angrily all over the Valley for the last hour and a half. The fact he hadn't eaten anything at dinner was kicking at his stomach so he went in and ordered a chicken salad. When he finished he felt better. Calmer, anyway. He dumped his plate and drink in the trash and headed for the restroom.

Sitting on the toilet he was amused to see a glory hole drilled through the wall to the next stall. Just as he finished, someone came in and took that stall. After a moment or two of the requisite silence, a finger darted ever so nonchalantly past the hole on the other side. *Oh, what the hell*, Roger thought.

He showed his finger briefly at the hole to indicate acceptance. The man in the other stall stood and moved to the hole, exposing Nikes below the stall wall. Roger's jaw dropped. They were blue and burgundy. A good-sized stiff penis poked through the hole and into his stall. It jerked upward a couple of times, tantalizingly. Roger smiled. He slid off the toilet to his knees and took the cock in his mouth. It was terrific. No wonder Janice was crazy about him. It was rock hard and veined and he could feel every irregularity with his lips and tongue. He began beating his own meat in a double-time rhythm to his bobbing head. He heard the man on the other side breathing irregularly, gasping, on the verge. Then, soundlessly, he came in Roger's mouth. The man pressed even harder against the wall, thrusting his dick as hard as he could at Roger, panting in short breaths. Roger shot his load, too. Half of it going on one of the online only, one-of-a-kind shoes. As soon as the man was done, he withdrew, zipped up, and dashed out.

Roger leaned back on his toilet and sat there smirking. He was right. Elliott wasn't as straight as the perfect Janice thought he was. But he did have a great dick and thick jizz.

Roger came home to find Elliott in the kitchen cleaning one of his Nikes with a cloth at the sink.

"Hello, Elliott," Roger purred as he poured himself a rum and coke. "Have a nice evening?"

"Yes, thank you. And you?"

"Yummy. Whatcha got there?"

"Oh, just taking care of a little stain."

Roger noticed Elliott was now wearing a pair of Timberland boots. "I see you changed into more butch shoes for late evening."

"No, I've had these on since after dinner."

"Oh, really," Roger said knowingly. He leaned in close enough to force Elliott to stop rubbing his Nike. "Then where have these been?"

"Wouldn't know," he shrugged. "I loaned 'em to your dad, ask him."

Tuesday, March 21st

The funeral was over and the mourners were leaving. "Didn't Mrs. Collins's nephew do a lovely job with the makeup?" Patrick said to as many of them as possible, making sure they all knew his mortuary was not to blame for the deceased looking like a cross between Ann Miller and a rodeo clown.

"Are you the owner?" asked an attractive thirtyish African-American woman.

"I am one of them," Patrick responded in a voice filled with professional sympathy for the occasion. "Did you know the deceased?"

"Not really. Wife of a colleague of mine. Only saw her at USC functions." She leaned in close, exuding confidence. "Although I never saw her look quite like this."

"Her nephew insisted. He has . . . a vivid palette."

"Um-hum. Of Magic Markers, apparently." Patrick decided he liked her immediately and smiled.

She had been counting on that. "My name is Sarah. I'm a filmmaker. Is there someplace we could talk?" she asked.

Mark Sparks, wearing only a white towel, was across town taking a break from bottoming at the Hollywood Spa bathhouse on Ivar. He ordered a Diet Coke and a Power Bar at the lounge café and sat down to do the *L.A. Times* crossword while waiting for some decent beefcake to check into the cavernous place. He looked up at the TV screen in the lounge to see himself. *Shit,* he thought watching his own Arthur report on the tube, *I gotta get a better gig.* He desperately needed to break a really big story to move up.

"— Fifty-two of the fifty-five Arthurs were found in a Thai Town dumpster by Eddie Bowling, a scrap-metal man who was looking for recyclable metal. Today he's finding that Arthur metal recycles into fame. Bob Davies of the Motion Picture Institute called Bowling to say he was grateful to have the famous statues back where they belong. As for the missing three awards, their whereabouts remain a mystery . . ."

"Not such a mystery," Sparks heard a Latino man at the bar say to the spa manager. "I know where one of them is."

Rudy had filled out a job application and was waiting there while the manager looked it over. Rudy was sure his prior experience at Flex would make getting this job a sure thing. He watched the taped Mark Sparks give his report and gestured toward the screen. "My boyfriend has one, a real Arthur," he told the uncaring manager. The real Mark Sparks was intensely interested.

"I need some phone numbers," the manager said. "Last employer and two references."

"How about my boyfriend?" Rudy asked.

"That'll do."

Rudy rattled off three numbers. Sparks quickly jotted them down in the margin of his crossword puzzle. *Please, God,* he breathed fervently, *let just one of these babies pay off.* His cell phone rang. He reached into his fanny pack on the table and grabbed it.

"Hello?" He gritted his teeth when he learned it was Phelps, his Department VP.

"Three missing Arthurs, where are they? Nobody knows, you with me, Sparks?"

"Yes," he tried not to growl.

"Eddie Bowling, junkman, found the Arthurs. I need you to get me a profile, Sparks. Eddie Bowling: man of the hour; from dumpster-diving to Arthur guest, getting the reward, instant stardom, it's the American dream. Think *Behind the Music,* think Lifetime *Biography,* think you can get it to me in two days?"

"Two days!?"

"That's what I wanted to hear, Sparks, you the man. Gotta go. Gimme twenty-two minutes on my desk, by Wednesday noon. Ciao."

Mark flung the phone back into his fanny pack. "Fuck!" He had to interview some junk man who thinks he's a hero because he has the amazing dumb random luck to fall over a dumpster full of Arthurs? Asshole probably kept the other ones for himself just to —

Mark gasped. Kept the *other ones* for himself! He stuffed the crossword into his fanny pack. In less than ten minutes, he was dressed and headed downtown for a date with a junk man.

Patrick and Guy were at Buzz, the coffee house next to the Virgin Megastore at Sunset and Crescent Heights. They were enjoying lattes and the intermittent stream of men — mostly industry, mostly gay, and all perfect — on the escalators either going to or just coming from the highly expensive and fashionable Crunch gym upstairs.

"Have I told you, Guy?" Patrick said breaking the reverie. "I'm doing a film."

"Porno?"

"Sadly, no, I suffer from the Irish curse. It's an independent film."

"Starring you?"

"Starring O'Leary & Finkelstein's Mortuary, for the moment. But I'm up for a part. Do you know anything about the myth of Parsifal?"

"Tragically, I was absent that school day."

"It's about crippled masculinity and carrying a father-wound."

"I'm guessing your film is not a musical."

"No, but if you can stop being a dick for two minutes I'll tell you what it is about."

Guy looked at Patrick who seemed uncharacteristically intense. "Proceed."

"Parsifal's father was a knight who died. His mother does everything in her power to keep him from going off like his father. Naturally, he goes off in search of the Holy Grail."

"Naturally, who wouldn't," Guy said. Patrick shot him a look. "Sorry."

"He meets the Fisher King whose kingdom is in ruins, but who tells him where the castle is that has the Grail and the Lance. Parsifal goes and enters the castle which is full of people hoping he can revive the kingdom by asking the right question, okay? He has a vision he doesn't understand so when he sees the Grail and the Lance he's unable to ask the question."

"What is the question?"

"Later. Okay, so the Grail disappears and everyone laughs at him and the Lance wounds him in his masculinity."

"Which means what?"

"It pokes him in the balls. It's symbolic of masculine wounding."

"Sweetheart, I want to be supportive, but *The Blair Witch Project* made more sense."

"These are archetypes." Guy continued to look at him blankly. "Indulge me. So the castle disappears and Parsifal spends years and years and years trying to become worthy of finding the castle and seeing the Grail again."

"Worthiness issues!" Guy exclaimed. "Okay, I'm there."

"Right. And along the way he fucks a lot of women, 'cause he's keeps needing to prove his masculinity."

"Because he got poked in the balls."

"Because his masculinity is wounded. But the more he fucks, the more empty it feels. Sound familiar?"

Guy remained silent. He knew that feeling all too well.

"All right, so one day this woman, Kundra, throws herself at him and he starts like he's going to fuck her, only he looks at her and she's all pathetic and desperate with lust — and he sees himself in her. He sees that's how he is. So with this huge realization he feels so sad for her, that he doesn't have sex with her. And that act of purity transforms her. She's made whole and so now can tell Parsifal where the castle is. And since because now he's pure, too, he can enter the castle where he sees the Lance and the Holy Grail. And because he's matured, he can ask the question."

"Thank God, the question."

"And the question he asks is, 'Whom does the Grail serve?'"

"That's it? Well, the answer better be good."

"The answer is, 'The Grail serves the Grail King.'"

"Who's the Grail King? The Fisher guy?"

"No. Parsifal."

"I don't get it."

"It doesn't matter, because he's touched again by the Lance, which heals his wound and the kingdom is revived and prospers. The end."

"And that's the movie you're making?"

"No."

"What? You give me some class in Medieval Shit 101 for nothing? I'm ordering another latte just to throw at your shoes."

"The movie is based on that. It's a modern re-telling, set in L.A. with a black perspective."

Guy affected a bad Irish accent to ask, "And what part o' this black perspective would you be, Mr. O'Leary, now?"

"It so happens there's a white man named Red in it," Patrick said indicating his hair. "Hello? Okay, look, you don't have to be excited for me. I wanted to share with you what I thought was an amazing story, one that spoke to me."

"Well, help me, Patrick. Tell me how."

"The searching for, for, I don't know what, but that feeling of searching . . ." Agitated, he got up and tossed his full coffee into a trash bin. "I need to get back. I'm letting the director use my office as a location. I gotta make sure everyone else is gone before they get there."

Guy watched him go with concern. This was not like Patrick. It was confusing.   And troubling.

Michael Foster Fowler turned off the *E! Entertainment* report and rolled over in dirty gray sheets. He resigned himself to spending the rest of this hideous day in bed, just as he had yesterday. He was mired in a sharp, severe depression he hadn't known since his first months at Desert Springs Restorative Treatment Center. God had given him a mission to find these icons and then two days ago snatched it away, dropping them by a dumpster in Thai Town. "Why?" he whispered again to the stained ceiling. "Why?"

Suddenly Fowler sat bolt upright. He'd been so stunned when he heard they were found that he hadn't considered the rest of the story. The black reporter on *E!* had just said it. Of course! They had not found all the Arthurs as had been first reported. They found fifty-two — but fifty-five had been stolen. Michael Foster Fowler saw it all clearly now. His part in God's divine plan was to find the three missing ones!

Mark Sparks had spent over two and a half frustrating and useless hours in Eddie Bowling's dumpy apartment that stank of other people's cast-offs, sucking up to this uneducated, smart-ass ghetto rube who, by a colossal fluke of the universe, somehow just happened to be rooting though the right filth at the right time. Sparks sighed and pretended to smile again. "Now, Eddie, when you retrieved the fifty-five Arthurs, did you bring them all here?"

"I told you there was fifty-two. I only found fifty-two. I told you that, like, three times. You take shitty notes for a reporter. No wonder you only at *E!*"

Sparks's cell phone rang. "Hello!" he barked into it.

It was Sparks's producer Madison. "Why don't I have a stack of obituary tapes on my desk? What the fuck are you doing?"

"Phelps commandeered me for a special assignment; it's not like I could tell him to go fuck himself."

"What 'special assignment'? Why didn't I hear about it?" Sparks enjoyed the paranoid panic creeping into Madison's voice. "Where are you?"

"Pacific Dining Car with Eddie Bowling. Heard of him? He found the Arthurs."

"Fuck you, Sparks! What about my update project? My obits?"

"Golly, I wouldn't know. Maybe you should ask Phelps."

"You are not going behind my back on this. You still answer to me and you will be on that update project first thing tomorrow morning or I'll take that to Phelps, you hear me?"

"Gotta go, our thirty-two ounce steaks are here." Sparks hit the End button, cutting him off.

"You know," said Bowling, "I actually have eaten at the Pacific Dining Car."

Sparks didn't even bother to look up. "At a table or in the alley out back?" He jerked his head toward the cameraman. "We're done here."

After getting thrown out of Flex bathhouse four days ago, Bob Davies didn't have the nerve to go back. But he did have the need for cock. That's why he was prowling the halls of the Hollywood Spa. A handsome Latino in a T-shirt and jeans came out of a room carrying a bucket and a wad of dirty sheets.

"Hey, look who it is," Rudy said. "What can I get you?"

"Oh, my God. What are you doing here?"

"That scene at Flex cost me my job, so . . ." Rudy shrugged and smiled at him.

"I'm sorry. I didn't realize."

Rudy laughed. "You looked pretty bad going to the hospital. We didn't know if you'd make it."

"I really appreciate you guys for doing that. If there's anything I can do for you, you'll let me know?"

Rudy cruised him. "Oh, I can think of something but I wouldn't have a job here when we got done."

Bob felt his dick give a little jump. This was more like it. The humpy towel attendant coming on to him. "What's your name?"

"Rudy Diaz," the handsome Latino said, reaching for a handshake deliberately calculated to last a little too long.

"Bob Davies." He took advantage of the lingering handshake to caress the man's hand with his thumb. He was pleased the gesture was returned. "What would you say to a real job? Say, in Beverly Hills?"

"What would I have to do?"

"I don't know yet. But it'd have better benefits than they're giving you here."

Rudy looked doubtful. "Illegals don't get benefits."

Bob nodded. He hadn't thought of that. He wondered how much clout he had in that area. "I could look into that. Interested?"

"Would I have . . . personal duties to perform?"

"I would expect, from time to time, that there would be duties of an occasional personal nature. Would that be a problem?"

He didn't want his boyfriend, Eric, to know but it sure beat the hell out of mopping up cum in this dump. Rudy smiled broadly. "I'm sure we could work something out."

Bob smiled back. He liked the idea of playing the Daddy. Especially with the Institute picking up the tab. "Where are you going to be in ten minutes?"

"Serving in the café lounge," Rudy told him.

Ten minutes later, Bob was fully dressed in his designer suit and ready to check out. Rudy was wiping tables when he looked up to see Bob coming down the main staircase. It was the first time Rudy had seen him really dressed and put together. Excellent Armani suit, Ferragamo crocodile loafers, he remembered the man's Mercedes. Shit, he just might get himself a sugar daddy out of this. Maybe more. A car, a better apartment, maybe even a green card. Who knows?

Bob gave Rudy his IMPAT card. "Come see me on Thursday. Call for an appointment. Dress a little better. You gotta look like a legitimate interview."

Rudy decided to press it. "Maybe you want me to buy some nice clothes?"

Bob good-naturedly brushed Rudy's goatee with his knuckles. "Don't get greedy. Show up first, and then we'll talk."

STEALING ARTHUR

Wednesday, March 22nd

Dave, a/k/a the impervious Frank "B.C." Powers, gripped the steering wheel in his car two floors below ground in the parking building near where his appointment had been at Cedars-Sinai. He was shaking. He couldn't donate a kidney to his sister after all. He had just learned he was HIV-positive.

The doctor had told him the news with a counselor in the room, and then left him with the counselor to talk about his feelings. The problem was he had no feelings because he was utterly numb. It wasn't real. It felt like it was happening to someone he was watching from across the room. He vomited in a trash can. The counselor asked if he had a friend he could call. No, no one. Or maybe . . . maybe he did now.

He called Roger. It rang and rang but the service never picked up. Christ, he had to get out of there. So he fled to his car where he was now, the windows shut tight. He heard only muffled sounds from the parking building where he was two floors below ground. Already buried. "Oh, Christ," he whispered trembling. "What now? What now?"

Big Ed booted his computer and idly explored new items on eBay. One caught his eye:

Pubic Hair of Madonna. Item number 3271447175
Starting bid: $100.
Current bid: $1,250.
Time left: 3 days 3 hours.
History: 19 bids.
Location: West Hollywood, CA
Description: One (1) blonde pubic hair from singer-actress Madonna. Harvested from bathroom of her private boudoir in her Los Feliz estate in Los Angeles. Approx. 1.5 inches long (measured while pulled straight). This seller prefers PayPal.
Place a bid: US $_____.

Big Ed winced at the price. Everyone had her tired coffee table book where she bared her bush ad nauseum, but who else could say they had an actual piece of the pie? Oh, what the hell. Considering what he was willing to bid on an Arthur at the Sotheby's auction last Friday, this was nothing. He bid thirteen thousand dollars and clicked over to check his e-vite to see who was coming to his Arthur party on Sunday.

Hm, nothing from Petey in West Hollywood yet. Going into Instant Messaging, he saw Petey was online and decided to IM him.

"Yo, Petey. What up. :) Come to my party Sun????" He hit SEND.

With a gling sound on Big Ed's computer, Petey sent his IM back. "Sorry didn't RSVP. Busy. BTW, can I bring guest?"

"As long as he's hot ;)" Send.

Gling. "LOL. I'll be there. See ya."

Petey got rid of the Instant Messages so he could finish downloading photos from hunglatinos.com. These macho Mexican mariposas had been his downfall in Vegas, and damn if he still wasn't a sucker for them here in L.A. But here it was all on his terms.

It was an elegantly hateful plan based on taking advantage of undocumented aliens. All over Los Angeles there were street corners where *jornaleros* gathered, men from Mexico, Guatemala, and other Central American countries, struggling to feed their families by getting day jobs for dirt wages.

Petey would roll up in his black Ford F-250 pickup truck, point at the hottest man in the group and say, "You." The man would run over and hop in the back of his truck, grateful for a job and a day's pay. Petey would take the man to a hotel room he had rented and, once inside, pull out his gun and tie the man down. Then Petey would fuck him, two, maybe three times over the course of the afternoon. He knew he could depend on the humiliation of a sodomized man in a hyper-macho culture to keep this disgrace to himself.

Petey called his goon Nicholas on his cell phone. "Where are you?"

"Finishing up some business in Brentwood. It will be a good week, I think."

"Good, 'cause I'm going to Vegas this weekend. Friend of mine is having an Arthur party. Can you handle the collections and deposits?"

"Boss, what do you think I am? Sure I handle for you. You have good time. Put a hundred bucks on Cameron Diaz and Kevin Spacey for me."

Petey chuckled in amusement. "You follow the Arthurs?"

"Eh," Nicholas said philosophically. "In Greece, nobody care. But here in this town everyone is crazy. I catch the crazy, too, so yes, now I follow Arthurs. Also a hundred on *Sixth Sense*, I think."

"I got you down. I'll see you next week to go over the books."

The days after sucking off his stepfather had been an emotional maelstrom for Roger. He was disgusted with himself. And with Bob, too, for cheating on his mother like his real father had. And cheating with Bob made Roger the other, what? Woman? Betrayer, certainly — but it was a mistake! Except for the desire for dick. Which was also wrong. He craved cleansing. He called a number he had only called twice before.

"Hello?"

"It's me. I need it again."

"Who is this?"

There was a beep from another call. He ignored it. "The college boy. Blond."

"Oh, yeah. The straight jock." The voice shifted lower. "You been dirty again?"

"Yes," Roger whispered.

"I can't hear you, boy. Say it."

"I've been dirty."

"Uh-huh. Then you know where you have to go?"

"Yes." Again there was the beep, and again he ignored it.

"Yes, what, you filthy shit?"

"Yes, Sir."

"That's right, you fucking maggot." There was a pause, Roger heard the man breathing. "We'll take care of this tonight, midnight. You got that, boy?"

"Yes, Sir." The beep sounded a third time. Roger shut his phone.

While waiting for his computer to boot up, Mark Sparks opened his briefcase. There was the crossword he had been working on two days earlier in the Hollywood Spa. *Damn*, he thought. The ordeal with Eddie Bowling had erased it from his mind. He looked at the three phone numbers he'd overheard the Hispanic guy give the manager.

As soon as his computer was up, he typed in www.anywho.com and clicked on "Reverse Search." He entered the first number and clicked. It was a spa called Flex. "Figures," he smirked. Okay, he thought, let's try the second number. Disconnected. Shit. He entered the last number. "Bingo!" he said with a sly grin. It was a residence on Westbourne in West Hollywood. Sparks wrote down the address.

At the end of a long shrill day at Margaret Atherton's, Eric took the #2 bus down Sunset to Ivar Street to meet Rudy at the Hollywood Spa. He arrived just as Rudy was punching out.

"We were so busy I didn't get lunch," Rudy said, "I gotta eat something right now."

"Okay," Eric said as they walked up the street, "but it's gotta be cheap."

Rudy made a dark face. "Shit, man."

"What?" Eric asked, annoyed at the attitude.

"You never have any money."

"I'm a temp, hello? And they've only paid me for a couple of days." They turned onto tourist-crowded Hollywood Boulevard. "Besides, I've had to grit my teeth and put up with Margaret Atherton bitching about 'those damned homos rooting through my papers' all day. I'd appreciate it if you'd cut the moody Mexican crap."

"What the fuck does that mean?" Rudy demanded, stopping for a face-off.

Eric knew he had stepped over the line. He also knew they were both in foul moods, so he tried to smooth it over. "I'm sorry, let's get you something to eat."

"I don't think so, you Anglo asshole." He shook his head. "Now it comes out, doesn't it?"

"What?"

"You just wanted to have a brown-skin boy, something exotic, didn't you?"

"What are you talking about? You were the one who put the moves on me."

"Still, Gringo gets to fuck the wetback."

"You're forgetting I'm the bottom here! If anyone gets fucked it's me." A flash camera went off. Tourists taking in the Walk of Fame had gathered for this little impromptu sidewalk show, but Eric was beyond caring. "And since I 'never have any money,' why don't you find yourself a sugar daddy?"

"Maybe I have," Rudy shot back, "Someone not such a twinkie hick. Somebody in the movies who can hold down a decent job, maybe. And God knows, someone a little more versatile in bed!"

Stunned, Eric reeled. "Rudy, all you had to do was ask."

"Ahh, *chinga tu madre*," he mumbled and strode through the small crowd around them.

Hot, confused, and upset, Eric ran through the tourists in the opposite direction. What the hell had just happened?

"Oh, honey, I guess it wasn't meant to be," Suze purred over the phone. "Anyway it was only, what, a week?"

"Nine days," Eric sniffed, trying not to cry again. "But I really liked him. Maybe more. What do you do when you get dumped?" he asked her.

"Self-medicate, but we don't need to go there. You need to do something that'll make you forget all about him." She thought a moment. "I know, get laid!"

"I don't know anyone else in L.A."

"That's why God made bathhouses and sex clubs."

Bathhouse memories just made Eric think of Rudy. "What's a sex club?"

"It's a place gay men go for a fast dirty fuck so they can get on with their lives. It's what hetero men only wish they had. Ask Guy, he'll tell you all about them."

"He's not here."

"Then just look in any local gay rag. Eric, sweetheart, I've gotta go. You find yourself a nice sex club and well talk tomorrow. Ciao!"

Eric disembarked the #4 bus in a dense lower-middle-class residential area. It was dark, streets were empty, and there were no signs anywhere. How was he supposed to find a sex club hidden in all this? He saw a figure in the shadows. As it walked past a streetlight, Eric saw the menacing shine of black leather from his cap and the intimidating glint of chain on his chest. *This may be more than I bargained for,* Eric thought nervously. The man turned the corner and was gone. "Oh, shit," Eric whispered, then ran across the street to follow him. He saw the man open an unmarked door on a blank looking building and disappear inside. *Well, I've come this far,* Eric thought. He took a deep breath, crossed the street and entered.

Eric showed his I.D., paid eleven dollars for "membership" to Prowl, and was buzzed in. Dozens of men were stalking one another in the shadowy dimness, both assaulted and driven by the pounding music. The smell of cowhide, poppers, and cigar smoke mixed with the heady scent of raw sex. Testosterone practically crackled in the air. He saw a man with an Ampellang piercing through the head of his penis using it to smack the face of another man kneeling before him in a black straightjacket. A man with an angel wing tattoo spanning his shoulderblades was being plowed against a wall by a man wearing only workboots and a gas mask. Eric climbed the stairs in the center of the space.

He was stopped by a darkly muscular man in a hood who simply reached out and held on to Eric's crotch.

"Been fucked yet, vanilla boy?" the man asked.

"Uh, no, I just got here."

"Then your lily ass is mine." Pulling Eric by the crotch, the man led him over to a corner room. "Drop 'em." Trembling with excitement tinged with fear, Eric followed orders. The man was wearing dirty 501 jeans with just the top button fastened so his dick and balls could hang out. He pulled off his black T-shirt to reveal a hairy chest and an American Indian tattoo on his left shoulder.

He roughly pushed Eric to his knees and thrust his genitals in Eric's face. "Work on those balls, boy." Eric was happy to comply, but he kept wondering, *How do I know this guy?* The man reached into Eric's mouth and pulled Eric up by his jaw. He took a handful of lube and slathered it in Eric's ass. He pulled Eric's head close and whispered, "You take it bareback?"

"No."

"Fine, it just takes twice as long." He ripped open a condom packet with his teeth and quickly rolled the rubber on his thick dick. "On your back." Eric did as he was told and put his legs up. The man leaned over him and in a guttural whisper said, "You are mine." He grabbed Eric's shirt and popped open all the buttons. Before Eric could say anything, the man had plunged deep inside him, taking his breath away.

Damn, thought Eric, riding thrust after thrust, *this guy is good!* He just wished he could remember where he had seen the man before. Suddenly he knew. "Oh, my god, you're Frank Powers!" Eric exclaimed.

"Yeah, so fucking what?" Powers said, not letting up a bit.

So what? thought Eric, *He's only the hottest man in porn. Only the man I've beat off to for years.* "Give it to me!" Eric shouted. *And he's fucking me!* Power's rhythm suddenly changed. He was groaning and pushing tight against Eric's ass. *And he's coming inside of me!* "Oh, God!" Eric shot over his shoulder and continued spurting on his belly. Powers fell on top of him, both of them out of breath.

Twenty minutes later, Eric was drinking a Diet Pepsi from the machine near the front. As he relaxed on a ratty worn sofa next to three bikers who were rimming each other, he was pleased at how rapidly he was becoming acclimated to Los Angeles. He figured there wasn't much more that could surprise him.

Then he went back upstairs.

He saw a noisy crowd of men gathered around a sling in one of the rooms. Standing at the edge he heard a young man moaning in what sounded like pain, with occasional cries of "Please!" and "Stop!".

The crowd of men jeered and cursed at him, "Take it, you pussy!" Eric maneuvered to the side where he could get up on a railing to see. A young blond college kid was forcibly held in a sling by four men. He was wet, red-faced, and writhing as a hulking man standing with his hairy back to Eric hammered the kid.

"How's it feel, straight boy?" the man grunted in a guttural growl while thrusting.

"Don't!" the kid begged.

"Shut up!" the man demanded, backhanding him hard in the stomach. The kid tried to double over, but the others held him down. He started to cry, whimpering. That only made the other man angrier. He spat in the kid's face. "I said shut up, you fucking breeder!" He leaned in, smacking the poor kid across the face.

Eric was aghast. *This is rape,* he said to himself, *this is wrong!*

"Let me go," the kid's face was distorted in fear and pain. "Please!"

"If you won't fucking shut up, I'll shut you up!" The man pulled out of the boy and pushed his way through the crowd to the other end of the room to get to the kid's face.

Eric gasped in shock. It was his roommate, Guy!

Grabbing the kid's matted blond hair, Guy forced him to swallow his condom-covered dick. The men pressing close cheered. "Eat it, frat boy," he ordered. His victim choked and gagged but Guy maintained his hold. "Clean all that ass juice off that dick. Yeah. You got a girlfriend? Tell her you know how to suck cock, too." The kid fell into a rhythm. "This straight boy's sucked dick before. Oh, yeah. Uh-huh. Oh, he's a good cocksucker. Oh, God." Excitedly, Guy withdrew, pulled off the condom and beat off, coming on the kid's face. After smearing it around with his hairy dick, he turned to the men holding the boy. "Let him go."

When he was released, the college kid slid to the floor. He hugged one of Guy's legs and jacked off in less than ten strokes. He kissed Guy's filthy work boot, repeating, "Thank you. Thank you. Thank you, Sir."

The rest of the group dispersed. Guy looked over. "Oh, hi, Eric," he said with a smile. "Having fun?" Eric remained frozen, his mouth and eyes open wide. "Oh, dear," Guy said. "You look like you just learned the recipe for Soylent Green."

"What," Eric finally found the words to say, "was that?"

"A movie before your time."

"No, I mean that!" he said gesturing at the wet sling.

"Oh." Guy came over and put a hand on his shoulder. "Let's get outta here and get something to eat. Degradation makes me hungry as hell."

Dave saw the kid coming up the stairs and grabbed him by the crotch. "Been fucked yet, vanilla boy?" The kid said no. "Then your lily ass is mine." He roughly took the kid to a corner room and yanked the boy's pants open and down. "You take it bareback?" The kid whispered he didn't. So he put a condom on his famous dick, the now-lethal dick, the dick of death. He told the kid to get his legs in the air, leaned over him and said darkly, "You are mine."

Fucking, fucking, like the city that had fucked him, giving him the virus. This kid who looked a little like Roger. Fuck Roger. Fuck everything.

"Oh, my God, you're Frank Powers!"

Dave kept plunging it in deep, balls slapping so hard they hurt. "Yeah, so fucking what?" A lot of fucking good that fucking did him. He withdrew completely only for a second.

Unnoticed, he pulled the condom off.

Then he went right back to plowing the kid, the kid who was going wild underneath him.

A half hour later, Dave had just pissed on the guy lying in the tub in the Prowl bathroom when Roger entered. "What the fuck are you doing here?" Dave demanded.

"Who the hell are — Dave?" Roger asked, stunned to see him here, confused by Dave's leather hood.

"Are you just getting here?" Dave said, noting Roger was fully clothed.

"Leaving. What are you doing here? I thought you had clients?"

"And that gave you permission to come here, Mr. I'm-Not-Gay?"

"You're the hustler and I have to be faithful?"

"I thought we were a thing," Dave raged at him.

"Yeah, whatever the fuck that is!"

"I needed you today."

"Oh, well, next time maybe you should make an appointment, like I was a client. How fucking dare you give me this shit? You have no idea what I've been through in the last couple of days."

"I'm HIV-positive!" The words named the disease everyone knew was present in this place. The words that were feared and denied at a level that made them unutterable in a sex club had been spoken.

"Shit," said the guy in the bathtub.

"I found out today," Dave said. "I tried to call you. I tried to call you but there was no answer . . ." He began to sob. "Oh, Roger, I'm so scared."

"Let's go sit down."

On the sofa by the Pepsi machine, Dave told Roger everything that had happened at the hospital, everything he was afraid of, money, insurance, clients, income, health, looks, reputation, death, pills . . . things he had never told anyone came pouring out. A couple of hours later, Dave was exhausted and grew quiet. Roger gently moved Dave around so he could lean against Roger and be held. After a silence, Dave said, "Oh, my God, I've been going on and on. What about you? What's going on in your life?"

Roger gave a half-chuckle. He owed thousands of dollars he couldn't pay to his bookie who had beat him up and threatened him, he had sucked off his mother's husband, he was wrestling with his soul over his sexuality, he had just gotten ass-fucked by the nameless dom he called when he craved punishment, and he was having an affair with a hustler he probably loved who just told him he had HIV. Everything felt like it was crumbling, but through the new perspective of Dave's HIV — and especially the warmth of Dave in his arms — it all fell away.

"Nothing," Roger said. "Absolutely nothing." Roger had equal measures of dread of the future mixed with contentment for the moment, this fleeting instant, that combined to make him feel okay. Not good. Nothing like good. But okay.

And in that moment, okay was enough.

※

It was past one o'clock when Guy and Eric pulled into the parking lot next to Pink's Hot Dogs on La Brea. They got out and joined the line in front of the open-air stand. "Eric, did you know I used to be married? I mean, to a woman?"

"You mentioned it once. Patrick said to let it go."

"Patrick is wise. Her name was Becky. Possibly the most fucked-up thing I ever did." They picked up their hot dogs and moved to the condiment stand. "I was taught that abortion, homosexuality, and women in pants caused the bloody wounds of Jesus to flow afresh."

"Eww," Eric said, having just covered his cheese dog with ketchup.

"Sorry. Anyway, I was taught that my thoughts of other men were 'vile.' I was an 'abomination,' blahblahblah, so I did everything I could to be straight." They found a table and sat. "I felt so bad I wanted to die, but if I died, I'd go to hell. Finally, I got to the point I figured hell couldn't be any worse than this, so I drank gas from the lawn mower."

"Ugh, gasoline?"

"I know, it's so trailer park, but that's what was on hand. When I woke up in the hospital, the chaplain asked me why I did it and, stupid me, I told him. He told me about Desert Springs Ministries, where all I had to do was give my life over to Jesus, and God would cure me of my hideous evil."

"They're an ex-gay group?" Eric asked, already on his second cheese dog.

Guy nodded. "I spent four years there learning to hate myself even more in the name of Jesus. Didn't help that one of my 'brothers in Christ' was quoting me scripture by day and fucking me in the ass at night." Guy's expression darkened as he recalled the spiritual violence.

"So what happened?"

"Huh?" Eric had jolted him back to the present. Guy quickly gathered his thoughts. "Well, eventually I had to prove I was changed by taking a wife. So I did."

"Where is she now?"

"No idea. And given how I treated her I'm sure she's glad to be rid of me. Not that she didn't have issues, but at Desert Springs, who didn't?"

"She was gay, too?"

"I don't think she knew what she was. Anyway, after that it took me another five years to come out to myself, figure shit out, and become a functioning human being. So you see why I have just a tiny amount of rage at the breeder world?"

"And that's why you were raping that straight man?"

"In a sex club? Wake up and smell the poppers. It's a scene, Eric. I get to work out my anger on these guys."

"But aren't you afraid they could have you arrested?"

"Honey, these guys come there looking for me. That blond kid tonight? He had a fucking appointment with me. Hell, I've had that boy twice before." Eric sat in silence as Guy finished his chilidog. Guy knew Eric had a lot of sorting-out to do. "C'mon, Grasshopper, let's get you home."

A quarter to two in the morning, Michael Foster Fowler was keeping watch in his car on Westbourne in West Hollywood. Guy and Eric drove past, turning into the drive by the purple house with the bougainvillea. "Now who would be coming home so late on a weeknight?" Fowler asked the plastic Virgin Mary on his dashboard. Anybody out this late was up to no good. These people would bear watching. Yes. Close watching.

Thursday, March 23rd

"Eric! Your little Madonna pube is up to over two thousand dollars on eBay."

"Seriously?"

"Come look," he said gesturing to the computer screen. The bidding was at $2,075. "That was over an hour ago, let's see where it is now." He clicked on "refresh" and the screen changed. Eric and Guy looked at it in shock. eBay had stopped the bidding.

Eric read aloud, "'The seller's claim cannot be verified.'"

"Noooooooo!" Guy roared.

Eric was confused. "They're saying we can't prove it's Madonna's?"

"That is total bullshit!" bellowed Guy. "Just clone the DNA and see if you don't get a trampy diva with a bogus English accent." Guy grabbed the monitor in both hands and shook it. "Fuck you, eBay! Fuck your ugly eBay wife! Fuck your mutant kids and diseased pets and awful clothes!" He slumped into the office chair. By the computer was an envelope marked "Madonna hair." Guy picked it up and sadly held it to his chest. "Eric, could I be alone for a while?"

In the car later, Eric comforted Guy. "I think we're doing the right thing." Guy was driving him to work by way of the funeral home on Santa Monica. "If it wasn't for Lee, I'd never have found the thing in the first place."

Inside they found Lee at the desk by the main door in front of the O'Leary & Finkelstein office. When they presented her with the Madonna hair, she let out a shriek that brought her boss out of his office.

"What was that?" he demanded.

"Hi, Patrick," Eric said. "We just stopped by to give Lee some pubic hair."

Patrick frowned at her. "When I hired you, I assumed you had your own."

"This is Madonna's!" she told him excitedly, waving the envelope.

"Yeah, but just try convincing eBay of that," muttered Guy bitterly. "Hey, Patrick, I wanted to apologize for the other day. Still don't know what I did, but I can't take you being pissed at me."

Patrick hugged him. "It's nothing buying me an overpriced lunch can't fix. Authentic Café, with drinks, noon?"

"All right, but at that price I want to run off a few Xerox copies while I'm here. I'm putting up missing-cat notices in the neighborhood."

"Pussy's still not back?" Guy shook his head. "Sorry to hear that," Patrick said. "Come on in and use mine, it's color."

STEALING ARTHUR

Back in the car Eric was considering the fact that he knew someone who ran a mortuary. He idly wondered aloud, "Is Patrick an O'Leary or a Finkelstein?"

"He's got red hair and a foreskin," Guy said. "You do the math."

"Who are the Finkelsteins?"

"Silent partners. They own something like half and let Patrick run it."

"How do you apply to run a mortuary?"

"He didn't. It was his dad's. His mom died, and then when dad kicked, his sister got all the money and Patrick got the business dumped in his lap."

"Where's his sister?"

"Utah, maybe. She married a Mormon, so they don't speak. I love Mormons. Ever fuck one?" Guy glanced over and smiled. "Oh, look who I'm asking."

Eric frowned. "So he got stuck with his dad's choice of business."

"Yeah."

Eric shook his head. "My dad wanted me to go into construction like him. I guess they think that's gonna make a man out of us. Whatever that is. Still, I keep trying. I don't know why."

"Me, too, and mine's dead."

"It's like we're all foraging, or hunting for whatever it is that we're supposed to find or be or do to become a man. Does anybody really find it?"

"Huh."

"What?"

"Just remembering a story Patrick told me the other day. About knights and getting a lance in the balls." They were silent the rest of the way until Guy pulled up in front of Margaret Atherton's house. "Okay, get out and get to work. With no Madonna muff, you've got rent to pay."

After lunch, Margaret Atherton's nurse, Ming, announced a surprise for both Eric and Margaret. "I've had it on order at Video West for weeks and it finally came in yesterday." He dug in his bag and came up with a VHS tape. "I've got an actual copy of *The Ring of Truth*."

"Why," demanded Margaret, "would you want to see that old thing?"

"Said the 'old thing' herself," quipped Ming. "I want to see what you're always bitching about the Institute Award over. You know, 'I was robbed,' and all that drama."

"I was robbed, you cocksucking coolie!"

"And I figure there's a good chance it'll shut you up. Besides, it's bound to be a hoot to watch."

"Fuck you. It's not a hoot."

"No? Let's put it in and find out," Ming said fitting it in the VCR slot. He pressed PLAY and got comfortable.

Ninety minutes later, both Eric and Ming were riveted to a sixty-three-year-old black and white melodrama. In it, Margaret Atherton was young and soft. She was an unpretentious, ethereal beauty, who had practicality and hard-as-nails strength. Her husband thought she had died in a shipwreck and had married a loving heiress to provide for the children. Kindness and heartbreak shone from a luminous face as she let them carry on in the bliss of ignorance, because she just learned she was dying of leukemia. "Treat them well," she says to the good-hearted heiress who discovers her truth. "I will be in God's hands in a very short time. Richard, Johnny, and Lisa . . . I leave in your hands." The music swelled. THE END.

"Oh, my God," Ming wailed in tears and snot, "it's too sad!"

Eric, too, realized he had been crying. He looked at the decaying, wheelchair-bound Margaret Atherton with newfound tenderness and awe.

"That's why I should have that fucking award," she declared smugly. "But those Hollywood assholes gave it to that dyke Luise Rainer." She wheeled herself away grumbling, "Fucking Hollywood faggots."

Roger sat in the USC coffeehouse long enough for his decaf to reach room temperature. How had his life gotten so fucked up? The debts, the boyfriend — was he a boyfriend? And now the HIV shit? More insanity he didn't need. But there was a part of him that did need Dave. Did he? Shameful. Lusting for a man. Stealing from his parents and begging for money. He felt completely out of control.

"I said hey." Dr. Sarah Utley was standing directly in front of him. "In your own little world, huh?" she asked with a smile.

Roger tried smiling back. "What are you doing here?"

She held up a bag with a sweet roll in it. "Breakfast and lunch. And I'm filling this out." In her other hand were three typed pages stapled together.

"School stuff?"

"Arthur ballot. For a party Sunday. There's a prize for whoever gets the most right." She thought of her own Arthur sitting at home. Her good-luck charm for the film she was making. She exuded confidence. Felt daring, even. She tilted her head at her student. "You wanna come to this party I'm going to?"

"As long as it's not a teacher-student thing. I hear that's frowned upon."

"Hey, if you're gonna give me grief about it —"

"I'd love to go." Roger replied. Dating a woman. This was normal. He could use a good dose of normal right now. "I'd like that very much."

"That's more like it." She smiled and got up to go. "I'll call you?"

"You have my number."

"Yes, I do." She leaned on the table. "Can we keep this on the down low?"

With the flickering glance at her breasts she had intended, he said, "Of course."

In West Hollywood, *E! Entertainment* reporter Mark Sparks was looking for an address on Westbourne. He eased his red Miata to a stop across the street from a purple house covered with fiery bougainvillea. Was it empty? Mark got out of the car and affected an archly casual stroll over to the gate in the low wall surrounding the yard. No car in the driveway. He entered the gate with a sense of déjà vu. Had he gone home with someone here? He sidled over to a window for a look inside.

Michael Foster Fowler was watching this while eating a Whopper Jr. in his car also staked out on Westbourne. Fowler tossed the sandwich aside and slid out of his green convertible. He hustled up the street, hiding behind bushes as he got close to the house. Through the thick arborvitae hedge next door he saw a short, sturdy black man in Polo khakis and white Façonnable dress shirt peering into the kitchen window.

Mark looked through the kitchen into the den beyond it. Suddenly his cell phone rang, scaring him half to death. "Jesus, what?" he whispered into the phone. "Look, don't give me shit about not being on your project, Madison, I'm on a story. I could be this close to finding the missing Arthurs, is that big enough for you?"

Fowler's eyes grew wide.

"No, no, no," Sparks begged, "please don't make me come in, not now. Okay, fine! I will!" He snapped the phone off, then yelled at it, "Fuck! You!" He jammed it in his pocket. Taking one last look inside the kitchen, he muttered, "You're in there, I just know it. And you're mine." He turned and stormed angrily to his car.

Fowler tiptoed around the hedge, skulking into the backyard of the purple house. On the deck there was a window into the den. Shading his eyes, he pressed his nose against it for a better look inside. Reflected in the glass of a framed poster for Ross Hunter's *Lost Horizon*, he saw a shadow of himself and, by moving a little to the left, shelves filled with books and knickknacks . . . and there it was!

Seemingly out of nowhere, a silver RAV-4 drove up the drive, radio blaring the Bow Wow Wow classic "I Want Candy." Fowler dropped behind a large jade plant, his heart thumping like mad.

The driver turned the car off, killing the music, but he continued to sing the chorus, only with different words. "I want Pussy . . ." He got out and opened the rear door and stacked several boxes on the rear seat. Then, still singing, he lifted them all in one load, shutting the door with his foot. "I want Pussy . . ." He was on the hefty side, not like most WeHo homosexuals. The boxes hid his face from Fowler's view. The man unlocked the back door to the house and entered as his phone rang.

Michael Foster Fowler crept back to the window. The stack of boxes was on the sofa and the man stood with his back to the door, phone to his ear.

"Oh, hi, Eric. Just now got back. Estate sale. Shitload of Christopher Radko." The voice seemed almost familiar. "High-end Christmas ornaments, the holiday homos eat this shit up. No, no Pussy yet." Fowler tilted his head, listening intently. The way this guy looked and talked, maybe he wasn't even gay. "Yeah, I put some more flyers up this morning, and after lunch I'm gonna check a couple of shelters. How's the old battle-ax? Yeah, I can hear her; sounds like you better get back. Okay. See ya tonight." The man beeped the phone off. He set it on the counter and turned around.

Fowler gasped in horrified recognition and stumbled backward. Him? In a panic he turned and ran blindly two steps before falling flat into a koi pond. He scrambled out and crawled behind a massive clump of birds of paradise as Guy Lanner — there could be no mistaking it — as Guy Lanner himself stuck his head out the back door to investigate.

"Kitty-kitty? Pussy?" Guy scanned the backyard hopefully. Fowler, dripping, held his breath. Guy gave a sad sigh and went back inside. Fowler crept around the other side of the house and scurried back to his car in a daze.

He sat there in his filthy and stinking wet clothes sopping into the car seat upholstery. "Not him," he whispered hoarsely. He leaned over in despair, pulling himself into a fetal position. He looked up through the windshield into the flat blue L.A. sky. "Oh, God," he cried softly. "Why are you doing this to me?"

"Because you're a filthy butt-fucking parasite, you giant gook!" Margaret yelled.

"Girlfriend," Ming said taking the cuff from the blood pressure monitor off her mottled arm. "I'm the only person in this town who gives a rat's ass if you croak or not."

"Bullshit. You're just as bad as the others."

"There's where you're wrong, Miss Thang," he said, putting the equipment away. "'Cause, as long as your tired, evil ass is among the living, I get a paycheck. Kiss kiss?"

"Fuck you!"

"Yeah, I know." He looked over at Eric sitting stiffly in a chair across the large bedroom. "I need a cigarette," Ming told him. "I'll be outside."

"I try to do good in this world," Margaret said, wheeling herself across the bedroom to Eric. "I give generously to my religious foundation. Deep down, I'm a good person." She smiled ever so wanly, waiting for a response.

"Okay . . ." Eric ventured suspiciously.

"Why, then, do people take advantage of me? I've had three husbands, and they all married me for my money."

"Oh, now, how can you say that?"

"Because they were all homos!" she snapped. "Jesus Christ, only one could get it up with me and that was only when Tyrone Power joined us." She turned her chair away in disgust. "You people take and take. Money, years, dignity. You touch my food, my body, you go through my things!" Shaking in fury she glared at Eric and shouted, "What do you want from me!"

"I don't want anything, Ms. Atherton, I just need a job, honest."

Margaret's head jerked backward and her expression suddenly changed to horror. "Augh, God!" She went limp in her chair. Eric knelt beside her.

"It's okay, you'll be fine," he told her. He'd seen similar performances from her before. "You just got overexcited. Take a deep breath with me now. Come on. In. Out . . ." She didn't respond. Eric stood and wondered if he should call Ming. Would he be finished with his cigarette yet?

Margaret Atherton fell out of her wheelchair face down on the floor.

Eric took a deep breath. "Miiiiiiiinngg!"

"Doris, hold my calls." Bob Davies ushered a nervous Rudy into his plush IMPAT office. "Sorry to keep you waiting, things are nuts right now. The telecast is in four days; it's a nightmare. Actors, producers, gift bags, the President's Gala. Next year I'm putting my own people in there, I don't give a shit who it pisses off. At least they found the damned Arthurs, huh?"

Rudy felt out of his league. What hope did he have of getting a job in a swank place like this? He felt foolish for being here.

Bob looked over Rudy's miserable test scores. "Types a little, but the computer's a washout."

Rudy burned with humiliation. "I'm not stupid. I'm good with computer games. My sister in Tijuana has some and I beat her all the time."

"Really?" Bob rooted through a sample gift bag for the Arthur presenters on a table by the window. He found a Game Boy, opened it, and gave it to Rudy. "Show me."

"*Prime Carnage*? I don't know this one."

"It's new, it'll be out in a couple of months. Try it while I answer some email."

In ten minutes Rudy had it down. Bob was pleased.

"Diaz, here's the deal. You have talent, but I can't hire you up here. Not yet. But I have a place for you down in the garage. It's eight bucks an hour, but if you'll take it, I'll get you computer lessons at night starting next week. You get proficient enough, in a couple of months or so, I'll transfer you up here as an office assistant. You get a job, a skill, and time toward a green card. And I'll get a smart, handsome, discreet new assistant. How's that sound?"

"Sounds like I'm just another Mexican in the garage, man." Bob handed Rudy a card from his desk. Rudy was confused. "Beverly Hills Formals?" he read.

"We have an account there. Go and get fitted for a tuxedo, then be at the Shrine Auditorium at noon Sunday wearing it. Your name will be on the list at the entrance."

"For what? What are you saying?"

"I'm saying this is how I intend to treat you. Your first assignment will be for the Arthur telecast, as a dark, handsome, tuxedoed seat-filler."

"What's that?"

"When a star leaves his seat for any reason, taking a piss, throwing up, line of coke, whatever, we need attractive people to fill that seat while they're gone so when we cut to a shot of the audience there are no empty seats. You have no skills right now, so it's the best I can offer. Will that make a couple of months in the garage more bearable?"

"You'd use me for that?"

"Why not? Besides," Bob winked, "you could be sitting next to Tom Cruise."

Rudy narrowed his eyes. If Davies was being honest, he could stick it out. And it beat the hell out of mopping jizz in a bathhouse. "How do I know I can trust you?"

"How do I know you won't waste my money and time by disappearing in three months? Or three days?" Bob shrugged. "I don't. But . . . here is a hundred dollars to seal the bargain." He stood face to face, only an inch or two away from Rudy. "Now then. What can you give me?"

Rudy smiled and cupped his new boss's genitals in his hand. Sliding down to his knees, he opened the Botany 500 slacks, and pulled out Davies's dick. He licked the sides, making it jump in anticipation, then took it all the way down the back of his throat.

Bob leaned back with a smile. Oh, this arrangement was exactly as he'd imagined it. An idle fantasy carried for years, now brought into reality. And into his office.

"Mr. Davies, you have a call," crackled the vintage intercom on his desk. The harsh unexpected sound caused him to jerk upright. "Ow!" he exclaimed, bending over and grabbing his cock. "No teeth!"

"Not my fault, man," Rudy protested, "You jumped!"

"Never mind," Davies said, clawing his way to the intercom on his desk. He pressed the talk button. "I said no calls, Doris!"

"Yes, sir, but you need to take this one," his secretary insisted.

"Fine," he said angrily, "put it through." He glanced down at his painful penis. At least there was no blood. "Fuck. Fucking fuck."

"We can still hear you out here, Mr. Davies."

Davies released the talk button as his phone rang. He answered it curtly. "What?"

"I'm so sorry to bother you, sir." It was Eric, his other recent hire, very upset. "I'm calling from Cedars. Your aunt had a stroke and, and, and she's here now and, and she's resting, and they're monitoring her I think, and I'm so sorry, sir, and, and, and . . ."

"Calm down, it's not your fault. Calm down." He jumped. Jesus Christ, Diaz was underneath him licking his balls. "Not now!" he rasped at him, covering the phone. On the other end Eric continued to say how sorry he was. "Look, I'll be right there, stop worrying about it. She's old. She was due." Overdue was more like it. He hung up and zipped his pants. "Really sorry about this, but I got a family emergency. We can do this some other time?" Diaz nodded, and Davies saw him out.

As Bob put on his coat to go to the hospital, all he could think was, *Bitch can't even let me get a decent blowjob.*

It had been a week and Ed couldn't wait any longer. He pulled the card out of his wallet and punched the number on his cell.

"Hello?"

"Hey, it's Ed. Big Ed? We met in Palm Springs. I hope it's okay to call?"

"Wow, yeah! I just didn't think you meant it when you asked for my card."

"Of course I meant it. Shit, Noel, you're the hottest man in the desert."

"Me? No, no, that would be the dude I'm talking to, ya big bad bear. Man, I'm really glad to hear from you. What's up?"

Big Ed considered his day. Two hours earlier that morning he'd been in room #1708 of his family's casino hotel snapping a man's neck for making a $1.2 million "clerical error" that had somehow ended up in a bank account in Brazil. Big Ed had folded the body three times — knees, hips, and spine — to fit in a large suitcase which he wheeled out right through the busy casino. He had just this minute come home. He sighed. "Oh, same old same old," he said. "Hey, I been thinking about you all week."

"I been thinkin' about you, too, big guy. God, you were a hot fucker. I'm gettin' a hard-on just talking to you."

Big Ed smiled, turning his computer on as he spoke. "Noel, I want you to come to Vegas."

"Don't know if I can. You know I got a partner."

"Bring him, we'll have a three-way. You said you two had an agreement, right? I just want you to get your tight ass to Vegas."

Noel laughed. "Oh, man, he's a major size queen, too, he'd go crazy over you."

"I'll put you up in a VIP suite. We'd never have to leave the room." He logged onto the Internet. "Give him a call and see if he's up for it."

"Well, he can't come until after the Arthurs and I've got a few more days here in Mexico."

"Mexico?"

"Sport fishing. But let's stay in touch 'cause I'd like hooking up with you again, for sure. I'll talk to you soon, okay?"

"You got it. Bye." He rang off and clicked on his bookmarked eBay page to check on his Madonna hair. There was a message saying eBay had stopped the bidding. "Aw, hell."

Friday, March 24th

Inside the Starbucks at Santa Monica and Westmount, Dave tossed the *L.A. Times* crossword aside. He had filled every space with an H or an I or a V, across and down everywhere it could fit. He pulled his cell phone out of his cargo pants and speed-dialed Roger. As he listened to it ring, he realized Roger's was the only non-business number he had on speed-dial.

"Hello?"

Just hearing Roger's voice made things feel better. "Hey, stud, it's me."

"Dave. Yeah, how ya doing? I've been so busy. You know, school."

"I'd like to see you again. When can I?"

"Oh, I don't know, um, it's just, I mean, I'm going through some, I don't know."

"Yeah, I know," Dave said. "Can we go through it together?"

"Look, Dave —"

"What are you doing Sunday, Roger? We can watch the Arthurs."

"I can't, I'm booked. It's a school thing with my film professor. It's gonna be boring, a buncha other teachers I'm sure, but I can't get out of it."

"What if I came with you?"

"I don't think so, Dave. Can I call you next week?"

"What about Saturday?"

"I can't."

"What about tonight? What about today? What about right now, damn it?"

"David —"

"Fine! I get it."

"Don't do this."

"Do what? Call me next week. I can wait. I got all the fucking time in the world." He pressed the END button hard, snapped the phone shut, and knocked back the last of his latte.

As he was angrily leaving the Starbucks his cell phone rang. He looked at the number displayed and recognized it. "Hey, Burt, haven't heard from you in forever. What's up?"

"Have I got a client for you!"

"I don't know, Burt, a lot's going on with me, I'm thinking . . . I'm actually thinking about, maybe I need to retire."

"Well, do it after Sunday, because you have a fan. A big fan."

"How big?"

"Two thousand an hour, six hours minimum," Burt said. "And if I know this client, probably more like all night long."

"Shit. Okay, then, who is it?"

Burt told him.

"Holy fuck."

Sunday, March 26th

"My name is Gwyneth," spoke the dark no-nonsense woman in a vintage Chanel suit. "You will obey me, or you will leave this place with speed and bloodshed, do I make myself clear?" The small army of thirty beautifully dressed male and female seat-fillers in the lobby of the Shrine Auditorium murmured assent. "You will line up in the order I will give you. When a seat is emptied, I will show the person at the front of the line the exact seat location like so." She shone a red laser pointer at a seating chart on an easel. "And I will give that person a slip of paper with that seat number on it. You will walk as quickly as you can to that seat and sit down. You will not speak to anyone. You will not look to see who's sitting behind or around you. You will face the front and give your attention to the stage until the owner of that seat returns. At that point you will get up, you will walk as quickly as you can back here, you will check in with me, and you will take your place at the end of the line. Is that understood? Say, 'Yes, Gwyneth.'"

"Yes, Gwyneth," they all answered.

She put a perfectly manicured fingertip to her headset and listened for a moment. "Thank you. All right, ladies and gentlemen, in five minutes we will have access to the auditorium for fifteen minutes. At that time we will rehearse the drill. You will line up in this order and you will go nowhere until I tell you. Got that? Say, 'Yes, Gwyneth.'"

Bob Davies came out of the auditorium to find Gwyneth doing her usual excellent job. "Hello, Gwyneth, how's your boss?"

"She is out of town," she told him flatly. "Ms. Ciccone does not have a good relationship with the Institute."

"Well, I'm glad she was kind enough to let us still use you."

"She understands a girl needs to work. Are you all right, Mr. Davies?"

A tuxedoed Rudy had just leaned out of line to smile and wave at him. He looked stunning. "Yes, excuse me." He went to his new employee and pulled him aside. "Damn, Diaz, you look amazing. I'm really glad to see you here."

Rudy shrugged, "Part of the job, right?"

Bob grinned. "Then you're accepting it?"

"Sure." He tugged at his collar. "Never worn one of these before."

"You have any idea how great you look in it?"

Rudy smiled, glancing down at the semi-hard-on showing through Bob's suit pants. "No, but I'm getting an idea."

With a guilty grin, Bob shifted himself. "You go get back in line, smartass, and I'll see you at work."

Eric worried about Margaret Atherton in Cedars-Sinai Hospital. She was doing extremely well, all things considered. Still, Eric was riddled with guilt. "If only I'd had some kind of medical training, I might have spotted some warning symptom," he said, moping around the kitchen.

"Here's a quarter," Guy said irritably, "play some other tune. You said yourself she was a homophobic bitch. So please do us both a favor and get over it in time for us to go to Patrick's Arthur party. It's at 5:00."

"The show doesn't start until 6:00."

"We have to watch Joan trash the red carpet. Otherwise it's just not the Arthurs."

By 4:30, Eric wasn't over it so Guy left him at home. After Guy left, Eric decided he couldn't bear to watch the show. He put on his plain tan Hunt Club jacket and walked to Cedars-Sinai to spend the evening outside Margaret Atherton's room.

☆

Patrick threw open his front door. "Oh, Sarah!" Patrick called out theatrically. "How awkward. Here you've come to my Arthur soiree and the Institute has tragically omitted your movie from the nominations."

Sarah laughed, kissing him on both cheeks. "Let's get it made first. I brought a guest, one of my students. That all right?"

"As long as he brought booze."

Roger shook Patrick's hand. "Hi, I'm Roger, and this is Jose Cuervo," he said holding up a bottle with his left hand."

"Entre vous!"

Guy's voice boomed out from the television room, "It's starting!" Roger froze.

"Places, everybody," Patrick said, shooing them all along. He stopped Sarah and Roger at the doorway and announced. "Everybody, this is my friend Sarah, our very own off-duty filmmaker for the evening."

"There is no place I'd rather be than right here with you," she spoke archly. Other guests applauded politely, acknowledging the *Mommie Dearest* reference.

"And this is her friend, Roger."

"Hi, Roger!" said everyone on the room except Guy who, at seeing Roger, stopped cold.

That little fucker, Guy thought. All his anger and disgust at the straight privilege this frat boy represented surged forward in an instant. *Does he think I'm gonna let him get away with that shit here?*

"Turn it up, it's Robin Williams!" Suze called out.

"You do it." Guy handed her the remote and came over to Roger with a calculatedly frightening smile. "Don't you look like you could use a drink," he smirked, turning him toward the kitchen. He couldn't resist using the guttural growling tone under his breath, saying, "March, boy." In the kitchen Guy backed Roger up against a corner counter. "My, my. Aren't we a long way from a sling at Prowl."

"You can't, you can't say anything —"

"Wrong! Because there's so very much I could say. Including corroborating physical details." He leered at Roger.

"Please, what do you want? What do you want from me?"

"This. That look of terror." Guy was inches from Roger's face. "That clammy feeling of 'oh, holy shit' and there's nothing you can do. Cause you're stuck here, straight boy." Guy smirked. "Straight my hairy ass. You don't get to pass tonight, not with me. Welcome to being my bitch, frat boy." He let that sink in, breathing hot, close breaths on Roger's face. "Now, then, what's my boy supposed to say to that?"

Roger could only whisper, "Yes, Sir."

Patrick shouted from the TV room, "Guy, come in here! You're missing the opening montage."

Guy leaned into the room where everyone was watching Robin Williams inserted into classic movies. "Hey, everybody," he announced, "Roger just volunteered to make the rest of the night's margaritas and popcorn."

Patrick nudged Sarah, "Cute and he cooks!"

"Don't you wanna see this, Roger?" Sarah called back.

Roger stuck half a head out just long enough to squeak, "I'm good!"

Guy pushed Rogers face back into the kitchen. "Let's find you a uniform." He opened a couple of drawers until he found what he was looking for. He turned to Roger. "Wear this," he demanded, holding up a frilly lavender starched organza apron with pink embroidery and white ruffles.

The extravagant femininity of it was mortifying to Roger. "Please, no."

In an instant, Guy was on top of him, pressing him hard against another cabinet. "Who the fuck do you think you're talking to?" he barked in a hoarse whisper. He angrily fumbled at Roger's zipper. "You want what you usually come to me for?"

"No! I'll do it, I'll do it." Ears scarlet with shame, he put on the ultra fem apron.

"That's better, pussy boy. Now it's refill time out there," Guy said handing him a pitcher of margaritas, his face less than six inches away from Roger's. "And one more thing." Guy spat a huge glob in Roger's face. Roger reeled, his mouth open in disbelief as the glistening spit clung to his nose and cheek. "Never refuse me again." With his hand, Guy wiped the spittle off Roger's face and shoved it into his still-gaping mouth. Disgusted, shocked, Roger tried to spit it out but Guy shoved him into the party room with the one-word order, "Go!"

Backstage at the Shrine Auditorium, Hiro gave his tuxedo a tug and checked his zipper for the umpteenth time. The stitches over his eye were out and makeup had covered the scar perfectly. This was the moment of heated brilliance he lived for all year — going onstage at the Arthur Awards! Hiro Yamamoto, Mel Finkelstein, and Ted Balch, the official vote-verifying accountants from PrattswaterfordDouglas, LLP.

For Hiro, being at the Arthurs was an entirely different experience now that he owned one. He had not died from his anal intimacy with Arthur, and the ordeal had taught him to grab for the things he'd always wanted to do but never before had the balls to try. He patted his breast pocket containing the list of those things, now with only a couple of items on it left for him to fulfill.

The stage manager motioned to them and the three men lined up at the very edge of the stage. The adrenaline made Hiro's skin tingle as it always did while waiting for the stage manager's cue.

"You're on!"

☆

"It's the Prattswaterford geek patrol, Patrick!" Guy announced as three tuxedoed nerds shuffled onstage to lend cosmetic credence to the Institute voting. "It's time!"

"Everyone stand and raise a glass," Patrick commanded of his guests. He spoke in stentorian tones. "Each year in this house we toast the pathetic Prattswaterford dweebs, symbolic representatives of the bean-counting geeks that make the world go round, and who use that mighty power to weasel themselves onto that Arthur stage once a year. And so, we drink to them and their otherwise meaningless, invisible lives. Salute!"

"Salute!"

☆

Hiro came offstage feeling twenty feet tall, vitally necessary and an integral part of the motion picture industry. Most importantly, he felt seen. He knew his partner Noel was watching so he had given a double tug on his ear as a private sign to his lover. Already Balch and Finkelstein were undoing their ties and loosening their collars.

"Thank God that's over," Balch said.

"Yeah," agreed Finkelstein, "now where's the bar?" They headed off to the Green Room.

Hiro wasn't about to go anywhere. Where else does air crackle with excitement and glamour like this? He blended in as one of the many official-looking tuxedoed men backstage who were assumed to be watching or guarding something or other. Unnoticed, he could remain close enough to breathe the very air of the stars.

☆

Patrick scrutinized the TV screen. "Look at the guy sitting next to Annette Bening. I could swear that's Eric's boyfriend."

"Ex-boyfriend," Suze informed him. "They broke up."

"Eric's ex is at the Arthurs?" asked Guy, squinting at the picture.

"Oh, please," Suze giggled. "How likely is that?"

"You're going to need more margaritas," Guy said to Roger as he passed. "Serve what you have and I'll help you whip up some more in the galley, you galley slave, you."

When Roger met Guy in the kitchen, he came angrily up to Guy and said, "I'm taking this damn apron off."

Guy grabbed him by the ear, twisting it hard, forcing Roger down to the floor. "What did you say?"

"Sir, please let me take this apron off, Sir," he whimpered.

"You don't want to wear my nice, pretty apron, you piece of shit?"

"No, Sir. Please, Sir, no, Sir."

"You wanna take it off, pussy boy?"

"Yes, Sir. Please, Sir."

Guy smiled. And it wasn't pleasant. "Okay, then," Guy said, releasing Roger. "Take it off."

Meanwhile, the telecast broke for commercial. Sarah looked over at Patrick and took a deep breath. She was invincible, she could do anything, she had an Arthur herself sitting back at home on her filing cabinet. She sidled over to him.

"Patrick, darling."

"Somebody wants something," Patrick said warily. "Yes, my lovely?"

"We're running a teency bit behind on filming."

"So you need more time at the mortuary. How long?"

"Five more nights." Patrick's eyes widened so she hurried to reassure him. "But not right away. I'm thinking Wednesday or Thursday?"

"And you would repay my insane generosity how?"

"By making you a star, of course. You know I'm just waiting for a location to come through to shoot your scenes."

Lee, who was sitting nearby, asked, "Are you really making a movie?"

"Yes," Patrick told her. "Only O'Leary & Finkelstein's is the star, it seems."

"What's it about?" she asked Sarah.

"It's a modern reinterpretation of the Parsifal myth for African-Americans."

"Uh-huh," Lee nodded. "And what's that in English?"

"I don't think we have time," Sarah demurred.

Lee glanced back at the TV. "They just gave Warren Beatty a microphone," she said. "Trust me, we have time."

"It's about a black boy named Junior in South Central L.A. His father was killed in a gang shooting when Junior was still a baby. As he grew up, he wanted to be a city councilman to do something about the neighborhood. One day he rescues a young black woman named Kundra from some thugs, and they have sex. He later learns she's the adopted daughter of Councilman Jimmy 'Red' Knight, who's white."

"That would be moi," Patrick interjected. "Or so I'm promised."

"No offense, Patrick," said Suze, "but you're playing a straight man?"

"I play one every day at work, young lady," Patrick said giving her the evil eye. "You don't grow up with the father I had without getting the swaggering macho bullshit down pat when needed, Missy." He turned back to Sarah. "Pray continue."

Sarah spun her story, enjoying the power of holding an audience. "Junior gets a series of jobs, eventually landing at a mortuary because that was the location available, thank you, Mr. O'Leary." Patrick raised his glass to her. "In the meantime he's screwing women like crazy because he thinks that's what being a man is all about."

"Tell me about it," Suze said.

"Of course doing that just makes him feel empty so he tries to hide in drugs but it all just gets worse until he hits bottom and —" Roger appeared from the kitchen with two full pitchers of margaritas. Everyone stared. Not only was the apron gone; everything was gone except for a pair of revealing black Joe Boxer jockey shorts. Sarah was the first to speak. "Child?"

"It's just, it's, it's only a joke," Roger said.

Guy followed him out of the kitchen. "I love this guy," he said, clapping him so hard on the back that it left a perfect red handprint. "Talk about spontaneous and wacky! All I said was, 'you'd be a real hit serving drinks in your shorts' and here he is. Sarah, your date's a stitch. Go on, Robbie, freshen drinks. Now, what do you say?"

Roger made it as jokey as he could replying with his required, "Yes, Sir!"

"Good boy," Guy nodded in smiling approval. He turned his attention to his gathered friends. "What's going on?"

"It's the movie I told you I was doing," Patrick told him, "and you've come in at the end of it so just keep quiet. Sarah? And hurry because they just cut to commercial."

"Right," Sarah said, dragging her attention back from Roger's surprisingly fine ass. "Okay, so he meets back up with Kundra at a substance abuse meeting, the spark is still there, and they go to his place for sex. Trouble is, the harder she offers herself, the more Junior sees himself in her crazy despair. So he decides not to take advantage of her. She recognizes this selfless act, and it heals not only Junior, but Kundra, too, making them each whole."

"Commercial's over," someone shouted from the TV room.

Sarah cut to the chase in rapid-fire delivery. "Long story short, she convinces him to run for councilman to replace her dad who's resigned in disgrace over a scandal. He wins, and enters the City Council Chamber at City Hall as an equal on his own merits. He returns to his old neighborhood to clean up the gangs, thereby restoring the kingdom blahblahblah. Everybody's happy, the father-wounds are healed, and I win for best directing and screenplay, the end!"

"Sir, you can't be here," one of the assistant stage managers told Hiro. "We need this area clear for the performers. Please go enjoy the show from the Green Room."

Hiro nodded and left dejectedly. Real stars never go to the Green Room. The elite have their own special private areas.

Alone in the Green Room, Hiro nursed his ego with a free Dom Perignon. He sulked, watching the telecast on the monitor over the bar.

※

There was a shot of Kevin Spacey in his seat. "Come out, Kevin! Come out, come out!" Guy called at the TV screen, "Forget Hollywood, I have a place for you!"

"Knowing you, it's face down," Patrick sniffed. "Who's winning?"

Suze consulted her pad. "This award just put Sarah ahead, followed by Roger."

Guy looked around the crowded room. "Where are they?"

※

Roger was straddled over Sarah in the guest bedroom. He was pressing her breasts together and urgently thrusting his penis between them. "God, I love your tits," he whispered.

"Fuck 'em," Sarah whispered back. *Maybe he'll come like this*, she thought, *and I won't have to deal with . . . that problem.* There was, after all, a reason she hadn't allowed herself to be with a man for so long. "Fuck 'em good," she added by way of encouragement.

Roger wished she wouldn't speak. It made him go soft and he was determined to fuck a woman.

Sarah closed her eyes, listening to his determined, rhythmic breathing. Did he just say, "Who's the pussy boy now?" She opened her eyes. He was working hard, thrusting between her breasts. He was losing steam. This was the point that men inevitably went where she feared. She tried to stall. "I want you to come on my face."

"Yeah?"

"Yeah. You close?"

Roger was nowhere near. Shit. "I wanna fuck your vagina," he said. *Do straight men talk like that?* he wondered.

Shit, here it is, she thought. There was nothing for it but to let him discover what he would. He moved down the bed and she opened her legs with anxiety. Sarah felt it starting in only a couple of strokes, this condition caused by excessive amounts of estrogen in her system which made her climax whenever she had sex. As the orgasm seized her, she shuddered, biting the back of her hand, hoping the pain would make the next one longer in arriving.

Roger paused in surprise. He made a woman come. And so fast. He was a man! He returned to thrusting because he was going to come inside her no matter what it took. What the fuck? She was biting her hand again. *Jesus,* he thought as she came again. *Only a straight man could make a woman climax twice in just a couple of minutes.* But he couldn't come in her. And he was getting soft again. "Turn over."

Sarah was happy to comply. At least this way she wouldn't be coming every thirty seconds. She positioned her buttocks for convenient entry. He used spit to lubricate her anus, then slowly and, she thought, with surprising expertise, entered her.

Roger positioned himself so he could thrust into her ass without having to see her breasts. This felt good, but it still wasn't happening. He glanced at a clock on the dresser. They'd need to get back to the party soon. Christ, how long is this going to take? He closed his eyes and saw Dave under him. Dave had never bottomed for him so Roger, if he really concentrated, could imagine he'd feel just . . . like . . . this.

Sarah was impressed by Roger's technique. He was gentle, building intensity slowly. Most men don't understand how to have anal sex.

But Roger was different.

Hiro slipped out of the lowly Green Room and maneuvered his way to the Press Tent where Hilary Swank had just been served up to the media for winning Best Actress in *Boys Don't Cry.* But her time at the press tent microphone was short, because only a few minutes later, Best Actor was announced and Kevin Spacey came out, dazed, to replace Hilary Swank.

She had been unceremoniously pushed off to the side, stunned at being so suddenly adored and then ignored. Hiro found himself next to her. "Congratulations, Miss Swank," he said, bowing deeply.

"Thank you," she said. She looked back at the press now converging on Kevin Spacey. "Center of attention one moment, a minute later . . ." She shrugged charmingly.

"It does not matter. From this moment on, you are forever an Arthur-winning, and I might add, Arthur-worthy actress."

Nothing lubricates conversation with an actor like praise. They sat down on wooden folding chairs. Hilary set her award on the chair next to her so she could better concentrate on Hiro's heartfelt gushing. It was all too brief because in only a few minutes Anthony Minghella won for Best Director and replaced Kevin Spacey at the microphone, bumping Kevin to the offstage area where Hiro and Hilary were chatting.

Hiro stood and held out his hand. "Congratulations on your Arthur, Mr. Spacey."

"Can you believe this?" Kevin said to Hilary, ignoring Hiro.

"We won!" Hilary giggled.

"We won!" Kevin shouted, holding his arms open wide. Hilary jumped up and hugged him, and they both jumped up and down.

Hiro, realizing his personhood was utterly eclipsed by such star power, sat down.

Right on Hilary Swank's Arthur.

Hiro yelled in surprise at the pressure of its head where he'd recently felt the same unhappy sensation from his own Institute Award. He tumbled sideways to the ground with a shout that caused all in the Press Tent to turn and stare at him. Horrified, he looked around the room in a moment of glaring silence.

Then Kevin came to the rescue of all, making a big show of exclaiming, "Oh, my God, do we have an injury?" He reached out as if to help Hiro up. Hiro extended his hand, his heart overflowing in gratitude. But Spacey had only feinted toward him. He veered past him to the chair where the Institute Award was lying on its side, and picked it up instead. He examined the Arthur then held it aloft. "No, it's perfectly fine!" he stated to all as he handed it grandly to Hilary.

There was laughter all around and the press gave Kevin a smattering of applause for his wit. Deeply humiliated, Hiro fumbled to his feet and scurried away. Sweating, shaking with dishonor, he fumed at such bad luck. That's what it was. More bad luck. His grandmother was right. Stolen items bring very, very bad luck. But it was an Institute Award. You don't just get rid of an Institute Award because it's unlucky. No, things would need to get much more unlucky before he could think of doing that.

At that moment, Big Ed was playing host to Sin City's gay mobsters in the VIP suite at Big Ed's family's hotel in Vegas. Nearly two dozen of the gay sons, nephews, and cousins of the rival ruling families mingled, betting on awards and outcomes. Not even Ed could call them friends, they were more like business acquaintances come together in an uneasy truce based on a sexuality that was counter to their macho heritage.

"Who needs another drink?" Big Ed asked loudly so the help would see him pointing to the glasses of his "friends," each from a rival family: Ricky Sorveno, Tony Napoli, and Jimmy "The Stump" Carson. "You having a good time?"

"Talk to me after they give out some freakin' awards," Napoli said tersely. "I'll let you know then."

"Petey! Glad you could make it," Big Ed said shaking his friend's hand. "Who's your handsome friend?"

Petey had a frightened looking young Mexican man with him. Petey shrugged. "Paco," he said, chucking the man under the chin. "They're all Paco."

On the wide-screen TV Robin Williams told the audience, "Bad news everybody, someone just stole the rest of tonight's Arthurs off the loading dock." The audience roared.

"What I wouldn't give to have one of those things," Jimmy the Stump said, hardly moving his rocky face.

"There's three just walking around out there somewhere," mused Big Ed. "Damn, I'd like to get my hands on just one of 'em, just one."

Petey was surprised to hear the vehemence in Big Ed's voice. "You're really into those things, huh?"

"Oh, yeah," Big Ed nodded, utterly serious. "I'd kill for one."

"You and me both," agreed Sorveno. "You get in on the one they auctioned off a couple of weeks ago? Sotheby's?"

"Luise Rainer's, *The Good Earth,* 1937," Napoli rattled off. The others grunted assent. "I bowed out at fifteen grand."

"Twenty-seven five," muttered Jimmy.

"Thirty-one," grumbled Sorveno.

Big Ed just nodded. He didn't want to tell them he'd bid eighty before letting it go. It seemed like one-upmanship. And after all, he was the host.

"Fuck it," said Napoli. "That one shoulda gone to Garbo anyway for *Camille.*"

"Are you shitting me?" demanded Jimmy the Stump. "She just sat there. Margaret Atherton, *Ring of Truth,* now there's a performance."

"Oh, my God," gushed Big Ed, "it's phenomenal! Margaret Atherton was amazing!"

"You telling me Garbo is shit?" asked Napoli.

"No! What are you sayin' I'm sayin' here? Of course Garbo's great. But Margaret Atherton, she was amazing in that. Blew me away," admitted Big Ed.

"Garbo is shit," said Jimmy the Stump.

Napoli bristled threateningly. "Look, you cocksucking mook—" He was interrupted by his pager going off to the strains of the Arthur winning song from *Titanic.* He fished it out of his pocket and read the text message. "Fuck. Thought somebody whacked that asshole." He stuffed the pager back in his pocket. "I'll be back by Best Director," he said heading for the exit. He threw open the door, turned for one last parting shot, roaring loud enough to be heard by everyone in the suite, "Don't you ever call Garbo shit!" He slammed the door behind him.

There was a stunned silence in the room.

Jimmy, Sorveno, and Big Ed all shrugged. "Eh," they said together.

Someone shouted, "Best Costumes, everybody!"

"And the winner is . . . Sarah, by five points over Lee," Suze announced.

"Did I win?" exclaimed a disheveled Sarah hurrying down the hall. "What did I win?"

"I'd say a roll in the hay," observed Guy as he pointed at where she had caught the hem at the back of her skirt in her belt, exposing her ass. Embarrassed, Sarah quickly yanked at her skirt and smoothed it down.

Roger entered as nonchalant as possible in his briefs. "What's going on?

"Apparently, you, darling," Patrick said. He glanced at Roger's wet, stained briefs and grimaced. "Trousers, please." Roger scurried away in sham shame, pleased everyone knew he'd heterosexually fucked his female date.

"Um, I believe I won something?" Sarah said to change the subject.

"Yes," Patrick said reaching for small golden gift bags. "First place is a copy of last year's Best Picture, *Saving Private Ryan*, and a fifty-dollar gift certificate to Tower Video. Sadly, they do not offer dry cleaning." Sarah took her bag and sat down, trying to become invisible. "Second place goes to Lee; a twenty-five dollar gift certificate and a copy of last year's biggest turd, *Armageddon*."

Lee took her bag triumphantly. "Thank you, thank you. I couldn't have done it without all you tiny, insignificant, unnecessary people." There was light applause.

"Third place is a ten dollar gift certificate and — wait, who came in third?" Patrick asked scorekeeper Suze.

"Roger. What does he get?"

"Something most apropos," Patrick said glancing in the bag. "*Babe: Pig in the City*." He held it out to Sarah. "Here, think of it as something you two can share."

"Like crabs," added Guy.

The party broke up as people hugged and said their good-byes. Roger caught Guy in the hallway coming out of the bathroom.

"I just wanted to say fuck you, asshole," Roger hissed. "Whatever you say now, I can deny, because everybody here knows I'm straight."

Guy shrugged, unfazed. "Whatever you say."

Roger remained tightly angry. "I am never calling you again, you sadistic shit. I never want to see you again."

Guy smiled. "Well, look who grew some balls. Maybe, just maybe, it won't be necessary to see me again." He held out his hand to shake. "Friends?"

"Fuck off," Roger muttered as he pushed past him toward the front door.

"Of course, I've been wrong before," Guy said to the empty hallway.

It was past three A.M., and the caterers for the President's Gala were packing things away in trucks behind the Exposition Hall. Rudy was there, waiting for his brother who had gotten work as a busboy. Rudy shivered in the cold night air and pulled his tux coat around him. A black stretch limousine glided by like a shark. It stopped about fifty feet past him, then backed up, drawing even with him.

With a whir, the passenger window slid down. Rudy stopped breathing. A handsome, world-famous actor with a mega-wattage smile greeted him. "Would you like a ride?"

"I'm, uh, I'm waiting for my brother."

"If he looks like you, he can have a ride, too."

"I think . . ." Rudy swallowed. "He might be a while, I think."

The door popped open. "Then why don't you wait for him in here?" The actor seemed to be alone in the car, without his equally beautiful and famous wife. Rudy hesitated. The actor turned to someone seated past the door. "Do you know Spanish?"

A man leaned forward into the dim light. Rudy recognized him immediately. Porn stars get buzzed in free at all bathhouses.

"*Me llamo Frank*," said the man. "*¿Cuándo te va a suceder algo como esto nuevamente?*"

The famous action star patted the seat next to him.

Rudy climbed in.

At 5:37 A.M. a long black limousine pulled in front of Rudy's dumpy little bungalow complex. Through the tinted glass Rudy saw his front door at the end of the walk, but he was busy being ass-fucked by the dazzlingly handsome star who commanded so much money per picture that only his own production company could afford him. Tweaking on crystal meth, Rudy was only vaguely aware of the sweat-covered icon pounding him. He vaguely recalled being picked up by the star outside of the Shrine, but the rest of the evening — spent entirely in the limo careening up and down Los Angeles freeways — was mere flashes of ecstatic abandon to the never-ending power of the chemicals in his cortex. Where was the other guy? Rudy looked behind him to see the hot hairy guy plowing the smooth movie star's ass even as the star, with synchronized action, was ramming Rudy. He remembered somewhere in a parking lot — was it in Ventura? — the driver joined them. Then somewhere with lights flashing by — Hollywood? — he had been on his back looking up at palm trees while the hairy guy fucked him. Then the two of them interlocking legs on the floor double-fucking the star. Seeing the perfectly trained body lowering, then rising and lowering again, both dicks in his ass while he grunted, his eyes clenched shut, the world-famous hair plastered to his forehead. Rudy looked around at the other end of the limo. Champagne bottles, someone's shirt. A box of condoms, opened and spilled. None of them were

opened. They hadn't been used. Not a one. All night long. Fuck it, who cares. The sublime deep rhythm of the cock filling his ass was everything.

Light was just beginning to show in the east, behind the court of bungalows. With a crisp thump, the limo door popped open. Rudy, holding his tux pants up with one hand, and the rest of his clothes in the other, stepped out into the chill air uncertainly. Steadying himself against the car, he gained his bearings and pushed off toward his front door. The black limo, the superstar, and the HIV-positive porn star sped away.

Monday, March 22nd

Early in the morning Suze called Eric. "You're back on the job," she told him. "The Atherton woman is going home tomorrow and Bob Davies wants you there."

"Ming's the nurse, she doesn't need me. Why would Davies want me there?"

"I think it's to make sure she doesn't crawl to a phone and bother him."

"Whatever."

Tuesday, March 28th

Michael Foster Fowler watched the sun come up over flat-topped apartment houses and garages laced together with ugly electrical wires. Since his shock of seeing Guy Fowler, he had felt utterly adrift, overwhelmed. He wrestled with it like Jacob and the angel, trying to understand.

He recalled the day years ago he had finally acknowledged his powerlessness to the black perversion of his soul. It had brought him to Desert Springs for a cure from his homosexuality, just as it had also brought Guy Lanner. Michael wondered whether it worked for Guy. *He got married afterward, so it must have,* Michael thought with envy. Followed by a sneering, *Then what brought Guy to West Hollywood?* Michael had been led to Desert Springs and to Guy by his sin. Now, years later, he had been led to Guy's house by the Arthur. The Arthur . . .

Suddenly he saw the confluence of all things in his life with crystalline clarity.

His past: Guy Lanner.

His present: His Arthur responsibility.

His future role in the cosmos: A new Mission — to rise above the shame of his past with Guy Lanner and embrace the honor of recovering whatever Arthurs remained at large. He would do this in full faith that these tasks would reveal unto him the next part he would play in a grateful God's plan, just like the presence of at least one of the Arthurs had been revealed unto him.

At Guy Lanner's house on Westbourne.

That same morning, when Guy dropped Eric off at the actress's house, there were two news trucks parked outside. "Looks like Death Watch 2000," Guy said.

"They're vultures," Eric said climbing out of the car with his gym bag. Inside the house he found the actress in the pastel green living room in her wheelchair. Her right eyelid drooped so low it almost closed and her mouth hung down on the right. Her entire right side was slack from the stroke. She hardly seemed like the same person.

"Hi, Ms. Atherton," he said. "I'm Eric. I work for you."

She made a series of determined but weak sounds. He had to ask her to repeat it several times before he understood she was saying, "I know. I'm fucked up, not stupid."

Eric smiled. "I brought you something." He opened his gym bag. "For the most touching, amazing, and totally awesome performance in *The Ring of Truth,* the winner is —" he removed the Arthur that Guy had bought for him in a flea market "— Margaret Atherton." He put the award in her left hand. "It's real. I think you deserve it." But she was too weak to hold on to the heavy award, so Eric took it from her and placed it on the mantle with her other, lesser awards. Then he turned the wheelchair so she could look at it. "I better go tell Ming I'm here." He patted her good shoulder and left the room.

He never saw the tear roll down her left cheek.

Eric found Ming in the study. He had opened every drawer and file and was going through stacks of papers.

"Jesus, Ming, I thought she was just going off crazy, but you are touching her stuff. What are you doing?"

"Investigating," Ming said, pausing to put a hand on his hip. "And you're not gonna believe what I've found."

"Whatever it is, it's none of our business," Eric said turning to walk away.

"Your community is your business, little Miss Back-of-the-Bus. Ever hear of Desert Springs Ministries?" Eric turned back in surprise. "Started in 1963. The prototype for all those other homosexual conversion stalags? The granddaddy of all ex-gay ministries?"

"She funds that?" Eric asked in horror.

"She founded it. Check it out." Ming turned an open ledger around for Eric.

What he saw made him take it from him. In disbelief Eric turned page after page. He grabbed another volume and ran his finger down the columns. He opened the next volume. His breathing grew short. He looked up at Ming. "Millions of dollars," he whispered. "All to keep her 'Restorative Treatment Centers' going?"

"It gets better," Ming said sarcastically as he opened a file cabinet. "Finally found the key to this one today."

Eric discovered annual files of reports in the drawer. He read off some of the file headings. "SUCCESS FOLLOW-UPS, SOULS SAVED."

Ming took out a file from near the rear of the drawer. "Look at these names under DIED IN THE LORD," Ming said pointing to a column.

"Deceased, age 34. Age 25. That's how old I am. Age 28, 31, 27. My God, there's over a dozen of them."

"And you're just looking at 1978. These other files go from '65 to present."

"This is like mass murder."

"It's not murder if you can get the homos to kill themselves." Ming shut the folder and stood. "Bitch deserves to die."

"No. Nobody deserves to die."

"What about all these people? Did they deserve it? What about the ones who didn't commit suicide but had their lives ruined by Desert Springs?" Eric had never seen Ming look so resolute. A calm, deadly anger emanated from this very large, strong man.

"I won't be a part of any crime," Eric told Ming. "And I won't be an accessory."

"Well, I've got something in my bag I'm not afraid to use."

Two minutes later Ming wheeled Margaret Atherton into the den. "Here you go, you dried up, droopy bitch." He pushed her to within a foot of the television. "Nice and close," he said, setting the brake. From the doorway Eric watched Ming reach into his bag and pull out a videotape. "I rented a bunch of classics over the weekend and forgot to drop them off yesterday. Suddenly I don't mind having to pay a late fee." He popped the tape in the VCR and hit play. Ming turned the volume up loud with the remote. "Wouldn't want you to miss anything, Cruella," he shouted over the strains of "We Are Family" as *The Birdcage* began. Margaret strained to move and made noises of protest. "What?" Ming yelled over the music. "Sorry, can't hear you!"

With the little strength she had, Margaret raised her left hand and with great effort extended her middle finger.

During the movie, Eric went back to the study to go through the papers for himself. As old as Margaret Atherton was and in her poor health, she clearly wasn't going to be around for long and there were some items he wanted to check up on.

Around 3:30, as *Priscilla, Queen of the Desert* was almost over, Eric closed the bankbook and went into the kitchen for a sandwich. Bringing it into the den he saw Margaret slumped over in her chair. He touched her shoulder but there was no response. And she wasn't breathing.

"Ming! Get in here!"

Ming came from the porch where he had been smoking. He felt for her pulse. "Shit," he said. "And I didn't even get to put on *Boy Orgy III*."

"Aren't you going to call 911?"

"She's dead, Eric."

"But —"

"But what?" Ming asked rhetorically. "I'm gonna finish my cigarette," he said, and he headed leisurely back to the porch.

Eric called 911 himself. In a moment of guilty panic he pushed Margaret back into the living room, away from *Priscilla*, the arguable murder weapon. When the paramedics came, the press crews from the vans outside came barging in as well. Ming dealt with all of that while Eric called Bob Davies to tell him the news.

"So she's dead?"

"Yes, Sir. The paramedics are taking her out now covered over with a sheet."

"Hallelujah," Davies said, "Halle-fucking-luja. Thanks for calling. You take care of whatever needs to be done."

"Don't you want to do that?" Eric asked. "I mean, you're her family."

"What the hell am I paying you for but to take care of her shit? She was a pain in my ass as long as she lived and now that she's dead I want to be rid of her. I'll handle the legal end. You make whatever arrangements you see fit, the estate will pay for it. Just do it." And he hung up.

Eric thought for a moment. Considering the discoveries of the day, he knew what he needed to do. He called Lee at Patrick's funeral home.

"Well, hey, baby," she said. "What's up?"

"I've got a dead actress on my hands," he told her, "and I want the works." When he was done arranging the details, he called Suze.

"Oh, sweetie," she said sympathetically, "what a day you've had. Tell you what. Meet me at The Abbey on Robertson in an hour. I'll buy you a well-earned drink."

By this time the paramedics had left with the body and the news crews were getting pickup shots of the room in which they assumed she had died.

Eric entered the living room. "Ming, do you know where The Abbey is?"

"What a fabulous idea! I am so up to celebrate. Help me get rid of these news creeps and we are there."

Eric grabbed his gym bag to go. On his way out he noticed his Arthur on the mantle. No use in it staying here now, he thought. He tossed it back in his gym bag, helped Ming push the cameramen out, and locked the door behind them. They got in Ming's open-air Jeep parked at the curb and headed for The Abbey.

Mark Sparks entered the *E! Entertainment* editing bay and slouched in the chair in resentment. He'd been ordered to edit Margaret Atherton's video obituary and tribute for that evening's airing. *Like I don't have enough bullshit to do,* he thought as he sullenly watched the new raw footage.

"What the fuck?" he said aloud. He had viewed the paramedics working on her and noticed the mantelpiece. He rewound to see it again. There, as plain as opening credits, was an Institute Award. But she never won an Arthur, he thought. He retrieved the tape of his home interview with her from a week or so earlier. There was no Arthur on the mantle and she was even bitching about not winning. Where the hell did that one come from? He scanned ahead to the end of the new footage. There was the mantle, but now no Arthur. Where did that fucker go? He replayed earlier footage noting the presence of her Asian nurse and the familiar looking guy he'd met during the interview. Later on, right at the end of the tape, there was a shot of that guy leaving with a heavy looking gym bag.

"Oh, my God," Sparks said to the room, "that twinkie son of a bitch stole it!"

※

Eric walked home from The Abbey a bit unsteadily. When he got to Guy's house, he sobered up immediately. The front door was standing wide open. Inside he saw the place was a mess. Books had been pulled from shelves. Drawers and cabinets were open with contents dumped on the floor. He froze in the den. Someone was rummaging around in the bedroom at the back of the house. Frightened, Eric crept down the hall toward the noise. Abruptly, Guy rushed out of the bedroom right into him. They both screamed in terror.

"Jesus, Eric!" Guy panted after he got his wits back.

"What happened?"

"Someone broke in."

"What did they take?"

"I don't know! I can't figure it out. But whatever it was, they wanted it bad." There was an authoritative knock from the front. "That'll be the cops."

Guy and Eric met two West Hollywood sheriff's deputies in the living room. One of them questioned Guy while Eric showed the other around the house. Guy's expensive computer, the TV and all the electronic components were untouched, likewise several credit cards left out on Guy's dresser.

The phone rang. Eric left his deputy to answer it. As if he wasn't already rattled enough, the caller was his mother.

"Eric, honey! How nice to finally hear your voice. Are you enjoying Los Angeles?"

"Mom, this is really a bad time."

"Oh, I know, did you hear about Margaret Atherton dying? She was so wonderful."

"Yeah, Mom, I heard. I have to go now."

"Something's wrong, I can hear it in your voice. Eric, are you all right?"

"I'm fine."

"Then what's going on?"

He cracked. "We've just been ransacked and robbed!"

"Robbed!"

"Yes! Well . . . we think. I really have to go. Bye, Mom."

The deputy returned from outside. "Did you guys see this?" He motioned for Eric and Guy to follow. He led them out to the garage.

On the side of the garage was a message spray-painted in three-foot high blood-red letters:

I KNOW YOU HAVE IT, FAGGOT!

Wednesday, March 29th

At 8:30 the next morning Eric stumbled into the kitchen after a fitful night's sleep. Guy was already in there, as awake as a pot of Starbucks Espresso Roast and half a box of Little Debbie Oatmeal Cakes could make him.

"GoodmorningEricIfigureditout!"

"Somebody's had way too much sugar and caffeine," Eric said archly. "Normal speed, please."

"Okay." Guy made an effort to slow down. "Whoever ransacked the house and painted that message on the garage was after something he didn't find."

Eric snorted. "Thank you, Jessica Fletcher."

"Hear me out. The only thing of value that wasn't here, was in your gym bag."

"My Arthur Award?"

"Thank you, Miss Marple. Someone knows we have it and they're pissed."

"Who would know that and how would they know it?"

"That I don't know, Eric, and neither do I care. But I do know this, I don't want some deranged Hollywood hit man! coming back here. I say we get rid of it."

"But it's worth thousands."

"Not if you're dead. In a town where people would kill for a part, what do you think they'd do for a genuine Arthur?"

The doorbell rang. "Do you think it's the robber?" Eric whispered fearfully.

"They don't usually ring the bell," Guy retorted, heading for the front door.

"Go ahead and make fun of me," Eric called after him. "All I know is that would be the last person I'd want to see today."

Guy returned. "You might want to make that the second-to-last person."

A stout blonde woman in her mid-fifties and a blue print smock dress followed Guy carrying a small suitcase. She was flushed and clearly upset by the debris still strewn on the floor.

"Mom!" Eric exclaimed. "What are you doing here?"

"Oh, Eric!" she said. "You hadn't returned my calls and last night you said you'd been robbed so I drove right to Saint Louis and got on the first plane to Los Angeles. Did they hurt you, honey? I'm so sorry! And the flight and the airport and I haven't slept a wink, and, and, oh, Eric!" She plopped on the sofa and began to cry.

"We're okay, Mrs. Burgess," Guy said. "You've had a rough night and I have just the thing you need."

"Ed! Eddie!" Big Ed's father lumbered down the hallway. The door to his son's room was closed. He threw it open and barged in. "Eddie, I need you to — what the fuck is this?" His six-foot-nine son was sitting on the edge of his bed holding a videotape and crying. "What's wrong?" Big Ed pointed to his computer screen across the room on his desk. His father peered at it. On CNN.com's entertainment news web page there was an obituary. "Who the hell is Margaret Atherton?"

"She's an actress," Big Ed said, wiping his face. "She was amazing. I just saw her in this." He held up the video of *Ring of Truth*. "She was so good. I didn't even know she was alive until I saw she just died." He made a painful effort not to cry.

"That's what this is about? Some cockamamie dead movie bitch?"

"She was an artist!" Big Ed said.

"Jesus, Mary, and Judy fuckin' Garland. How'd you turn out to be the biggest fag act since Siegfried and Roy?" He snatched the video from Big Ed. In massive hands used to snapping necks, he wrenched the plastic case into splinters. He threw the ruined tape across the room, crashing against the dresser mirror. "Three weeks!"

Big Ed was shocked, confused. "What?"

"Three weeks you were in an incubator when you were born. God, how your mother and I worried." He shook his head. "For *a frocio*, a cocksucking *busone*. What a waste of time. What a fucking waste of money."

"Pop?"

"What a fucking waste you turned out to be." He left in disgust.

Ed sat there for several minutes, stunned. His father had never liked having a gay for a son, but he'd never blown up like this before. The black ribbon of videotape lay unspooled across his dresser. The broken casing on the floor.

He had to move out. Now. Leave.

He'd get a suite at the hotel. Maybe later when he'd thought things through, he'd finally do it. Maybe it was time to move to West Hollywood. He'd get up with Petey and get the hell out of Vegas. Set up shop in L.A. Maybe there he could come up with some action that would get him away from this bullshit. Something that would make a difference, make some real money.

And that would finally make his father proud of him.

Thursday, March 30th

When Eric's mother woke up it was still morning. She tried to smooth the wrinkles from her dress and came into the kitchen where Eric was eating. "I see you picked up the house during my nap," she said. "And you've changed into your nice clothes, too."

"It's Thursday, Mom. You've been sleeping for twenty-three hours."

"No!"

"You were kinda upset. We gave you a Valium. How do you feel?"

"Well, confused, but really rested."

Eric smiled. "Good. Do you think you'll be okay coming with us?"

"Where are we going?"

Guy strode merrily into the kitchen in his dark suit. "To a funeral, Mrs. Burgess. In Hollywood."

"Ooh! Will there be stars?"

"I can guarantee you one," Eric said.

Mrs. Burgess was all aflutter. She gulped down breakfast and scurried off to change into her best dark brown dress. Eric and Guy went over the plan they had agreed on the previous day. They would slip the stolen Arthur into Margaret Atherton's casket and it would be out of their hair.

"She'll finally have the award she always wanted but never got."

Guy grumbled. "I just hate giving it to that homophobic Desert Spring bitch."

"Shh!" Eric hissed at him, gesturing toward his mother down the hall.

"Oh, shush yourself. If you had any balls you'd have told her you were gay by now. You're going to have to come out sometime."

"Come out where?" asked an excited Mrs. Burgess who had just come into the room. Guy merely looked at Eric, enjoying the awkward moment.

"Come out . . . to the car," Eric said finally. Guy shrugged and led Mrs. Burgess out the front. Eric grabbed his gym bag with the Arthur award still in it, and hurried out the door.

From his rusty green convertible across the street and one house down, Michael Foster Fowler watched Guy Lanner and two other people come out of the purple house and get in the RAV-4. An older woman and that younger homo who was carrying the same heavy gym bag he had when he came back to the house night before last. Fowler had been furious at not finding an Arthur anywhere in that damn purple house.

"It has got to be in that bag," he muttered. He let the RAV-4 get half a block away, then he started his convertible and followed.

At O'Leary & Finkelstein's Mortuary, Eric introduced his mother to Lee at the front desk and to Patrick who came out of his office to greet them.

"Did you ever find Pussy?" Patrick asked Guy.

"No, and I've looked everywhere," he replied sadly.

"Maybe," Mrs. Burgess suggested sweetly, "if you didn't objectify women like that, you'd find a nice girl." Patrick and Guy looked at her. "That's what Oprah says."

"Mom, Pussy is his cat."

"Oh. Oh dear," Eric's mother stammered, turning deep crimson.

"Besides, there are entirely other reasons I don't need to find a nice girl," Guy said smiling. He offered her his arm. "Shall we go view the guest of honor?"

Seated by the door inside the chapel was *E! Entertainment* reporter Mark Sparks. *Of all days for that asshole to fuck up!* he thought, seething at his idiot cameraman who hadn't shown up. Still, he was convinced he was on his way to career gold.

As soon as Eric entered with his heavy gym bag, he knew his intuitions had been right on the money. He slipped outside, already tasting the publicity he'd get for this. Grinning, he flipped open his cell phone and quietly called the police.

☆

Guy was standing by the luxurious mahogany casket that was covered in layers of ornate brass when Eric joined him. "I was hoping I wouldn't still hate her when I saw her dead," Guy said with a frown. "Jesus, what tacky flowers."

"I know. I ordered extra glitter just for you," Eric said.

Guy looked around and noticed Eric's mother in the back, chatting with the only other people in attendance, a woman and her child, both dressed in chic matching black, complete with identical dramatic hats and veils. "Oh, please," Guy commented to Eric. "Mother-daughter mourning wear? *Vogue* has gotten completely out of hand."

"But who is it?"

Guy shrugged. "In this town, who knows? I wouldn't be surprised at anyone who showed up." Suddenly his jaw dropped. Eric followed his stare.

A manic looking man in a rumpled gray jacket and stained scruffy blue chinos stood in the entry. His dirty hair was a mess and he badly needed a shave. Guy blinked at him. "Michael?" he asked.

"God has sent me to you. Sinner. Sodomite. Thief."

The worst three years of Guy's life came surging back in his memory like a wartime flashback. All the pain, recrimination, and shame. And the rage. Rage like an unchained monster seized him in unforgiving talons. Shaking, he spat the name again. "Michael!"

"Yes, meaning 'who is like God.' And I have been sent!"

"Like hell you have, you shit!" Guy growled, marching up to him in a fury. "You lying bastard, you hypocritical prick!"

Patrick ran in. "Quiet! Both of you. What the hell is going on here?"

"This asshole was my sponsor at Desert Springs," Guy hissed. "He convinced me I could be straight if I called on Jesus. But most of my calling on Jesus was while this sanctimonious shit was butt-fucking me at night!"

Patrick collared them both and pushed them down the corridor. "I have two other services, three viewings, and a hangover going on. Whatever your problem is you will take care of it in here." He shoved them through an unmarked door into the embalming room. There were odd smells, equipment, and two stainless steel embalming tables — one of them occupied. "And keep it quiet!" He left, slamming the door behind him.

"I barely recognized you," Fowler sneered. "What with the extra weight, the thinning hair, that queer goatee thing."

"Yeah, seeing me healthy and not bound up in your religious bullshit probably would throw you off."

Fowler shook his head. "You were a weak vessel, Guy. You failed because you weren't strong enough in the faith."

"And you succeeded? What's this, you being straight?"

"Fuck you!"

"Oh, you did, Michael. Often, if you remember. You did a damn good job of that."

"Liar! Tempter! Shut up!"

Guy smirked. "What makes you hard? Jesus? How 'bout a six-foot angel with his ass in the air? Or a devil with his thick dick in your mouth?"

"Stop it," Fowler said, putting his hands over his ears.

"But you think about it, don't you? Don't you, faggot? Answer me, you pansy." Michael Foster Fowler was red-faced and the cords on his neck stood out. "How many other guys did you fuck, queer boy? Homo. Fairy. Cock! Sucker!" Fowler made a guttural cry and ran blindly at him. Guy whipped him around, pinning his arm and holding him around the neck. He growled into his ear, "You screwed me up for years, you sick bastard. Now you're mine."

Releasing Fowler's neck, he punched him twice in the face. Fowler jammed his elbow into Guy's ribs, breaking free. He turned and got a stranglehold on Guy and they stumbled against the table with the body. Guy punched Fowler in the stomach again and again, but Fowler wouldn't let go.

"Die!" Fowler shouted. "Die in your depravity!"

Guy managed to get a hand on Fowler's face, pressing with his thumb as hard as he could in Fowler's eye. Fowler yowled in pain and let go. Gasping, Guy backhanded him with such force that Fowler fell on top of the body on the embalming table.

Fowler bared his teeth like an animal. He charged Guy, colliding with him and sending them both into metal shelves laden with embalming equipment. The huge clatter of metal shelves, buckets, and implements brought Patrick rushing into the room.

"What the fuck is going on here?"

Guy stood and tried to explain. "This guy —"

"I don't care!" Patrick said, cutting him off. "This is a place of respect. Now, both of you, keep it quiet or get the hell out," he demanded. "I have to go explain a fistfight to people in three viewing rooms and two chapels." He strode out, the door thudding shut behind him.

Guy took Fowler's wrist. "Come on, asshole. Up."

"I can't," Fowler wept. Nothing had gone the way he imagined it. Not the Arthurs, not Guy, not his mother, not Jesus, nothing in his life. He had thought he had a purpose, a reason to live. But it had all been so many false hopes. He was sobbing so hard he had to fight for air. He was broken utterly. A Job with no God to make things right. At last he looked up at Guy. "I want to die." Guy hoisted him to his feet, but he leaned on Guy crying. "I just want to be straight," he sniffed. "But it's so hard. It's always so damn hard."

"Of course it is, Michael. It's not natural for you."

"No, I mean my . . . manhood. Every time I'm near a man, it's hard." Indeed, Guy had thought that he had felt something, but feared it might be a gun. He reached down and pressed his hand firmly against Fowler's crotch. "Don't," Fowler yelped, flinching.

"You sad bastard," Guy said. "And I thought those Desert Springs shits had fucked me up."

"But they were right."

"Were they? Does their ex-gay crap feel right? Or does this feel right?" He squeezed the dick in his hand and Fowler moaned. "How about this?" With a jerk at Fowler's zipper and belt he opened Fowler's pants. Fowler grimaced and shut his eyes, but he didn't move. "And how about this, you fucker?" He yanked Fowler's pants down to his knees.

"Please."

"Please?" Guy snorted. "Please don't?"

"Please . . . Sir."

Sir? A new understanding crossed Guy's face.

Down the hall, Mark Sparks reentered the chapel where movie star Margaret Atherton lay. With a confident sneer he walked over to Eric standing by the open casket. "I think she's got on less makeup now than when I interviewed her two weeks ago."

Eric looked at him. "Hey, you're the guy from *E!*, aren't you?"

"Uh huh. And you're the guy," he said pointing to Eric's gym bag, "with the stolen Arthur." Eric's look of shock obliterated any doubts Sparks might have had. He smiled serenely. "You're trapped in here, mister. And don't even think about leaving. I'll just be waiting outside for the police." He turned and went out to wait in the hall, passing Bob Davies who walked briskly up to the casket.

"At least something's going right," Davies muttered. He peered in the coffin at his dead aunt. "Bitch." He glanced at the flowers. "Jesus, that's a lot of glitter." Then Davies looked at Eric. "Thanks for handling everything. You did a good job, Eric. Let me make a note to give you a bonus." He patted his empty suit pockets. "Damn. Diaz!"

His assistant dressed in a black suit hurried in. Eric was even more surprised.

"Rudy?"

"Eric!" the handsome Latino exclaimed with a smile, then hugged Eric.

"Oh, my," salivated Davies, "that brings back memories." Then to Rudy, "Make a note to get him a bonus. And maybe we can find him a real job at the Institute."

"He could use it," Guy said, entering the chapel for Kleenex for Michael, currently in a fetal position back in the embalming room.

Davies glanced at his watch. "Shit. I gotta get back to the lawyers. You know what I get out of fifteen years of dealing with that old battle-ax? Furniture." He turned to go. "The remainder of the estate goes to her precious damn Desert Springs." And he had gone.

"What?" shouted Guy.

"Not now," Eric said in a tone meant to shut him up. "Rudy, it's good to see you."

"You, too," Rudy nodded sadly.

"Diaz!" Davies called from down the corridor.

"Gotta go," Rudy said to Eric, brandishing the car keys. "Adios, amigo." And Rudy chased after his new boss.

Guy exploded. "I can't believe that hate-run ex-gay crusade of hers is getting everything!"

"Guy, there's no time for that." Eric took him by the arm and explained about Sparks. "The cops are coming and we're trapped in here with a stolen Arthur award. What the hell are we going to do?"

"I thought we were just going to put it in the coffin next to her."

"Oh, like they wouldn't look there!" Eric's voice was higher and panicky.

"All right," Guy said trying to calm him, "I've got an idea, but I need a diversion.

From where he had stationed himself outside the chapel, Mark Sparks saw the two uniformed policemen come into the lobby. "This way!" he called out to them. "I've got the thief cornered in here with the goods." At her reception desk, Lee sensed trouble and left to find her boss Patrick.

Suddenly Eric shot out of the chapel clutching his gym bag to his chest. "That's him!" Sparks shouted as he ran after Eric. He tackled him as the cops come running up. Eric fought hard to get away, but Sparks already had a grip on the gym bag. The policemen pulled them apart. In the scuffle, Sparks won the bag.

In triumph he opened it and dumped it. Only gym clothes and a Walkman fell out.

"The Arthur must be inside," Sparks told the policemen. "He must have hidden it in the chapel!" He rushed into the chapel where Guy was sitting calmly with Mrs. Burgess, who was seated next to the lady and the little girl in matching black mourning veils. Sparks looked between and under the seats. "Where . . . where?" he breathed, thrusting aside curtains. Then he looked at the display up front.

The *E!* reporter rooted through the hedge of luxuriant floral tributes, silver glitter sticking to his dark skin. "I know it's here!" he shouted at Eric who shrugged at the officers. Sparks looked at the casket and a grin spread across his face. "Of course!"

He boldly marched over to it and started feeling around inside. Nothing. *No!* he thought, *it has to be here!* He opened the portion of the casket that covered the body from the waist down. Bupkis. He frantically fumbled all around the dead actress. He was pulling and tugging at her clothes when Lee and Patrick appeared in the doorway, both aghast.

"That will cease immediately!" Patrick boomed.

Sparks froze. Looking up he saw five mourners, two policemen, a receptionist, and the owner of the mortuary staring at him caught mid-rummage on the corpse of an elderly Hollywood star. Maybe no cameraman was a good thing. Hot with shame and humiliation, Sparks stormed out.

The officers followed him. "Sir, you want to explain why you called the police?"

An officious olive-skinned woman in a chic Donna Karan business suit entered past them and made her way to the mother and daughter in black. As she whispered to the mother, Eric recognized Gwyneth. What was she doing here? Unless that woman was — "Oh, my God," Eric whispered. The mother got up and took the four-year old by the hand and led her over to Eric. She offered a gloved hand. Eric took it in awe as she said only three words.

"That totally rocked." Then she and her daughter left.

Eric stopped Gwyneth on her way out after them. "Was that Madonna?"

"I am not at liberty to say," Gwyneth answered, registering who Eric was. "But I can tell you I'm no longer Ms. Ciccone's Assistant's Assistant. I'm now her Assistant."

"What happened to the old Assistant?"

"She was fired for using Ms. Ciccone's private exercise equipment."

"Oh," Eric said, recalling being chased by guards through the singer's home. "The Soloflex in the bedroom?"

"No. The pool boy in the cabana." A car horn tooted. "Goodbye, Eric."

"Such a well-mannered child she had," Mrs. Burgess remarked. "But what a struggle it must be raising her as a single mother. Not to mention the financial burden. Did you know her?"

"Not exactly," Eric said, "but I've been to her house."

Guy drove Eric, his mom, and a still quivering Michael Foster Fowler back to the purple house on Westbourne. Mrs. Burgess was most concerned about Fowler and tried to soothe him in the backseat by straightening his clothes and hair.

"Please, lady," he said, making himself as small as possible against the door opposite her, "you remind me of my mother."

"Oh, well, thank you," she said, smiling.

Averting his eyes he squeaked, "That wasn't a compliment."

When they arrived, Mrs. Burgess headed for the kitchen while Eric and Guy helped Fowler inside, taking him to Guy's bedroom. They sat him on Guy's bed where he rolled over into a tight fetal position again.

"You think bringing him home is the best idea?" Eric asked skeptically.

"Look at him," Guy said. "What else could I do? The man's a fucked-up wreck."

"Yeah, one who just tried to kill you."

"If you remember, I once tried to kill me. We both got sucked into that Desert Springs bullshit, so I have a pretty good idea what's going through his head. Why don't you go help your mom pull some food together before Patrick and Lee get here?"

"Can I call Suze?"

"Why not? Hell, see if Madonna's available." Eric left and Guy shook his head at Michael. "What am I gonna do with you?" he wondered aloud.

"I have no purpose," Michael said in a low moan. "I'm a failure. In every part of my life a failure. Let me go home. I promise you'll never have to see me again."

"Oh, please. 'I wanna die, I wanna kill myself.' Boo fucking hoo. It's not happening today."

"Why not?" Michael sat up. "I do want to die."

"Because it's stupid, because it doesn't fix anything, and because I've got a houseful of people here for lunch, not a suicide. So get over it and pull your shit together." It wasn't working. Michael could only look at the floor. Broken. Empty. Guy took a deep breath, knowing it was time to take complete control.

He jerked Michael upright to speak to him nose to nose. "All right, boy, get a grip. You want a purpose? You serve me. You do exactly what I say, when I say. You got that?" Michael, wide-eyed, just looked at him, not knowing what to think. "I said, you got that?" Michael nodded. Guy stepped back, arms folded. "As of now you are my boy. You don't think. You don't worry about what to do. I tell you where to go. I tell you where to sleep. I tell you when to get up, and what to be. Right here, right now, there is no other purpose but me, boy. As of now, you can stop thinking." He softened his tone. "You want focus, you want decisions made, for the time being you come to me." He reached out and caressed Michael's cheek. "Okay, boy?"

Fowler reached up and held Guy's hand against his face. His eyes were closed tightly. He breathed a couple of times. He nodded as a tear fell from his eye. "Thank you," he barely whispered.

"'Thank you' what?" Michael looked at him quizzically. Guy explained, "If you agree, this is how it needs to be."

"Thank you . . . Sir."

Guy acknowledged the consent with a nod. "Now comb your hair and wash your face, boy. And go make lunch."

Guy entered the kitchen to find that Patrick and Lee had arrived. They merely leaned against the wall watching Eric and his mom arranging plates of cheese and fruit.

"What, you can't help out?" Guy asked Patrick.

"It's not like I'm having any of that," Patrick said gesturing toward the food. "You know I never eat anything solid before dinner. Which begs the question, where are the adult beverages?"

Just as the first pitcher of screwdrivers was mixed, Michael Foster Fowler came to the edge of the room with his head bowed. "I'm ready. Sir."

"Ah, the relief staff has arrived," Guy announced. "Let us take what we have and repair to the sundeck." Lee and Patrick helped Eric take the food outside. "You, boy," he said to Michael as he pulled a chef's apron out of a drawer and tossed it to him, "put this on and make sandwiches."

"Yes, Sir. Thank you, Sir."

Mrs. Burgess smiled at Michael as she passed with her pitcher of screwdrivers. She leaned in to Guy and said, "I didn't know he worked for you."

"I didn't either until about five minutes ago," Guy said, "We'll see how it goes."

After calling Suze, Eric went back out on the patio where Guy was ranting about Atherton's money.

"It pisses me off the bitch can die and still benefit those ex-gay assholes at Desert Springs."

"Trust me," Eric said, pouring himself a screwdriver, "she won't. Ming and I got our hands on her bankbooks and all. The house was triple mortgaged so forget that. All told, there was only about twenty thousand in cash left."

"That's still twenty thousand too much for those bastards."

"Will you chill? Davies put me in charge of all the final arrangements, I made sure we spent every dime on the funeral."

"And God love you for it!" Patrick said, toasting him. "Eric, when you croak, I'm giving you a free flowers and a casket upgrade."

Guy was grinning widely at Eric. "You sly pedigreed dog. And here I thought I was rooming with Opie."

A couple of minutes later, Suze arrived. "Oh, honey!" exclaimed Mrs. Burgess hugging her, "I haven't seen you since you left Rosebud. Eric, you didn't tell me Suze was out here. Are you two getting together again? That would just be perfect!"

"Uh, not exactly, Mom," Eric told her.

"You have got to tell her!" Guy whispered to him. Eric shot him a dirty look and hissed, "Shhh!"

Suze was thrilled to learn of Eric's possible job at IMPAT with Davies, but sorry to hear Guy's cat, Pussy, was still missing.

Guy shrugged, "You can't have everything."

Michael Foster Fowler, wearing the chef's apron over his rumpled clothes, came out of the house and stood by Guy with his head bowed. "Sir, I put sandwiches for your guests in the den, Sir."

"Good boy," Guy said, patting him on the head.

"Thank you, Sir." And he went back in to start coffee.

The TV was on in the den, showing a sullen and still slightly glittered Mark Sparks reporting entertainment news. "Turn it up!" Eric shouted, grabbing a sandwich.

". . . has learned that Madonna is currently in negotiations with Tim Rice and Elton John for a musical version of the life of Margaret Atherton with Disney as a possible studio. Elsewhere, scrap metal dealer Eddie Bowling, who found fifty-two of the fifty-five Arthur awards that had been stolen from a loading dock in Downey, California, informed the Institute of Motion Picture Artists and Technicians he was owed the reward money that had been offered. As yet, the other three missing Arthurs remain," here Sparks breathed a bitter, resentful sigh, "at large."

"We know where one of them is," remarked Guy.

"Well, I don't, dear," said Mrs. Burgess. "I mean, we saw you at the casket, but with all those flowers, who could see?"

"Yeah," Patrick wondered, "Exactly what did you do with it?"

"It's where it belongs," Guy said, "with Margaret Atherton as Eric wanted."

"But Sparks felt all around in that coffin," Eric reminded him. "What did you do, ram it up her ass?"

"No," Guy said slyly, "but you're getting warm."

Eric's eyes got huge. "Oh, my God!" he cried. "You mean to say you shoved it up her —"

"Pussy!" shouted Suze, scooping up the orange cat that had come in the open door to the patio. "Look, Guy, she's back!" And Guy was instantly at her side, petting and kissing his cat, unsuccessfully trying to mask his tearful gratitude for her return.

Eric noticed his mother looked rather nonplussed at learning about the Arthur. "I'm sorry if it's a little shocking, Mom. It's not always like this here."

"Oh, that's okay, son," she said, "After a day like today, there's not much that would surprise me."

At that, Guy looked up from nuzzling his cat to catch Eric's eye. Eric understood his meaning, and nodded resolutely. He took his mother's hand. "Mom," he said gently, "come into the next room." He smiled tenderly at her. "There's something I think it's time I told you."

Friday, March 31st

Guy drove Eric and Mrs. Burgess to the airport. The morning had been tinged with sadness from learning the truth about her son, and breakfast conversation had been strained. In between struggling silences, she had asked naïve, sweet, worried questions of her son. "Are you . . . healthy, Eric?"

"Yes, ma'am," he replied respectfully. The fact that his mother now knew he was gay made it new and uncomfortable for him, too. The drive to LAX felt interminable. His mom watched buildings and streets go by.

At last her dark fears burst through. "Son, I just pray you haven't had unprotected sex with Greg Louganis."

Guy almost hooted, but Eric's mom looked painfully ready to cry. Guy bit the inside of his cheeks as hard as he could.

"I promise you I haven't. I don't do anything unsafe and I always use condoms." That last word had made his mother wince, and fall silent again. At last they arrived at the terminal. Guy got her suitcase from the back to check it with a skycap.

Standing at the terminal entrance, a bit of panic touched Eric. "Mom. Please don't hate me, mom."

"Hate you? Oh, Eric, how could you not know? I loved you before you were born. I loved you before I met your father. When I was a little girl and playing with dolls and wanting a real baby, I loved you then. I'm your mother, how could I not love you always?"

Guy returned with her baggage claim. "Some mothers find a way, Mrs. Burgess."

"Well, that's not right," she said. "With me it's not even a choice."

"It's not a choice with me, either, mom."

"I don't know if I understand that, honey. But I'll just say I love you, okay?"

Eric hugged his mother. "I think that's enough."

"I think it's supposed to be enough for everything," she said, hugging him back. "We just don't say it, or really mean it, enough."

When Eric got back home, he found messages on the phone from Suze.

"Where have you been?" she scolded him when he called her. "You need to get your ass over to IMPAT ASAP. This Bob Davies friend of yours has another job for you."

"Did you tell him what a washout I am in the skills department? Unless, of course, he's got a farm."

"Yes," Suze admitted. "But he said he'd find a position for you."

"Other than bottom?"

"Don't knock it. It got Pia Zadora a Golden Globe. Just get over there, okay?"

⭒

"The people at Star Temps tell me you're not exactly office-qualified," Bob Davies told Eric two hours later. "But I know you're dependable, honest, good in a pinch, and most important, discreet. That alone will take you far in this town. I was also reminded by a mutual friend that I said I'd look for something for you. A non-temp job. Which I'm offering to you if you'll take it. It's parking attendant, downstairs. Not much, but it's what I have. And," he added with only the slightest hint of a leer, "I'm sure I'll be seeing you up here again in no time." He punched a button on his retro '50s intercom. "Diaz." The office door swung open and Rudy came in dressed in his black driver's uniform. "Take him downstairs, introduce him around. Make sure the other guys don't kill him."

Rudy nodded toward the door and headed out. Dazed, Eric followed. In the elevator, Eric found his voice. "You got me this?"

Rudy shrugged. "It's not that much of a job."

Eric frowned and shrugged back. "I don't have that much of a resume."

"You can drive a car, can't you?"

"Yeah. Hell, I can drive a dump truck, forklift, thresher, tractor —" The elevator door opened up on the first parking level to reveal tandem-parked Mercedes, Rolls, Porsches, Jags, and Bentleys.

"We don't get a lot of tractors down here." Rudy brought him over to the car park staff of three who were huddled around a radio listening to a soccer game in Spanish. When the distinguished older man with the gray mustache saw them, he turned the volume down.

"What's this?" he asked.

"New man, Señor Rangel. Eric, this is Carlos, Jesus, and boss man, Señor Rangel. They all habla English, so don't let 'em pull that shit on you. Guys, go easy on the gringo, okay? Eric just came to L.A."

"Hey, me, too," said Carlos.

"What's a white boy doing down here?" Jesus asked suspiciously. He tilted his head at Eric. "Can't even let us have the shit jobs like this?"

"Davies owes him a job," Rudy explained somewhat cryptically. "So he starts at the bottom, just like me and you."

Señor Rangel shrugged. "Get him a jacket and show him how we run this." He went back to the soccer game, turning the volume up to echo in the cement car park.

Rudy leaned in to Eric's ear. "Just play it very straight down here, know what I mean?" As he walked over to the key cabinet and grabbed a single key on a chain, he said, "I'm taking Davies out to Malibu in fifteen, so I'll see ya around."

"You're working for this Davies guy again?" Guy asked Eric at home that evening.

"And why parking cars," asked Patrick. "I mean, let's face it, the only successful item on your Los Angeles vita so far is killing off bitchy Arthur also-rans."

"If you must know, Rudy got me the job."

"Rudy!" Guy said smacking his forehead. "Now I get it. You two getting back together?"

Eric looked down at his untouched Diet Coke. "I doubt it."

Michael Fowler entered the den with his head bowed. "Sir, dinner is ready, Sir."

"Thank you, boy. C'mon, we need to chow down," Guy said shooing them all into the kitchen. "Patrick is taking us on the set of his movie tonight."

After dinner, Patrick and Guy with Eric and Michael Fowler in tow arrived at O'Leary & Finkelstein's where Sarah Utley had assembled an after-hours cast and crew. It was not going well. Sarah was struggling with sound problems. Bored, Guy asked Patrick, "So what's supposed to be happening here?"

"Okay, see the black guy back there with the suit?" Patrick said, pointing. "He plays Junior, the lead. He's the Parsifal character."

"Parsifal is hot," Guy commented.

"He's also straight, so let it go. At this point he's screwed up his relationship with my daughter and me and is on his own, now working — ta-dah! — in a mortuary. He's supposed to be consoling mourners and what-not. But instead, he's preying on their vulnerability."

"That dawg! And this has to do with all that wounded masculinity stuff you were spouting to me . . . how?"

Patrick sighed. "He's misusing his gifts. And he thinks fucking women equals being a man." Both Guy and Fowler's mouths fell open. "Yeah, I thought you Desert Springs divas would pick up on that."

Sarah called for places. "Let's try and get this before our mic goes out again."

Two hours later, there at last came a break. Sarah turned to Patrick with a proud smile. "We started out in the crapper but we're in clover now. Thanks again for letting us use your place."

"As long as nobody knocks over an occupied casket, it's not a problem," Patrick responded graciously. "Any word on when you'll be filming moi?"

"Still looking for your house, darling."

"What kind of house are you looking for?" Eric asked.

"Rich, tasteful, out of my league," she answered. "The well-appointed home of a city councilman and shitloads of time to shoot in it. For free. For some reason that's hard to find."

"I might know a place," Eric offered.

"You?" Guy asked in surprise. "Where?"

"I'm thinking Davies might let me have Margaret Atherton's for a few days." Then to Sarah, "I worked there for a while."

Sarah was awed. "Oh, my God, Margaret Atherton was huge. That must have been really special."

"Yeah. Pretty much. I'll ask on Monday."

"Bless you, child!" Sarah kissed Eric on the forehead and returned to her crew.

"How much longer do you have to hang around here?" Guy asked Patrick.

His friend nodded toward the crew and actors. "As long as they're here."

"In that case I'm taking my guys home."

Patrick raised an eyebrow. "Michael Fowler is one of 'your guys' now?"

Guy sighed. "I took him back to his apartment this afternoon. Patrick, it was shit. We picked up a couple of things and came back to my place. I'm putting him up in my office, just for a while."

Patrick took Guy's arm and led him a few steps away to whisper, "Jesus, Guy, how many sob stories can you take in? And this one tried to kill you. He's dangerous."

"He's me, Patrick." Guy glanced over at Fowler standing hunched over next to Eric, looking small and lost. "And right now he needs structure and something that'll keep him from thinking and turning that on himself." Guy turned and shouted, "Boy!"

Instantly Fowler was attentive, the call to a task giving him life. "Yes, Sir!"

Guy threw a set of keys at him, which he caught. "Get the car."

"Sir, thank you, Sir," he said and he was gone.

Patrick noticed the chain with padlock around Fowler's neck, the sign of servitude. "That's the kind of structure he needs?" Patrick asked.

Guy smiled and shrugged. "What, there's a rule it can't be fun for me? He'll earn his keep doing housework, cooking, chores. I showed him how to post on eBay this afternoon, he picked it right up."

"Oh, my God, he's permanent."

"Just until he gets on his feet."

"You're giving him on-the-job training! And this dominant/submissive shit?"

"Patrick, back off a little, huh? You've never understood that dynamic. I know you think the whole Desert Springs mindfuck thing is driving this, but that was ten years ago. I've learned a few things since so give me a little credit, huh? Trust me, all right?

"No. You trust me, Guy, he needs professional help. Where do you get off saying he 'needs' being bossed around?

"The same way I knew I needed to take in some young blondie from Buttfuck, Missouri, I'd never met before," he said gesturing toward Eric. "Or the other guys. It just comes to me. And when it does I can't say no."

Patrick frowned unhappily. "You take in more strays than Betty White."

Michael Foster Fowler ran in the entrance and over to Guy with his head bowed. "Car's here, Sir."

Guy rubbed Fowler's head like a dog. "Good boy. Tell Tractor Boy he's shotgun, you get in the back."

Without raising his head, Fowler smiled. "Thank you, Sir." He scurried off toward Eric and they both went outside.

"How do you know he won't attack you in the middle of the night?" Patrick demanded.

With a grin Guy shrugged and headed toward the door. "I don't."

Part Two

Saturday, April 1st, 2000

The uniform shirt was perfectly skintight and tailored to show off his physique. Dave, as Frank Powers, pulled on the matching dark blue stretch trousers designed to hug his legs and ass. He arranged his cockringed genitals for maximum effect, and zipped the fly up carefully. He stood in front of the full-length mirror as he added the black belt, the holster, and the mock gun. He attached the silver lieutenant bars to his collar, and pinned the regulation-legit L.A.P.D. badge to his chest. The shoes, hat, and baton completed the uniform. He curled an uncaring lip at his reflection. Not scary enough. He snarled HIV rage at the mirror. That was it. He was hot. He was ready. He was dangerous.

In his dead-on L.A. cop outfit, Dave spent his evening at the Faultline bar ignoring the hands that reached out to caress his torso and crotch. He caught his sneering reflection in the mirror above the bar. He knew he was built solid enough to stand out from the other cops, highway patrolmen, MPs, marines, cadets, sailors, and borderline S.S. storm troopers populating the place, all trying not to be caught staring at him, the porn star. Between the constant attention, groping, and drinking, Dave-as-Frank was actually able to chase away thoughts of the virus that ran in his veins.

☆

By 1:35 A.M. that night, Hiro was lying naked, spreadeagled on his back on the filthy, sticky, wet floor of the room right at the top of the stairs on the second level of Prowl in Silver Lake. Although he had already come four times on this first thrilling visit to a sex club, he was beating off again, watching the sexy, sweat covered Latino standing over him who was about to be the last of a group scene of at least fifteen guys to ejaculate on him.

"Aah, aah, *madre Dios!*" the man said as a ropy spray of semen hit Hiro on his chin and chest.

With his free hand, Hiro wiped it all over his face as he writhed, consumed in his own almost painful orgasm. He lay there, eyes closed, breathing, trying to collect himself, vaguely aware of how raw his dick felt, not minding in the least. He was exhausted yet exhilarated, having reached a state of orgiastic sexuality that he had never visited before. It felt transcendent. Although he had discarded his to-do list days ago, this was unequivocally the single best item he had written on it.

When he retrieved his clothes from his locker downstairs he put them on right over the mass ejaculate in various states of stickiness. The wetness stained through his shirt and pants like badges of raunch. As he exited the club he noticed the larger wet areas, his chest, his crotch, steaming slightly in the cool early morning air. He smiled.

Luxuriating in the taboo of his shamelessness, he sauntered to his car. Opening the trunk of his BMW, he took out his Arthur, the very thing that had led to tonight's amazing experience of wallowing in sex. Without removing it from its burlap sack, he set it on the passenger seat next to him as he got in.

Dave was feeling the effects of too many beers and too many men feeding off his sexual energy. He lurched out the door and onto the Melrose Avenue sidewalk. He was parked on Vermont, so he walked toward the intersection where he waited for the light to change.

Hiro traveled west on an empty Santa Monica Boulevard, inhaling the smell of sex rising from his warm, deliciously slimy body. He put his hand under his shirt to rub his cum covered belly as he turned south on a deserted Vermont. He pulled his hand out from under his shirt and looked at it in the glare from streetlights and neon signs moving by. It was shiny, dripping with jizz from more than a dozen men. He cupped his hand over his face, closed his eyes and greedily breathed it in. The smell was pure, intense sex. He exhaled and opened his eyes. He had just enough time to shout, "Shit!"

His BMW smashed into another car. His front airbags deployed with a bang, scaring him as much as the awful impact. He felt his car careening off at an angle, so he hit his brakes. As the airbags deflated, Hiro looked quickly around to see what the damage was. "Oh, God," he moaned, "Oh, Jesus Christ." In his mirror he saw a white station wagon knocked diagonally across the intersection into the curb.

"Holy fuck!" shouted Dave from the corner, instantly sober. Steam came from under the station wagon's hood. The blue-black BMW sat in the intersection, the front of the car as well as the left fender now a mass of jagged metal. He ran to the station wagon praying the driver was alive.

Hiro thought in horror, *Oh, Christ, what about that poor driver?* He pushed the limp airbag away, turned off the engine, and glanced down at his left hand as it grabbed for the door handle. He froze. No, no, no, no, no! A deeper panic began filling his gut. *I'm covered in semen!* "Oh, Jesus, God, Christ what have I done?" he whispered in horror. "I cannot be seen like this!" At the gas station on the corner he saw a policeman running to the other car. Oh, fuck, oh fuck! Trembling, Hiro looked at his sex-sopped clothes. He heard someone shouting. It was the cop by the station wagon, pointing at him. The panic surged from his stomach, gripping his chest, choking his throat, and filling his head with one paramount, intense, demanding thought: *Get away!* Hiro threw his car into drive and stomped on the gas. His tires squealed, leaving rubber behind him.

STEALING ARTHUR

Waving his hands frantically, Dave shouted at the BMW, "Stop! Stop!" The blue-black BMW tore away, going south on Vermont toward the freeway. "You fucking shit!" Then Dave cursed himself for having been too shocked and upset to get a license number. But he didn't have time for that right now.

Inside the station wagon there was a black woman with blood on her face. "Oh, Jesus," Dave breathed. "Are you all right, lady? Are you all right?" She was dazed, staring at him with her mouth partly open.

Sarah's eyes were so wide Dave could see her entire irises. "Can you move, lady?" Numbly, she unfastened her seatbelt with her right hand. Her left arm fumbled for the door handle. She opened the door and stumbled out.

Sarah stood, wobbling between the car and Dave. She looked at the destroyed rear half of her station wagon. "My props," she said weakly.

"Lady, you're bleeding."

She turned her head to face Dave, as if seeing him for the first time. "Someone hit my car, officer."

"What?" He had completely forgotten what he was wearing.

"I've been hit," Sarah mumbled, wiping the blood off her forehead. She saw the red wetness now on her hand. She looked at Dave again. "Officer, can you take me to the hospital? I don't feel . . ." She collapsed, falling against Dave.

Dave scooped her up in his arms and hustled to his car nearby. He set her down in the passenger seat and fastened her seatbelt. He climbed into the driver's side and took off going north on Vermont, speeding toward Hollywood Presbyterian Medical Center at Sunset, only a dozen blocks away.

Sarah regained woozy consciousness on the way. "Thank you, officer," she said, working hard to focus on Dave's L.A.P.D. badge. "Officer Fister." She noticed the civilian dashboard. "This is a police car?" she asked looking around the interior of Dave's Audi.

Dave had no clue how to reply. How do you explain fetish wear to someone depending on you to be a cop? "Yeah. Undercover."

"In a uniform?"

"Uh, the . . . car's undercover, not me," he said, swerving past a slow moving taxi.

"That doesn't make any —"

"Don't try to talk, ma'am." He wondered what the hell the emergency personnel were going to think of a cop not waiting for an ambulance but bringing an accident victim in his car. He figured there was only one way to play this.

At the Hollywood Presbyterian emergency entrance he pulled right up to the door, blaring his horn. An angry security guard came running his way, but Dave jumped out of his Audi and began yelling. "I've got a black female adult in here, mid-thirties, bleeding from a car crash! You turn right around and get me a doctor!" He strode into the emergency room and barked at the nurse on duty, "I need a gurney out here *stat*! Move it, move it, *move it!*" Somehow, miraculously, it worked. Two nurses and a doctor came quickly. They expertly removed Sarah from his Audi and wheeled her into the hospital.

Dave hopped in his car and drove the fuck away.

Once home, Hiro pulled his damaged BMW into the garage, closing the garage door quickly so neighbors wouldn't see. Feeling defiled by his semen-stained shirt and pants, he shucked his clothes right there in the garage, sealed them in a trash bag, and put it in the trash. Inside, under the sink in the bathroom, he found a spray bottle of Formula 409 and an unopened pint of Lysol. He sprayed the 409 on his legs, arms, and torso, turned on the shower as hot as he could stand it, and climbed inside. He lathered all over with soap and rinsed. Twice. Then he reached for the Lysol. It wasn't so bad — until the cleanser hit his abused, raw penis. The pain caused him to howl and dance.

And slip and fall, splitting his chin open on the side of the tub.

Between the trauma of the car accident, his bleeding chin, and his now throbbing penis, he knew he'd probably need a Valium to sleep.

That night he took two.

Sunday, April 2nd

Through groggy eyes, Hiro could see it was 6:30 by his alarm clock. He felt around for the remote on his nightstand and turned the TV on to see if that was 6:30 A.M. or P.M. It was A.M. because they were finishing the morning traffic report. He shifted and the remote fell to the floor. Fuck it. He rolled over to sleep some more.

". . . speaking of traffic, early this morning there was an encounter of the vehicular kind at the corner of Melrose and Vermont," the snarky morning show host gushed.

What? Hiro fought through the Valium to sit upright in bed. *What was that?*

"When police arrived, not only had one of the drivers sped away, but the other had disappeared as well," the host chuckled. "Officers searched the surrounding area fearing the driver could be wandering the neighborhood, possibly turning up on someone's yard dazed and incoherent."

"Ooh, how Margot Kidder!" smirked the co-host. "Did they find the driver?"

"That's the strange part, Diane. She turned up at Hollywood Presbyterian Medical Center with a story that didn't make sense how she got there. Police are hoping when she's released her memory will improve. At present, the only witness is a gas station attendant."

Hiro literally rolled out of bed, falling to the floor. He fumbled for the remote.

"So be on the lookout for that. And speaking of cars, Eddie Bowling, who found the Arthurs that had been stolen off a loading dock in Downey, says his first purchase with his reward money is going to be a new —" Hiro had found the remote and clicked the television to blessed blackness, silence.

He held his head to think. There was some woman injured bad enough to be in the hospital. He could have sworn he saw a cop. And there was a witness. What the fuck was he going to do? What if the woman died? Such guilt on top of such deep shame for the way the wreck had happened. That must never come out.

Never, never, never. Too much shame. Too much bad luck. He desperately needed to do something, but what?

Other than a four-inch gash on her scalp, a cracked rib, and some internal bruising, Sarah was okay. The doctor had mercifully prescribed Percocet because, despite being healthy enough to go home, any movement hurt so much it made her cry.

In order to be released from the hospital she needed a way home. Her mother didn't have a car, and hers had been totaled. So she had called the only person she could think of.

Roger stood in the doorway. "You ready to go?" he asked expressionlessly.

"Oh, baby, I'm so ready to leave," she said, smiling through the Percocet.

Sarah needed him to drive her by her house to pick up some things, and then take her to her mother's home where she could rest up for a few days. Sarah lived on Holly Knoll, a narrow winding street in the hills below Los Feliz.

Once there, Roger helped Sarah out of the car in front of her tiny, immaculate stucco house. The front door was practically on the street and the rest of the house followed the steep slope of the hill down. The stairs between the living, dining, and kitchen floor and her downstairs bedroom, bath, and office made recuperating there impossible.

Immediately inside the house there was an alphanumeric home security keypad. Sarah had to fight through the painkiller to disarm the alarm. Roger watched her slowly press A, then R, then T, H, U, and R.

"I gotta get some stuff from downstairs," she told him. "Could you help me down the stairs?" Roger put his arm around her waist, and helped her make her painful way downstairs.

"Thank you," she said. "There's a little red suitcase in the closet, if you'd get it for me." Roger opened the closet and flicked on the light, knocking a house key labeled "spare" off a gold cup hook above the light switch. Roger replaced it and pulled the suitcase out. "I want you to put some things in it for me." Sarah directed Roger where to go in her dresser and bathroom for panties, bras, sweat pants, T-shirts, lipstick, toothbrush, and other personal items to take to her mother's. He packed it all in the red suitcase, and helped Sarah slowly, gingerly climb back up the stairs.

At the front door, Sarah remembered something. "My brush! I need my hairbrush. Baby, would you go back down and get it?" Roger nodded and headed down the stairs again. "It should be in the right-hand top drawer," she called out after him.

Alone downstairs, Roger accidentally opened the left-hand drawer. His eyes became quite large.

He had been to enough Hollywood parties to know exactly what he was looking at. He opened the drawer below it to find even more. Serax, Xanax, Tranxene, Hycotuss, Zydone, Tylox, Valium, Librium, Tuinal, Fiorinal with Codeine, Restoril, Vicodin, Vicoprofin, OxyContin, Morphine-IR, Duragesic, Seconal, Dolophine. Holy fuckinol. None of this was for personal use. They weren't in prescription bottles but in plastic bags. His film teacher was a pill pusher.

Roger's gambling demon saw a shitload of money in pill and capsule form just sitting here. And he was a man with debts, a man who needed money. Bad.

"Find it?" Sarah called down.

First things first, Roger thought. He shut all those drawers and opened the top right one. He grabbed the brush. Then he opened the closet and pocketed the key from the gold cup hook. "Got it!" he shouted back.

Monday, April 3rd

Hiro's cell phone rang at ten the next morning. It was his assistant, Jenean, calling because there was an important partner meeting about to start and she was concerned. Was it already Monday? He told her he couldn't come in because of food poisoning. "Have Finkelstein cover for me."

"Will do, Mr. Yamamoto. But, golly," Jenean said, her voice full of genuine sympathy, "first that spill you took in your office and now this. I swear, you're just having the worst luck."

"You have no idea." He pressed the off button. He stretched and sat up. Physically, he felt surprisingly better. All he had to do was figure out a way to deal with one and a half tons of incriminating metal in the garage.

Being a thrifty accountant, he also wanted the insurance company to pay for the car. It needed to be a way that couldn't be connected to the accident. Maybe even a way to have someone else get rid of the car for him.

A cunning plan began to bloom.

Roger parked several houses away on Holly Knoll. With a Trader Joe's grocery bag folded under his arm, he walked to Sarah's house and inserted the spare key in the lock. He stepped inside and, using his knuckle, pressed A-R-T-H-U-R on the keypad, disarming the alarm. He put on a pair of rubber gloves.

In the bedroom he loaded the paper bag with two dozen plastic bags of assorted highly illegal prescription drugs. Then he went exploring. The jewelry box on the dresser was full of crap: plastic earrings, African tribal beads, a locket with worn gold plate. Adjacent to the bedroom was a guest-room-slash-office. Props, lance painted with blood, computer, file cabinet, printer, Arthur statuette, video equipment . . .

What?

An Arthur? On top of the filing cabinet? He picked it up. It certainly felt real. He turned it over to look for the trademark stamp on the bottom. He wrinkled his forehead. How the hell did a USC Film History 101 professor have an Arthur? It hadn't been inscribed. Holy shit. It had to be one of the missing ones.

It just seemed natural to take it.

"This is not good, Roger," Nicholas said. A sudden, powerful fist slammed into Roger's gut making him double over and fall backward between cars in the USC parking lot. The asphalt was hot against his scraped skin. He lay there gasping for breath as Nicholas calmly walked around his car to stand over Roger's head. "I am very disappointed." He put his foot on Roger's neck with enough pressure to make him choke. "I told you two thousand. You bring five hundred to me and a bag full of shit?" He reached down, grabbing Roger by his hair, and yanked him to his feet. "I told you two thou or I break something." Nicholas gestured to Roger's body. "You pick what I break."

"There's gotta be three, four thousand in there in drugs alone," Roger coughed. "Please, it's worth more than two thousand. That's gotta count for something."

"I am a good American worker," Nicholas explained as if to a child. "I work for a boss. He pays me to collect money — not shit!" he roared.

Roger flinched as spittle hit him in the face. "That's not all that's in there," he said trembling. "I have an Arthur."

Nicholas raised a thick eyebrow. "You?"

Roger nodded. "I think it's one of the missing ones."

Nicholas chewed on that. "If you are shitting me, I break two things. You shit me?" Roger shook his head vigorously. "Dump out the bag on your car seat."

Roger opened his car door, reached in and emptied the contents of the Trader Joe's bag onto his passenger seat. Clear plastic bags of pills plopped onto the floor and filled the seat. The Institute Award fell out on top of the bags. Roger picked it up. "It's genuine. Here's the stamp on the bottom, it's real, I swear it's real."

Nicholas's mouth twitched. He pulled out his cell phone and called his boss.

"Nicky, Nicky, Nicky," Petey said once he understood what this call was about. "You know we can't do the drugs; that's another family." Fucking Greek was turning soft on him. "Just follow procedure, okay? Demand more money next week, beat the shit out of him, and move on, can you do that?"

"There is something else. He has an Arthur."

Petey snorted. "Yeah, and I got a twelve-inch dick."

"This is real."

Petey frowned. Okay, so it was ridiculously unlikely. But what if it were true? There were three floating around, they had to be somewhere. And this could cement his relationship with Big Ed who had a major hard-on for Arthur. "Put the kid on."

Nicholas handed the phone to Roger.

"Every Arthur gets engraved after the ceremony," Roger explained. "This one's blank. It's one of the missing ones, but it's real."

Petey grunted. "Gimme Nicholas." Roger passed the cell phone back to Nicholas. "Take it," Petey told him. "And the drugs. Call this week paid in full. Bring it all to the boat tomorrow at three."

As Nicholas put his cell phone away, a worried Roger asked, "What did he say?"

Nicholas smiled, clapping him hard on the back and holding him uncomfortably tight and close. "Spit for good luck, my friend," and Nicholas did. "I hope tomorrow for the kind of luck you have today."

Tuesday, April 4th

Hiro called in sick again and went into the garage to survey the damage to his BMW. The first thing would be to remove all the parts that had white paint that could link him to the white station wagon he'd hit. The bumper would have to come off, maybe the fender, as well. Aesthetically, he hated the look of the deflated airbags, too. He selected a large pair of shears and climbed inside to cut them out. While there he accidentally kicked the Arthur, still in its burlap bag protruding from under the passenger seat. Hiro picked it up.

"You," he sneered at it as he slid out of the car, "have caused enough trouble." He absently set the gleaming statuette near the front edge of the workspace shelf. He noticed a crowbar on the wall, and grabbed it.

The bumper would be the first thing he attacked. He found a likely place, inserted the crowbar, and pulled. The bumper gave a little, and Hiro was encouraged. He pulled harder, putting his back into it. The metal groaned but held. Annoyed, he climbed up on the bumper and grasped the crowbar with both hands. Braced against the bumper itself, he pulled with all his might.

The crowbar shifted suddenly and unexpectedly, ripping his left hand and causing Hiro to fly backward. He smacked the back of his head against the counter with such a force the Arthur bounced and wobbled right to the very edge of the shelf above him. In an animal rage there on the floor and with all his strength, he beat the bumper with a single mighty blow from the crowbar. The heavy bumper fell off the car — crushing Hiro's left ankle just below it. The blinding pain caused him to jerk upright, smashing the top of his head on the underside of the counter. Knocked farther forward, the Arthur teetered dangerously on the ledge. In frustration, Hiro fell backward, again hitting the base of the counter.

The nine-and-a-half pound solid metal statuette wavered on the ledge, then toppled, hitting Hiro squarely in the crotch like a brick. He rolled on his side gasping for air, holding his injured testicles.

The slap of water against hundreds of boats, the clang of halyards against masts, and the cries of gulls greeted Nicholas as he walked down a dock of Pier 44 Marina in Basin G in Marina del Rey. The sun was bright, a nice breeze cooled his olive skin, and a forest of masts filled his view as he walked past millions of dollars of catamarans, sport fishers, ketches, yachts, and old wooden yawls. Tied up in its slip near the end of the dock was a thirty-foot Fiberglas Bayliner. On board, Petey, in a tropical floral shirt and shorts, was making final preparations to set sail.

"You bring it?" Petey asked. Nicholas raised the Trader Joe's bag. "Lemme see."

Nicholas stepped off the dock and onto the boat. Petey pulled the Arthur out of the bag and examined it. "Well, fuck me sideways," he muttered. He pulled out his cell phone and called Big Ed. No answer, he'd have to leave a message. "Yo, this is Petey. Eddie, you are not gonna believe what I got for you, pal! This is so big that I am gonna be your new best friend forever. So you gimme a call ASAP, okay?" Petey snapped the phone shut with satisfaction. "All right, I'll get the aft. You untie the bow lines so we can cast off."

"What? You mean like out into the water?" Nicholas couldn't swim, and he didn't like the ocean. He also didn't like Petey much. Or trust him. "No, I stay on land."

"No, you pilot the boat."

"I don't know how."

"We'll get out in the water, you'll see it's just like driving a car." Petey caught the angry flash in Nicholas's eye and his tone became all business. "You are piloting the boat, got it?"

"Why not you? It's your boat, where will you be?"

Next to the helm, Petey opened the companionway door leading below deck and called out, "Paco!"

Below, a handsome young Mexican repairing a joker valve in the marine head came into view.

"¿Qué?"

"*Vamos afuera a calar los motores.*" Paco, almost certainly not his name, looked apprehensive about leaving the safety of the dock. Petey fished a crisp hundred-dollar bill out of his shirt pocket and held it out to him. "Okay now?"

The man hesitated, but finally took it. Petey smiled. "*Muy bien, continúa mi amigo.*" The man grinned and nodded and went back to his work. Petey looked at Nicholas and said, "We're heading out. You'll pilot because I'll be busy below."

Nicholas had heard of Petey's *jornalero* habit. He now knew what he was there for, just as surely as he knew this young man spoke no English and had no idea what was coming. Nicholas also knew Petey was boss and there was nothing he could do.

They cast off and Petey maneuvered past hundreds of slipped boats, into the main channel, and out past the breakwater. There was an open ice chest near the wheel with Corona beer chilling in it. He laid the Arthur in the ice chest so as to enjoy seeing it shine in the sun as he swigged a Corona. Once in the open ocean, he revved the engines, heading far out into Santa Monica Bay. A thin mist of salty spray covered the boat.

About twenty minutes out, Petey pulled back on the throttle, slowing to only a few knots. He gave a nervous and agitated Nicholas a brief lesson in navigation. Leaving him at the helm, Petey went aft. Just before he went below, Nicholas saw him draw a gun out of his Tommy Bahama shorts.

Nicholas heard the frantic noises from below. His eyes were fixed on a point near the dark blue horizon, his lips were taut, and his knuckles white where he gripped the wheel.

He was twelve years old again. His uncle Ari opened the door to Nicholas's bedroom in the middle of the night. Uncle Ari stepped out of his white boxers and slipped under the covers. The Hugging Game, he called it. But it always ended with Nicky making the same terrified muffled yells as the poor Mexican below. Just like when he was a child, time stopped.

He was surprised to find Petey standing beside him. Nicholas realized he'd been at the wheel a long time because he noticed his arms were sunburned.

Petey nudged him with an elbow. "Hey, I said, you want a go at him?" Petey asked, grinning in the glaring sun.

Nicholas pushed Petey in the chest so hard he slipped on the moist deck, falling backward. "Keep the fuck away from me," he growled.

"Jesus Christ, you stupid Greek," Petey yelled, scrambling to get back on his feet. "Who the fuck do you think you're talking to?"

"What you do is evil!" Nicholas shouted at him, trembling with fury. "You are sick, evil person."

"Oh, yeah?" he said, pulling his pistol from his shorts. "Well, I'm the sick fuck with a gun, you shit." He smacked Nicholas across the face with it, sending him to the deck, spilling the ice chest. Petey shoved the gun in Nicholas's face. "Whaddaya think about that, huh?"

With his right hand Nicholas felt for a beer bottle among the ice but grabbed the Arthur. With his left hand he knocked the gun away from his face, and with his right, he clocked Petey with the Arthur solidly on the side of his head. The gun went off, grazing Nicholas's ear, but the impact of the Arthur made Petey lose his grip and the gun landed on the deck. Nicholas kicked the gun away and it skittered down the step to the aft deck. Both of them lunged for it, flopping like landed fish. Petey ended up with it.

"Back off!" Petey snarled as he himself backed away. He wanted to get a safe distance from his crazy henchman as well as a good aim at him. Defeated, Nicholas got to his feet breathing heavily, the gold award still in his hand. "What the fuck is wrong with you?" Petey yelled at him. "You work for me, asshole, me!"

The companionway door burst open and the Mexican flew out, naked, wielding a long knife from the galley and screaming in an insane rage. In his fury he attacked the first person he saw, a surprised Nicholas, slicing him deeply all the way down his right forearm. Nicholas howled in pain. With an angry upward swing of his bloody right arm he smashed the Arthur into the poor Mexican's jaw. The man dropped to the deck.

"Shit," Petey said staring down at the man. "I tied him down good. How the hell did he get out of the ropes?"

"You are wrong, asshole!" Nicholas cried. "I do not work for you. I quit!"

"Quit?" Petey asked dryly. "You're fired." He shot Nicholas in the left collarbone, shattering it. Nicholas tumbled overboard from the impact, golden statue still in his right hand. "Oh, fuck!" Petey ran to the side of the boat. Nicholas flailed in the water. Petey reached out, "Give it to me! Come on! Give it to me!"

Nicholas raised the award, shocked he still had it in his bloody grip. Choking in the water he screamed, "Fuck you!" He went under, but thrashed his way back up for air, but mainly for another, "Fuck youuuu!" Suddenly there was a sharp pain just above his right elbow. He raised his right arm. It was a bloody, severed stump. Panic took over and he beat the water like a madman.

There was a jerk on his foot. He felt for it with his remaining hand. Most of his foot was gone. Nicholas began screaming. He screamed and gasped until he sank into the darkening water.

The Mexican man had pulled himself up on a seat to witness the horrible death of Nicholas. With terrified eyes, he saw Petey shift his gaze to him.

"You couldn't stay where I left you," Petey said with annoyance and frustration. "You had to come up and see all this."

The man slid to his knees and folded his hands, begging. "*¡Por favor no me mate, porfa, señor, no me mate!*" through tears.

Petey indicated the transom, the top edge of the back of the boat. "*Aquí. Siéntate aquí.*" Shaking and weeping, the man sat where he was told. Petey looked at him and shook his head. "So damn hot, too. Shit. You realize this is your own fault. Right? Right?" With one swift move, he brought the muzzle of the gun up between the man's eyes and pulled the trigger. The back of his head exploded into chum. He fell backward into the bay and sank.

Petey's cell phone rang. He felt his pocket, but it was empty. He glanced around the deck for it. He retrieved it from under the step up to the helm. "What?" he barked.

"Big Ed here. Got your message. What's up?"

"Message?" He was bleeding from a gash on the side of his head. "It's been a crazy day. Remind me."

"You were gonna be my new best friend 'cause I wasn't gonna believe what you had for me."

"Oh, that."

"Yeah, so what is it, old buddy, old pal? Whatcha got?"

"Nothing now," he said with disappointment. He glanced over the stern at the roiling darkly red water. "Things kinda fell through."

"Oh, good, you're awake," said the blurry man in the white coat. "I'm Dr. Ng."

"Mmm?"

"No, Ng. It's Vietnamese"

Hiro blinked and remembered lifting the bumper and crawling into the house to dial 911. "How am I?"

"Well, we monitor all head injuries, so you're spending another night with us, just to make sure. But if all goes well, we'll let you go home tomorrow." The gist of it was that Hiro's head was bandaged to cover the ten stitches in the back of his head and the eight in front. His left hand, swathed in gauze, had a cracked knuckle and a gash with a couple of staples closing the wound. Plus the bumper had fractured his left ankle, which was now in a cast.

"Your skull's intact," Dr. Ng told him, "so I think you'll be fine. There'll be someone else to talk to you about your hand and foot."

"Who?" Hiro asked. As the doctor consulted his paperwork, Hiro hoped it would be someone whose name he could pronounce.

"Dr. Fira Raznoshchikova."

Hiro closed his eyes. "If I am allowed pain medication, I would like some now."

"Just gimme seven back," Sarah's mother said to the cab driver, handing him a twenty. She turned to her daughter while the cabbie made change. "You gonna need help getting out?"

"I'll let you know," Sarah said, opening the door and carefully swinging her legs out. Holding on to the car's roof, she managed to pull herself out and stand on her own. She still ached all over.

The cab drove away leaving Sarah and her mother holding the little red suitcase of her things. Sarah unlocked the door, stepped inside, and disarmed the alarm.

"Child, you need to open some windows. Stuffy in here."

"Go for it. I'm going see if I can manage these stairs," Sarah said, taking the suitcase. She headed carefully down to her bedroom, her left hand holding solidly on to the banister. She went to her dresser and put the hairbrush in the top right drawer.

She noticed the top left drawer was just slightly open. That was odd. She pulled it open.

Empty.

She jerked the one below it open. *Shit,* she thought, seeing it empty as well. *Oh, shit, shit, shit!* She tried the drawer below that. *Fuck!* She leaned against the dresser trying to put together what had happened.

Robbed. Someone broke in, knew exactly where to go, and cleaned her out. Who knew she was dealing? And what else did they take? She rapidly opened jewelry boxes and drawers to see what else was missing. Just the pills. What about her office?

She rooted through the things on her desk — it all looked undisturbed. She yanked open a filing cabinet drawer. It, too, looked undisturbed. She pulled open another. Untouched. She shut the drawer and for the first time realized there was nothing on top of the file cabinet.

"No. Oh, no. No, no, no, no, no!"

"You okay, baby?" her mother called from upstairs.

She felt violated. And scared. Someone knew she was dealing drugs. They'd stolen her stash, the source of her movie funding. And her Arthur!

She put her hands to her head. What could she do? Call the cops, tell them thieves had stolen her cache of black-market drugs? Oh, and a hot Arthur, too? She was fucked and there was nothing she could do or say.

"Baby?"

"I'm fine, Momma." *God damn, shit, piss, cock sucking, fuck!* "Yeah, everything's just fine."

Thursday, April 6th

After his assistant Jenean had taken him home from the hospital and left, Hiro was determined to complete his plan to get rid of his wrecked car. He retrieved the Arthur from the garage and set it on the fireplace mantle where he picked up his car keys. Fortunately it was his left foot that was in a cast, so he could drive the mangled BMW to East Los Angeles.

Forty-five minutes later he parked his car on North Hazard, two scary blocks off Cesar E. Chavez Avenue. He exited the car, deliberately leaving the keys in the ignition and the window rolled down. On crutches, he hobbled to a tired, depressing convenience mart on the corner to get a cup of coffee and call a cab to take him home. Juggling wretched coffee and his crutches, he shuffled outside to use the payphone. Looking down the grim and grimy street, his heart became light. His car was already gone. For the first time in days, Hiro smiled. He finished his coffee contentedly in front of the convenience store before calling the police.

It took more than three hours for the police to come. But after filing a stolen-car report, at least the officers were kind enough to drive him home. At last, things were going right. Once home, he slid out of the police car, and waved to the policemen as they drove away into the early evening.

Then he realized he had forgotten to remove his house keys from the key ring he'd left in the BMW. He was crippled, on crutches, and locked out of his own home. Plus it was getting dark.

He limped around the house to find the best window to break, selecting the medium-sized low one on the side of the living room. He wedged up a brick from the back patio Noel had laid, and lobbed it through the glass, sending glittering shards all over their fine living room. He broke off a stick to beat out the pieces still attached to the bottom of the window frame. Carefully he braced himself on his good foot and stuck his left foot, the one in the green cast, up and through the window. He pulled himself up to the sill and tapped around in the near darkness with his left foot until he felt the floor through the cast. He shifted his weight inside, but the hard cast slid on the bare wooden floor and he reached out with his right hand to catch himself. He sliced it open on a three-inch knife-like piece of glass in the side frame.

"Aaauughh!" he screamed as he tumbled into the living room. "God, shit, fuck!" So unlucky. He saw the Arthur up on the mantle, gleaming in the last light. That unlucky, unholy, golden, Goddamned award mocking him. Hiro made his decision.

Holy Grail of Hollywood be damned. He was getting rid of that fucking thing.

Five miles off the coast of Ensenada, Noel cracked open a cold can of Tecate beer. He was greatly enjoying this last of his Mexican vacation on a sport fisher he had hired. They'd been out in deep water for over two and a half hours without so much as a nibble on his line, and he was just fine with that. He was very happy to be on the sparkling blue Pacific on a calm day, luxuriating in the variations between the warm sun and chilly breezes.

He was also enjoying his daydreams of Big Ed, whom he had met in Palm Springs. Usually the really big American guys don't go for the smaller, smooth, brown guys, but Ed was something else. And he'd actually called like he'd promised. Noel looked forward to hooking up with him again this weekend in Vegas. His partner, Hiro, was bound to know he was seeing another guy, but they had their understanding. In the meantime, Noel wanted to focus on enjoying his last full day in Mexico.

He certainly enjoyed watching the boat captain's two teenage sons. Their father would shout out orders to them and they scrambled ably to comply. They baited his hook, cast for him, and handed him the long fishing rod. They were a bit scrawny for his taste but they wore thigh-length cut-off jeans and deliciously clingy white A-shirts. They were straight, but eye candy is eye candy. He wondered if it would get hot enough for them to take off their undershirts.

Noel was jerked back to reality by a sharp, hard tug on his line.

Fifty yards out the water roiled. The dorsal side broke the surface and they saw the telltale fin of an enormous shark. Adrenaline shot into Noel's system. The captain spoke rapid Spanish, indicating Noel should cut his line. "No! ¡Me gusta! ¡Me *gusta!*" he shouted back. Noel hadn't expected to catch anything, and was thrilled at catching a shark. He wanted to bring it back to the dock so everyone could see. And get photos, too, to impress Hiro. He adjusted his stance and continued to reel it in, fighting the beast but by-damn winning by inches.

At last the shark was at the stern, his snout exposed. The teeth, rows of angry daggers, snapped at the air. The captain dashed up to the helm, returning with a sawed-off shotgun. Leaning over the back of the boat, he pressed the muzzle to the shark's head and pulled the trigger. Instantly the shark was still. The captain gave orders for his sons to tie up the shark for towing back to port.

On the dock at Ensenada, it took a winch to haul the nine-foot bonito shark out of the water and hang it from the weigh station crossbeam. He paid one of the captain's sons to run to the marina store and buy a disposable camera.

He gave an older man five dollars to take photos of Noel, the captain, and his two sons all standing by the landed shark. Grinning, Noel thought, *Hiro is just going to shit.*

The captain handed Noel a long, ugly looking knife, and pointed at the belly of the shark. Noel still felt flush with excitement, and it was so *Jaws*. Noel took the knife and plunged it high up, into the shark's belly. He was practically flying from the testosterone rush. With all his might, he pulled down hard and fast. Seawater and blood spilled out along with fish, a crushed Coke can, a human foot, an arm, and an Institute Award.

The Institute Award didn't make sense. Sarah could understand someone stealing the drugs, but her Arthur? Did they think it was a fake and just take it for a joke? Or if they knew it was real, what did they think they could do with it?

"Okay, Ms. Utley, we're almost ready."

With a start, Sarah came back to reality. "Oh. Thank you. Tell the actors to get touched up and I'll be right there." The undergraduate grip nodded and left. Sarah surveyed the lights, reflectors, cables, and crew crowding the late Margaret Atherton's living room. She saw Guy, Michael Foster Fowler, and Eric come in the front door, and frowned. More people in the way. But it was the blond kid who had made this house available, so she needed to make nice.

"We wanted to watch if that's okay," Eric said. "We promise to stay out of the way and be quiet."

"Of course you can stay," she effused, giving him a big insincere hug. "You are my hero, mister. I have you to thank for all this."

Patrick walked over nervously, demanding, "What are you all doing here?"

"Um, lending support?" Guy answered, surprised.

"This is a movie set, not a theater," he insisted nervously, smoothing his suit jacket. He turned to Sarah. "They have to go away. I can't handle this."

Guy called out to the room, "Can we get a fresh tampon for Debbie Diva here?"

Sarah took Patrick aside. "I have to let them stay; they got us the location." She saw Patrick was still unsettled. "What's wrong?"

"It's this scene, it's upsetting enough," he said, looking worried. "And I don't need the added pressure of them hanging around."

"I'll take care of it, okay?" Sarah told him. "You're sweating like crazy." Patrick dabbed at his forehead with a handkerchief. "Get some water, take a breath, and go see makeup. I want to shoot in the next five minutes, okay?" Patrick nodded, smoothed his jacket again, and hurried off. Sarah returned to Guy and his two roommates. "Why don't you come into the den? That's where I'll be, watching it on the monitor."

Guy, Eric, and Michael Foster Fowler were herded into the den where they waited while Sarah went over the scene with Patrick and the young woman playing Kundra, his daughter, in the living room. Eric pointed to a spot in front of the television.

"That's where Margaret Atherton died," he said, still guilt ridden about it.

"Really? All the video showed the living room," Guy noted.

"No, we moved her in there because, well, we killed her in here."

"What?"

"Ming and I, we forced her to watch gay videos," Eric whispered sadly.

"Are you telling me the founder of Desert Springs bit the big one watching homo porn?" asked Guy incredulously.

"No. It was *Priscilla: Queen of the Desert*."

"Ah, I understand," Guy nodded sagely. "Death by ABBA."

"Sir?" Michael asked, looking spooked. "Founder of Desert Springs?"

"It was her money," Guy said. "She was a chief founder and contributor."

Michael's eyes darted around the room. "No, no, no," he whimpered. "I think I'm gonna be sick."

Guy gripped him by the shoulders. "Look at me," he said in a stern, fatherly voice. "She's dead. You saw her body at the funeral. She can't hurt you. It's okay now. She can't hurt you anymore." Michael looked intensely into Guy's eyes, and slowly became calmer. "That's good. That's my boy. You all right now?"

"Yes, Sir. I think so."

Guy gave him a firm bear-hug and sat Michael down in a beautiful heavy black rocking chair where he looked extremely small. Guy came back to Eric. "That's some rocker."

"It's ebony. The whole place is filled with quality stuff."

Guy looked around at the rich paintings on the wall, the built-in cabinets. "This is the kind of place my wife wanted." Eric raised his eyebrows and looked at him. Guy never talked about his wife. "Tasteful. Moneyed." Guy shook his head. "What was she doing with me?"

"Same as what you were doing with her." Guy shot Eric a warning look. "At least from what you told me."

Guy relaxed and took a breath. "Yeah. Two fucked up homos trying to be straight. One of the smartest people I ever met, too. God, I hope I never see her again."

Eric cautiously decided to pursue it. "She was that bad?"

"Her? No, it was me," Guy said quietly. "Things I said and did.

Unforgivable. But, by now I'm sure she's become the person she wanted to be. Least I hope so."

Sarah entered with a couple of grips. "Looks like we're ready to roll!" she said.

Positioned in front of the camera, lights, and hand-held sound boom in the living room, Patrick and the actress playing Kundra were ready. At last they heard Sarah from her monitor in the den call out, "And action!"

"You will not embarrass this family like this," Patrick roared with an intensity that surprised even him. "I didn't raise you to be a whore to some piece of trash!"

"Don't you call him trash. He loves me. And I love him, so you may as well call me trash, too!"

"Maybe you are queer, you disgusting little ingrate," he sneered. "I'd have your mother to thank for that."

From the den came Sarah's voice shouting, "Cut!" She came into the hallway where she could be seen. "Queer?"

Patrick seemed lost. "What?"

"You said 'queer.' It's 'trash.' The line is 'Maybe you are trash, you disgusting little ingrate.'"

Patrick pressed the heels of his hands to his eyes. "I'm sorry. It's too much like my father." He pulled his hands away and looked at her. "I don't think I can do this."

"I want another take and I want to do it now."

"Sarah —"

"You're shaking, Patrick, you're practically out of control. That is exactly what I need from you. Now, can you do this?"

Patrick took an uncertain breath and nodded.

She touched his face. "Thank you, baby." She turned around. "Okay, places!"

Back in the den, Michael stiffened to attention when he heard the director's name for the first time. He leaned toward Eric to ask, "Did he say Sarah? Is her name really Sarah?"

Eric nodded. "Yeah, why?"

"She's a Sarah," Michael whispered like a prayer. "Mother, she's a Sarah."

And a desperate hope took hold.

Friday, April 7th

After being released from the hospital around three that morning, Hiro cleaned up the glass and gore in the living room in a Vicodin stupor. He fell asleep on the living room sofa, never making it to bed. At 8:45 he was awakened by a call from the cops telling Hiro they'd found his car, stripped, in an ally in East L.A.

Hiro had it towed to the scrapyard in El Monte. By three, he was in a taxi, headed there. He still had his head bandaged and, of course, the cast on his left foot and leg. Now, though, both of his hands were wrapped in medical dressing, his right one freshly sewn up with eleven stitches.

On the seat next to him in the cab was his once-precious Arthur statuette, tied securely inside the burlap bag. He had wanted an Institute Award all his life. Now, after having one for less than a month, he couldn't wait to be rid of it once and for all.

Arriving at the scrapyard, Hiro instructed the taxi driver to wait. Hiro then met with the owner of the yard and was taken to the burned-out husk of what had once been his beautiful BMW. He firmly wedged the bagged Arthur into the hole where the glove compartment used to be.

At a safe distance, Hiro watched intently as a crane with an enormous electromagnet swung over his car. The electromagnet dropped onto it with a crunching sound. The current switched on and the crane lifted the remains of the BMW, swinging it in an arc over to the car-crushing machine. The current switched off and the car fell into the machine with a crash. Hiro felt deep, grim satisfaction as the hydraulics started up. With eerie, yet satisfying creaks and groans, the car was loudly and completely crushed. The crane lifted a three-by-three block of solid, twisted metal out of the machine and deposited it on a stack of others. Somewhere inside that mangled cube, Hiro's Institute Award was eternally trapped, safely entombed until melted down one distant day into steely liquid.

On the way home in the cab, he thanked his ancestors for allowing him to be unburdened, uncursed, and out from under the shadow of the stolen Arthur Award's evil. After paying the cab driver, he used both hands to turn the spare key to his front door. He stepped inside, and what he saw made him drop the key.

There was a shining, golden Arthur on the mantle.

"No!" he shouted in shock.

It couldn't be, it wasn't possible. It was the Vicodin. Or the stress. Or maybe he was hallucinating. He stumbled toward the mantle and reached out. No, it was solid and real. But it didn't make sense. The room seemed to spin. Hiro sank to his knees. How could this happen? How could this be?

"How?" he wailed. "Howwww?"

Saturday, April 8th

There was a union grip working on Sarah's film whom everyone called Dan the Man. Guy, who was visiting the set, naturally gave his ass a generous ogle.

"And what are you lookin' at?" Dan the Man huffed in rather theatrical offense.

"Nothing," Guy replied with an arched brow. Dan the Man snorted and left the room. "Okay, I'm officially bored," Guy announced. He turned to Eric. "I'm going home while I'm still young. You?"

"Yes!" Eric responded in a groan. "I had no idea making movies was so dull."

Guy turned to Michael, holding out the keys. "Boy, the car."

"Sir, I would like to stay, if I may, Sir," Michael said respectfully.

This was the first time Michael had expressed anything other than total subservience. Guy smiled. It was a sign Michael was beginning to heal enough to make his own wishes known.

"Of course you can. Patrick can drive you home. See you at the house, boy."

"Yes, Sir."

After Eric and Guy left, Sarah came into the den to work out some light-rigging details with a grip. When she was done, Michael approached her.

"Hi, my name is Michael," he stammered. "Foster Fowler? I'm a friend of Guy's. Living there. That's all. Nothing else."

Sarah answered as if talking to a small child. "That's very nice."

"Thank you. Anyway, I know your name is Sarah, and would you like to have coffee with me sometime? Sarah?"

Sarah glanced around at cables, wiring, crew, props, all urgently needing her attention at the moment. "Um, I'll have to get back to you on that later, okay? The film and all. You understand."

"Sure. That'd be great," Michael responded, hope dancing behind his darkly ringed eyes.

"Good." She patted his arm and returned to the living room where her Kundra and Red were rehearsing a scene that simply was not working. Sarah chewed her lip, thinking, *What's gonna give this the punch it needs? Punch?*

"I've got it!" she exclaimed. "Fuck the dialogue, all of it." She pointed at Patrick. "You gotta beat her."

"What?" Patrick asked nervously. "No! I've never hit anyone in my life."

"And you're not starting with me," Kundra said.

"Don't worry," Sarah reassured them. "I can do it all with camera angles and stage slaps, I'll show you." She turned to the cameraman. "Give me a tight two-shot in the chair," she ordered. Turning back to her actors, she demonstrated how the stage slap would work. Kundra would keep her hand hidden on the other side of her face from the camera so Patrick could hit it forcefully with his hand.

"I can't do it," Patrick apologized. "I can't hit her."

"Oh, don't be such a baby, it's only her hand."

"Go ahead," the actress said, "Practice a few times."

Patrick tried once, barely tapping her. "Gotta be harder than that," Sarah told him. He tried it again. "Harder!" Patrick backhanded the actress's hand with a resounding smack. "All right!" Sarah looked at her crew. "Let's do it!" She scurried behind the cameraman. "Action!"

Just as he had rehearsed, Patrick stage-popped her good. "You can do better than that!" Sarah shouted, determined to push him to the limit. "Keep rolling and do it again!" Patrick did, gritting his teeth into a grimace of fury, he hit her harder. "Keep rolling! Come on, bigger!" she yelled. "Smack the shit out of her! What the fuck is wrong with you?"

Suddenly Patrick was a nineteen-year old freshman, home on Thanksgiving break, standing in his father's kitchen. In the foolish, naïve joy of his first real crush, he had just told his father he was gay. His father looked at him with such black contempt and disgust that it shocked him.

"Daddy?"

His father's arm flashed out and knocked him to the yellow linoleum. "Don't you tell me that shit!" he bellowed. "Get up!"

"No!"

His father kicked at him. He scrambled backward where he was trapped in a corner. "Get up! I didn't pay for college to turn you into a faggot! What the fuck is wrong with you?" He beat Patrick's face, breaking his nose. And he kept beating him, and beating him . . .

Kundra screamed. Sarah was shouting, "Cut! Cut! Jesus Christ, Patrick, cut!" A grip pulled Patrick off Kundra. Patrick was breathing hard as he looked around covered in cold sweat. He saw Kundra in the chair, her back to him, upset. He pulled free of the grip and went to her.

"What happened?" he asked, frightened to know the answer.

"Keep him away!" shrieked the actress.

Her nose was bleeding, there was a welt already appearing over one eye, her upper lip was split. Patrick looked at his right hand in horror. There was a smear of blood on it from the actress. "Oh, my God," he cried, trembling. "Oh, my God."

He strode to the front window and deliberately thrust his hand through the glass.

Michael Foster Fowler took Patrick to the emergency room where he received twenty-three stitches in his right hand. Driving Patrick's car, Michael brought him home. Once inside Patrick's apartment, Michael walked him to the bedroom and sat him on the bed.

"Are you okay, now?"

Patrick shook his head looking at his blue-gray carpet. "I am not remotely okay. I'm wondering if I've ever been okay. And I thought you were crazy."

"Well, I kind of am."

"Me, too. I just didn't know it." He began to cry.

Michael sat next to Patrick and held his good hand. As his mother had done when he'd been sad, he sang the song he believed all mothers sang to their little ones:

Hush little baby, don't you cry,
Momma's gonna never ever die.
And if your crying doesn't stop,
Momma's gonna marry a big fat wop.
And if that man should leave us, dear,
Momma's much better, so don't you fear . . .

Patrick looked at Michael. He knew three things. One, he was just like Michael, only the social coping skills differed. Two, the drinking wasn't working anymore.

. . . As far away as you might be,
You'll never, ever, ever get away from me . . .

And three, this was the most fucked-up lullaby Patrick had ever heard.

Sunday, April 9th

Big Ed had a limo pick Noel up at the Las Vegas airport and drive him to the family's hotel. He met Noel at the door of the suite naked, hard, and already lubed. He yanked Noel's shirt open. Noel shucked his pants, but not fast enough for Ed who ripped his Tommy Hilfiger boxers neatly down the seam. The enormous man picked him up, carried him to the couch, and threw him face down on it. Noel raised his ass toward Ed, gasping in exquisite pain at being filled by a very Big Ed.

After dinner, they watched *The Ring of Truth* on Turner Classic Movies. Noel was curled up in Big Ed's arms — until the end when Ed had to run to the bathroom crying.

"God, you're a pussy," Noel said when he returned.

"I can't help it. It's just damn good."

"Yeah, she was pretty much robbed of the Arthur that year."

"I know! Yes! That is so true! And I can't believe you know that."

Noel shrugged. "It's my job. I work for E.I.S. Entertainment Investment Services. We work with Credit Lyonnaise, Intermedia Film Equities, all the big movie investors." He sat back down and lounged on the couch.

Big Ed pricked up his ears. "Really? How does that work?"

"Studio gets a property, they go to the bank to finance it, and the bank calls us in. We consult, see if it's a good fit for the bank, you know, who's starring and all that."

"Wait, you're saying they come to you? They ask what movies to make and you tell 'em?" Noel nodded at him. "But I thought that was the studios."

"The studios are run by egos. But in the end, it always comes down to who's got the bucks, and that's the banks. Banks don't know from movies, so they call us to advise them as to what films to back."

"I didn't know anything like that existed."

"Just one of the many jobs on the fringe of show business. And we've said yes to some pretty big pictures. *Fargo, Toy Story, The English Patient.*"

"Oh, my gosh, that's . . ." Big Ed did some quick mental calculations. "That's ten Arthurs on those movies alone."

"All that and we don't even get invited to the Awards. If it wasn't for my partner I'd never even get in."

"What's he do?"

"Hiro? He's a VP at PrattswaterfordDouglas."

"The guys who count the votes?"

"Yeah, he's in charge of that. Well, that and a lot of other things, but that's the thing that gets us backstage. He's one of the guys they trot out during the ceremony."

Big Ed stood up. "You're telling me your partner counts the votes for the Institute Awards? And you decide what movies get financed and which ones don't?"

"There's more to it than that but, yeah, basically." Noel sat up as Ed began to pace "What's wrong?" he asked.

"Nothing,"

But Noel noticed Ed's eyes looking off into space. Ed was putting things together, thinking, calculating...

Monday, April 10th

"*¡Quiubo, vato!*" Eric said, sticking his head into a small cubicle at IMPAT.

"Eric!" Rudy said with a smile, looking up from his computer. "*¿Qué pasa?*"

"*Nada, tranquilo,*" Eric said. "Where is everyone?"

"Some luncheon meeting at the Director's Guild. Thought I'd snag some time on a computer while they were out."

"Yeah, the guys downstairs took the limo to Del Taco. I brought my lunch."

"Me, too. Let's see if the conference room's open."

Five minutes later Eric and Rudy were having lunch on the long custom cherry conference room table.

"If I'd known you cooked like that, I'd never have let you break up with me," Eric said noting Rudy's homemade arugula salad with red pepper, asparagus, mandarin oranges, chicken, and chèvre.

"And look at you with the chicken flautas? You make that yourself?"

"*Sí,*" Eric said proudly. "*Todo lo que yo hago es rico.*" He enjoyed making Rudy laugh. "The guys in the garage are teaching me *español.*"

"More like *mexicano,*" Rudy said with a chuckle. "*Mi güerito.*"

Eric laughed back, "Hey, you know, this weekend's the gay rodeo. Guy wants me to see it and Patrick's coming along, too, and so is Michael."

"Who?"

"A guy living with us now. Wanna come with us? I'll buy you a churro," Eric said archly.

In response Rudy fed Eric one of his asparagus spears dripping with vinaigrette. "I just might let you do that."

"You're in the Mafia?" Noel screeched, pale and wide-eyed at Big Ed. "The real gambling, extortion, killing-people Mafia Mafia?"

"Well, yeah, but it's not like I applied for it or anything." Big Ed tried to think of a way to lessen the impact. "It's more of a family issue, really."

"Yeah, the Corleone family! Jesus, I've been going down on a Gambino."

Big Ed sat on the edge of the bed, looking as small as his hulking bulk would allow. "I know you're gonna need time to think about this, but I want you to know why I told you. Please sit down." Noel took a chair, one far across the room. "Here," Ed said, sweetly patting the space next to him on the bed. Noel rose and came to him warily. He sat gingerly and stiffly next to Big Ed. "Noel, I'm only telling you this because I trust you," he said putting a massive arm tenderly around the small Filipino. "I mean, you think I blab this to just anybody? I feel like I can talk to you. Tell you things."

"Please, don't tell me anything."

Big Ed laughed heartily. "Come here, you," he said, rolling over onto the bed with Noel in his arms. Effortlessly he folded Noel into himself so they lay there spooning. Noel figured he had little choice in the matter. Big Ed spoke softly. "See, I wanna do business different than my dad. Better. Smarter. Fewer people getting hurt. But I didn't know how — until tonight. You gave me the idea, and I wanna let you in on it. You and your partner."

"Wait," Noel stammered. "He's innocent, he doesn't know anything. He doesn't have to be part of, of whatever this is."

"You're both part of it, you both deserve a cut."

"A cut?" Noel said raising an eyebrow. "Okay. What is it?" he asked warily.

Big Ed snuggled in closer. "It's a three-point plan. Part one is you. You advise studios and banks what kind of movie to make, right? You could advise me. I got money connections. You just tell me where to put it and we'll back our own films. Part two needs some work 'cause we need to get the movies we make nominated."

"For Arthurs?"

"Yeah. You know somebody?"

Noel rolled his eyes at the impossibility of pulling this plan off. "No."

Big Ed shrugged. "I'll keep working on that. Anyway, once the movies are nominated, your partner 'tabulates' the votes so our films win. 'Cause when our movies win those awards, that always ups the box office, so we make even more money." Ed sounded very pleased. "We don't even have to kill anybody. Least not that I can think of. So it's big money, it's no killing, it's big stars and movies, and they have to let us go to the Arthurs 'cause it's our movies up for the awards. And winning 'em, too." Ed was absently playing with Noel's nipples through his shirt. "All we gotta do is figure out that middle part. I know a guy in L.A., Petey's his name; I can get him working on that. And once we get it rolling," Ed said, nuzzling his nose in Noel's straight black hair and inhaling the scent, "finally, I'll make my father proud of me."

Noel slid out of the sprawling round bed with butter-slick black satin sheets where Ed was snoring. He tiptoed into the bathroom, shut the door, and sat on the edge of the Jacuzzi tub. He dialed his home number.

"Hello?" Hiro's voice seemed tired, as if he hadn't slept in a week.

"Hey, honey, it's me. How are you?"

"Unlucky. It's been a hard couple of days. You?"

"Good, good. I'm in Vegas. Did you get my present for you on the mantle?"

Instantly Hiro's voice was alert, sharp. "You? That was you? You put that, that thing on the mantle?"

"Yeah, how do you like it? It's real, you know."

"Yes, I know. But how? How the hell did you —?"

"On the way back from Mexico. I dropped by the house on the way to Burbank to catch my flight to Vegas. You were gone. Bet you were sure surprised, huh?"

"You have no idea."

Noel was annoyed that his partner wasn't more effusive about finding a by-damn Institute Award over the fireplace. "Well, you're welcome."

"I'm sorry, but I said it's been rough. Many unlucky days." Hiro made the effort to sound more enthusiastic. "It's quite something. Where did you get it?"

"Long story. Look, I want you to come to Vegas. It's really important."

"Please, no."

"Trust me on this. There's someone you need to meet. Can you do that?"

Hiro was in no condition to argue.

Friday, April 14th

Noel met Hiro at the Las Vegas airport with a bouquet of cherry blossoms, not that his partner could hold them. "What the hell happened to you?" he asked in alarm as soon as he saw Hiro hobbling toward him on a crutch with a bandaged head and hands.

"As you said, long story. I'll be fine." He hugged Noel with his crutch arm. Then he indicated the briefcase tucked under his other arm. "I brought it, although it felt very unlucky. I expected the plane to go down in the mountains."

On the way to the hotel, Hiro told the story of his Arthur, what happened to his car, and explained his injuries. "But now that this second Arthur has come to me maybe my luck is changing. Maybe I'm supposed to have one."

Noel grinned. "How would you like to have a dozen or more?"

When Noel opened the door to the suite for Hiro, Hiro didn't move. His accountant's eyes quickly tallied the cost of a hotel room this sumptuous and knew A) it was way out of their league, and B) something fishy was up. "Whose room is this?"

"The person I want you to meet," Noel said, pulling him gently into the suite. "His name is Big Ed."

"Oh, my God, he bought you. Like Robert Redford in *Indecent Proposal*."

"Not exactly," Noel said, crossing the room, "although there is money involved." He knocked on the door to the bedroom. "Ed, we're back."

Noel saw an Italian giant in an Armani suit open the door, flashing a smile. "Hiro!" he exclaimed warmly, striding toward him. "I've heard so much about you." He hesitated in his reach for Hiro's hand because of the bandages. "Wow. Um, well, here." He reached above the bandages to shake Hiro's arm. His massive, furry hand completely wrapped around Hiro's forearm. Hiro could understand Noel's attraction.

"You're fucking my partner?" Hiro asked him point-blank.

"Only sometimes. Sometimes it's the other way round." Suddenly uneasy, Big Ed dropped his smile. "Uh, I understood you had an arrangement for this."

"We do," Noel said pointedly to Hiro.

"Our 'arrangement' was not to talk about it. I would extend that to include not parading our tricks in front of each other."

"Hiro, I'd never do that. This is a business deal."

That caught his ear. "Business?" The cost of the room took on a new dimension. "What kind of business?"

"Hollywood business," Noel said.

"Although," added Big Ed, blatantly cruising the battered though cute, compact, firm Japanese man, "I wouldn't want to completely rule out the tricking."

There was a knock at the door. "Room service," called a voice outside.

Noel let in three servers with two carts. They swiftly set the table and when they were done, Big Ed tipped them lavishly. They bowed in unison, and left.

"Shall we?" Big Ed held out the chair for Hiro and then for Noel. He removed the domed covers to reveal yakitori, steaming tonjiru, cucumber seaweed salad, and savory smelling minced beef cutlets. Hiro pawed helplessly at his chopsticks. Noel scooted his chair over so he could feed his partner while their host explained his plan for highjacking the Arthurs.

Hiro boggled at what he was hearing. Not because it was wrong or immoral, or even illegal, but because after hearing all the jokes year in and year out about how he could throw the voting and who would know, ha ha ha, he had never really, seriously, actually considered it before. For one thing, the other parts of the plan would have needed to be in place. It had never occurred to him that his partner Noel would be one of those parts. And more than that, here was a man (a really big man, what were those, size fourteen Bruno Maglis?) who was willing to make all that happen. Eventually, Ed excused himself to go to the bathroom.

"So, what do you think?" Noel whispered.

Hiro took a breath. "Something has happened in the last six weeks. Everything was normal, then it all went crazy. I made a list of things I've never done but always wanted to do, and I did them. I never did such a thing before. Why did I do it now? That," he said gesturing with a swathed hand at the gleaming Institute Award set as a centerpiece on the table. "It has made my life . . . unsettled. Different and painful and stupid sometimes. And scary. But exciting. We may end up in jail."

"We may end up rolling in dough. And on the A-List."

"I know," Hiro said, his eyes focused dimly off on future red carpet events. "We would be the people we've always sucked up to."

"Stars would be kissing our ass for a change. Oh, and speaking of, you haven't lived until you've had Ed give you a rim job."

Hiro came back to the present with a thud. "Excuse me?"

"The best. And don't look at me that way; you don't like to do it. Besides, it's obvious he has the hots for you, too."

"Oh, great, another Anglo with a jones for Asian men."

"Like that ever stopped you. Besides, Mr. Size Queen, he's not called Big Ed because he's a crime boss."

The door opened and Ed returned to the table. "Well? Thoughts?"

"I want a business plan," Hiro said simply. "And I want to know how we nominate our pictures. It will take time to get all the elements in order and that cannot, must not be rushed. Then a trial run. Pick a category for next year, something small, best score maybe, see if we can pull that off. If, *if* we can do that, I'm in."

Big Ed grinned and shrugged theatrically. "Hey, you're the Prattswaterford man, without you there is no plan. So, sure. Everything your way."

"And no killing," Hiro added. "While you are in L.A., I don't want any killing."

"Done," Ed lied.

Saturday, April 22nd

Saturday brunch was at the Silver Spoon on Santa Monica. Patrick was demonstrating his deftness with a fork in his uninjured hand.

Guy was duly impressed. "So you've learned to do everything with your left hand since your little 'accident' on the set?" He leaned in archly, "Everything?"

"If your smutty little mind must know," Patrick said with a definite edge to his voice, "that hasn't been a part of my life for a long, long time."

"Oh, my God, are you serious?" Guy asked, taken aback. "How long?"

Patrick thought for a moment. "When was that god-awful Barbra Streisand movie? You know the one."

"The one? Um, *A Star Is Born*?"

"*Up the Sandbox*?" suggested Eric.

"*For Pete's Sake*?" Michael offered.

"*All Night Long*?"

"*Nuts*?"

"*What's Up, Doc*?"

"*A Star Is Born*?"

Eric swatted Guy. "You already said that."

"I know but it really sucked. So what was it, *Yentl*?"

"No!" Patrick said with annoyance. "The one with Lauren Bacall up for an Arthur."

As if sucking lemons, they all said together, "*The Mirror Has Two Faces*."

"That's it. I just remember watching that Arthur show and thinking 'I have no interest.' Cuba Gooding, Jr. was there, Ralph Feinnes, Edward Norton, and I felt nothing. All these beautiful men, Woody Harrelson, Tom Cruise, and I didn't care. And that's how long it's been." There was silence at the table.

Guy's tone was of genuine concern. "Patrick, sweetheart, that's not normal."

"I haven't touched myself in six weeks," Michael said quietly, trying to help.

Everyone looked at him. Guy returned his attention to Patrick, "I rest my case."

"I know it's not normal," Patrick admitted, "but as long as I act above it all and I'm funny and let's face it, drunk, I can pretend it doesn't matter. But it does. Something has to change."

"All you need to do," Guy said, "is start whacking off like a normal person and you'll be just like you were!"

"I don't want to be like I was, Guy," Patrick said urgently. "I don't even want to be like I am."

Guy stood, putting on his light windbreaker. "I gotta tell you, Patrick, it's this fucked-up movie you're doing. Ever since you started you've been all withdrawn and weird and I don't like it." He crossed his arms in frustration. "I mean, how would you like it if I suddenly got all internal and introspective and shit?"

"I don't know," Patrick admitted. "Maybe you should. Maybe it's time you did."

Guy drew himself up coldly. He addressed only Michael and Eric. "If we're gonna make the 3:30 *Rules of Engagement* at the Beverly Center, we need to go now." He exited the restaurant as Eric and Michael scooted out of the booth to follow.

"What's up his ass?" Eric asked Patrick.

"No one," Patrick replied. "Which could be a big part of the problem." He watched them leave, then caught the waiter's eye to order another cup of coffee by himself. He became aware of the conversation in the booth behind him.

"... running the Bereavement Group at the church but I'm the biggest fraud in the world. These people tell me stuff; I don't know what I'm supposed to do. I can't go on like this. No connection or direction. Something has to change."

There was a silence. Patrick heard the other man put his fork down and take a thoughtful breath.

"Ezra, have you ever heard of the California Men's Gathering?" Ezra must have shaken his head. "It's three hundred mostly gay men in the woods. They create a safe space where you can bring your vulnerability and leave all the usual daily macho bullshit behind."

"So, what do you do there?"

"Workshops, rituals, swim naked, meet people. Sounds to me like you're ready."

"For what?"

"You're at a crossroads, sweetheart. Overflowing with potential and love and desperate for direction. At least think about it. Go online to www.theCMG.org and check it out."

Patrick jotted "theCMG.org" on a napkin.

Monday, April 24th

As Dave was going down on him that morning, Roger tried not to think about the fact that Dave, as Frank Powers, had spent most of the night at a client's house in San Marino. Or the fact that it had been an uncomfortably long time since Nicholas had told him when his next payment was due. He decided to give over to the professional expertise of his lover's mouth. The purely physical sensation had him climaxing within minutes. But Dave hadn't stopped sucking, he was swallowing his load.

"What the fuck are you doing?" Roger shouted, shocked at the risky behavior.

"Oh, please," Dave said wiping his mouth. "As if it mattered at this point."

"It does matter. Are you swallowing your clients' jizz?" He watched Dave move away sullenly. "You wanna get reinfected?"

"It's less risky behavior, okay? Besides, why should you care?"

"Because I care about you, asshole, in case you hadn't noticed. What else are you doing out there?"

"Earning a living," Dave snapped back. "You should try it sometime."

Stunned, Roger could only stare at the man who had turned his life upside down by asking him to move in only a week ago. Softly, deadly, he said, "Try caring for someone who doesn't give a shit about himself."

Driving to USC, Roger replayed the morning's drama. *Less risky?* he thought angrily. You want risky behavior, give over to a porn star hustler. He was in way over his head. He'd told his mother and stepfather he was moving in with a college buddy. It all felt out of his control. He parked his still-dented Lexus in the USC lot, grabbed his backpack from the passenger seat, and got out.

"Hello, Roger."

He froze. He turned to see who it was. He didn't know the man, but he recognized the professional menace.

"My name is Petey," he said with steely, sinister coolness. "And we need to talk about a payment."

The color drained out of Roger's face. "Where's Nicholas?" he breathed.

"Nicholas's fortunes have . . . sunk." Petey smiled like a car salesman. "I'm your new loan officer."

Wednesday, April 26th

Sarah felt sure this was a bad idea, but this Michael guy had been so insistent that she agreed to meet him. She made sure it was in a crowded, well-lit public place.

"Grande decaf low-fat mocha, please." She looked around at the patrons of the Starbuck's at Westmount and Santa Monica hoping he'd be a no-show. But there he was at a small table in the corner. He saw her and stood. *Damn,* she thought. She got her mocha, plastered a reserved smile on her face, and went to meet her date.

"Hi," he said. "I wasn't sure you'd come, and I really needed to see you."

"Yes, I got that from your phone call." She sat down reluctantly.

"My name is Michael Foster Fowler. Your name is Sarah," he said awkwardly. "You remember me from shooting your movie at that movie star's house?"

"Vividly," she said. She reminded herself to be polite; after all, he might simply be mentally deficient. "That's where you first asked if you could see me."

"Uh-huh. Hey, uh, maybe we could see each other again?" Michael gave her the best smile he knew.

Sarah wondered why the man was grimacing at her. "Don't you think we should see how this meeting goes first?"

"Oh. Okay." He watched her take a sip of her mocha. "I like your name."

"Thank you. It's from the Old Testament, it means 'princess.'"

"Hebrew princess," Michael amended. "Michael means 'who is like the Lord.'"

"Ah," was all she could think of to say.

"It's the name of one of God's archangels in the book of Daniel. He had special charge of Israel as a nation. In Jude 1:9 he disputes with Satan about the body of Moses and in Revelations 12:7-9 he warns against 'that old serpent, called the Devil, and Satan, which deceiveth the whole world.'"

"Jesus Christ," Sarah said in shock. "I mean, he, uh, Jesus Christ, was um, announced by angels, too. I think. Right?"

"Uh-huh, but that was another archangel, Gabriel," Michael smiled. This was going even better than he'd hoped. "I think of Gabriel and Michael as the angels who are best friends."

"Oh, really."

And he could trust her! "I never had friends, so I imagined Michael and Gabriel would come and sleep with me even though I was a mortal sinner." Her eyebrows were arched very high. He was infinitely pleased to be impressing her with his knowledge of angels. She was a woman, she was a Christian, she could discuss the Bible and, most importantly, her name was right. "Oh, Sarah, this is going great," he gushed. "We can go out again, don't you think? Let's go out again."

Sarah set her mocha down. "Michael," she began as gently as she could, "I don't think so."

Michael was crushed. "But why?"

She took his hand. "Because you're gay."

The shame returned and ripped through him like Saul falling on his sword in 1 Chronicles 10:4. "I am not! And how can you tell?" he begged her. "I don't dress that way, I don't look that way."

"We're in a Starbucks in West Hollywood, Michael. The friends you live with who were at the shoot? — all gay. You have a slave chain around your neck with a padlock. And, baby, that haircut?"

Michael silently cursed Guy for taking him to Blades. "But I need you. I need you. Sarah. I need you to save me from that. You're my last chance, Sarah."

"Going out with me isn't going to turn anybody straight," she told him as nicely as possible, gathering her purse and standing. "Believe me, I have experience with this."

"No, don't go. You have to be the one. You're Sarah."

"Yes, I am. And, dear one, there's no other way to put this. You are mental."

"I know that. But I'm not gay. I love God and the Bible and Jesus. I'm Christian, I can't be gay!"

"Honey, I'm sure you love Jesus. But your archangels have sleepovers. You're gay."

Saturday, April 29th

Guy had been driving twenty minutes in silence. Finally Patrick could stand it no more. He turned in his passenger seat. "Michael, why did you shave your head?"

Wedged in the backseat beside Rudy and Eric, Michael looked at the floor and mumbled, "I didn't like my haircut."

Patrick turned to Guy behind the wheel. "Honestly, Guy, you should have taken him to Blades." Guy held up his right hand palm out, the universal gay gesture indicating a sore subject not to be broached. Patrick took the hint.

"How is your hand, Patrick?" Michael inquired.

"Healing nicely, and thank you for asking. I look forward to frightening you all with my disfiguring scars inside of a month." They rode on in silence, save for Faith Hill on the radio reminding them to "Breathe." Out of the blue Patrick announced, "I'm going to a men's gathering."

"What the hell is that?" Guy asked. Patrick told him what he'd read on the California Men's Gathering Website. Guy snorted. "Great, just what gays need; our own New-Age bullshit cult."

"It's not a cult," Patrick bristled. "I'm hoping it'll help me sort out what's going on in my head. It's at the end of May over Memorial Day weekend."

"How nice," Guy said with sarcasm. "So it's a three-day mindfuck?"

"Maybe I'm not the only one who could use a good mindfuck," Patrick replied tartly. "At least I'm looking for something, somewhere, somehow to shake me out of my rut." He folded his arms and sulked. "If that takes going off for a mindfuck, I'll give it a shot."

Rudy leaned forward. "When the person is ready, the mindfuck will find them."

"And what are you," Guy asked, "the foul-mouthed fortune cookie?"

"My grandmother always said when it's time, your perfect disaster will fall from the sky. It comes and you will never be the same."

Guy shook his head. "Rudy — and I say this with love — you are so full of shit."

Rudy shrugged.

They had parked and were just entering the Gay Rodeo when a somewhat short, wiry man in his late thirties with a sparse beard shouted at Guy from the entrance. He was dressed all in denim with a red bandana around his neck, and real cowboy hat, chaps, and dust-encrusted boots. "Guy! Oh, my God, can that really be you?" The man deftly wove his way through the steady stream of people coming into the rodeo grounds.

Guy put his hand out. "That's me." The man tossed his head back and laughed heartily. Guy noted a little tuft of chest hair peeking out from his shirt.

"You've put on a little weight but it suits you. You look happy. People call me Buck. Damn, you're looking good, Guy. These your friends?"

Guy introduced Patrick, Michael, Eric, and Rudy. Buck shook hands all around.

"Can't stay and talk. My competition's up soon and I gotta get saddled up and ready."

"What's your event?" Eric asked.

"Calf roping. Wish me luck!" Buck waved and disappeared into the crowd.

"So, who was that?" Patrick asked Guy who was staring off after Buck and looking perplexed.

"Hell if I know."

Rudy and Eric had gone off to look at the vendor booths, leaving Michael and Patrick sitting on some grass where they could drink lemonade and watch the burly crowd go by.

"I love looking at the giant guys who just stand there, posing, looking like 'we're all too good for you.'" Patrick observed with disdain. "Nobody goes up to them except other muscleheads. What a sad, pathetic, tiny world that must be. Thank God I drink."

"Patrick," Michael blurted, then hesitated. "I think I'm gay."

Patrick was about to make a smartass comment, but refrained when he saw the pain on Michael's face. "Well, I think so, too. But, I think that's okay."

"I thought there was a way out. But the woman my mother told me about turned me down. She said I was gay."

"I don't think our mothers have anything to do with it."

"My mother wanted me to be good," he said, "and to love Jesus. But you can't love Jesus and be gay."

Patrick grimaced. "Look around here. Do you want to be with any of these men?" Michael stared at the ground and nodded in shame. "And do you still love Jesus?"

Michael whispered, "I do."

"Well, honey, I don't know about the Bible or what you've been told, but it sounds to me like you're living proof that all that bullshit is wrong." He put his arm around Michael. "I mean, really, why would God make you gay just to make you miserable?"

"Why would God allow His only son to be nailed to a cross?"

Patrick leaned back to regard Michael anew. "Honey, you and I have very similar issues. Except for the part with me not giving a shit about God." He rattled the ice in his lemonade. "But then, what the hell do I know."

Guy appeared out of the crowd. He strode directly over to Michael and unceremoniously plopped a brand new black cowboy Stetson on his head. "I got you a hat."

Michael took it off to admire it. "Thank you, Sir. But why?"

Guy frowned. "Because you shaved your head, you're in the sun, and you've got no hair. I'm gonna go watch this Buck guy in the calf-roping event." He plucked the hat from Michael's hands and stuck it sternly back on his head. "You wear your hat, boy, or you'll fry your bald head." He turned on his Tony Lama black bull-hide heel and left.

Michael touched his fine new hat. "He wants me to get therapy."

"Darling, we all do."

"He wants to pay for it."

"Then you'd be stupid not to."

"But he can't afford it. He has me doing all his eBay stuff, so I see what comes in. It's not enough to make a living."

Patrick chuckled. "That eBay crap is just one of his two hobbies. His grandfather invented blister packs in the '60s — you know, those pills in the plastic and foil wrappers you can't open? So Guy has a small trust fund. He can afford to keep your dysfunctional ass in therapy for a good little while. Of course the irony is he won't get therapy himself."

Michael let that sink in. "What's his other hobby?"

"Strays. Like you. Like Eric. Of course Eric just needed a place to stay, while you needed global disaster relief. You're just the latest in a long line. But I give you kudos for being the most spectacularly fucked-up thus far."

"What do you mean?" Michael asked, somewhat miffed.

"Oh, come on, sweetheart. You were the first to ransack his house, to attempt to kill him, to be his slave boy, to have sex on an embalming table, stop me anytime . . ."

"All right, all right," he said sulkily. "I'll do the therapy."

"Good. Now let's just enjoy the scenery," Patrick said, nodding toward a group of cowboys coming their way.

Michael turned to see them just as they passed. A dark one in a sleeveless open flannel shirt looked directly at him and gave him a wink. It had never before crossed his mind that anyone might think him attractive. It felt warm like syrup on his mother's pancakes. It felt huge, like possibility itself. It felt like Jesus smiling.

Eric and Rudy were trying on leather paraphernalia in one of the booths. Rudy had shucked his T-shirt to see how he looked in a black leather bar vest. He gazed critically at himself in a mirror. "What do you think, Eric?"

Eric saw the animal hide framing a beautiful, deeply caramel-colored chest and torso on the man who had once sent him home singing after one night of love. "I can't do this, Rudy," he blurted. "I thought I could handle just being friends, but it's too much. All I do in the garage is think of you and wonder what you're doing upstairs. I'm not even talking about Davies. It's how is your day going and is he learning stuff and does he miss me." He paused. "It hurts too much, Rudy. I'm quitting Monday."

"No!" Rudy said in alarm putting his arms around him.

Eric wriggled away. "Don't. Just don't touch me."

"But why?"

"Because that's all you have to do, okay? All you have to do is touch me and I'm hard. Shit." He adjusted himself in his pants.

"Eric, you know what I do at work two, three times a day? I come down just to see what you're up to. Señor Rangel thinks I'm spying on him."

A thin ray of sunlight peeked through Eric's clouds. "Why didn't you —?"

"Because I have a deal with Davies. I didn't think you'd want me like that."

Eric gave it some thought. "It is just a deal, though, right?" Rudy nodded. "Nothing else?" Rudy shook his head. His short, luxuriantly thick black hair reflected millions of beautiful tiny prisms in the brilliant sunlight. "Then you know what?" Eric said. "I can live with that."

And they kissed with such abandon that the people in the nearby line for sno-cones applauded.

Michael was confused at seeing a man wearing only a jockstrap and boots while carrying a sign for a new video and

DVD release. "That movie won two Arthurs," he remarked to Patrick. "Why would they need to advertise like this?"

Patrick peered over his sunglasses. "I think you misread the sign, dear. It says *Good Will Fucking*." He sat upright. "That's Frank Powers."

"Who's that?"

"Only one of the biggest porn stars in the business. Literally. Come on!"

Before Michael knew what had happened, he found himself standing next to a stunningly beautiful nearly naked man with a Viagra erection pushing his jockstrap away from his body. Michael was so flummoxed he had no idea where to look, or not look.

"Mr. Powers," Patrick said, "I have a proposal for you."

Dave as Frank Powers was all friendly professionalism. "Thanks, but all personal business must be handled through my Website, FrankPowers.com."

"Not that kind of proposal. I have a friend who needs a place to edit her independent feature. You and Bad Boiz work with Cha-Cha LaBouche, who I know has editing facilities because how else would we enjoy your astonishing come shots replayed from three different angles?" Patrick turned theatrically to Michael. "Six to eight major spurts, every one over his partner's shoulder." Michael wanted the earth to swallow him. "Anyway," Patrick continued to the porn star, "I'm sure my friend would be willing to pay a finder's fee to help us arrange editing facilities at a reasonable, which is to say negligible, price." He gave Powers his card. "Call me. If it works out it's a couple of hundred for you for a few phone calls."

"Okay," he said bending over to stick the card in his boot. Michael made an involuntary strained noise at the perfect buttocks facing him. When Powers came up he asked, "You okay?"

"Oh, he'll be fine," Patrick said. "He's just new to being gay. He's never seen your work."

"Well, hell, then," Powers said as folksy as he could be. "Meet the Monster." In one deft move he freed his chemically induced erection from his jock and plopped it in Michael's hand. The poor man gaped at it in mortified horror. It not only filled his hand, but continued another five inches toward him with a slight curve to the left. Mercifully, Powers stuffed it back in his jock. "Can't be seen doing that," he said with a friendly wink. "Gotta move on." Powers walked off, smiling and waving at the crowd.

Patrick looked at Michael who, still staring at his hand, appeared stricken. "Breathe," Patrick reminded him, "breathe."

After the calf roping, Guy perched himself on a rail fence near the contestants' entrance waiting for the wiry-looking man in denim, chaps, and red bandana to come out. When he saw him, he called out, "Hey, mystery man!"

Buck looked around in time to see Guy hop off the fence. "Hey, Guy. D'ja see the calf roping?"

"Yes, I did, and you rock! Congratulations. Third place. Very impressed."

"Thanks," the roper smiled. Guy liked the crinkles around his eyes.

"Buy you a beer?"

"Love one." They ambled toward the beer tent.

"I think you'd have won if you had a little more weight on you," Guy said. "Those other guys were just bigger."

"Well, this here's all I got, but I'm real happy with it." Buck rubbed Guy's back in a friendly way that seemed oddly familiar to him.

"Where do I know you from?" he asked. "I have racked my brain, and I'm sorry, I just can't place you."

"Oh, I don't think the past matters, Guy. It's the 'right now' that's important. And right now it is really good to see you."

After grabbing beers, Guy indicated a nearby hay bale. "Sit down?"

"Just for a minute."

"Since you won't tell me where we met," Guy said, "how about telling me where you live and what you're up to, here in the 'right now'?"

"Well, in the right now I'm on a ranch out in Santa Barbara County. The work's fine, but the pay sucks. So I'm also part-time security guard for the outlet mall. But lately I'm thinking of moving back to L.A. You?"

Guy gave Buck his standard "What do you do?" speech, but had a hard time doing it. He was far too distracted by this man, this real-deal cowboy with the adorable wispy beard, twinkling eyes, and that tantalizing tuft of chest hair at his collar promising more below. Guy realized he was just staring at Buck. "Oh, shit, I stopped talking, didn't I?" he said in embarrassment.

Buck nodded and laughed. He glanced at his watch. "Whoops. Gotta get back in time for the graveyard shift at the mall." He stood and hugged Guy. "I'm really glad to know things turned out all right for you." He stepped back and smiled warmly. "I hope I see you again." He waved, took off through the crowd, and was gone.

Guy stood there in a kind of afterglow — until he remembered: "Shit! I didn't get his number!"

Wednesday, May 3rd

Dave hung up the phone in his kitchen, surprised to find out Patrick's my-friend-needs-an-editing-bay story wasn't a line. So he called Cha-Cha LaBouche, who was very open to the proposition. Too open. Something was up.

"Dave, my dear, I know I've got you scheduled, but I'm pulling you out of both *The Cider House Tools* and *Bods & Monsters*."

Dave was stunned silent as a fear gripped him. Finally he asked, "Why?"

"I think it's time you moved into production. And you know I love you so I'll pay you what we agreed for *Cider House* and *Monsters*. But let's talk next week about seeing where you might fit in, okay, sweetie? Gotta run."

For a moment Dave just stood staring at the linoleum, pale, and breathing in shallow staccato breaths. It could mean only one thing. He hung up the phone and went to Roger in the next room. "Cha-Cha knows I'm positive. And if Cha-Cha knows, everybody knows." He turned a black look at Roger. "Who have you told?"

"Are you accusing me?" Roger said in disbelief. "I can't even tell anyone about you, let alone your HIV status!"

Realization hit him like a punch to the gut. *Oh, shit,* he thought. *The meds.* Someone must have recognized him at the gym and seen the pills in his gym bag. "I'm sorry, Roger, I'm sorry," he said moving to hug his partner. "But I'm just so scared. This is my job, my income."

"There's other jobs, you know," Roger said, hugging him back. "Ones that maybe don't involve fucking men."

"Roger, I worked at Fatburger for three months when I was sixteen. My manager paid me to let him suck my dick and I never had another job. It pays for this house, my car, my sister's dialysis. It's why people want me, why they like me. It is me, Roger. What else am I good for?"

Friday, May 5th

Big Ed had just given Noel and Hiro the tour of his new West Hollywood condo. It was over-decorated in glass, mirrors, glass, chrome, and more glass. "Do you like it?" Big Ed asked proudly as they moved toward the door to go out for dinner.

"Yes," Hiro lied. "It's very . . . Fortress of Solitude."

"Yeah, masculine," Big Ed agreed. "I think Pop will like it."

Noel's eyebrow rose as he remembered what Ed had told him about his father. "You really think your father's gonna come visit you in Boys Town?"

"Why not?" Ed said optimistically, as they exited the condo into the corridor. "I told him I lived in the straight part of West Hollywood. Shit. Keys."

While Ed went back inside, Noel asked Hiro, "What's the 'straight part' of West Hollywood?"

"Barney's Beanery."

Ensconced later in a private booth at La Bohème, Hiro told Big Ed how, with a judicious firing or two and a massaging of the protocol for tabulating the Arthur votes, he could, in essence, be the one who verified the final total. "There's been talk of reforming the process anyway, so I'm working on that. If I can head this up — which I think I can if I can get Finkelstein, who's our VP of Special Projects, out of the way — then only I will have full knowledge of the vote tally for any category."

"Hiro's been there for seventeen years," Noel added. "Eleven of those years doing the Arthurs, so they trust him completely."

"Sounds like a plan," Big Ed nodded. "How long do you think it'll take?"

"Six months for refining the process, maybe a year to get rid of Finkelstein. That will be the hard part."

"Maybe you could come up with something to speed that along?" Ed suggested. He turned to Noel. "How 'bout you?"

"Pretty much the same. I gotta reassign a couple of people, get some kids so they'll be eager to let me train 'em. Bring 'em up to speed, I'm thinking six to nine months. What about your end?"

Big Ed leered. "My end is yours anytime you want it."

Hiro and Noel exchanged glances. "Yeah, about that," Noel began carefully. This was the part of the evening they had not been looking forward to and, given Big Ed's background, they needed to tread very lightly. "Hiro believes —" Hiro shot him a dirty look — "and I agree," he added hastily, "that it's one thing to be 'in bed' together as business partners —"

"Oooh, yeah," grinned Big Ed, not at all sensing where this was going.

"— and something else again to be, well, actually in bed with each other."

Big Ed was at sea. "What do you mean?"

Noel looked to Hiro for help, hoping for a tactful way to put it. Instead, what he got from Hiro was, "Business partners cannot be fuckbuddies."

Big Ed looked hurt. "But I love you guys."

Hiro remained firm. "Believe me, that is appreciated. But down the line, if something goes wrong when I am on my back, it could adversely affect things when we are on our feet."

"So, you're saying no more sex?"

Hiro nodded. Ed looked sadly at him, including the pink places where the stitches had recently been along Hiro's scalp. What could he do? At last, Big Ed shrugged sadly and said, "Okay."

"Thank you, Ed," Hiro said with what he hoped was the right amount of deference mixed with professionalism. "Now, let us return to the subject. Can you tell us what you have found out about the nominations process?"

Sunday, May 7th

Patrick and Sarah sat in the lobby of Bad Boiz Productions located over a furniture store on La Cienega Boulevard. Other than the door through which they entered, there were two other doors at opposite ends of the stark, white room. Every once in a while, someone would come through the door marked STUDIOS revealing a portable chrome tower of computer and video equipment and beyond, the graphic live sex of a young man Sarah could swear she'd sold drugs to, engaged in a dildo scene for streaming live Internet video. A technician had come out for a soda from the machine in the lobby.

"I can't look," Sarah murmured, "but I have to know. Did he get the black one in?"

As the technician went back into the studio, Patrick glanced inside. "I don't know how to tell you this, but he has the black one down to the third knob . . ." Sarah winced. ". . . and a nightstick."

Sarah covered her face with a dog-eared magazine, repeating, "It's for the film, it's for the film . . ."

There were footsteps trudging up the stairs from the parking lot, followed by Dave coming in the front door. "Sorry I'm late. Boyfriend problems." Seeing Sarah, he paused a moment. "You know, you look very familiar. Have we met before?"

Sarah felt similarly, but couldn't place him. "You have a brother who's a cop?" He shook his head. "Well then, maybe a past life," she offered.

Patrick led the introductions. "Sarah, this is Frank Powers."

"Hi, call me Dave. Frank's a stage name."

"Oh, are you SAG?" inquired Sarah, forgetting where she was.

"It's a nom de porn," Patrick explained. Sarah felt like an idiot.

"Well, let's see if Cha-Cha's here," Dave said affably and disappeared through the door at the other end of the room marked OFFICE. From her angle, she saw that the walls inside were plastered with porn posters.

Patrick looked at Sarah with concern. "Are you all right?"

Sarah smiled a little too hard, eyes a little too wide and nodded manically.

Dave returned and waved for them to follow him into the office area. He led them into a room with shelves stocked with numerous copies of porn titles and explicit posters. "This is our media and mailing room," he told them. "Right now we're sending out review copies of my latest film..."

Sarah had no idea where to look — until she spotted a door labeled EDITING. "What's in here?" she asked, moving toward it quickly so as not to see anything else.

"That's edit room two," said a pudgy man in his mid-forties wearing a brown suit. He proffered a rather dainty hand. "I'm Cha-Cha. Out of drag today so I'm rather plain William Helprin."

Dave, Patrick, and Sarah followed Helprin into his stark white office. Dave introduced Patrick, who introduced Sarah, who explained her project. As Dave listened to the plot of her movie, he felt himself getting pulled into the story. Learning about the main character's absent father, his search for masculinity by indiscriminate screwing, and his desperate search for wholeness spoke to Dave. It was like hearing his story in another person's clothes. He was riveted, but unable to keep silent. "Red throws him out? But he can't! I mean, he gives him another chance, though, right?" he asked worriedly.

Somebody shoot me, Helprin thought as Sarah droned on about her *facacta* movie, feeding on Dave's interest. Why is he so into this? He remembered seven years ago hiring Dave as one of his own discoveries. Dave was a talent, prodigious, professional, a powerful presence. But his winning quality was his genuine sweetness. A flicker of a smile touched Helprin's lips as he watched Dave hang on every detail. The fact Dave now had HIV pained Helprin in a place he was surprised to learn could still feel.

"I'll give it to you," he said, interrupting Sarah's spiel.

"What?"

"You want an editing bay, right?" Helprin reminded her, blowing his nose. "It's yours. In six months. Beginning of November I'm out of town running a two-week *Butt Pirates of the Caribbean* cruise out of Port Canaveral. I'll be shooting *Butt Pirates III* on the ship during the cruise. So other than the live porn you'll have the place to yourself."

Monday, May 8th

Sarah, energized by her editing bay coup of the previous day, was doing reshoots at Margaret Atherton's house this evening. She was setting up a shot with Patrick when Rudy came by to talk to her.

"Just letting you know," he told her, "Davies has a possible buyer to see the house tomorrow, so make sure you leave it spotless."

"Got it," Sarah said, "thanks. Patrick, let me see you hit your mark."

Rudy gave Patrick a wave and watched him work with Sarah for a few minutes until a big blond collage-jock-gone-to-seed nudged him with his elbow.

"I bet you'd be hot," he said.

"What?" Rudy asked incredulously.

"It's cool," the fortyish man reassured him, casually coiling electrical cable. "They call me Dan the Man. I can tell you're gay and that's totally cool."

"Thanks," Rudy replied, not at all thankful. The guy just stood there looking at him with a slimy smile. "Can I help you?" Rudy demanded with sarcasm.

"Oh, you could help me just fine," Dan the Man said, dropping the cable in a professional heap. He hooked his thumbs in the waist of his well-worn jeans so his fingers, including the one with the wedding band, could point to his crotch.

Rudy laughed at his display. "You can't be serious."

"As a heart attack." Dan the Man leaned in close. "Seven inches if you want it."

"What kind of gay bar does that line work in?"

"Dude, I'm not gay."

"You're asking me to suck your dick, Dan the Man, that's pretty damn gay."

"Just a mouth, dude. Close my eyes while you do your thing. You get a big, fat, juicy dick, I get a blowjob. We both go home happy."

"No," Rudy said. "I'm going home happy. You can go home and fuck yourself." He headed out.

Dan the Man swaggered after him a few steps to shout at him, "If I could do that, I sure wouldn't be asking you, asshole!"

Wednesday, May 24th

Michael was in his second therapy session. Dr. Larry probed him with an unforgivably intrusive question: "How are you today, Michael?"

He had no idea how to respond. Waves of fear, resentment, embarrassment, helplessness, and shame pulsed through him. Still Dr. Larry sat there, waiting. Shame won out. "I failed in keeping my word," he blurted.

"What word was that, Michael?"

"That I would find the Arthurs, the ones that were stolen. I promised I would do it, and I failed. All I do is fail."

"How does that make you feel?"

Tears pricked his eyes. "Like I let down God."

"How so, Michael?"

"My father wouldn't keep his word, so Mother said I had to. She said when you make a vow it's a bond and if you don't keep it, it's a sin. It's like you lied to God."

"Can you tell me about a vivid memory you have about your mother?"

Michael thought back to a time when all he had to do was love her. "I was in my cabinet in the kitchen. Watching her making something I think. She was going back and forth between the refrigerator and the sink. I like watching her when she can't see me."

"You're in a cabinet, you say?"

"Yeah, next to the sink. I had to go in the cabinet when I was bad."

Dr. Larry sat up. "Was your mother abusive to you, Michael?"

"No! She never once hit me, she'd never do that. I just had to spend time in the cabinet if I was bad."

"For how long?"

Michael thought about it. "Depends. If I was late home from school or something, it was just maybe for during dinner or until midnight. If it was bad enough to break my mother's heart, it was usually overnight or until lunch. But she never hit me. When I got older and did something bad, I'd go in the cabinet myself because I knew I needed to pay for my sin. Once, I stayed there for two and a half days."

"What did you do that made you give yourself that much time?"

"Nothing. But man is born in sin so I knew I would eventually do something and when I did I'd already have punishment time saved up. Later on, I just liked being in it. So I'd curl up inside and watch things through a crack in the door."

"And when did you stop going in the cabinet?"

"After eleventh grade," Michael said sadly. "I didn't fit anymore."

Friday, May 26th

Patrick took the 101 Freeway going west out of L.A. The directions on his California Men's Gathering materials took him quickly from suburban malls to a twisting two-lane black top that forced him to slow down as he entered Malibu Canyon. The late afternoon sun threw shadows across beautiful exposed western rock and steep chaparral-covered canyon hillsides. Pale yellow yucca bloomed among the rock, flecking the landscape. He found the entrance to the site of the gathering, and turned off the road.

There he was met by a grinning man with a clipboard and walkie-talkie. He wore a tie-dyed sarong around his waist, two "CMG Volunteer" stickers over his nipples on his otherwise bare chest, bright orange sandals, and matching floppy sun hat on his flowing black hair. Patrick gave his name, was duly checked off the clipboard, welcomed, air-kissed, and cleared for parking down the road. What the hell kind of gathering was this?

After parking, he lugged his gear down the dusty road to claim dusty space in a dusty cabin. At various points along the way there were men stationed to greet, welcome, and hug all arriving attendees. He politely but firmly declined all hugs. He made his way to the Dining Hall where he was registered. After receiving his materials, he was pointed toward the picnic tables just outside where he was invited to decorate his nametag. Did they honestly expect him to do that, let alone wear it around his neck? He crumpled it and threw it in the trash.

He wandered glumly over to the tables covered with all manner of provided glitter, stickers, stars, pens, paints, glue, scissors, feathers, string, and of course, dust. There was a gaggle of men at one table all screaming and laughing and hugging each other (*what is it with the hugs?*), so he chose the other one with only a single person absorbed in whatever he was doing with a glue stick. The man looked up and smiled.

"I think I know you," he said. "You from L.A.?"

"Yes," Patrick answered taking in the large and heavy Samoan. "You look familiar, too. I've seen you at funerals. You're from the MCC church?"

"Yeah. I'm Ezra," he said shaking Patrick's hand.

Patrick now had unwelcome silver glitter fixed to his palm. "Patrick O'Leary. O'Leary & Finkelstein's."

"Right, that's it. This is my first time here."

"Mine, too," Patrick said frowning. He looked unforgivingly at the dusty trees and dusty tables and aggressively flamboyant, oh-so-damn-chummy, happy people. He brushed grit off his pants. Good God, the dust.

Ezra looked around at the very same things and sighed. "Isn't it beautiful. It's just a magical place. Feels like anything could happen here."

After a dinner of predictably wretched camp food, drumming came from the main lodge at the other side of the camp, calling all to the opening ritual. Twinkle lights lit up the darkness, marking the path across the wooden bridges over the stream to the meadow.

It was too stupid for words. Once inside the main lodge, there was mumbo jumbo from the presenters as a live trance band played. The noise rose in pitch and volume as a long colorful cloth object was lowered from the ceiling. Hundreds of spangled ribbons hung from it. At a signal, men placed around the room pulled the object open like a giant flower blooming over and high above the gathering of men. It was a parachute brilliantly hand painted with intricate symbols of masculine sexuality. Phalluses, wriggling sperm cells, swords, and wands in reds, blues, greens, and white filled the symmetric spaces around twelve larger images drawn in black at the outer rim of the parachute. From the edge hung the ribbons and he now saw see that each ribbon had a brown card attached to it. One of the leaders announced that the images in black were archetypes.

"The cards hanging all around the outside of this parachute mandala correspond to these archetypes," the leader intoned. "They represent the Teacher, Explorer, Child, Revolutionary, Fool, Ecstatic,

Sage, Healer, Alchemist, and others. As we lower the edge of the mandala, let one of the cards choose you. That will be your archetype to explore for this weekend!"

Three hundred joyously eager hands reached up to pluck a card from the ribbons. Oh, what the hell, Patrick decided. He grabbed a card that practically hit him in the face. It was an image of an androgynous face with a definite come-hither look. Confused, he turned the card over to read what was on the back:

The Prostitute

Shadow Side: The one who has sold his integrity, soul, and self to be what he believes others want him to be in order to feel accepted/loved/right. His journey is to put that aside, learn who he is, and take back his power.

Empowered Side: The one who is known for his integrity/wholeness and refuses to compromise his talents, values, and freedom. He lives his own life on his terms.

Consider: To whom do you sell or give your power?

Sunday, May 28th

By the second full day of the gathering, Patrick found that being around so many friendly and very earnest men had lifted his spirits and he was actually able to enjoy himself. If only these people weren't so damned touchy-feely. He headed toward the Group Rebirth space under the open parachute mandala because it was the only workshop that didn't sound like it required having to get naked and/or be touched.

Minutes later Patrick was lying on the floor with over thirty other men — none of them touching — but all of them breathing like mad, deliberately hyperventilating as the workshop leader had instructed them to do. According to the facilitator, conscious connected breathing hyper-oxygenated the body causing excess oxygen to reach the brain cells and unlock unaccessed memories and other stuff Patrick couldn't be bothered to take seriously. It was all so much New Age hocus-pocus, but he was there.

His mouth was utterly dry from forcing air in and out at such an accelerated rate. His fingers and feet tingled and he felt pleasantly dizzy, as if floating, or high. Colors swirled behind his eyelids, shifting shapes, alternating intensity. Forms began to coalesce as parts of his body drifted away leaving only the awareness of a wide plain. At first he thought there were trees, but they were men, dozens all around him. In an instant he realized that they were him, each one a different aspect of himself, but with one thing in common. They were all angry at him.

"Why are you so pissed off?" he asked them. They only continued to glare at him. Patrick saw they were stuck fast in some kind of hardened mud. That's why he had thought they were trees. Somehow he understood he had done this to them. From the midst of them, a golden man came floating toward him. He wore a white sarong around his waist, with a crown of white flowers in his flowing black hair, and he held before him an ax. He hovered there in front of Patrick with tears streaming down his face, silently pleading, thrusting the ax toward him, but Patrick had no arms to take it. The man faded, the hundreds of men around him melted away.

He had forgotten to keep breathing and his body was returning to its normal oxygen level. The parachute mandala overhead came into focus and he became aware he was crying for no reason he could understand.

Several hours later, after another despicably bad camp meal, Patrick was still too rattled to go to that evening's talent show in the main lodge. He decided to turn in early and began down the path to his cabin. He saw Ezra sitting in the doorway of the cabin across from his.

"Not going to the show?" Patrick called as he approached.

"No," Ezra said with a soft smile. "I just wanted to sit here and be still for a while. What about you?"

"Same here. I had kind of a strange experience this afternoon in a workshop."

"Yeah? Me, too," Ezra laughed. "You okay?"

Unexpected emotion flooded Patrick and he was barely able to say, "I don't know," before crying again.

Ezra jumped up and caught Patrick before his legs buckled. "It's okay, come on over here." He set Patrick down in the doorway and sat beside him with his big arm around him.

"I'm sorry," Patrick said, roughly wiping his eyes in embarrassment. "I've been doing that all afternoon."

Ezra rubbed his back gently, up and down. "It's okay. You should have seen me yesterday after the father issues workshop." They sat there silently for a while. Ezra's other hand began to stroke Patrick's arm absently as they both looked up at the stars.

Patrick became aware of Ezra holding him. It was a hug, but not a hug. He could tolerate it. He could sit with this large man for this moment. He could allow himself to be held here. He touched the back of Ezra's hand to feel the smoothness of his skin.

"What?" Ezra asked?

"Nothing." He rubbed his fingers along Ezra's stout caramel colored forearm. He caressed it with his hand. He became aware that Ezra was looking at him. He raised his hand to Ezra's face, hesitating. Ezra took Patrick's hand and placed it against his cheek, leaning his face into Patrick's hand.

It was the warmth of Ezra's hand that made Patrick feel so suddenly unbearably sad that he had to catch his breath. It was the awful realization that in the past three years the only people he had allowed himself to touch had been deceased. In that revealing instant he knew that his own body had been as dead as the corpses he buried. Touching Ezra — touching life — made him see how dead he had been. And he felt a desperate need to drink from life. He brought his other hand up to cup Ezra's beautiful round face. Ezra leaned forward and kissed Patrick softly. Patrick felt blood flowing where it had heretofore refused to go. He kissed Ezra back and felt something that had been gone so long he had stopped missing it — desire.

Ezra wrapped both of his arms around Patrick. Ezra felt his body welcome a need that excited him to think he could meet. He realized the gift of this tall, thin man reviving a spirit that had been too long dormant. He pulled away to look at Patrick's face, so pale it seemed almost luminous. As he outlined his features with his thumbs he felt the wetness below Patrick's eyes. Ezra kissed the tears tenderly in the darkness. He whispered, "Let's go inside."

Saturday, June 3rd

"I want each of you to have a part of something very special," Patrick said as he opened a shoebox for the guests in his living room. Guy, Michael, Eric, and Rudy leaned forward uncertainly to peer at the shredded silk rags painted in greens, blues, reds, black, and white inside. "Our beautiful parachute mandala was ritually destroyed in the closing ceremony. We were told to take the pieces with us, so its energy could go out into the world," he told them with emotion he no longer cared to hide under a cover of cleverness. "Go ahead, take one. I want each of you to have a piece."

Bemused, Rudy and Eric looked at one another, but each took a tatter to be polite. Guy didn't bother. With a dismissive snort he went back to his chair on the other side of Patrick's den and flopped in it.

"I wish I could have been there," Michael said reverently. "It sounds beautiful."

"It sounds like a bunch of hysterical hooey," Guy grumbled.

"Don't you want a piece, Michael?" Patrick asked, ignoring him.

"I can't," Michael apologized. "It's not Christian."

"It's love," Patrick reassured him. "I think that crosses over into all religions." Michael reluctantly fished a hand into the shoebox. "And I had an astonishing —" he found himself suddenly embarrassed to say vision "— dream, too."

"Can I have another piece?" Michael interrupted. "This one has a penis on it."

"Now, that's a piece I'll take," Guy spoke up. He came over and grabbed it from Michael who took a different piece out of the box.

Patrick continued. "In my dream — what is it now, Michael?"

"This piece has a big sperm drawn on it," he said abashed.

Patrick snatched it from him and gave him another. "Here," he snapped.

"What was your dream, Patrick?" Rudy interjected. Patrick told them about all the men trapped in the mud and the man with the ax. "You know what that is, don't you?" Rudy asked.

"Sure," Guy said with arms folded. "Disturbing. Overwrought. Psychotic."

"You are stuck," Rudy told Patrick. "And only you can take the ax and free those parts of you by chopping them off at their feet."

"Ow!" Eric grimaced.

"Freedom's always painful," Rudy explained to Eric. "Think how scary it was when you came out to your mom."

"Yeah, well, how can they be free with no feet?" Guy said with scorn. "They can't even walk anywhere."

Rudy smiled at him. "You do not need feet to fly."

"Okay," he said standing. "Enough carnival bullshit for me. I'm going home."

At home, Guy stormed straight into the kitchen. He took the vodka out of the freezer and poured himself a good stiff drink. Guy saw his reflection in the microwave door. He had that fucking piece of that stupid mandala still sticking out of his shirt pocket. He yanked it out and glared at it. The sink, he thought, yeah. He turned the water on full blast and shoved the fabric down the drain. He flipped the disposal on. It made its comforting grinding sound. There was a wooden spoon on the counter. He jammed the handle down into the disposal again and again to make sure the fabric was thoroughly destroyed. In his intensity, the spoon snapped off in his hand, the handle rattling around and around in the drain like crazy. Shocked at himself, Guy quickly hit the switch to the disposal, turning it off.

Jesus Christ, he thought fearfully. *Why the hell am I so angry?*

Sunday, June 4th

Big Ed was curled up on his white leather sofa, happily watching the east coast cable feed of the Tony Awards. It wasn't the Arthurs, but it was a close runner-up.

There was a metallic rattling at the front door. "What the fuck?" The doorknob jiggled hard. Ed was on his feet and reaching for the black and chrome buffet where he kept his living-room gun when the first impact shook the door. He had the gun and jumped over the sofa to land in a roll that had him aiming at the front door as it burst open, kicked in by — "Pop?"

His father glanced around, taking in the apartment. "What the fuck is this?" he asked with a sour look.

"Jesus, Pop, I coulda killed you!"

"You killed me three years ago when you told me you were queer. Fucking key wouldn't work."

"You don't have a key," Ed said standing up. "You go to someone's home, you knock on the door."

"Don't you tell me what the fuck I do. Where do you think you got the money to pay for this?" Dancers swept across the stage on the giant TV. "What the hell is that?"

"*Jesus Christ Superstar,* Best Revival of a Musical nominee."

His father spat. "Somebody fucking kill me."

Big Ed found the remote and hit the mute button. He sighed and put the gun in his pants pocket. "Pop, I don't wanna be like this. Let's start over. Why are you in L.A.?"

"There's rumors going around you got a Arthur. That true?"

It wasn't his exactly, but he felt he had a share in it. "Close enough."

"Then you got big trouble 'cause somebody else wants it, bad enough to kill."

Ed's mind was reeling. Other than Noel and Hiro, who else knew? Did Petey know? "Who wants it?" he asked.

"Ricky Sorveno, Tony Napoli, and Jimmy the Stump."

"What?" They had all been at his Arthur party just two months ago. "I thought they were my friends."

"Son, a little wisdom. Just 'cause somebody likes pussy like I do don't make 'em my pal. Just 'cause they suck cock like you don't make 'em yours."

"But why would they wanna share an Arthur?"

"They don't wanna share, you retard. They each want it."

"So whichever one gets it, the other two are left out and —?"

"Bang, bang. Like I said, big trouble."

Big Ed sank to the sofa. He remembered the Arthur party. *I would kill for one. Literally,* he had said. *You and me both,* Sorveno had agreed. Ed had been kidding, but shit, these guys were serious. Deadly serious. Napoli was certifiable, and Jimmy the Stump wasn't far behind. And no matter whom he gave it to, the other two would be crazy-nutcase dangerous.

"Okay, I just thought you should know," his father growled. "I got some appointments and then I'm going back to Vegas." He gave the apartment a parting glance and rendered judgment. "Goddam pansy palace."

Monday, June 5th

Hiro took their communal Institute Award off the mantle and handed it to Ed. "Take it."

"No!" Noel shouted from their kitchen. "It's ours!"

"Let them have it. It's bad luck."

"That's bullshit," Noel said from the doorway, wiping his hands on a dishtowel.

"It doesn't matter," Ed said. "Whichever one of those guys we give it to, the other two are coming after us."

"'Us'?" Hiro repeated.

"I asked around," Ed told him with a frown. "They know I have partners."

"Bad luck, bad luck," Hiro mumbled wandering away.

"Look," Noel said to Ed, "this isn't what we signed on for. You got us into this, you gotta get us out."

"No, you look," Big Ed said loudly, poking him with a meaty finger, "any operation involves risk. You were happy to be in when it was all Arthurs and getting rich. Suddenly you wanna back out the moment we hit a snag? Calm down!"

"This is not a snag," Hiro hissed. "Unless you can pull three Arthurs out of your ass pronto, we could all be killed!"

"And he knows about pulling Arthurs out of his ass," Noel said. Hiro shot him the blackest glare. "Sorry, nerves."

Ed had an odd expression on his face. "Boys," he smiled, "I think you just solved our problem."

Tuesday, June 6th

Big Ed adjusted his bulk in the confining office chair. Through phone calls from the L.A. airport he had arranged this appointment here in Chicago. He was seated across the desk from Barry Siegel, VP of Manufacturing & Sales in Siegel's nice, but hardly plush office at D.L. Paul & Co., the manufacturers of the Institute Award statuettes.

"What you're asking is out of the question," Mr. Siegel told him with a professional smile that stopped somewhere around the eyes. "We get these kinds of requests from time to time and we always say no. Most recently from a singer and actress I can't mention but," he leaned conspiratorially across the desk to whisper, "she has an album coming out in September."

Big Ed nodded understandingly. Then he got up out of his chair to lean his massive frame over the desk, his hard black eyes inches away from Siegel's, to whisper back, "I don't give a shit, you pissant little mother fucker!" ending with a roar. It had the desired effect, as Siegel blanched and drew back. "I want three Arthurs, I want 'em fast, and either you're gonna make 'em, or you're gonna wish you had." He sat back in his tiny chair, once again the affable guest. "I'm not an unreasonable man. I'll make it worth your while. Ten thousand dollars each, for a total of thirty grand."

Outrage played across Siegel's small white face. "How dare you come in here and threaten me," he said in a low cold tone. "Get out."

Wednesday, June 7th

Barry Siegel kissed his wife, picked up his briefcase in the hallway, and stepped out the front door of his suburban Winnetka home into a beautiful North Shore Chicago morning. He pointed the automatic car lock on his key ring at the silver Mercedes CL600 in his driveway.

The blast from the explosion threw him against his door. The porch windows shattered inward. Flames and metal debris flew past him to litter his yard. In shock Siegel picked himself up to look at the charred remains of his Benz. Car alarms all over the neighborhood were shrieking. His wife opened the front door in panic. Seeing her husband alive, she hugged him, crying hysterically.

"Oh, my God, my God," she wailed. "What happened?!"

"I don't know," he said terrified, looking around the neighborhood for sources of more possible horror. Frightened neighbors up and down the street were peeking out of their doors and windows. His cell phone rang. Still clutching his sobbing wife with one hand, habit allowed him to open his phone with the other. "What?"

"You know," the large man's voice from yesterday said, "I'm thinking now that I want all three for only twenty thousand dollars."

"You! You fucking maniac!" he yelled into his cell phone.

"Now, now, an ugly temper's only gonna cost you. My offer's down to nineteen thou."

"You almost killed me, you Goddamned fucker!"

"But I didn't. I am a professional at this, you know. And we're down to seventeen five now."

"Stop that! Stop it! Why are you doing this to me?"

"Fifteen thousand. It'll buy you a new car if you're willing to downsize."

"Shit! Fuck! All right! All right! God. All right! Fuck. I, I, I gotta have some time. I can't just, I gotta set it up, okay?"

"How long?"

"I don't, I, uh, uh —" Siegel had no idea, but he knew he'd better come up with an answer. "A month." A couple of blocks away a police siren was approaching.

Ed figured he could keep Sorveno, Napoli, and Jimmy the Stump at bay for a few weeks. It made sense Siegel would need to finesse a few things to pull some out-of-season Arthur making. "A month then. I'll be in touch." Ed heard the sirens pulling up. "And about the cops?"

"What?"

"My advice is be vague."

Sunday, June 11th

"This is the police! Open up!" Patrick shouted beating on Guy's front door. "All West Hollywood citizens must attend the Gay Pride Festival or go to jail!"

Guy opened the door. "You've got the wrong house, officer, we're all heterosexuals here."

Patrick pushed past him. "Then you'll have to move. We have zoning laws, you know." Inside he clapped his hands like a camp counselor. "Children! Fag Fest 2000 awaits." He found Michael online in the office which was also his room. "How can you sit in here shackled to a computer when the boulevard is lined with acres of cunningly displayed flesh?"

"I have to list all these eBay items for Guy," Michael answered. He gestured to two large boxes of garage sale and flea market finds. "You go and have a good time. I think I should stay here."

"Wrong!" Patrick pronounced closing both boxes. "Because I think you should get out there and meet your tribe." Guy was standing behind Patrick in the doorway. Michael looked at him for an okay. With a nod from Guy he got it. Patrick continued down the hall to Eric's room, knocking rudely on the door. "I know what you two are doing in there and it's illegal in thirty-eight states!"

Eric opened the door, fully dressed. "Actually, we stopped doing that around four-thirty or five." Behind him on the bed, Rudy, also dressed, looked up from tying his Nikes to wave at Patrick.

"God, I hate you two," Patrick declared. "Now go help Guy with brunch so we can stake out a space for the parade."

The gay Pride parade in West Hollywood is second only to Macy's Thanksgiving Day Parade in the number of entrants, participants, and length. But the Pride parade was scheduled to begin at noon and it was past one o'clock with no sign of it yet. One thing the Macy's parade does not have to contend with is Gay Standard Time.

Knowing the parade would be late, Patrick had brought the Sunday *L.A. Times* crossword. "What's a four-letter word for 'extend across'?"

"Cock," Guy replied impatiently. "It's my answer for everything." He took a sip from his spiked orange juice. "Cock and adult beverages."

"Yes," Patrick muttered, returning to his puzzle, "and look where it's gotten you."

Guy glared at him, then angrily bellowed up the road, "Where's the goddam parade!"

When the parade finally did start, Eric was overwhelmed by its enormity. This loud, ongoing dance of pride and flaming festivity moving past him reduced Eric to tears.

"You all right, *mi vida*?" Rudy asked.

Eric could only gesture at the great color and freedom of the parade marching by and squeak, "I didn't know."

Patrick noticed Guy scowling. "Who pissed on your pancakes?"

Guy nodded toward Eric. "Look at him. God, I'm jealous," he said. "I've been to too many Prides. I'm too jaded. I can't remember that feeling. I know I had it once because I cried, too. I just can't remember how it feels." He looked at Patrick. "How could I lose that? What washed it away? Where did it go?"

"I can't answer for you," Patrick told him. "But I went to that men's retreat because I have that same empty 'what happened?' feeling in every single part of my life."

"Yeah, and you came back with rags and no answers." Guy turned to watch the Sisters of Perpetual Indulgence float lurch by. "Is it too late to get your money back?"

"Actually I left with a clue. But if you don't want to know . . ." he said, pointedly turning his attention back to the parade.

"Oh, for God's sake," Guy said petulantly turning back to him. "Spill it, bitch."

"Those feelings of wonder and awe? They never left me." He looked at his friend with deeply sad eyes. "I left them."

A large Samoan man broke ranks from the Metropolitan Community Church contingent and ran over. "Patrick!" he shouted, scooping him up to hug him. "Oh, it's good to see you! How are you doing?"

Patrick was taken aback, both by seeing Ezra again and by the earnestness of the question. "Oh, my God, you really mean that, don't you? Uh, not bad, considering. I miss you and everybody and, I guess I miss the Men's Gathering."

Ezra reached into his back pocket and pulled out his shred of the mandala. "Me, too." Patrick pulled out a matching piece of torn fabric from his own pocket, and they both laughed.

"I gotta go," Ezra said as he jogged back to the MCC contingent. He shouted over his shoulder, "Good to see you!"

When Ezra was out of earshot, Guy leaned over to Patrick. "Have we 'done' MCC's pastor?"

"A lady of gentility, taste, and refinement never tells, you cunting whore bitch," Patrick said demurely, calmly retaking his place on his folding chair. "And he's not the pastor. He's a deacon. A pastor-ette."

Behind the MCC group was the P-FLAG contingent. "Sir!" Michael asked with urgency, "who are these people?"

"Parents and Friends of Lesbians And Gays," Guy told him.

"Parents?" Michael asked in disbelief, clutching Guy's arm.

"Parents?" It had to be so. One sign carried by an older straight couple read, WE LOVE OUR LESBIAN DAUGHTER! Weak with emotion, Michael slid out of his folding chair to his knees on the asphalt. Open-mouthed, he stared at a father walking arm-in-arm with his diesel-dyke daughter. There was one son walking happily with his parents while holding hands with his boyfriend. Simple. Open. Honest. And utterly inconceivable to Michael. Healthy, happy gay people with parents who loved them? He wrapped his arms around Guy's leg and sobbed.

Guy rubbed Michael's head tenderly. He saw Eric off to the side, not much better off. The P-FLAG group always got to the crowd. They always brought forth the loudest applause and the most tears.

And he wished like hell he could feel it again, too. Some of it. Any of it.

Sunday, June 18th

"Are you fucking with me, Barry?" Big Ed said into his cell phone, stirring lemongrass and *nam pla* into the soup he was making in his kitchen.

"Absolutely not," Barry Siegel said from Chicago. "Nobody wants this over more than I, but it's still going to take four days. We have to sneak the molds out of the vault, cast the metal, grind down the seams, then there's the plating process and hours of polishing. I had to get two guys to help me out."

Ed chuckled. "What's that gonna cost you?"

"Two early retirements with major benefits plus cash, not that you'd care."

"Okay, so it's four days. How you gonna manage that? Two weekends?"

"No, it has to be done all at once so it has to be July Fourth weekend. The Fourth is on a Tuesday so we're giving everyone Monday and Tuesday off. We have Saturday through Tuesday to do this."

"Barry, I am so impressed I wanna come by and watch you work. Pencil me in for a visit to your office on Friday before the holiday. Three o'clock. We'll spend the Fourth together, make some Arthurs, have some laughs, it'll be great. Until then, ciao." He hung up and tasted his soup.

Wham! Wham! Wham! The pounding on the front door made Ed start so violently that he hit his head on the stove hood. He grabbed his gun from the cupboard.

"Big Ed DeLello!" shouted a darkly accented voice from the hallway outside.

"Who the fuck are you?" he bellowed at the door.

"I got a message."

"Who from?"

"Tony Napoli."

"Prove it."

"Garbo is not shit."

Ed opened the door. "What the fuck you doing, yelling in the hall? Get in here." An intense looking, tall and extremely thin Latino in sunglasses and a black Yves Saint Laurent pinstriped suit with wide lapels entered. "Jesus," Ed muttered, pocketing his gun, "why don't you just wear a sign?"

The man ignored him, making a sour face. "Stinks in here. Like Chinatown." He was followed inside by another Latino, a heavyset goon, also in a suit, but something off the rack at some knockoff shop. Ed found it hard not to stare at the guy's large mole over his right eye, like a wad of gum.

"They call me El Palo," the tall, thin man told Big Ed in a noticeable Mexican accent. "And the message from Mr. Napoli is that he would like to have something that is currently in your hands."

"Too bad," Ed scoffed. "'Cause it ain't available for another two weeks."

"Mr. Napoli is not going to like that."

"My heart bleeds. Look, El Pollo —"
"Palo!"
"I don't have it. And I'm not gonna have it until after the Fourth of July. The good news is, I actually like Tony Napoli. So you tell him, from me, that because I value our friendship, I will be happy to give it to him as a present. In two weeks. But he's gotta keep it under his hat 'cause I don't want other parties that might also be highly interested to think I'm playing favorites, you understand? It's a social and business thing. Can you tell him that?"

El Palo sucked in his already gaunt cheeks as he considered this. The action made him look like a Dia de los Muertos gangster doll. "I will tell him your message."

"Then our business is concluded?"

"For now."

"Then get the fuck outta my house, you shit-eating errand boy."

El Palo's eyes flashed in anger. He considered shooting Ed in the foot just for his insolence. But gunshots in an apartment building . . . residents . . . witnesses . . . a bad idea. Instead he nodded sharply to his henchman who opened the door and walked out into the hallway. El Palo followed. Big Ed stepped out, too, just to say, "As long as you're running errands, El Polly, tell Napoli to grow a pair and see me himself next time."

In less than a second El Palo had his gun pressed hard against Ed's temple. "You do not call me errand boy," he whispered with scorching hoarseness, "or El Pollo, you *maricón*." His other hand snaked into Ed's pocket, removing his gun. "It is El Palo!" He pulled his right hand back and swung, smashing his gun into Big Ed's face, knocking him into the wall. "That is to help you remember." He turned and dashed down the hall to the stairwell, his large goon running after him, struggling not to lag behind.

Ed lurched into his apartment. He ran cold water from the kitchen faucet over his profusely bleeding face. It was still numb from the trauma. Ed pressed a dishtowel to his temple with one hand and fumbled for his cell phone with the other.

"Ay, Ricky Sorveno!" he said, wincing as feeling began to return to his gashes. "Big Ed here. Hey, I hear you'd like to get your hands on a little statue I may or may not have. Yeah, I thought so," Ed said. "You got a birthday end of July, right? Oh, the 15th? Right, okay being how you and me are such good close friends, I would like to give it to you as a gift. Yeah, a birthday present." He glanced at the dishtowel. The bleeding was beginning to slow. "Listen, I'll bring it when I'm in Vegas next month, okay? Only we keep this between you and me because there's others that want this and we don't want to hurt nobody's feelings, right? These other people are crazy, they might come knocking on somebody's door, know what I'm saying? Good, I'll see you in about a month. Ayyy, who's your new best friend? Right!" He closed his phone and went down the hall to the bathroom to dress his wound. Later he'd call Jimmy the Stump and promise him an Institute Award, too. So many balls in the air. Ed just hoped he could keep everybody happy until after the 4th of July.

Wednesday, June 21st

"I inherited failure from my father," Michael told Dr. Larry.

"How so?"

"He was unable to provide my mother's necessities from day one, she said. And I grew up like him. I fought it. I tried so hard. But I break vows and I'm a failure, too."

"What vows did you break?"

He looked at the floor and mumbled, "That I wouldn't be a homosexual. God spoke to my mother and said I would find a woman named Sarah who would make everything fine. I found a Sarah, but she said I was a homosexual. I failed by growing up to be just like my father."

"Your father was gay?"

"He had a best friend who my mother figured out was more than that."

"How did she react?"

"She was defiled because she had taken an abomination into her bed and received his seed."

"Did they divorce?"

"Of course not. God declared He hates divorce in Malachi 2:16. It didn't matter though, because God made His judgment known. My father had type one diabetes and he died of DKA a month after mother found out he was a sodomite."

"DKA?"

"Diabetic ketoacidosis. No insulin in his body."

"Wasn't he taking insulin?" His client nodded. "How old were you?"

"It was four days before my second birthday."

Dr. Larry was confused. "You remember all of this and yet you were only two?"

Michael nodded. "I'm special. I only have a birthday every four years."

"Were you a leap-year baby?" His client nodded again. "So you were really eight."

Michael shook his head. "Mother only allowed birthday parties when my birthday happened."

"How old are you now, Michael?"

"I turned nine this year."

"You're thirty-six, Michael, you're thirty-six years old." Michael made a painful expression. "Does that make you uncomfortable?" Another nod. "Why is that?"

"It's not right. It's not what mother said." He crossed his arms, hugging himself in a distressed manner. "I want, I want to —" He broke off with a grimace.

"What is it you want, Michael?"

He started rocking back and forth. "I want to go back in my cabinet in my mother's kitchen."

"Why, Michael?"

"You make me upset," he said, looking up at the ceiling, fighting back the tears. "All of this frightens me. And the dream came back. Only worse."

"How was your dream different?"

"The house I'm in that's floating on an ocean of some sort of liquid? Well, it's blood. And it's not just at the door now, the blood is coming in." He turned from the ceiling to look Dr. Larry in the eyes. "And it wants me."

Wednesday, July 5th

Noel let Big Ed in. Ed was carrying a metal briefcase and followed him into the kitchen where Hiro was preparing dinner. Ed set the briefcase down on the counter.

"Check this out," he said, almost giggling as he clicked the latches. He opened the briefcase to reveal a gray foam-rubber block that filled the case. Ed removed the top layer of foam rubber. There, nestled in perfectly fitting hollows, were the gleaming awards. "Siegal even had records of which ones weren't recovered. So these are perfect right down to the serial numbers!"

"Great," Hiro said from the sink where he was washing bok choy. "So now you can pay off your mob friends."

"And this will mean the end of crazy people coming after us for Arthurs, right?" Noel asked, glancing at Ed's fresh scar from where El Palo had pistol-whipped him.

"I can't imagine why it wouldn't be," Big Ed beamed.

Noel and Hiro gave each other sidelong looks. They weren't so sure.

Saturday, August 19th

With a crash there was coffee and a broken *Wizard of Oz* mug on the floor. "Fuck!" Dave yelled. He had stumbled against the corner of the kitchen table.

Roger rushed into the room. "Are you all right?"

"I'm fine, it's just . . . Shit, my sister gave me that mug."

Roger was already reaching for paper towels. "Sit down, let me get it."

Dave did as he was told, not because he wanted to, but because he was still a little dizzy — something he wasn't about to tell Roger. It was the fucking meds, he was sure of it. Or stress from the rampaging fear. Whatever, he woke up every day feeling more and more drained.

Roger put the shards in the trash without saying a word. In the last two months Dave had been sleeping later and later and having these little accidents with more and more frequency. And no matter what Roger did, he couldn't get Dave to so much as smile. He felt like Dave was miles away in a depression he couldn't crack. *Maybe it's my fault,* he thought. *Maybe if I wasn't so fucking distracted by the new gambling losses on top of what I already owed, I could be there for him.* Feeling like a failure, he put the paper-towel roll back in the rack, and willed the tears back. When he had them under control, he turned around. "Let's go to the beach." There was no reaction. He put his hand on Dave's shoulder. "Hey."

"What?"

"We're going to the beach. It'll be good for you. Both of us. It'll be good to get out, get some sun, fresh air."

"I don't feel like doing much of anything today."

"That's why we're going to the beach," Roger said, raising his voice. "You need to move, you need to do something, damn it, anything." He strode to the side door and went into the garage. He opened his car trunk and got a Sav-On bag. Coming back into the house, he tossed the bag on the table.

"What's this?" Dave asked listlessly.

"Beach toys. I bought them in June and forgot I had them in the trunk." He took out two oversize Hello Kitty towels. There was also a beachball in flat plastic wrapping. "We're going to the beach."

"I don't have any sunblock."

"I'll go get goddam sunblock!" Roger shouted. He caught himself, startled by the outburst. "I'm sorry. I'll go to Sav-On now and get us some." He tore the plastic off the red, blue, and orange beachball. "Here, blow this up while I'm gone."

Roger turned off the ignition in the parking lot of the Sav-On. Just as he went to open the car door, a black Ford F-250 roared into the space next to him, screeching to a stop so close he couldn't open his door.

Petey hopped out and sauntered over to Roger's passenger side. The window was halfway down so he snaked his hand inside, unlocked the door, and yanked it open. "Looks like you're going to have to get out this way," he said.

Roger was surprised, terrified, and unable to move. All he could think of was $368,750, the amount he owed. Petey reached inside, grabbed Roger by the front of his collar and physically pulled him out. Roger fell face-first onto the sandy asphalt. As he tried to get up, Petey kicked him in the ass so hard it sent him stumbling forward, gouging his head on the headlight of the Mustang facing them. He flopped on his back, the breath knocked out of him. Roger felt Petey's foot on his neck.

"You're late, my man," Petey snarled. "But I'm giving you twenty-four hours. Here's the address," he said stuffing a piece of paper so far back into Roger's mouth he gagged. "Be there with twenty thousand bucks and we'll go from there." With that, Petey walked away.

Roger didn't dare move until he heard the F-250 peel out of the parking lot. He got up, shaking. The beach wasn't going to happen today. Or any day.

Roger called Dave and lied about a family emergency. *How many more lies can I tell?* he wondered, loathing himself. But Roger couldn't afford to think about that.

It took him until nightfall, but he found a used car dealer who worked out of a trailer in Gardena who would buy Roger's Lexus LS400 for cash, now. The man had bad teeth, a lazy eye, and a nose that instantly smelled the reek of desperation coming off Roger. He gave Roger $18,500, about a third of what the car was worth. With the $1,200 he had saved from hocking some of his parents' jewelry he'd stolen and what he'd saved from bartending instead of going to school, it would just cover his immediate need. He watched the man put stacks of cash in a Del Taco bag for him.

Roger called a cab and went back to Dave's house in Culver City. It was just midnight and Dave was asleep. In the darkness Roger stumbled over the now-inflated beachball he'd told Dave to blow up. He felt for the closet door, opened it, and kicked the beachball inside.

He collapsed on the couch. He left the curtains open so the morning light would wake him. He wanted to be out of there before Dave got up and saw him with the scabs on his face. He'd need the time to come up with some good fresh lies to cover those.

Sunday, August 20th

Downtown Culver City was practically deserted this early on a Sunday. Roger walked down Washington trembling and nauseated, clutching the Del Taco bag with twenty thousand dollars cash. He found the alley and walked down it slowly, cautiously, fearfully. Suddenly there was a squeal of tires at the end of the alley and Roger's heart began pounding. Petey's black F-250 was hurtling toward him. Petey hit the brakes and turned the wheel, sending the pickup into a deliberate sideways skid that stopped only a few feet from where Roger was standing too stunned to move.

Petey jumped out of the driver's side laughing. "You got some cajones, boy!" He snatched the Del Taco bag from Roger. "This better be it," he said. He walked over to the passenger side window and tossed it in. Without stopping he circled back to Roger and punched him just below the sternum so hard it cracked three ribs. Roger bent double, vomiting. With a right uppercut to Roger's jaw, Petey sent him flying backward, falling against a filthy dumpster before sliding down into a fetal position on the hot, stinking asphalt.

"That's for being late," Petey snarled before striding over to kick him hard in the kidney. "And that's to get your attention, asshole."

He bent down beside Roger and waved a map page torn out of a Thomas Guide in front of him. It had an amount and an "X" on it, both marked in red. "This is your next payment. Seventy-five grand by Friday. Ten A.M., Griffith Park. Here's directions. You got that?" Roger could only make a gurgling sound on his side. "Good enough." He turned on his heel, heading for his truck, not bothering to look back.

Wednesday, August 23rd

Bob Davies had had a long, rotten, and stressful morning meeting at NBC in Burbank. He decided to stop off at his home in nearby Toluca Lake before getting back to his office. He'd have the house to himself, make himself a sandwich, maybe even jerk off to relieve some tension.

The first sign something was wrong was the unfamiliar Audi in the driveway. He parked behind it and entered quietly. He heard soft, slight sounds upstairs. He went up the stairs cautiously. The noises were coming from Betty's and his bedroom. Holding his breath, he carefully peered around the corner. "What the hell are you doing?"

Roger was bent over a pile of jewelry on his parents' bed. The top drawer of Bob's dresser was open, as was his wife's jewelry box. "Nothing," was the best Roger could manage. "I'm taking everything in for cleaning. At the jeweler's. It's a surprise."

"How stupid do you think I am?" Bob demanded. He noticed the scabs on Roger's face. "Oh, Christ," he said as another thought struck him. "You're into drugs, aren't you? You're stealing to pay for your habit."

"No!"

"Where's your car? Why is there an Audi downstairs?"

"Mine's in the shop. That's my roommate's. He let me borrow it. To go to the jeweler's."

"Jesus, what the fuck do you take me for? Roger, what is going on here?"

In a breath, it came out. "I'm in debt, dad," Roger said. "I'm in bad, bad debt."

Bob remained suspicious. "What kind of debt?"

"Gambling. I owe over three hundred and fifty thousand dollars; my next payment is for seventy-five thousand in two days. If I don't pay this guy Petey, I don't know what he'll do to me."

Bob took a closer look at the wounds on his stepson's face. The gash in his scalp. "My God," he whispered. "What happened to you?"

"I was late with a payment."

"It's that serious?"

In response, Roger unbuttoned his shirt and took it off painfully. There was a great black bruise at the bottom of his ribcage. He turned around to show another over his left kidney along with scabbing where Petey had kicked him so hard his boot had broken the skin. Roger opened his pants and pulled them down to reveal another bruise on his ass from the Sav-On parking lot, this one already going a sickening green.

Bob was horrified. Appalled. "This Petey person did all this to you?"

Roger nodded, pulling his pants up. "I have a tooth I might lose, I don't know yet. And it hurts to breathe."

"We'll call the police."

"No! If I call the police, he will kill me. This isn't TV, this is the fucking Mob."

Bob's head was swimming. "There's gotta be something. Your car. Sell it back to the dealer, they can deduct —"

"I sold it four days ago to make the last payment."

"You said it was in the —"

"I lied!" Roger shouted. "I'm an addict, I lie and I steal, it's what I do! You should know I haven't been going to school either. I gambled away that money long ago. I'm a bartender at the fucking Olive Garden in Westwood." He stood in front of his stepfather half naked, utterly helpless, and for the first time in months, completely honest. "I'm a liar and a thief," he said. "And I am scared. I am in some deep shit and I don't know what to do. Can you help? Will you help me?"

Bob could only look helpless. Thoughts in his brain refused to connect. "I need something to eat," he mumbled. In a daze, he turned and fumbled his way downstairs and into the kitchen, where he stood staring at a loaf of bread.

What could he do to save Roger from this god-awful thug? The tuition for the kids was tied up in trusts, doled out only as arranged. Everything he made at his job was pretty much spent by the time he got paid because, even at his salary, he had gotten used to living paycheck to paycheck. Just last month he'd had to ask Bernice not to cash her check until the 15th. The Davies's dirty secret was that everything went to maintain this façade. The savings account? Some money there. Not a lot. Some money would be better than no money. This Petey person would have to understand that. Bob decided he would withdraw whatever was in their savings account.

He went to the foot of the stairs. "Roger?" he called upstairs. His stepson appeared at the top. "Put your mother's things back. You can take mine. Put your shirt back on. We've got an errand to run."

Fifteen minutes later they were at the bank. Bob used his debit card to check the balance in the family's saving account at the ATM by the door: $22,192.16. They walked inside and Bob closed out the account.

Friday, August 25th

Unable to hide his wounds, Roger had to come clean to his partner about the trouble he was in. It was infinitely worse than telling his stepfather. When he was done, he asked Dave, "Do you hate me?"

Dave, who hadn't shaved or bathed or eaten much of anything in five days, shook his head. "It makes perfect sense," he'd said, rolling back over in the bedclothes. "I'm just another one of your rotten bets."

Roger borrowed Dave's car. He turned off Los Feliz into Griffith Park. He drove to the Bird Sanctuary, the place designated on the map where he was to meet Petey. He parked in the small nearby lot and looked at the In-N-Out Burger bag with the money on the seat next to him. He closed his eyes and prayed for the first time in years.

Dear God, please let this be enough.

Selling Bob's gold and platinum cuff links, diamond tie pin, silver studs, and a couple of rings, had gained him roughly five-thousand dollars. Twenty-seven thousand and change. Nowhere near the seventy-five thousand demanded, and that knowledge dug a black, fearful hole in his guts. But it's what he had. Better some money than no money, right? He sure as hell hoped so.

And please, please don't let him kill me. Amen.

There was a trail that made a loop marked on the map between two steep hills. The In-N-Out Burger bag tightly gripped in his hand, he trudged uphill. Being a weekday, there was no one on the sycamore and cedar-lined trail. The stillness made him edgy. Now and then a gray patterned lizard would skitter across the path in front of him or to the side, causing him to jump. He smelled the dusty earth and dry leaves as he walked, his heart beating ever louder both from the climb and fear.

Petey was sitting casually, leaning back on a bench taking in the sun where the trail looped to go back down the ravine. As Roger approached, Petey turned his head to assess the In-N-Out bag. "Doesn't look very big. Better be some very large bills in that sack, or I'm gonna be very disappointed."

Roger was visibly shaking. "It's everything I could get, everything I have."

"But it's not seventy-five grand. Is it." Ashen, Roger shook his head. "Roger, Roger, Roger. What do I gotta do to impress on you that I'm not fucking around here?"

"Jesus Christ, it's twenty-seven, almost twenty-eight thousand dollars! That's gotta mean something. I'm trying to get it to you. Shit, I'm doing everything I can." He thrust the bag at Petey. "Just take it. I'll get more, but take this, it's almost twenty-eight thousand for God's sake."

Petey didn't even look at the bag. "Almost twenty-eight is not seventy-five, Roger." He stood up from the bench menacingly. "So now I gotta do something I didn't wanna do."

Hysteria overwhelmed Roger. "What? Kill me?" Roger shouted wild-eyed. "Then fucking do it! Just get it fucking over with!" He threw the bag in the dirt. "Come on, do it! Just do it and end it all right now! Kill me, you fucking asshole! Do it!"

Petey backhanded Roger across the face, spinning him around and dropping him to all fours. He knelt down beside Roger. "I'm not gonna kill you 'cause there's more money in you. You're just not being resourceful. Now pick right or left."

"Right or left what?" Roger asked, rubbing the snot away with a dirty hand.

"Arm. I gotta break one. It's so you understand the seriousness of our talk."

"Oh, Jesus, God," he sobbed.

"Take off your shirt," Petey ordered, tugging at it. Roger allowed Petey to pull his T-shirt over his head. "Roll over." Roger was too upset to hear, much less comply, so Petey pushed him over with his foot. Roger was lying on his back among the leaves on the dry trail, weeping at the sky. His mouth was open in a silent wail to no one who could help him. Petey forced as much of the T-shirt into Roger's mouth as he could stuff inside. "Now, right? Or left?" Shaking with sobs, Roger weakly held his left arm out. "Good choice, kid." Petey took the In-N-Out bag with tightly stacked twenty-dollar bills inside and positioned it under Roger's left wrist, raising his forearm a good five inches off the hard-packed dirt where his elbow lay. "If you hold still, it'll be cleaner break." Petey stood, took a step back, then, with all his body weight behind it, stomped on Roger's forearm, snapping both bones.

Roger's body arched as he let out an animal howl no one could hear, his face contorting so hard that it broke blood vessels around his eyes.

It was after seven o'clock that evening when Roger was released from Hollywood Presbyterian Medical Center. Bob drove him home to Toluca Lake in a silence of grief and self-recrimination. First had been the shock of Roger's cell phone call. Then, at the hospital, Bob had seen the x-rays — shattered bones within shadowy flesh bent at an unnatural angle. There was the interminable waiting for Roger to be released. And finally, there was that look of brokenness on his stepson's face, even though his eyes were shut. They were still closed even now as they coasted downhill on Barham Boulevard into the Valley.

"Are you tired, son?" Bob asked.

Roger shook his head. "So ashamed," he whispered.

Bob turned off Barham into Toluca Lake furious with himself. How could he have been so utterly naïve, so dangerously foolish as to think this thug would be satisfied with only partial payment? How could he have let Roger walk into that? This was entirely his own fault. No doubt Roger was in even more danger. He only hoped to God he could keep Roger from getting killed, but right now could only bring him home.

Entering the driveway, Bob saw Betty at the front window watching for them. Bob had called her from the hospital, explaining everything. She came out to help them inside. Her eyes were clearly red from crying, but she was by-damn going to keep them dry now that she was needed.

Upstairs, they put Roger to bed. He still wore the pained, shamed expression, unable to speak to or look at his mother, eyes closed tightly, wetly, as Betty and Bob gently pulled his dirty jeans off. His mother covered him with a blanket.

"I'll get you some juice. Just to have if you need," she said, leaving the room.

Bob stood there, still holding his stepson's jeans. "Son," he confessed. "I am so sorry this happened. I didn't know. I'm so sorry, son."

"Me, too. Oh, dad, I'm so sorry, too." Roger cried softly for a moment. "What about the car?"

"Don't worry about it."

"It's Dave's."

"Your roommate? I'll have my driver Rudy take care of it," Bob said, grateful to be able to do anything, no matter how small. "Keys in the pocket?" Roger nodded. Bob searched the pockets. He found Roger's wallet and set it on the dresser. There was a wadded piece of paper in the other back pocket, and the car keys were in the front right. "Got 'em." Just before he tossed the wadded paper in the trash, he checked to see if there was anything important on it. There was.

REST OF THE $75,000
MONDAY HERE
SAME TIME
<u>ALL</u> OF IT.

Saturday, August 26th

Bob Davies signed a personal loan for one hundred thousand dollars at his bank on his way to the Mercedes dealership on Van Nuys Boulevard. There he would sell his car, then go across the street to the Nissan dealership and buy a Sentra. Used. To hell with what people would say. It would give him approximately $165,000. He glanced at his watch to see if he had time for lunch at the Studio City Chin-Chin's. His watch! Hell, it was a Rolex. Why hadn't he thought of that days ago? There was another twelve to fifteen thousand. Bob smiled. He was going to make this work.

He hadn't mentioned finding the message to anyone. He would meet Petey. He would make things right.

He could fix everything.

Monday, August 28th

Rudy wondered why he was driving his boss to a location in Griffith Park at 9:45 in the morning in a company limo.

"Should be right around here," Bob said as they came out of the tunnel in the park. Over the last couple of days he had gotten enough details from Roger to know where to go, and what to look for. He saw the sign that said Bird Sanctuary. "Park there."

Rudy did as he was told, being wise enough not to ask any questions.

"Wait here," Bob said, getting out with a briefcase in hand. Rudy noted it wasn't his usual briefcase. "If I'm not back in twenty minutes, I want you to call the police."

Bob was panting for breath as he made his way up the trail. He paused, perspiring in the heavy, still August heat in his black Corneliani suit. Gnats danced around his face. He waved them away and continued up the hill.

There was only one other person on the trail. He was sitting on a bench, leaning back with his eyes closed, catching the sun on his face. He opened his eyes when he heard Bob's footsteps stop near him. Surprised by whom he saw, he instinctively reached for his pants pocket.

"I have money," Bob blurted before the gun was drawn. "I'm Roger's father. I brought money," he said setting the briefcase on the ground in front of him and taking a step back. "It's the rest of the money for today. And more beyond that."

"If you're a cop, you're fucking dead," Petey said, looking apprehensively at the woods around him.

Bob held his hands up. "I'm not a cop," he said trembling. "And I'd like to —" he found he had to swallow to keep from throwing up in fear — "I'd like to work out a deal. A payment deal."

Petey snorted. "I make the rules here, asshole."

"Of course. Of course you do. But we're both professionals. We can do this calmly, on a regular schedule, so there'll be no need for more, um, unpleasantness?" Petey smirked, which Bob decided to take as a smile. "I'd like to give you my card."

"Okay," Petey said. Bob didn't move, his hands still in the air. "I said okay." Bob looked painfully uncomfortable, and the pause became awkward for them both. Finally Petey barked, "Why the fuck won't you give me your card?"

"Because if I reach in my coat, you'll think I have a gun and kill me."

"Oh, right," Petey said nodding. "Which pocket?"

"Inside left breast."

Petey carefully felt inside the fine silk lining and fished out a business card. His eyebrows went up as he read it. "You're a fucking VP at the Institute of Motion Picture Artists and Technicians?" Bob nodded. "No shit? So like, you're the guys who do the Arthurs every year, right?"

"We give out the awards, yes."

"You mean like balloting and shit and all that, too, yeah?" Bob nodded again. Petey narrowed his dull eyes. "Just how much are you involved in this?"

"It's, well, that's my baby. It's what I do. My bailiwick." He saw Petey looked confused. "Job. It's my job."

Petey looked back and forth from the card to Bob several times as a real smile slowly came to his face. "Well, whaddaya fuckin' know."

Rudy was wondering why, immediately after they got back from Griffith Park, Davies had sent him to pick up an Audi at Hollywood Presbyterian. He took Carlos from the garage with him in the limo. When they arrived and found the car, Rudy got in the Audi and drove it to the Culver City address he'd been given, Carlos following him in the limo to drive them both back to IMPAT afterward.

Rudy was standing on the stoop of a modest, sunny yellow house on Motor Avenue, only a few blocks from Sony Studios. It was very hot and Rudy was hungry for lunch. Why wasn't anyone answering the doorbell?

At last the door opened. "What?" Dave asked dully. He looked an unshaven disheveled mess.

"I was sent to return your car," Rudy said, holding out the keys for him to take.

"Right," Dave said, taking them. "Thanks." He looked at Rudy more closely. "I think I've seen you before. Do I know you?"

Rudy would have remembered someone who looked this bad. "I don't think so."

Dave looked past him at the limo waiting by the curb. "The limo. Yeah. Arthur night. We got it on in a limo with —"

"Oh, my God, you're right." Rudy smiled at the hot memory. He laughed. "That was an amazing night."

"Yeah, we got pretty fucked up."

"Yeah, crazy! We did some wild shit that night. You're Frank Powers, right?"

Dave shrugged and nodded sheepishly. "Yeah."

"So, dude," Rudy asked gesturing toward him, "what happened?"

Dave didn't know where to begin to answer the question. At last he simply replied, "You might want to get tested."

Tuesday, August 29th

"There are two gentlemen to see you," Doris said over Bob Davies's vintage intercom.

Bob glanced up from his figures to look at his appointment book. There was no one scheduled. *Fuck 'em*, he thought. He pressed the button to speak back. "Tell them to please make an appointment, I'm booked solid right now."

A man's voice came over the speaker this time. "Hey, Mr. Davies, it's your friend Petey."

"Oh, shit!" he hissed to himself. He jumped up from his desk and hurried to the door. Opening it he said with great deference, "Why, Mr. Petey —" and he caught sight of the hulking six-foot-nine goombah with him, "— and friend! Won't you both come in? Doris, please hold my calls," he said as he closed his office doors.

Petey introduced the giant mook as "the man I work for."

"Hello, I'm Ed DeLello," that man said, reaching a massive paw toward him. He shook Bob Davies's hand like it belonged to a rag doll. "People call me Big Ed."

"I see," was all Bob could think to say.

"Petey tells me you run the Arthur Awards."

"Yes," Bob answered, already not liking where this was going.

"He also tells me that, financially speaking, you're in a compromised position with my business."

"He's in deep shit," Petey smirked.

Big Ed held up a hand to Petey, indicating decorum was called for. "Mr. Davies," he said leaning forward, "I can't tell you what a thrill this is for me to be here."

That was unexpected, Bob thought. "O-kayyy?"

"Did you know I was handicapping the Arthurs for my dad at age fourteen?" Ed said, smiling at the memory. "That was the year Cher showed up in that Bob Mackie punk Marie Antoinette outfit with a neckline down to her pubes and a three-foot-tall wig with jewels and feathers for days. I don't remember what won, but I remember Cher. And even though I was only fourteen, I thought, 'Motherfuck, I wanna be a part of that!' And here I am now, sitting in the Motion Picture Institute itself, talking with the man who puts it all on."

"Uh, actually, I'm more of a coordinator, really," Bob said. "I just serve as go-between for all the various guilds."

"It must be difficult," Ed said admiringly, "keeping all those egos satisfied and yet, telling them what to do."

"Well, yes, it does take a certain amount of finesse," Bob admitted, surprised, "but then, I've been doing this for over twelve years. I like to think I've established a certain amount of respect in the film community. It's the kind of reputation money can't buy."

"See, there's where you're wrong, Mr. Davies," Big Ed said with a friendly smile, "Money can buy anything, including reputations. In fact, I'm here to purchase yours. Your son owes me a great deal of money. I could make that go away. The debt erased, no more worries. And, because I respect you and the Institute, I wanna enter into a relationship with you. Make you a partner in my Hollywood dream."

"Partner?" Bob asked uneasily.

"Absolutely," Ed assured him. "Because I see this as a give-and-take, long-term thing. See, I already have certain other key people already in place." Ed leaned back on the loveseat with great satisfaction. "You are the last piece of the puzzle."

After hearing the plan, Bob Davies could only sputter. Struggling to gather his wits, he explained that it wasn't like he could simply whip up a list of films and nominees in his office. The nominations took place in bits and pieces all over town. There was the Directors' Guild that nominated the directors, the Writers' Guild that decided the writing nominees, every category would have its own individual group to influence. There were fourteen branches in the Institute to deal with plus the President's Board. Impossible!

On the other hand, he had to admit he liked the idea of all these guild assholes he'd had to placate and cater to over the years being duped and/or strong-armed into going his way. Only it wasn't his way, it was the Mob's. This was unthinkable.

But what the hell is an Arthur, really? Bob asked himself. A lump of metal and a coiled steaming load of hype. When Bob weighed that against Roger's freedom from debt and further violence, there was no contest.

"I'll do it," he said, having no idea how he was going to accomplish any of it.

As they were leaving Bob's office, Petey walked ahead to get the elevator. Bob tapped Big Ed. "I know I'm not in a position to ask anything," he said, "but there is one thing I'd like."

"If I can do it, I will," Big Ed said, putting his hand on Bob's shoulder.

"I deal with you," Bob whispered, then indicated Petey with a glance. "Not him."

"Done," he said offering his hand to shake. "I'll be in touch." They shook on the deal, and Ed joined Petey in the elevator.

As the elevator was closing, Doris said, "There's a Mr. Cohen here with your son's cell phone." She indicated Dave seated off to the side.

"Hi," Dave said, rising a little unsteadily as Bob greeted him. Dave knew Roger's stepdad worked here at IMPAT and had come because he knew of no other way to establish contact. At great effort he had even bathed, shaved, and dressed in clean clothes for this visit. "I've called Roger over a dozen times in the last few days. I'm his roommate," he explained, watching his words. "I was worried, a little." He pulled out the cell phone. "And I found this in my car. Guess that's why he didn't return my calls." He couldn't hold back any more. "Can you tell me how he is?"

Bob smiled at him. "Why don't you give him a call at the house? I'll give you the number. I think he'd like hearing from you." He steered Dave into his office.

The elevator opened again and this time Eric got off in his parking attendant uniform. He found Rudy in an office down the hall. "Wanna do lunch?"

Rudy looked up from his computer screen. "Oh, yeah."

On the way out, Eric said, "I think your days doing Davies might be numbered."

"Why do you say that?"

"I just saw him taking Frank Powers into his office. You know who he is?"

Rudy recalled his disturbing meeting with him just yesterday. "The porn star?"

"Yeah. Wanna know a secret?"

"Okay," Rudy said warily.

"I did him," Eric bragged. Rudy looked at him ominously. "Oh, don't be so upset," Eric said. "It was the day we broke up. I went to a sex club to get over it and, well, it was Frank Powers, so what was I gonna say?"

"Frank Powers fucked you?"

"Within an inch of my life," Eric laughed. "On the stairs!"

"Did you use a condom?"

"Well, of course. He's a porn star, so, yeah," Eric replied. "I mean, who wouldn't? You'd have to be high not to, right?"

Petey was in his black pickup cruising east on Third. If Big Ed didn't want him handling this Davies prick, then fuck 'em both. At least he'd finally learned exactly what Ed's plans were. He pulled out his cell phone and dialed a Vegas number with his thumb.

After three rings, there was a voice on the other end. "What?"

"It's me, in L.A."

"What do I care?"

"I know what Ed's up to here."

"Yeah? So talk to me."

Petey outlined the whole plan, as outrageous as it seemed, to take over the business of the Institute Awards. He included the financial components of bet rigging and investment in the films nominated. How things looked to be falling into place, even though it was going to take time to work out all the details and make it happen.

"If he does," the voice in Vegas said, "it won't be his for long. Keep me informed."

Petey hit the end button as he approached a paint store at La Jolla. There were a dozen *jornaleros* on the corner, hoping for work. He noticed a particularly handsome tall one. Petey slowed down to pull over, grinning to himself. "You are mine, Paco."

Betty Davies padded up the stairs to ask if Roger's roommate, Dave, would like to stay for dinner. She paused outside Roger's room, politely listening to make sure she wasn't interrupting anything.

"I thought you'd left me," Dave said in a hushed voice. "Not that I'd blame you. But I thought you were gone."

"Dave, I never left," Roger replied quietly. "But it's felt like you've been leaving me. I've been watching you spiraling down. I couldn't compete with the depression. Besides, after the stupid, stupid shit I've done, I figured why would you want me anyway. So I didn't call."

"I'm sorry, Roger. I'll get out of bed, I'll dress, I'll get some antidepressants, just tell me you'll come home." His voice cracked. "I'm so scared. I need you home."

"You need me?" This time it was Roger choking up. "Dave, you're the one thing in my rotten life, even with all the shit and the problems and the virus, you're the one thing I can see through to. You are home to me."

Outside the room Betty held her breath. She heard the bedsheets rustle and muffled tears. Her son Roger was a homosexual.

There would be no grandkids here. At least this explained why Roger had always been so sullen, quick to explode, and secretive. Well, that and owing hundreds of thousands of dollars to the Mafia. How could she let her son know she knew, and that it was all right? At least this boy, Dave Cohen, seemed like a nice Jewish boy. Clearly interested in a committed relationship. Weepy, but sincere. Why, for all she knew, he probably just come out of the closet, as well. That must be why he needed antidepressants. She gasped. *That's it!* she thought, and scurried down the hall.

Two minutes later Betty knocked on Roger's door as she gently opened it. Dave and Roger instantly ceased their embrace, moving guiltily away from each other.

"It's okay," Betty said. "I know. And these are for you." She gave them each of the surprised men a small brown prescription bottle. "It's Xanex. My favorite," she said, beaming. "They're wonderful!"

Wednesday, August 30th

"I notice you don't talk about your father, Michael," Dr. Larry remarked in their usual Wednesday afternoon session.

"He was a liar and an adulterer and an abomination."

"Do you know this or is it what your mother told you?"

"She said he cheated on her with another man. That's what I know."

"Those are her memories, Michael. Do you have any memories of your father?"

"No. Except that God killed him for his sins."

"Before he died, did you ever do anything together?"

Michael tried to think of an example, but gave up. "Mother said he never really loved us."

"Don't think about her, think about your father. Try closing your eyes."

Michael did, but there was nothing except that all-too-familiar black monolith in his mind blocking all memory. "I don't see anything."

"Keep thinking. You're very young, in your bedroom. Is there a smell you recall? Or a sound? An image that comes to mind?"

There was nothing he could see. But there was a sound, coming from the other side of the monolith, making itself heard around it. It was a tune, a familiar melody he was hearing. Lost in the memory he began to hum it. He knew how it went, but he'd never sung it himself. The words were still hazy, though, something about packages wrapped in brown paper and string. When he got to the chorus he remembered the name of the song. "My Favorite Things," he said opening his eyes with a surprised start. "He sang to me. He sang goodnight songs to me when I went to bed."

"Does that sound like something someone would do if they never loved you?" Michael couldn't speak, could only shake his head. Dr. Larry smiled. "Can you remember any other songs?" Michael didn't know if he should dare for more. "Go on," Dr. Larry urged him.

Michael closed his eyes tightly to concentrate. In a flurry the songs came back, like swallows returning from a long, bleak winter. "Try to Remember." "There's a Place for Us." "On the Street Where You Live." "It Only Takes a Moment." "Feed the Birds." And he heard his father's gentle voice in them all. For the first time in decades, he heard his father in his heart.

"Your dad only sang you songs from musicals?" Guy asked him when he got home. "No wonder you're gay."

"They're from musicals?" Michael asked.

"Oh, my God, you didn't know?" Michael shook his head. "Lucky for you, boy, I have every filmed musical known to man on DVD and/or VHS." Guy turned his head and barked out at the sundeck, "Patrick, get in here! We're saving a life!" He turned back to Michael. "Get yourself a sandwich, I'll pop some corn, and we'll start your musical education tonight."

Michael hesitated. "Did your father sing, Sir?"

"Yeah. He sang 'Buffalo Gals.' But he'd only sing it to my sister. He said men didn't sing to men; it was effeminate." The memory caused him to pause as well. "Every night I'd hear him sing it to her, though."

"But not to you?" He watched an ugly cloud pass over Guy's face. "That must have made you very sad, Sir."

"I gotta make popcorn," he muttered and went into the kitchen as Patrick entered from the deck with a large — and largely empty — martini glass.

"Did your father sing to you in your bed at night?" Michael asked him.

"No," Patrick said. "But he'd stop at the door and say the same poem to me every evening at bedtime. It went like this." He cleared his throat. "'*Get yer nose outta that goddam book and go to sleep before I smack you!*' Least I think it was a poem. Here's to you, dad," he added, and knocked back the rest of his drink. "Thanks for the haiku."

Amid a clatter of pots and pans, Guy called out from the kitchen, "Patrick, find *Sound of Music* and put it on."

"I shall require another adult beverage to endure such syrup," Patrick called back.

"Oh, quit yer bitching, it won a slew of Arthurs. One of them for Hottest Nazis."

Two hours, several martinis, and a giant bowl of popcorn later, Patrick was leaving, claiming "allergies." Both Guy and Michael plainly saw it was the emotion of all the von Trapps making it from picture-perfect Axis Austria into picture-perfect neutral Switzerland without losing so much as a single Liesl along the way. Guy laughed and taunted him mercilessly as he left.

"Pussy!" he hooted after him from the front door. "You big pussy!" Guy's cat came running inside to weave around his legs. "Oh, Pussy!" he said, picking her up. He brought her into the den. "So, did you like it?" he asked Michael.

"It's kind of odd," Michael remarked. "People singing all the time."

"Yeah, but it's wonderful, don't you think?" Guy plopped down beside him, stroking Pussy.

"But why is that gay? What makes musicals gay?"

Guy thought about that as he scratched his cat's head. "We've had to make up our own reality for so long, I think it seems natural to us," he said quietly. "And I don't know about you, but having spent a lifetime living in this hurtful, shitty, hate-filled reality, I think I prefer a world where love is so big you simply *have* to sing it." Pussy climbed down off Guy's shoulder and went to her food bowl. "Looks like Eric's at Rudy's again. No sense in waiting up." He stood and stretched. "I'm going to bed."

"I'll clean up, Sir."

"Good boy."

After tossing and turning for an hour, Guy became aware of a shadow in the doorway to his bedroom. He saw the person moving in the darkness slowly, stealthily toward him. It was Michael. *Oh, shit*, Guy thought. Patrick had warned him only a couple of months ago how unstable and dangerous Michael was. Michael crept closer. Guy tensed, his heart pounding.

A slow, hoarse, barely audible whisper came, "Are you awake?"

Guy's mind raced. Had the therapy been too much for him? Or too soon? Had Michael secretly hated the slave thing? "Michael?" Guy asked warily.

"I have something for you," came the reply from the dark.

Oh, God, he thought fearfully. Guy swallowed with a dry throat. "What is it?"

Standing next to Guy's head, Michael loomed directly over him. Softly, he sang.

He kissed Guy on the forehead. "Goodnight, Sir." And he tiptoed out.

Friday, September 15th

Dave had just left the L.A. Gay & Lesbian Center in Hollywood where his doctor had given him the results of several tests and so much information that he couldn't comprehend it. "So he tells it to me all over again only this time it's like he thinks I'm retarded or something," Dave told Roger on his cell phone angrily. "Finally I just said, 'gimme a damn Xerox of all my records.'" He glanced at the stuffed manila envelope over on the passenger seat. "So that's what I left with."

"Don't worry," Roger said. "When you get home we'll go over it together."

A vw van pulled out of a parking space directly in front of Dave. "Shit!" He slammed on the brakes, just missing the van. He leaned on his horn while shouting out his window, "Asshole!"

"What happened?"

"Fucker pulled right out in front of me."

"Well, get off the phone so you can drive safely," Roger advised. "I'll be here waiting for you."

"Thanks. Love you."

"Love you, too."

At the next light Dave began to wonder exactly what was in the manila envelope, now lying on the floor from the sudden braking. He reached over for it, but his seat belt restrained him. "Damn it." He unbuckled his seat belt and reached again, far across and forward to retrieve the envelope. The light changed and the car behind blared its horn. "All right, already!" Dave came back up and sped forward.

A few blocks farther on, the traffic slowed to a snail's pace, so Dave opened the envelope and pulled out his records. One particularly thick stack was held by a small black binder clip. Keeping one eye on the stop-and-go traffic, he leafed through that stack. Pages refused to cooperate and kept flipping back. "Fuck this," he muttered as he yanked the binder clip off the stack and put it in his mouth, holding it with his lips. Scanning the pages he wondered if he should stop and pick up a medical dictionary. He turned west onto Washington Boulevard. Almost immediately there was another red light. He stopped in time, but the car behind him didn't.

It was only a moderate impact, but it caused him to gasp, inhaling the binder clip. The angular metal clip lodged in his trachea as Dave clawed at his throat. He coughed as his body desperately attempted to eject the clip, but it wouldn't budge. He couldn't breathe. He bent over, beating his head against the steering wheel to try to dislodge the obstruction. Nothing. Frantic for air his body arched backward, pressing his foot against the gas. The tires spun, squealing against the asphalt before finding traction and roaring through the intersection at high speed. The car jumped the curb and crashed into the cinderblock wall of a car repair shop. Having unbuckled his seatbelt earlier, Dave was thrown through the windshield, killing him instantly.

Sunday, September 17th

Lee was in the Repose Chapel handing out memorial cards when Patrick stuck his head inside to check on the mourners. "My God," he muttered viewing the bunch in the back rows, far from the closed casket. "I haven't seen so many porn stars in one place since *Falcon Pack 5*."

"That's a porn star?" Lee asked her boss, nodding in the direction of the short pudgy, somewhat effeminate man in the dark brown suit.

"That's a porn producer-director," he told her. "William Helprin. Professional name's Cha-Cha LaBouche. We're lucky he's not in drag." He pulled out his cell phone and made a call. "Sarah? It's Patrick. Whatever you're doing you need to get here right now." He explained the situation and signed off. Turning back to Lee he asked, "Have we seen the rabbi?"

Lee nodded toward the bearded avuncular man talking with the Cohen family. Patrick put on his yarmulke and professional demeanor and approached.

"Hello, are you doing all right?" he asked Mr. Cohen.

"Fine," Mr. Cohen replied stoically.

Patrick looked at Mrs. Cohen, who appeared shell-shocked, and at the younger yet worn-looking woman who was the sister of the deceased. She glared at Patrick in furious grief. "Can we get this damn thing over with?" she growled.

"Of course," Patrick said. He turned to the rabbi. "If you're ready?"

The rabbi nodded and said, "Just let me make a few notes in the hall."

Seated across from the Cohen family were Bob Davies and his wife Betty, with Roger, his left arm still in his cast, between them. Bob got up and went over to the Cohens. "I'm so sorry for your loss," he told Dave's family.

"Thank you," was all Mr. Cohen could say.

The sister asked, "How did you know my brother?"

"My son was his . . ." Bob panicked, *do they know?* ". . . roommate."

The young woman leaned forward to look at the man's son. Roger was heaving great silent sobs on his mother's shoulder. No roommate is that upset. Bob watched her putting the picture together.

"I should get back to my seat," he whispered and slunk away.

Mercifully, the rabbi came to the front with his hastily scribbled notes. With presence and grace he took the few facts he had just learned about the deceased from the family and turned it into a thoroughly adequate eulogy. When he opened the service up for mourners to stand and speak of any memories they had for David Allen Cohen, there was the usual awkward moment before anyone spoke.

At last William Helprin rose majestically, and spoke sincerely. "I am proud to say I worked with Dave for many years, and I can say he was a consummate professional. Dedicated, dependable, a joy to work with. He had a sweetness, a kindness, and vulnerability you don't often meet. And I shall miss him terribly."

After a brief silence, Dave's sister rose. "I'm Katrina; Dave was my brother. He called me Trina. When my husband was killed six months ago, he dropped everything and came and he helped me get through it," she said tearfully. "Dave was always there for me. When we were kids. Then school. Then when I got kidney problems, bad, and he helped with, well, everything. And I don't know what I'm going to do without him." Crying, she collapsed in her seat.

Sarah, who had slipped in the back across from Helprin and his boys, stood. "Dave Cohen reached out to help me when he did not have to." She looked directly at Helprin, locking eyes. "He helped set up a service so I could complete my movie. And I will always be grateful for that."

After that, things grew silent, and after an appropriate time, the rabbi closed the service with the Kaddish.

When it was over, Sarah sidled over to Helprin. "We are still on for the editing bay, right? End of October, first of November?"

"My dear Ms. Utley," he replied, "it's the last thing the boy ever asked me for. How could I say no? But sweetheart," he added, "bringing it up like this? Now?" He simply mouthed the single word, "Tacky." He patted her arm and joined his entourage who were extremely anxious to get the hell out of the presence of death.

As people made their way to the exit, Trina maneuvered her way over to Roger. "I'm not surprised you didn't give a testimonial."

"No," was all he could say.

"Yeah, you were too broken up over your 'roommate.' You think I can't see what you are? Thanks," she spat with sarcasm. "Thanks for helping kill my brother. Thanks for luring him into your poisonous lifestyle, I hope you fucking die." She turned to stalk away, then whipped around to face and point at his entire shocked family. "Do not come to the graveside! You've done your damage, now leave us alone!"

Monday, September 18th

"Happy birthday, dear Eric," Patrick, Michael, Rudy, and Suze sang to him, "Happy birthday to you!" All applauded as Guy brought the triple-chocolate-death cake from Sweet Lady Jane's out onto the deck in his backyard. The twenty-six candles on it illuminated the icing with FELIZ CUMPLEAÑOS ERIC DIAZ written on it in white icing.

"Muy funny," he said grinning, before blowing them out. "Now bring on the presents!"

Guy handed Eric a CD. "It's Madonna's newest, *Music*," he said as Eric unwrapped it.

"Wow," Eric said, "That's, uh, great. Thank you, Guy."

As Eric hugged him, Guy added, "It doesn't even come out until tomorrow. I had to blow a guy at the Virgin Megastore."

"Like you'd need an excuse to do that," Eric laughed.

Rudy pulled Eric away from the table for a more intimate hug. "I'm taking you out to dinner tomorrow," he said kissing Eric. "But there's something else I really want us to do together."

"Anything, as long as it's with you," Eric murmured, kissing him back.

"I want us to go together," Rudy said looking into his lover's eyes, "and get tested for HIV."

Eric pulled away from him. "Why? What have you done?"

"Nothing. But I've never been tested. Have you?"

"No."

"Well, if we're serious about each other, I think we should do it."

"You don't think I'm serious?"

"Of course I think you are. And so am I. That's why we should do this," Rudy reasoned. "Are you all right?"

"No," Eric said, "I'm not. It's like, 'Happy-birthday-and-you-might-have-HIV.' It kinda came outta the blue, you know?"

"I'm sorry," Rudy apologized, stepping closer to kiss him on the cheek. "Will you think about it?"

"Later," Eric said, pushing away. "Damn. Right now I just want to have my party, okay?"

Tuesday, September 19th

Roger lay in the bed he and Dave had shared, feeling lost. He hadn't changed clothes since the funeral. For the last two days he hadn't eaten and had barely slept, but he felt had no reason to get out of bed in this closed, dark house. Then he heard the front door being unlocked and opened. Voices. A woman's and a man's. Roger didn't give a shit who they were, he was angry at having his grief violated. Were they pulling the blinds up? He got himself together, shoved himself out of bed and marched into the living room where he found Dave's father and sister, their backs to him, assessing the room.

"We can take the desk, the couch, TV, and cabinet this trip," Mr. Cohen said, picking up two lamps from the end tables. "I'll put these in the front."

"What the hell are you doing?" Roger demanded.

Both Trina and her father jumped. Trina sputtered, "I thought, we thought, I mean, I expected, we thought nobody'd be here."

"I live here," Roger replied.

"Or that you'd be at work, then, or else busy," she said.

Roger looked at them incredulously. "I am busy. I'm grieving, how about you?"

"We don't have to listen to him, Katrina," Mr. Cohen said. "Everything in here belongs to us."

"Not everything!" Roger shouted, infuriated. "This is mine," he said grabbing a stuffed bear from the bookshelf. "Dave gave it to me after we met. And this, this was ours." he said, snatching a framed photo of himself with Dave at Santa Monica Pier. "And this, and this . . ." He continued saving items around the room.

"The furniture belonged to David," Mr. Cohen said implacably. "It's ours now."

"Take it!" Roger yelled. "If that's what's so important to you," he stormed back toward the bedroom with his items clutched to his chest. "Fucking vultures."

That pissed off Trina, who came right down the hall after him. "Oh, yeah? If we're vultures, you're a fucking murderer, you pansy faggot."

"You don't know jackshit, so just shut the fuck up."

"Fuck you! Fuck you for making Dave queer! Fuck you for ruining his life!"

Mr. Cohen appeared behind her. "Honey, don't make it any worse, let's just get what we came for. We'll get the rest of Dave's things later."

"You want Dave's things?" Roger said, his face white with anger. He pushed past them both and went into the bathroom. He grabbed the pink plastic wastebasket and opened up the medicine cabinet. "Epivar, one pill twice a day with food." He tossed it into the wastebasket with such force the bottle bounced and clattered inside. "Zerit, one, twice daily with food; Viracept, two pills three times a day, empty stomach," and he threw those into the wastebasket as well. "Here's Valtrax, once, daily; Lomotil, one pill, twice daily; Bactrum, one pill four fucking times a day, and we're not even talking about the injections!" He turned to face them. "Ruined his life? Who the fuck do you think was keeping him alive when he was too God damned depressed to swallow? Keep 'em, take 'em all with you," he said, "because they're Dave's things." He threw the wastebasket at Mr. Cohen who fumbled it, spilling the drugs everywhere.

"If it wasn't for you he'd never have needed this stuff," Trina yelled. "If it wasn't for you he wouldn't have AIDS."

"Me?" Roger laughed sardonically. "I'm negative, girlfriend. But let me show you a few more of Dave's things." He grasped Trina's hand firmly and marched her down the hall, through the kitchen, and into the garage. Trina stumbled behind him in surprise, scrambling to keep up. "Time you learned just how he supported you through all your 'tough times.' Check it out," he said gesturing to a long line of DVDs on a shelf. He pulled one out for her. "This one's called *Bear Fuck Party Five*, see, there's your brother, the one with the cock in his mouth. Here's *Father-Son Weekend*," he said throwing it at her. "Here's *Online Hook-Ups, Homo House Party, Serving Pvt. Ryan, Nut Busters* . . ."

With each title he lobbed the DVD at her. She backed in horror against the wall as he kept naming and tossing, naming and tossing. ". . . *The Big Guns, Beer Can Dicks, Sex Shooters, Cum Guzzlers, Fuck My Ass, Malibu Orgy, Lockdown, Trucker Daddies, House of Leather, Altar Bound, Saved By the Balls, Strokin' & Smokin', Jawbreaker, Sling Party*, take 'em all," he shouted throwing the rest of the stack at her. She looked down at her feet in shock, standing there in a pile of her brother's pornography.

Mr. Cohen was in the doorway looking aghast. "What's the matter, Mr. Cohen?" Roger sneered. "Don't have a DVD player? Then these are for you!" With a single great sweep of his hand he scooped dozens of VHS videos off the shelf in one gesture. They clattered cacophonously on the concrete garage floor. He smacked the garage door switch with his palm.

"Take 'em," he shouted over the grinding noise of the opening garage door. "Take it all, you ignorant, stupid fucks. I don't need his things. I have him here," he said pointing at his heart. "And not even you can take that away and pack it up in your truck."

He spun around and marched into the glaring sunlight. He stormed across the lawn to the street. He had no idea where he was going. As long as it was far away from those two, that was good enough for him. He broke into a run, tearing down the middle of the street as hard as he could go. He was done with crying. He was too damned angry to cry ever again. He would run instead. As far and as long and as hard as it took to make everything go away, just make it all go away.

Saturday, September 23rd

"Hey, Eric," Guy said at the breakfast table, "could I borrow that Madonna CD I gave you? I wanna listen to it while I do some gardening this morning."

Eric looked up from his cereal sheepishly. "Oh, Guy, I'm sorry, but I don't have it. I took it back. I exchanged it for Luis Miguel's *Romances*. I hope you're not mad?"

"Exchanged it? Why didn't you tell me you didn't like Madonna anymore?"

"You once said your ex-wife would tell you if she didn't like something, and you hated that. So I didn't tell you," Eric said getting up from the table.

Guy considered his motive. "Good call."

"I love *Romances*, though. To me, that's your gift, and I love it," Eric said, putting his empty cereal bowl in the dishwasher. "Oh, sí, me gusta Luis Miguel muchísimo," he added dreamily before walking back to his room singing "Bésame, Mucho."

Guy shook his head at Michael across the table. "The kid's gone native on me."

Tuesday, October 31st

When Guy opened the door, there was a knight in armor standing there. He opened his visor for a better look and saw it was Patrick. "Hail, Knight of the Woeful Countenance," Guy proclaimed. "Don Quixote?"

"Parsifal, you ignorant rube. Can't you see the yearning in my eyes as I'm questing for the Holy Grail?"

"Sorry, I thought that was the Halloween vodka."

"That's there, too."

"And what, pray tell, is your Holy Grail?"

"Fuck if I know," Patrick said, making his way to where Guy kept the liquor. "But with any luck it'll have a nine-inch dick."

"All right!" Guy shouted in triumph. "See, I told you didn't need New-Age crap, you needed a hard cock." He yelled back into the house. "Boy! Are you dressed yet?"

Sheepishly, Michael came into the den. He was wearing only army boots, a black leather pouch thong, and a studded leather leash attached to the padlock and chain he'd worn around his neck since he had arrived at Guy's. As best he could he was covering himself with his hands.

"Where's the harness?" Guy asked.

"I couldn't figure it out," Michael almost whispered. "Please, Sir, don't make me go out like this."

"Oh, my God, Michael," Patrick said in surprise. He turned to Guy, "He's a hot little furball! Who knew?"

"Turn around," Guy said smiling. Michael did as he was ordered.

"He's a walking carpet, front and back," Patrick exclaimed going over to him. "Oh, honey, the bears are gonna be all over you."

"Please don't make me go out like this, Sir. I'm gross, I'm too hairy."

"Come here," Guy said, going into the living room. Michael obeyed reluctantly. Guy turned him toward the large mirror by the entrance. "Look at that." Guy stood behind him and put an arm around his waist. "Go on." Michael raised his eyes, loathing what he saw. Guy set his chin down on Michael's tufted shoulder. "Michael, I wish you could see what I see," he spoke softly, looking into Michael's eyes in the mirror. "I see a man who's been through hell. A man who needs healing, who has given me the gift of his trust. I've never seen anyone work so hard to be good. When we go out tonight, I am proud to be seen with you. I don't know much about the Bible or God, but I do know we're all supposed to be children of God, so that includes you." Guy rubbed his hand over Michael's torso. "And it's time somebody told you this, too: you're one hot bearcub."

"I'll drink to that," said Patrick from the doorway.

"Now let's go celebrate that," Guy said.

"I'm not so sure about your costume, Guy," Patrick said as they hit the Boulevard in all its raucous, randy Halloween tumult. "No offense, but you're a somewhat chubbier child of God than Michael."

"Go fucketh thyself," Guy shot back at his friend in the rented plastic armor. "If I'm asking him to go practically naked, I have to be willing to do the same." Guy had on army boots, a black jockstrap, bar vest, black leather eye mask, and nothing else. With one hand he kept his bar vest closed to cover his love handles, and with the other he held on to a leash connected to Michael's neck chain. "Walk proud, boy," he ordered.

For this night, Santa Monica Boulevard was closed to traffic from Robertson to La Cienega for the de facto parade that fills the wide street with the most fabulous costumes in Los Angeles. It was a party with masquerade couture and dancing crowds so thick that Guy, Michael, and Patrick had to elbow their way politely down the happy, noisy street.

In addition to the usual bawdy excuses for near or simulated nudity, they passed numerous Erin Brockoviches, gladiators, and Roman Catholic priests and bishops chasing white-robed altar boys screaming in mock horror through the crowd as street theater. Guy's and Patrick's favorite, though, was three men who towered over the crowd in gold lamé unitards, their feet in gold boots screwed to three-foot high black balsa wood platforms cut down the middle so they could lumber slowly through the applauding, cheering throng.

"Look!" shouted Guy, "It's the three missing Arthurs!"

"Bet you wish you had one of 'em," a man behind him said.

"Nah," Guy replied, "they're more trouble than they're worth." He turned around to see who had spoken and was shocked to see who it was. "Buck! Oh, I do love a man in uniform," he commented, noting Buck's security guard get-up. "But is it really a costume if it's what you wear to work?"

"I could say the same for you," Buck laughed, looking at Guy's skimpy leatherwear. "Actually, I don't wear this to work anymore, I quit. In fact I'm moving to L.A. next month."

"Great!" Guy said enthusiastically. "I'd love for us to see more of each other."

"Me, too," Buck said pulling open Guy's bar vest for an assessing view. "'Course there's not all that much more left of you to see."

"Let me give you my number," Guy said, instinctively feeling his bare ass for where he usually kept his wallet. "Shit. Do you have a pen?"

"Nope."

Guy looked over to his boy. Michael didn't even have a place to carry paper, much less a pen. "Hey, Patrick —"

"Do I look like I have pockets?" Patrick said, his arms folded over his breastplate.

"Don't worry about it," Buck said smiling. "I'll look you up when I get settled. You're in West Hollywood, right?"

"Right. It's under —"

"Guy Lanner, I know. I'll call. See ya!" And Buck was lost in the crowd.

Guy waved after him. Then he thought, *When did I ever tell him my last name?*

"Ezra!" Patrick shouted.

"Hey," Ezra shouted back, and ran over for a hug. "So is the armor metaphorical or is it a journey thing?"

"He thinks he's Parsifal," Guy volunteered.

"A journey, then!" Ezra declared. "Hey, what's attached to your leash?" Guy stepped aside to reveal Michael, who had been hiding behind him and Patrick as best he could. Ezra was stunned. "Holy shit!"

Michael cringed. "I know. I'm sorry my body looks like this," he said trying to cover his shame with his hands.

"Why?" Ezra asked. "Oh, man, what I wouldn't give to have that much hair. God, that's beautiful. You are a totally hot man! What's your name?"

"Michael."

"Michael," Ezra repeated, wanting to remember this one. He looked back at Guy. "Are you and he —?"

"No!" Guy and Michael both said loudly at the same time.

Ezra came up with an old ATM receipt and scribbled his phone number on it. "Here, take this. I know it's pushy. And someone who looks like you do probably gets this all the time, but I'd love to sit down with you."

Michael had no idea how to respond. He really didn't think he should talk to someone so lustful of the flesh. Yet, he'd never experienced someone being lustful of his flesh, and that was exciting, albeit in a scary way. Flummoxed, he took the number just to make Ezra go away.

But Ezra didn't. He just stood there staring at him with a big goofy grin. Michael was desperate for anything to say. Finally Michael blurted, "I like your costume!"

Ezra laughed again. "It's not a costume. I really am a deacon." He pointed at the Metropolitan Community Church a few dozen yards away. "We always have open house on Halloween and Pride. In fact, I should get back. It's really nice meeting you, Michael," he said as he headed back to the church. He called over his shoulder, "I mean it: I really hope to hear from you!"

Michael's mind raced. A gay man of God? Well, there were lots of those, but an openly gay man of God? Wanting to talk to him? Maybe the lust was a joke. Maybe he should call. Maybe Ezra could be his Christian friend.

At that moment a pack of large, burly, bearded men clutching teddy bears and wearing nightcaps and open long johns came by. One of the men caught a glimpse of Michael and shouted, "Whoa! This cub's mine!" The others saw what he was talking about and swarmed Michael in highly tactile admiration, rubbing his hirsute body with a dozen hands. They gave appreciative growls punctuated by many versions of "Woof!"

"Don't!" he shouted, panicking. "Sir! Siiirrrr!"

Guy waded into the good-natured bears shouting, "Take it easy, guys! You're too much for him." The men pulled back and moved on. "You okay, boy?"

Michael stood with his hands in fists at his side, head bent down, eyes tightly closed. "Take me home, Sir," he said, upset. "Sir, please take me home."

Guy knew it was time. "Come on," he said quietly, and the three of them headed back.

The ATM receipt with Ezra's number on it lay in the street.

Saturday, November 4th

Gay Day at Wonderworld in Anaheim was cool and overcast as thousands of highly exuberant gay men and lesbians, wearing red shirts to identify themselves, poured into the Enchanted City with great hilarity and joy. They mixed merrily with tourists from Omaha and Big Bend who wouldn't figure out what was going on until well after they had spent several hundred dollars in admission to get their families into a park infested with festive homos. The downside was that Wonderworld was now full of its regular jostling crowds of tourists plus an equal number of lesbians and gays.

Noel snorted. "We've waited an hour and a half to go on freaking PlanetMan's Quest?" he sulked. "I didn't even like the movie."

"Yes, but you thought Major Jay PlanetMan was a hot cub," Hiro reminded him to no effect.

"Aw," Big Ed said as if speaking to a child, "does Noel want to hook up with my Major Jay PlanetMan?" He pulled the plush toy out of his shopping bag. "Man, look at the package in those space pants; I think he has a planet-sized hard-on."

"Good," Noel said, determined to be petulant, "then he can go fuck Uranus."

"After this ride," Hiro said, heading off the escalating argument, "I think we should go . . . relax."

Noel instantly brightened at the way Hiro emphasized that last word. "You brought some pot?" Hiro nodded. Noel kissed him saying, "I knew there was a reason I loved this man!"

"Well, hell, let's blow this pop stand and spark up a real major jay," Big Ed said. They left their place in line and headed for Pirate Island in Maroon Lagoon.

A large Latino man with a prominent mole over his right eye had been shadowing them all day. He, too, left the line to follow them. He and his boss had been humiliated by Ed the last time they'd met. Now he'd been sent to do a job he was going to enjoy.

"This is good shit," Noel squeaked, retaining as much of the sweet marijuana smoke in his lungs as he could. They practically had Pirate Island to themselves. Noel and Hiro led Ed to their favorite pot-smoking grotto, the one completely protected from sight. All three were toking with great pleasure. Finally Noel had to let the smoky air out of his lungs. "Now you know what makes this the merriest place on earth," he said to Big Ed, smiling dreamily. Hiro giggled.

Ed released his lungful, snickering. "I wish I could feel like this all the time."

"Me, too," Noel agreed. "I'm flying."

"Just like Major Jay!" Big Ed giggled, pulling out his PlanetMan doll. He made whooshing sounds as he "flew" him. "The butchest space cub in the universe!" he shouted, causing the others to crack up. Enjoying the appreciative audience, he brought the smiling PlanetMan up to his face. "Gimme some sugar, astro stud," he said, tonguing the doll's plastic space helmet for comic effect.

Suddenly the hefty Latino jumped out from behind an ersatz rock. With a wire in his hands, he whipped it over Big Ed's head to pull it viciously tight around his neck. But he hadn't counted on the PlanetMan plush toy being in the way, and the wire caught on the doll. Ed shot his elbow into the confused Latino's ribcage, causing him to stagger backward. Hiro and Noel screamed and leaped back. That gave Ed room to swing his large fists into the man's face in a one-two punch that knocked him to the ground. Ed grabbed him by the shirt, picked him up, and pinned him to the grotto wall. He recognized him as the fat goon that had been with El Palo at his apartment.

"Who the fuck sent you?" he demanded. He slammed the guy hard against the wall again. "Napoli again? Who!"

"Fuck you!" the man snarled and kneed Ed in the groin, causing Ed to drop him. Landing on his feet, the man put his hands together, and swung them into Big Ed's face, spinning Ed around and making him fall. The man scrambled for his dropped wire on the ground near Noel, but Noel swept it away with his foot sending it into the lagoon. "*¡Baboso, hijo de tu puta madre!*" the man bellowed as he stood.

"*Andate a la mierda*," Noel said, with a sharp punch to the man's Adam's apple.

The Latino clutched his throat as he staggered backward, falling over Ed. Big Ed rolled on top of him and straddled him, pinning him to the ground. He grabbed the man's thick black hair and began pounding his head against the concrete floor of the grotto.

"Who sent you!" Ed yelled in the man's face. He slammed the back of the man's head against the concrete with each word. "Who! Sent! You! Fucker! Who! Sent! You!"

"Ed!" Hiro shouted. "You're killing him!"

Ed paused in his fury. He lifted the man's head to look at the back. It had been pounded flat. There was blood mixed with bits of bone on the ground. Ed saw white matter inside the crushed skull. "Shit," he said, tossing the dead man's head back down. "Motherfuck!" He got to his feet.

"This is terrible, terrible luck," Hiro whimpered, his hands covering his face. "What are we going to do?"

"Where's PlanetMan?" Ed demanded. They looked at him in confusion. "Where's the doll?" he roared. Noel retrieved it from where it had been thrown in the fight. Ed took it by the feet and smashed the head of it against the side of the grotto, breaking the doll's clear plastic space helmet. He collected a couple of the larger, sharp pieces from the ground. He then stood and addressed Hiro and Noel. "I need some time to do something. You two get out there and make sure nobody comes this way."

"How?" Hiro squeaked.

"I don't care," Ed said, ripping the shirt off the corpse.

Neither one of them wanted to know what Ed was up to, so Hiro and Noel scampered to the opening of the grotto and stationed themselves there.

"Someone's coming!" Hiro called back to Ed. "Oh, shit, it's a whole family!"

"Keep 'em out!" Ed roared back.

Noel saw a mother and father and four rambunctious kids ranging in age from fifteen to six headed their way. There was nothing else to do. He grabbed Hiro and kissed him deeply. Hiro pulled away.

"What the hell are you doing?"

"Shut up!" Noel ordered and kissed him again, standing directly in the path leading back to the grotto. For added effect he shoved his hand down Hiro's pants.

The father and mother stopped cold. "Kids, we're outta here!" the father shouted. "Come on, we're catching the next raft back, now!"

"Disgusting," the mother whispered, before joining her brood in full retreat.

After several minutes of careful watch, it became evident they were the only people on the island. They tiptoed back to the grotto to see what was happening.

"Oh, my Jesus Christ and God!" Hiro said in horror, holding his queasy stomach. "What did you do to him?"

Ed had sliced signs and letters into the skin of the body's bare torso, front and back. "Gang symbols," Ed explained, washing his hands in the lagoon water. "If it was just a murder, the park might report it. But there's no fucking way in hell they'll take the chance of it getting out there's gangs in the park. Trust me, they'll make damn sure this never happened."

"What about evidence?" Noel asked. "Where's PlanetMan?"

Big Ed tossed him the plastic bag in which he'd put the broken doll. "In here," he said. "All the pieces, too. Along with what's-his-name's ID and jewelry."

Hiro touched a wet spot on Ed's T-shirt. "You have blood on your shirt."

"Yeah, but it just looks wet," Noel said. "Good thing we wear red on Gay Day, huh?"

"Yes, lucky," Hiro deadpanned.

Once outside the park entrance, all three broke into a run to get to the car. Suddenly Ed stopped so unexpectedly that Hiro and Noel collided into him. Ed looked at them apologetically.

"Guys," Ed said contritely, "I'm so sorry. I promised you no killing in L.A."

Noel and Hiro looked at each other in disbelief. Noel turned to Ed to shout, "It's Orange County! We'll get over it!" He grabbed Ed's hand and they all sprinted for the parking tram.

Tuesday, November 7th

Hiro, seated at a corner table in Kate Mantellini's, was finishing his early lunch, savoring a cup of coffee while mentally reviewing his morning meeting with Big Ed. Both he and Noel had presented to Ed and Petey exactly where they stood in regards to fixing this year's Arthur race.

Noel had established contacts with readers at production firms and studios around town. That would give them an inside track for what movies were in the pipeline.

Over the past six months Hiro had managed to rotate certain people quietly out of his division, replacing them with employees whose accounting skills were passable, but whose curiosity and imagination were nil. That left the one VP he was having difficulty getting around. Mel Finkelstein was aggressively intelligent, curious, imaginative, and worst of all, ethical. Big Ed said that something would have to be done about him. Petey suggested Finkelstein should "disappear." After the scene in Wonderworld three days ago, Hiro shuddered, and asked for more time. After all, they had until March.

"Hiro!" a familiar voice called out. Jolted back to the present, he turned to see his friend Bob Davies advancing on his table. "Don't usually see you in Beverly Hills," Bob said, shaking his hand.

"I had a morning meeting," Hiro explained.

"Join you?"

"Sure, for a few minutes, then I have to get back."

"I know the feeling," Bob said, sitting across from Hiro. "I've got a meeting myself in half an hour, thought I'd grab a bite first." He smiled at Hiro, feeling like an utter traitor to his friend. He wondered what Hiro would think if he knew he was conspiring to subvert Hiro's beloved Arthur. It would crush him.

"How is Betty?" Hiro asked, struggling to make small talk. All he could think was how he was betraying his friend Bob whose entire livelihood depended on the Institute Awards. One of the still-missing ones was in Hiro's briefcase under the table at that very moment. But if Bob knew what he was doing to the Arthur process, Bob would hate him, quite rightly, forever.

"Betty's great," Bob said, trying to remember the last time he'd seen her. "She's learning to cook Greek this month, so we'll try to have you and Noel over for a Hellenic feast," Bob said with a brittle laugh.

"And your family?"

Bob's stepson Roger was eking out a zombie-like existence in that now almost-empty house he'd shared with Dave. He half expected any day to get a call that Roger had killed himself. "Family's great."

Hiro noted that odd look on Bob's face. Did he suspect something? No, that was ridiculous, but Hiro's shame became too much to bear. "Good to hear it," he said getting up. "Gotta get back downtown." Hiro shook his hand and left quickly.

Bob wondered if the swiftness of Hiro's departure was because he could tell Bob was lying. He made a mental note to work on his poker face.

Especially since his after-lunch meeting was to be with Big Ed. Bob could report having excellent relations with those on the nominating committees at the Directors and Screenwriters Guilds, but was floundering at the Screen Actors Guild which nominated in four categories. The music and technical awards would be work, but he felt he could have some effect there if he offered the right people the right perks. Junkets to premieres in Europe. Tickets, and possibly escorts, to exclusive big name charity galas. Such was the legal tender of his office. But that was merely influence; he could guarantee nothing at this point. He prayed that would be enough for his mobster boss.

Tuesday, November 21st

"And when," Guy demanded loudly above the overbearingly tinkly music in the Robinsons-May Christmas store at the Beverly Center, "just when were you going to tell me we weren't spending Thanksgiving together?"

"Oh, put a Christmas sock in it," Patrick sniffed. "I would have told you sooner but you get so negative. I'm going to another California Men's Gathering."

"Oh, for God's sake," Guy snorted in disgust.

"See? That's exactly why I didn't tell you. I'm going to the CMG fall gathering outside of San Diego and you can just get over it."

"You're choosing some wank-fest-in-the-woods mindfuck over me?"

Patrick turned and faced him down. "Here's a news flash. Thanksgiving is not all about Guy Lanner. I'm trying to find some answers, okay? Why can't I think about my father without going into a rage? Why is it that the person I most hate being alone with is me? Why is this ugly ornament seventy-five dollars?" he said sticking it back on the tree in irritation. "And why am I not getting any support from my so-called best friend?"

"Patrick, if you want answers, don't go off howling at the moon with a bunch of strangers, get therapy like normal sick people."

"Oh, I need therapy? That's the pot calling the kettle beige," Patrick sniffed. Resolutely adding, "I'm going to the Gathering tomorrow."

"Fine," Guy sulked. "I'll have Thanksgiving with Eric and Rudy and Michael."

"I need to spend Thanksgiving with Rudy's parents and cousins," Eric told Guy at home. "We're going down to San Diego with his brother's family to see them."

"But I bought a twenty-pound turkey," Guy whined.

"I'm sorry, but Rudy wants to introduce me to the family so it's kind of a big deal for him. For me, too. You understand."

"Yeah. Of course. That's terrific." Guy pulled himself up and decided to be big about it. "You guys have a great time. Michael and I will do Thanksgiving."

Wednesday, November 22nd

"Here's your coffee, Sir," Michael said as Guy shuffled into the kitchen in his bathrobe.

"Good boy," Guy mumbled, taking the cup with the perfect mixture of strong hot Starbucks Ethiopian Blend, cream, and four packets of Equal. He took a delicious sip. Michael was still staring, smiling at him. "What."

"There's something I want to do, Sir," Michael said eagerly. He opened the newspaper and pointed to an ad in the first section.

Through bleary morning eyes, Guy read how the Los Angeles Mission wanted help feeding the poor and homeless on Thanksgiving Day. "You want to donate?"

"Well, yes, only since I don't have much what I really want is to go help serve."

"On Thanksgiving?"

Michael nodded. "If it wasn't for you, Sir, I think I'd be one of those people."

Damn, shit, piss, hell, fuck, Guy thought. But he merely nodded instead, saying, "Knock yourself out."

Thursday, November 23rd

Guy sulked watching the Macy's Thanksgiving Day Parade in his underwear. He turned off the TV and flipped on his computer. On the L.A. Bearclub Website calendar page, there was a listing for a Thanksgiving potluck at a house in Culver City starting at noon.

After jumping in the shower, he threw on a tank top calculated to reveal chest hair, and an open shirt to hide the love handles.

It was 75 degrees outside so a pair of camp shorts and flip-flops completed the look. Twenty minutes later he was at the potluck.

Bears are a friendly bunch, so there was a lot of good-natured pawing, groping, and backslapping in between grabs at chips and pumpkin pie. Still, Guy felt awkward around a bunch of men he didn't really know. The bears got into the bowl game on TV so Guy drifted back to the kitchen where he busied himself with angrily cleaning up while wondering why the hell he had come.

"Guy Lanner, you are stalking me," said a familiar voice from the doorway.

Guy turned, and instantly brightened. "Buck!"

"Good to see you," Buck replied, coming forward to hug him. "Mmm. You still feel good. What are you so pissed off about now?"

"All my friends dumped me and it's Thanksgiving," he said, wondering yet again where he knew this guy from. "And as if that doesn't suck enough, I'm cleaning somebody else's damn kitchen."

Buck chuckled and shook his head. "Fix me a plate and you can tell me all about it."

Saturday, November 25th

Guy hated dates. They made him feel awkward and stupid and ugly. In fact this one with Buck at Benvenuto on Santa Monica was the first time Guy had gone on an actual date in almost a year. "I know I know you from somewhere."

"Okay, it's true," Buck admitted. "We knew each other in a past lifetime."

"Past lives?" Guy said, twirling a forkful of chicken linguine Alfredo. "Please tell me you're not one of those New-Age guys into past-life regression and out-of-body whatevers. I got a friend this weekend at some men's gathering getting in touch with his feminine inner child or something."

"Don't you want to be in touch with your feminine side?"

"I'm gay; didn't that came with the package?" He washed the Alfredo down with some chardonnay. "Why? Are you all in-tune and tight with your feminine side?"

Buck smiled privately, looking only at his spaghetti. "Pretty much."

Guy leaned forward over his plate for intimacy. "Well, you'd never know it. There is just nothing girlie or femme about you," he grinned. "You don't look like some WeHo gym bunny, or a model, you look like a man. A real guy. I like that. A lot."

Buck leaned back surprised. "Guy, you don't know it, but that is possibly the nicest compliment you ever gave me."

"Gimme a chance for more," he leered. "Wait, what do you mean, 'ever gave me'?"

Buck just chuckled and reached across the table to grasp Guy's hand gently but firmly. "Let it go, Guy. It doesn't matter. Just enjoy what's in front of you."

That night at home, Guy pulled out every high school and college yearbook he owned, searching for a young Buck's face. Old photographs in shoeboxes were consulted. With a magnifying glass in hand he scanned the backgrounds of birthday parties, Boy Scout camping groups, the church choir, friends' wedding pictures, trips with old boyfriends, photos of the guys he'd put up at the house and helped get back on their feet, old and recent parties, that RSVP cruise four years ago, and more. Finally, long past midnight, Guy glared at the pile of his life's memorabilia and gave up in frustration.

Buck was in there. Just not where Guy was looking.

Tuesday, November 28th

"He doesn't cheat on his wife or abuse his kids," Hiro told Big Ed glumly while chopping water chestnuts for turkey stir-fry. "I've been snooping for months. He doesn't drink or smoke, do drugs, gamble or embezzle."

"Well, just how important is he?" Noel asked, glad to see the last of the damn Thanksgiving turkey going into the stir-fry.

"There were three of us who count and verify the votes. I got Ted Balch out by restructuring the department, but Finkelstein's too close to the project to eliminate. Hand me the sesame oil."

"We're only four months from the telecast," Ed reminded Hiro, passing him the oil. "What are you gonna do with this guy?"

"I don't know," Hiro said frowning.

Ed watched Hiro skillfully pour the oil into the hot wok and add the chopped vegetables. They steamed and hissed and smelled wonderful. *Another delicious creation,* Ed thought. *Creation?* He cocked his head. "Maybe we need to create some dirt on this guy," he mused. "Or find someone who could do that for us."

"Like what?" Hiro asked him. "And how?"

Ed's eyes narrowed. "Tell me all about your computer guys."

Friday, December 15th

For Roger the Christmas season felt like an unending painful war scene in a movie which he, as the main character, walked through untouched by the exploding fusillades of merriment around him. The house was nearly empty. In the bedroom there was only a mattress on the floor and a few boxes of his clothes. The living room echoed its vacancy as he walked through it into the kitchen.

He lifted his gaze to the calendar on the refrigerator. It was three months to the day since Dave had died. Exactly ten months since they had met.

He thought that he should cry, that right now he would really like to cry. But he knew that he could not. He had been unable to cry since that day he'd left the house for the Cohens to pillage. He felt like the house. Lifeless. Ransacked. Empty.

Saturday, December 16th

"So, if you're dating this guy," Patrick asked as they entered the crowded courtyard of the Art Deco styled Alex Theater in Glendale, "why isn't he among us?"

"Buck is working nights now through Christmas," Guy replied. He distributed tickets to that night's performance of the Gay Men's Chorus of Los Angeles Christmas concert to Patrick, Michael, Eric and Rudy. "They're on me. Merry Christmas, everybody."

They took their seats in the auditorium that was already buzzing with happy spirits and excitement about the Chorus. The lights went down and the curtain went up on over one hundred and fifty gay men in tuxedos with bright red cummerbunds and holly-and-berry boutonnières.

The program included everything from "It's the Most Wonderful Time of the Year," to "Rise Up Shepherd and Follow" to the 1942 Arthur winning "White Christmas." For Eric, hearing one hundred and fifty gay men singing "Merry Christmas, Darling" put a completely new and healing context to the song.

During intermission, Ezra sipped a Diet Coke near the Alex Theater's bar alone in the merry crowd. He saw Patrick, and waved him down.

Patrick hugged him and asked, "What's up?"

"Oh, not much. Except that I'm part of the Christmas Eve service at the church," Ezra said. "You're in the neighborhood; you should come. Candles at midnight, carols you already know and afterward, pastries donated from Victor Bene's. You'll love it."

"Sorry," Patrick said gently, "too much Christ for this pagan. I've been beat up too many times in the name of Jesus to go down that road again."

"Believe me, I understand," Ezra told him. "I'll pray for you."

"Do that. I'll sacrifice a goat for you."

"Ooh, bring it to church! I've got a great Samoan recipe!" They both laughed and Ezra left him.

STEALING ARTHUR

Patrick watched him disappear into the crowd. *He'll make somebody a nice husband*, he thought. *Too much God shit for me, though.* Religious baggage was Michael's psychosis, not his. *Wait a minute*, Patrick realized with a start, *Michael eats up that Bible crap like crazy*. And Ezra's brand of God was a hell of a lot more sane and inclusive than most. And didn't he have the hots for Michael in that harness and leash on Halloween? Hmmm . . . !

Monday, December 17th

"I have to admit I'm surprised by this," Jimmy B said as he was seated at the very clubby, very expensive Water Grill in downtown L.A. for lunch. His quick brown eyes noticed the third plate set as he opened his napkin, vaguely wondering who would be joining them. He was short, thin, and milky pale, with closely cropped curly black hair framing a sharp-featured but attractive Russian face. "Don't get me wrong, Mr. Yamamoto," he quickly amended, "I'm flattered, it's just unexpected."

Hiro smiled and nodded as he set his briefcase containing his Arthur by his chair. "You're a bright young man." Hiro told him, seating himself. "You could go far in the company on your own. But with an ally, who knows how much farther?" His guest smiled, abashed. "Jimmy B, there is something I need from you." He leaned forward to make his point. "I need Mel Finkelstein fired. Swiftly and irrevocably."

Jimmy B was completely bewildered. He tried to laugh. "You're kidding, right? I mean, Mr. Finkelstein's Vice President of —"

"I know his position," Hiro cut him off tersely. "That is why the cause of his firing must be shocking, indefensible, and so shameful he will not fight it and the partners will keep it quiet. It must also be undetectable. That's why you're here." Hiro gave his guest time to begin making some sense of this and compose a response.

"Mr. Yamamoto, with respect, this, this sounds like a personal thing between you and Mr. Finkelstein. I really can't get involved."

From nowhere, massive hands clapped down on his shoulders causing him to yelp.

"Yes, you can," Big Ed said, his tone as firm as his grip.

"Jimmy B, this is Mr. DeLello," Hiro said. "He goes by Big Ed."

Ed came around and took Jimmy B's smallish hand in his bear-sized grip, squeezing just a little too hard and shaking it a just a bit too roughly for effect. "Glad to meet you, Jimmy. I hear you're the computer whiz," he said, taking his seat. "Sorry I'm late. Parking."

Rattled, Jimmy B could only gawk at this mountain in a custom Ermenegildo Zegna suit uncomfortably close to him. "I'm in I.T.," was all that came out.

"I've told him our needs," Hiro reported.

"And?"

"He has reservations."

"I understand," Big Ed said sympathetically to Jimmy. "You're a good man, I appreciate that. But sometimes we have to do things we don't like. Lemme show you what I mean." Ed reached into his jacket. "Oops, wrong side." Jimmy B's eyes widened just as Ed had intended when he saw the gleaming black handgun. "Ah, here we go," Ed said, retrieving an envelope from the other side of his jacket. He opened the envelope and showed Jimmy B a series of photos taken in the just the last two days. "See this guy?" Jimmy B blanched. "Name's Marcos. Handsome. Hot, even. But illegal. Yeah, undocumented from Guatemala. He could get immigration off his ass and stay here if he married his American girlfriend." Here Ed showed a photo of Jimmy B with the handsome Latino. "Problem is, he's got a boyfriend, so that won't work. Another problem is, I know where to find him, and I've got the I.N.S. on speed-dial."

Hiro craned his neck to admire the photo. "How long have you been together?"

Stunned and frightened, Jimmy B was only barely able to croak, "Three years."

"Nice."

"All this for Mr. Finkelstein?" Jimmy asked Hiro uncomprehendingly. "What did he do to you?"

"That is irrelevant," Hiro said.

Big Ed put his lips to Jimmy's ear, then spoke in a deliberately normal tone causing Jimmy to wince. "Get him fired." He stood. "Gotta go. Double parked." He jerked Jimmy's chair around to face him. "Make it good, Jimmy B. And don't tell Marcos." He reached out, grasping the chair-back at Jimmy's hips. He lifted the chair with Jimmy in it three full feet off the floor to be eye-to-eye, and nose-to-nose. People all around gawked. "'Cause if he disappears, I know where to find you."

Tuesday, December 18th

The next day Jimmy B came in to work early. He logged onto his computer. From there he accessed the company's email, and disconnected Finkelstein's email. At 9:06, Mel Finkelstein called to report he couldn't get his email. Jimmy B told him he'd get working on it right away. He waited fifteen minutes, then went up to Finkelstein's office.

"I've located the problem, Sir, but I have to take care of it from your terminal."

"This going to take long?" Finkelstein asked, annoyed at the inconvenience.

"Five, maybe ten minutes."

Finkelstein gave an irritated sigh and relinquished his executive's chair to Jimmy B. "Fine."

Jimmy sat and started closing programs. "I gotta reboot and I need to be you to do this. What's your password?"

"SchindlersList, no apostrophe. I'm getting some coffee."

Ten minutes later, Jimmy was back in his office. He reconnected the email account and called Hiro. "I'm going to need time when I know Mr. Finkelstein's away from his computer."

"Piece of cake." After hanging up, Hiro called Finkelstein. "Mel, I need to go over some numbers with you. Could you come up to my office? Oh, that will be most excellent." Next, he dialed Jimmy's extension. "I can keep him in here for an hour. I will call you when he leaves."

Jimmy waited ten minutes, then disconnected Finkelstein from the network. His position allowed him access to everyone's I.P. address, so it was easy for him to take Finkelstein's and, using the password he'd learned earlier, assume it. With that, as far as the PrattswaterfordDouglas network was concerned, he was Finkelstein. All the websites visited would be recorded in the history as such.

He began surfing for something truly and unforgivably ugly.

Sunday, December 24th

"For a man with religious issues," Eric said, admiring a small gold wire tree devoted to Faberge reproductions, "you sure know how to put on a display."

"I adore Christmas," Patrick said. "It's the most beautiful holiday and also the saddest. It's everything I am — all glitter and glam façade." He raised his glass to Eric and Rudy, Michael and Guy, and to Suze, Lee, and Sarah. "A merry co-opted Pagan holiday to you all. May none of you need my services in the coming year."

"God bless us, everyone," Guy said, "especially Doctor Doom." They all sipped their champagne.

Patrick smiled and rubbed his hands together. "And on that cheery note, let us gather in the grand salon for carols."

Guests moved toward the living room or to the kitchen for drink refills first. Patrick motioned to Michael for a private conversation. Patrick took a small unwrapped box from under his tree. "Merry Christmas." Michael, who never thought anyone might give him a Christmas present, was unable to speak. "Go on, open it," Patrick urged.

Michael removed the top of the box and found a small antique silver cross on a matching silver chain. He wanted to say how beautiful it was and much it meant to him. Instead, what came out was, "But you don't like Jesus."

"Yeah, well. You do." Patrick hugged Michael who closed his eyes tightly and thanked God intensely for his friend.

Guy found himself cornered in the kitchen by Rudy and Eric. "What?" he asked suspiciously.

"You've been so nice to me," Eric began, "letting me stay in your home, helping me get started in Los Angeles, being such a great friend and more —"

"But you're moving out," Guy said, finishing the sentence for him.

Eric was caught off guard. "Yeah, how did you —"

"Because that's the speech I always get," Guy said putting his arm around Eric. "I take people in and they leave. It's what happens. I'm gonna miss you, Eric. I assume you're moving in with your *caliente* stud muffin here?"

Eric took his partner's hand, beaming at the prospect. "Yeah. I'll be out of the house by the first part of January," Eric vowed.

"That's fine, you two," Guy said. He put his hands on their heads and blessed them with a simple, "Mazel tov."

"*Gracias, señor,*" Eric replied.

"Thanks," Rudy said, hugging Guy.

They moved into the living room where Patrick was playing vaguely seasonal tunes at the baby grand piano. The piano top was crowded with photos, as was every available shelf on the bookcase.

"Who are all these people?" Suze asked, admiring a picture of a handsome man and his dog on the beach.

"These are friends of mine," Patrick said softly. "Friends I buried who died of the virus." Rudy and Eric looked at each other in apprehension. Michael, Lee, and Sarah looked at the dozens of framed faces with a new gravity.

"Oh, honey," Sarah whispered. "So many. So many beautiful men."

Patrick continued to play the piano softly, lightly. "Yes. There are more, too, that I don't have pictures of. The ones I didn't know, who died and had nowhere else to go so . . ." He shrugged. "Well, someone needed to bury them." He nodded toward the group on the piano. "More than a few of these ended up that way, too."

"O'Leary & Finkelstein's gave them free funerals?" Lee asked incredulously.

"Hush, child. The partners do not need to know about that," Patrick said meaningfully to her as he continued to play. "Some people say they've buried a lot of their friends. But when I say it, I mean I buried 'em, honey."

"Why didn't we see these when we were here for the Arthurs?" Suze asked.

"Too many ghosts," Patrick replied. "I only bring them out at Christmas. Like the tree and the reindeer and the little baby who'll grow up only to get nailed to a cross. Sadness runs so deep at this time of year, if it wasn't for all the wrapping and tinsel it'd be unbearable. And the songs, of course."

"Play the one I like," Guy asked gently.

Surrounded by his living friends as well as all the photos of departed ones, Patrick sang "Have Yourself a Merry Little Christmas."

As his guests were leaving, Patrick took Guy aside. He pointed toward Michael and whispered, "Get his furry butt to church." And he quickly explained why.

So as Guy, Michael, Rudy, and Eric were walking home Guy made sure they walked past the Metropolitan Community Church.

"Look, everybody," Guy proclaimed. "They're having a midnight Christmas Eve service! Let's go in," he said, insistently shoving Michael, Rudy, and Eric inside.

Familiar carols were being played in the sanctuary, so they grabbed seats in the back. Michael was apprehensive, but Guy held his hand firmly. As the candles were lit during the final hymn, "Silent Night," even Guy's face was streaked with tears.

Afterward, Guy found Ezra in the crowded lobby. "Hey!" exclaimed Ezra. "You came!"

"Not quite," Guy said, steering him toward his friends, "but I did get a little precome-y. Here we are. This is Eric and Rudy, and this is Michael. You remember Michael," he said undoing another button on Michael's shirt to expose thick chest hair, "from Halloween?"

"Oh, yeah, I remember Michael! Hi, there," Ezra said, hugging him. "Why didn't you call me? I knew it, I was too pushy, right?"

"No, I . . ." Michael could only stare at Ezra's deacon's collar. "I lost the number. I'm sorry. Maybe you could, if it's all right, give it to me again?"

"I've got a better idea," Guy said to Ezra. "We're all having Christmas at my house, it's just two blocks down Westbourne. Why don't you join us for Christmas?"

"Oh, I can't," Ezra said. "I'm taking teddy bears to the kids at Cedars-Sinai, it's one of our ministries. Takes all day."

There was a long awkward pause.

"Take me with you," Michael blurted as Guy, Eric, and Rudy looked at him in shock. "Please? I would like to do that with you."

"Yes, you should," Guy said. He turned to Ezra. "He should do that. He spent all Thanksgiving feeding the poor downtown. Swear to God. Fed shitloads of homeless."

"Oh, right!" Eric added, finally figuring out what was going on here. "So you know he has experience."

"Please?" Michael felt compelled to beg.

"Well, okay. If you think you're up to it," Ezra said, "meet me here tomorrow morning at 8:30."

Monday, December 25th

At 7:45 A.M., Michael crept down the hall from his room so as not to wake anyone. He was surprised to find Guy in his bathrobe sitting at the kitchen table with a cup of coffee and a key in front of him.

"Merry Christmas, Sir," Michael whispered. "I didn't think anyone would be up."

"I have a few little Christmas things for you and the guys later," Guy said softly. "But I wanted to be up so I could give you this in private before you took off." He slid the key across the table to Michael. "I think it's time."

Michael touched the padlock that had been around his neck for the past nine months, that had become a part of him. "Are you sure, Sir?" he asked nervously.

Guy nodded. "I think you're ready. Come here." He picked up the key and stood. "From this moment on, you do not need to look to me for what to do. You're able to make your own decisions. And you don't need to call me Sir anymore." He inserted the key in the padlock at Michael's throat and turned it. The lock sprung open. Guy removed the heavy steel chain from around Michael's neck. "There, it's official. I'm no longer your Master. Just your friend."

Michael rubbed his neck where the padlock had been. "It feels strange."

"I'm sure you'll get used to it. Merry Christmas, Michael."

Michael hugged him. "Thank you for giving it to me. And thank you for taking it off. Even if it does feel odd." A thought occurred to him. "Oh! I'll be right back!" he said and tiptoed quickly back to his room. A moment later he came back with the antique silver cross that Patrick had given him hanging around his neck on a delicate silver chain. He showed it proudly to Guy. "I've gotten used to having something there," he explained. "Besides, if you think about it, it's kind of the same thing. Just a different Master."

Michael met Ezra at the church at 8:30 on the dot. Ezra was dressed in black pants, white shirt, deacon's collar, and a Santa hat, loading boxes of stuffed bears into the back of his rather battered Neon.

"We've collected about two hundred bears," Ezra told Michael, fitting in the last of them. He slammed the trunk shut and turned to Michael with another Santa hat in his hand. "Now, we're going to be seeing some really sad kids. You have to promise me this: no crying, not in front of the kids. Got that?" Michael nodded seriously and Ezra put the hat on him as he continued. "Remember, we're there to cheer them up and let them know they're loved. So we laugh, and we smile, and we hold the hands of the ones we can touch." He adjusted the hat on Michael, gently brushing his hair aside. "If they cry, we can sympathize, comfort, maybe even hold them, but no tears from us. Can you do that?"

"I promise," Michael said somberly.

After arriving at Cedars, they put half the stuffed bears into a great red cloth sack that Michael carried as Ezra's assistant. They met up with the hospital chaplain on duty who led them on their rounds. Going from room to room, they gave bears to thrilled little boys and girls. Some of the children in the cancer ward were bald or balding from the treatments. Most of them were scared from being in a hospital. Some were too weak to sit up, but strong enough to hug their bear and smile as Ezra talked with them.

After a quick lunch, they got the rest of the bears from the car, refilling Michael's red sack. That afternoon they met children who had suffered fires, car accidents, child battering, or other traumas. There were broken limbs and bandages, IV drips and feeding tubes. In one room the parents sat next to a bed where a gaunt little girl lay with eyes closed. The parents were startled when Ezra and Michael entered. "We're giving bears to the children," Ezra explained.

"We want one," the mother said, with wet, red eyes.

The father said, "Honey —"

"She might wake up," the mother snapped, her chin trembling. "She could."

Ezra reached into Michael's sack for a bear and put it in the mother's hands. "Then I think you need to hold on to it for her."

There were several times Ezra had expected Michael to go running to the bathroom and cry, but he didn't. Michael stayed with him the whole time, fully engaged in talking with the children. He seemed able to empathize with their being frightened without exacerbating it.

When they were finally done, Ezra invited Michael to his apartment near the church for a bite to eat. The day had been supremely satisfying, but exhausting. As soon as Michael sat down on Ezra's couch, he collapsed into sobs for the dozens of suffering faces he had seen all day long. Ezra understood and sat next to him, holding Michael with comforting *I know*s and *It's all right*s.

Feeling safe in Ezra's hands, Michael lay fully across his lap and let the sadness of the kids, the season, and his own past Christmases pour out in tears. Ezra felt privileged to hold him and cried, too. Doing this together, the grieving felt like grace itself.

Part Three

Monday, January 1st, 2001

It had been an overwhelming week for Michael. Ezra's need to be needed was perfectly met in Michael whom he recognized as a profoundly wounded soul with a deep thirst for God and a beautiful chest he ached to bury his face in. But he held back, filling the hours with much talk of a loving God. Not that Michael heard or understood, but in looking at Ezra, he saw that Ezra saw Jesus in him — and that was undiscovered territory for Michael.

Tonight after a fervent dialectic on the summation of liberation theology inherent in Revelation 22:17, Ezra suddenly skipped to verse 20. With a "come, Lord Jesus!" he wrapped his wide hands around Michael's rapt face and brought it to his lips.

Michael had known lust with men, but never anything like this. Not filthy or vile, it was pure, with an intensity like falling, no, flying! Soaring, spinning. The feeling reached down from his giddy brain to caress his heart, then plunged through his guts to the root of his being. With a spasm that shook his body, he ejaculated in his pants.

But Ezra would not let him go. With Michael still quivering and breathing erratically, Ezra held him firmly in that kiss. He held him in that passionate grip until Michael slowly released his embarrassed tension and give over to being there unashamed.

Tuesday, January 2nd

"My associates wish to move cautiously and most deliberately with this," Ed told Bob Davies at their private breakfast meeting. "Therefore, we have selected one category to test the waters with. Best Original Song."

Bob shifted in his seat but responded, "I think that's do-able."

"Good," Ed replied curtly. "Get as many of these songs nominated as you can," he said, sliding a list of unlikely tunes across the table. "And in the meantime, continue creating meaningful relationships with those involved in all the other categories. Because if this works out, you're going to be a very busy man this time next year."

Friday, January 5th

"Today's the fifth anniversary of my mother's passing," Michael said during lunch with Ezra.

"Oh, sweetheart, I didn't know. Would you like to go visit her grave?"

"Yeah. There's something I'd like to do, and I'm kind of nervous about it."

"Would you like me to come with you?" Ezra asked. Michael nodded.

An hour later, at self-storage unit #925, Michael lifted the garage-like door with a metallic rattle that echoed down the corridor. "Hello, mother," he said. He picked up the urn with his mother's ashes from among the stored furniture and haphazard assortment of boxes of her things. "I want you to meet Ezra." He held the urn out to Ezra.

"Hello, Mrs. Fowler," Ezra replied as if he met people in urns every day.

"He's my —" Michael hesitated, "— friend." He shifted the urn to carry it in his arms like a baby. "I know you're in heaven, Mother, with Jesus and the angels," he said to it, "but I miss you. I miss Daddy, too, even though I know you won't like that. But my life is changing, and I think it's for the better."

He paused, rubbing his thumb along the urn's lid. The long linoleum corridor was filled with fluorescent lighting and thick silence. Michael took a deep breath.

"And, Mother," he whispered, "I'm gay."

After a long pause, Ezra put his hand on Michael's back. "What was she like?"

"She had visions," Michael told him. "Like Daniel or Ezekiel. Only her vision for me didn't come true."

Ezra's interest was immediately piqued. "Tell me about her visions."

"One was after my father died. Mother caught me looking at pearl divers in *National Geographic* and touching myself. I was sent to my cabinet until the next morning. Because what I'd done had pained her, she had to take one of her pills. She went into the bathroom crying and opened the medicine cabinet. A great holy light flooded the bathroom and there was an angel inside."

"An angel in your medicine cabinet?"

"Yeah, and it said, 'Why do you weep?' And my mother said, 'I fear that my son is a homo.' And the angel said, 'Fear not; Michael will be fine once he meets a Sarah.'" Ezra put his hand to his mouth, but Michael continued, not noticing. "For years I've looked for a Sarah to make me right. I finally found a Sarah, but she told me I was gay." He looked at Ezra and saw he was pale with a look of shock. "What's wrong?"

Ezra swallowed. "People call me Ezra, but that's only how you say it in English. It's actually spelled E-S-E-R-A. On Samoa it's pronounced *uh-sair-uh*. Like Sarah, only with an 'uh' in front of it. Esera."

Michael stared at him in amazement and awe, not daring to breathe. Then he began to laugh. "Mother!" he shouted to the urn, "I found a Sarah!"

Wednesday, January 10th

When Michael came over to Ezra's apartment, he noticed a shopping cart outside full of street junk. He climbed the stairs and rang the bell.

"Oh, hi, Michael," Ezra said answering his door, "come on in. Say hi to Thom."

"Hi," Michael said.

Thom looked up from his soup and asked, "Is my cart still downstairs?" Michael nodded. "I have thirty-five Coke cans, ten Pepsi, two Dr. Pepper and one Sprite. Nobody drinks Sprite anymore."

"I found him last night in front of the church," Ezra explained to Michael. "Hungry, filthy, off his meds, just a mess." He shrugged. "What could I do?"

Thom was dressed in an old pair of khaki pants and a denim shirt. "I have your clothes," he said to Michael.

Michael realized that indeed, he was dressed exactly the same, a coincidence that drove home the point that there were only slightly altered circumstances separating them. "Small world," was all he could think of to say.

"But full of things," Thom said. "He has four plates and saucers and cups but only three bowls and eight sets of forks, spoons, and knives, twice as many as he has plates for."

"I've got him some meds," Ezra explained, "but I can't get him into housing unless he has some kind of job."

"Guy knows a woman named Suze who works at a temp agency."

Ezra glanced at Thom who was counting paper napkins, and shrugged with little hope. "Anything's worth a try."

"All we're asking, Suze, is that you give him a shot," Guy said. He had brought Thom with him at Michael's insistence.

"But what can he do?" Suze asked.

"He can keep simple records," Ezra told her, "as long as he's on his meds." He saw Suze roll her eyes. "And basic cleaning up, straightening, low-level stuff."

"There's ninety-two wooden stirrers in the box by the coffee," Thom announced from across the room. "I could make something with those."

"Please don't," Suze begged him. "Sweetheart, please just sit in the chair."

"He needs a chance," Michael said. "Like Guy gave me. He's gotta have a job or they won't allow him into decent housing."

"Then he'll be back on the street," Ezra added. "He'll be off his meds, and who know what'll happen to him."

"Please, Suze," Guy implored. "Isn't there anything you can do?"

Suze gave in. "All right, all right. Bring him in tomorrow and I'll do what I can."

Thursday, January 11th

It was only 8:30 and already Suze regretting taking on Thom. She'd put him to work cleaning the restroom and storage area, but by noon his constant counting was driving her and the other two temp placement women crazy.

A job order came in and it was just nonspecific enough that Suze was willing to risk losing the client to get Thom the hell out of the office. "Do you know how to get to Beverly Hills?" Suze asked him.

Thom nodded. "Number 20 or 21 bus, five times an hour each, ten times an hour for both, that's one every six minutes."

"Okay, here is an address right down Wilshire. It's Neiman-Marcus, do you know where that is? Good. Ask for the personnel office. When you get there, ask for Mr. Harthen. I've written it down for you, can you do that? Great. He'll tell you what to do. Can you be there in half an hour?" Thom shook his head no. Her shoulders slumped. "Why not, Thom?"

"Bus fare."

"I think we can come up with that for you."

It was 5:15 when Suze hung up with Mr. Harthen. Before she could process what he had told her, the phone immediately rang again. "Star Temps, this is Suze."

"Hi, it's Michael. How did it go with Thom?"

"I sent him to Neimans. You're not going to believe this. He's actually got a job and they love him," she told Michael. "It's doing inventory. He counts things!"

Wednesday, January 17th

"I notice you keep returning to that particular day, Michael," Dr. Larry noted. "What do you think it holds for you?"

"My friend, Guy, has been educating me on movie musicals. Last weekend we watched *Bedknobs and Broomsticks*. When I saw it, I remembered that was the movie my mother took me to see that day. My father was very sick. When we came back, he was dead in the kitchen. Mom called the ambulance."

"Why don't you go through that day?"

Michael closed his eyes to remember better. "I'd had thoughts that morning about stealing money for ice cream, so I went in my cabinet. I heard Mother come in so I peeked out." The images came back with an intensity that put him back in those moments as if they were happening now. "She's angry. But she opens the fridge and takes out something small. Two small things." He wrinkled his forehead as he concentrated harder. "It's, it's my father's diabetes medicine. Two small bottles. It's the two different kinds of insulin. One has the clear medicine, the other has the cloudy. She's at the sink. She's got a syringe and she's putting it into the clear, then putting it into the cloudy. It looks like she's putting the clear medicine into the cloudy bottle."

"She's altering your father's insulin?"

"Must be. She throws the needle away. Now she's praying."

Dr. Larry summoned all his professional manner to keep Michael from hearing alarm in his voice. "What happens next, Michael?"

"An hour or so later daddy comes in. He opens the fridge. Takes the cloudy bottle. Injects himself. Leaves. I fall asleep." Michael shifted in his seat, becoming agitated as he remembered his past. "It's later when I wake up, because Daddy is upset. He's sick and he's looking all over the kitchen. Knocking things over. He needs something sweet bad. But there's nothing in the cupboards. His hands are shaking and he moves funny."

"Where is your mother?"

Michael gasped in realization. "She's there! She, she won't let him leave. She pushes him back when he tries. He can't move right. Shouting. Falling! On the floor, shaking! Can't get up!" The memory terrified him, pulling him into a fetal position. "Oh, God!"

"What is it, Michael?"

"She sees me! Yanks open the door. Pulling me out. 'Go to your room!' Daddy keeps jerking on the floor. Reaching at me. 'Go!' In the dining room, watching. The skillet. Oh, dear God!" Michael cried, his hands over his head in horror. "She hit him! Hit his head! He's moving a little, but not much. Mother opens the fridge, takes the medicine out. I run to my room. She comes in wearing her coat. 'We're going to a movie, Michael, would you like that?' 'Yes, ma'am.'" Michael opened his eyes, a stricken look on his face. "When we got back . . ." his face screwed up and he wept.

Dr. Larry let Michael sob himself out. After many minutes he said, "Are you going to be all right?"

Spent, Michael sat there considering the question for a couple of minutes. "She killed him for being queer," he said quietly, staring at the floor. "I understand it now."

"What do you understand, Michael?"

"My dream. You know, about the floating house with the water coming inside? Then later I realized the water was blood?" Michael looked up at his therapist. "It was his. It's my father's blood."

Thursday, January 18th

"So his mother murdered his father and got away with it?" Patrick asked over a gigantic overpriced sour apple martini at The Abbey.

"Apparently the cops figured he hit his head while convulsing from radically low blood sugar and never checked about the insulin," Guy told him.

"That is so bitchin'," Patrick declared. "Screwed up beyond belief, but totally bitchin'. Where is he now?"

"At Ezra's. They're full-on boyfriends now. They begged me to help get a job for some homeless guy the other day with a counting obsession. With Suze's help we actually did it. Inventory at Neiman's."

"Inventory can't last forever," Patrick said.

"Ah, but this is L.A. at the beginning of awards season. He's now at this place that puts together gift baskets for the stars. He's in OCD counting heaven. Think of it, x number of free Rolexes, purge bags, and coupons for Janet Jackson coffee enemas placed in x number of baskets going to x number of alleged celebrities: it's perfect."

Patrick noticed Guy craning his neck. "Who are you looking at?"

"Oh, that table of bears. Thought Buck might be here."

"When are you going to take that cowboy out on another date?"

"When are you going to take anyone out on a date? Ever?"

"Another!" Patrick called out imperiously to a passing waiter, pointing at his empty glass. "And if it'll help fit in more alcohol, I can do without the apple wedge." He turned back to Guy. "Where the hell are Eric and Rudy? I thought they were joining us."

"It's moving day. They found a closet-sized apartment in Park La Brea, near the museum. They're practically living in one of the tar pits."

"Ah, l'amour. "

"Yes, I wish them success. Actually I wish Rudy would make a hard-core porno movie, but for today I wish them success."

"Speaking of cinematic art," Patrick interjected, "Sarah's finished her film and she's pushing it at the American Film Market in Santa Monica next month. It's like a low-rent Cannes with buses to Malibu. Wish her success, too. If she gets a buyer I could be coming to a theater near you."

"Oh, dear," Guy said with a smile. "I might have a hard time dealing with a thirty-foot tall Patrick."

Patrick took a deep breath. "Yes, well, I find I have a hard time dealing with the life-sized model." The waiter returned with his martini. "Fortunately," Patrick said, lifting it to his lips, "I find this helps immensely."

Wednesday, January 31st

Guy came home around midnight after catching a late showing of *Gladiator*. He found an ornate covered container on his kitchen counter. It was dusty, so he rinsed it out and dried it off. He held it up to the light to assess the workmanship and shine. "Fifty, maybe eighty bucks on eBay," he murmured to himself. Hearing the front door open he set the container on the counter and called out, "Michael?"

"It's me," his housemate said. Michael came into the kitchen carrying a large baggie half-filled with sand and dust. He opened it and dumped it into the container on the counter.

"Hey!" Guy said, "I just washed that."

"You washed my mother's urn?"

"Oh, my God!" Guy shouted as he dived for the sink to scrub his hands frantically. "I have death on me! Get it off!"

"It's just dust," Michael said.

"It's dead woman!"

"No, only dust. 'For dust thou art, and unto dust shalt thou return.'"

"It's creepy shit, and I want it off me!" He pointed at the empty baggie. "What were you, taking her for a walk?"

"Kind of. I was spreading her around West Hollywood."

Guy looked at him dumbfounded. "Please tell me why."

"I've been thinking for years about what I should do with mother's ashes. After tonight's therapy session I was really angry at her. I got her ashes so I could spread them all over gay-infested West Hollywood just to spite her." He shrugged. "But it felt sinful and didn't make me feel any better. So I came home. I'll just wait until I come up with a better idea." He took his jacket off and headed toward his room. "Oh, and there's another thing," he said turning around. "Guy, you've been so great to me, really. Taking me in, letting me stay here, therapy. I can never repay you."

"Oh, fuck," Guy said. "You're moving out."

Michael nodded. "You said I should make my own decisions. And Ezra asked me. He's the first person ever to ask if I wanted to live with them." He gave a little smile and a shrug. "What could I do?"

Friday, February 3rd

"Oh, quit your bitching, you knew he'd move out," Patrick scolded Guy. "They always do when it's time; it's called success."

"But it's so empty with both him and Eric gone," Guy whined over the phone. "I need that life, that distraction. Do you know what I'm doing?"

"Yes," Patrick said, leaning over his kitchen counter, the better to hold his head. "You're forcing conversation at eight A.M. on a man with a hangover."

"I'm making pancakes. Everything I'm doing revolves around comfort food."

"Mmm, comfort food. Good idea. Think I'll join you."

Over the phone Guy heard the ice clinking into a glass. He frowned but decided to ignore it. "Just when I get these people livable, they leave me. And once again I've got nothing."

"Oh, spare me your soap opera, at least you have someone."

"Who? Buck? Are you serious? I don't have Buck."

"Damn it, Guy, you have possibility. Your life has possibility. Me, I have Stoli and orange juice and a workplace full of death.

For which I need to dress, I might add. So I'm hanging up now. Love you, don't ever change."

Guy stirred his pancake batter, thinking about Patrick's words. He found Buck's number in a pile of papers by the phone. He dialed it.

"Y'ello."

"Hey, Buck, Guy Lanner. Not too early, is it?

"Not for me. What's up?"

"Would you like to go to dinner sometime?"

There was a pause on the other end. "You asking me for a date?"

"If that's okay?"

Saturday, February 10th

One of the things Guy liked so much about Buck was his sense of peace. It put him at ease even as he envied it. The man was undeniably sexy, too, sitting there in Cobalt Cantina finishing his skirt steak on garlic mashed potatoes.

"Take me home with you," Guy said dreamily.

Buck continued chewing, with a devilish glint in his smile. Swallowing, he said, "I think it's a little soon, darlin'." He scooted his chair away from the table. "Be right back." He got up and headed for the restroom.

A woman came around to the table selling roses. Guy bought one and placed it beside Buck's plate. When Buck returned he said, "What's this?"

"For you."

Buck picked it up saying, "Thanks. But why don't you keep it. Flowers aren't my thing." He put it next to Guy's plate. He couldn't miss the dark scowl that crossed Guy's face. "Did I do something wrong?"

"My ex-wife used to do that. If I gave her something she didn't like, she couldn't just be nice about it, she had to tell me. Made me crazy."

"Oh, ho!" Buck chuckled. "He admits he was married!" Buck leaned back in his chair. "So tell me, whatever became of your ex-wife?"

"No idea. And honestly, I hope I never see her again."

"Why not?"

"Because she was smart, and talented, and everything I wasn't, that's why. And I treated her like shit because I hated myself for being gay. Of course, she was gay, too."

"You think so?"

"I know so. We met at Desert Springs, one of those ex-gay concentration camps. Yes, Jesus was going to cure us of our homosexuality. And if we married we could even cure each other! Such bullshit. So I don't know where Becky is and that's fine because I couldn't look her in the eye anyway."

Buck shifted so he could lean across the table. "If you met her there," he said quietly, sincerely, "it's safe to say she had some pretty serious issues, too. You don't end up at a place like Desert Springs unless you're pretty messed up to begin with."

"You know Desert Springs?"

"I do."

"Is that where we met?"

"Guy, let it go. You survived. What's the point of carrying the anger?"

"I don't know," Guy said. "But there's one thing I do know." He leaned in to meet Buck. "The more I get to know about you, the more I want to make love to you. I find you incredibly sexy. I want to pull your clothes off and hold you. I want to kiss you all over. And, oh, honey, I want to suck your dick."

"Well . . . ," Buck said with a sly smile, "that's not going to happen."

"I apologize, you're right, that was totally inappropriate. But I love being with you. And I kind of need to know if this is all one-sided on my part. Am I moving too fast? I'm not your type?"

"Oh, no," Buck told him enthusiastically. "No, I've always been attracted to you. I just don't think it's right yet."

Sunday, February 11th

"And the really sick, disgusting, and perverted part of this is that I think I'm falling in love with him," Guy told Patrick over brunch at the French Market. "And it scares the shit out of me because you know my pattern. I take on people and they end up leaving me."

"Yes, darling, but those aren't lovers, they're projects," Patrick pointed out. "You don't have a lover pattern mainly because you've done everything you could to avoid having a lover at all. One tiny thermonuclear catastrophe with a hetero marriage and you put up barriers all over the place. How this man got through is a miracle. I'm thinking my little Guy Lanner may be ready for the R word — relationship."

"I don't know. Have I told you about the sex?"

"Is it hot? Should I get another mimosa?"

"No, because there hasn't been any sex!"

"Oh, dear," Patrick said. "This is serious. This is not like you at all."

"I've tried, but he keeps stalling me. He's all 'I don't think it's right yet.'"

"Maybe he's on to something. Maybe we should get to know people better before having sex." A thought occurred to Patrick that made him sit upright. "Or maybe — maybe he has HIV!"

"Oh, my God," Guy said, struck by the possibility. "That could be it. He could be HIV-positive and doesn't want to tell me. He might think it'd scare me off."

"Would it scare you off?"

"I don't know," Guy said perplexed. "I've avoided any kind of relationship for so many years. Do I want to get involved now with someone who's positive?"

Tuesday, February 13th

It was 4:45 in the morning when Big Ed's alarm buzzed. He put on his bathrobe and shuffled into the living room where he turned the TV on. He made coffee while he waited for 5:00, when the Institute Award nominations would be announced live.

With a steaming cup of dark roast warming his hands, Ed slouched on the white sofa watching Institute President Brian Buter and Catherine Zeta-Jones read all the Arthur nominations. Mainly a lot of *Crouching Tiger, Hidden Dragon* and *Gladiator* plus the usual smattering of small surprises. But when it came to Best Song, Ed sat up.

"'I've Seen It All' from *Dancer in the Dark*, 'My Funny Friend and Me' from *The Emperor's New Groove*, 'One In a Million' from *Miss Congeniality*, 'Things Have Changed' from *Wonder Boys*, and 'Where Are You Christmas?' from *How the Grinch Stole Christmas*."

Ed grinned and took a deliciously satisfying slurp of coffee. Every single one of the songs he'd given to Bob Davies was nominated — and he'd deliberately picked some true stinkers just to test him. Now all he had to do was decide which song he wanted Hiro to make win.

"Y'ello."
"Hi, Buck. Guy. Not too late, is it?"
"Not for me. What's up?"
"You, uh, want to go out tomorrow night?"
"You mean Valentine's Day?"
"Yeah."
"You realize that's practically a proposal."
"Look, I'm kinda nervous about this. So, do you want to go out or not?"
"Sure."

Wednesday, February 14th

"No peeking," Ezra warned Michael as he guided him into the tiny kitchen. He pulled his hands away, saying, "Tah-dah!"

Michael stared in amazement at the heart-shaped cake with pink icing and the words MICHAEL BE MINE in red. "You made this for me?" he whispered. His boyfriend nodded with glee. "I don't know what to say. I haven't had a cake since I was eight. Thank you."

"Stay with me and you'll have lots of cakes. I'll make one for your birthday."

"Well, I don't have a birthday this year, but I'll still stay."

"You don't have a birthday?" Ezra snorted. "When were you born?"

"February 29th. Mother said I only had a real birthday every four years. That way I'd be her little boy forever."

"Yeah, well, we've learned Mom's not the best authority on normal behavior. As long as I have anything to say about it, you damn well will have a birthday — and another cake — and it's going to be on March 1st," Ezra declared. "Expect a Duncan-Hines chocolate cake in two weeks."

"Okay, but please, don't do anything else, okay? No presents or anything. I don't want you buying me presents."

"Fine!" Ezra sighed. Giving in to his weird boyfriend made him unexpectedly happy. "I promise not to buy you anything but it's on one condition: that we do something together that you'd like to do. Deal?"

Michael was abashed. Not used to negotiating kindness, he acquiesced. "Okay, then, I'll try to think of something."

"You do that," Ezra told him followed by a kiss. "Now cut that cake!"

"That's about the biggest piece of cake I've ever seen," Buck told Guy. They had ordered a single gargantuan slice of the Seven Layer Blackout Cake for dessert at The Cheesecake Factory in Marina del Rey.

"I know," Guy said, already lusting after it, fork poised to dig in. "It's the only reason I come here. God knows it's not the straight yuppie beach crowd that calls to me." They both attacked the cake. Buck made closemouthed moans of chocolate ecstasy. Guy gave Buck a devilish leer. "I also ordered it because chocolate is an aphrodisiac. Maybe I could make you make noises like that."

Buck laughed. "Guy, you are too much."

"I'm serious, Buck. Let me take you home with me. I know I'm not the hottest man in L.A., but I pay attention to what I'm doing, and I really, really want to please you."

Buck set his fork down. "Guy, I'd love to, but it's a lot more complicated than you think."

"Give me a chance," Guy implored. "I've really thought about this, and I don't care if you're HIV-positive. I'm fine with safe-sex. I just want to make love to you."

"Oh, Guy," Buck said softly with surprise. "That might be the most generous thing I've ever heard you say."

"But no, right?" Guy asked. Buck nodded at him. Again frustration seized him. "What is it? Just tell me! Am I rushing things? Is that it? You're not ready for this?"

"No, Guy, it's not me," Buck said simply. "I don't think you're ready."

"Who the fuck does he think he is!" Guy shouted in rage in his car driving home. "Of all the fucking ego! I'm not ready? What does he want from me?" He drove home the long way, down Washington Blvd. *What's he being so goddamned coy about?* he wondered angrily. *Is he HIV-positive? Or is he just a shit.* At a stop light at the edge of Culver City he punched the dashboard shouting, "Why aren't I good enough!"

Guy saw a Ralph's grocery store up ahead. He'd been too upset to eat any more of the cake at the restaurant, but now, having working himself around to feeling truly rotten, he needed a large bag of Nutter Butter cookies. And maybe a can of frosting.

Roger shuffled up and down the aisles at Ralph's, putting items into his hand-held basket. His life was in the shitter, it hardly mattered what he ate. This morning, though, he had a craving for peanut butter and ice cream. He was coming from getting a jar of Peter Pan chunky when he turned the corner to the frozen-food section. There between the upright cases of frozen foods was an intimidating sixty-foot long open freezer filled with dozens of flavors, kinds, and brands of ice cream.

"Jesus Christ," he mumbled, daunted by the overwhelming selection. There were too many to choose from, and he felt the panic rising. "It's okay," he told himself, trying to hang on, "I'll just get vanilla."

But there were so many kinds of vanilla. He began to breathe hard. There was regular vanilla, extra-creamy vanilla, natural vanilla, soy vanilla . . . his chest began to tighten . . . French vanilla, lowfat vanilla, vanilla ice milk, vanilla with pieces of vanilla beans . . . it was too much. He dropped his peanut butter to the floor. Gripping the side of the giant freezer for support, he completely broke down.

Tears slid down his face, dripping onto the cartons of ice cream. For the first time since David's death, he was finally able to cry. Indeed, he was unable to stop. He watched the tears hit the ice cream cartons and become solid. Cold, hard pebbles. Looking at his frozen tears, he realized that was what he had been for the past five months, frozen. He wept for David, he wept for himself.

"Dude, are you all right?" Guy asked the poor man sobbing into the ice cream.

Roger was only able to choke out a "No!"

"Roger?" Guy said. *Good God, he looks awful,* Guy thought. "Come here, it's okay," he said gently, turning the kid around to face him.

Roger leaned into him, letting himself go in this man's arms. He told Guy about David's death. How he was going to have to leave the house because he couldn't pay rent. How frightened he was. How useless he felt. Lonely. Shamed. So Guy did the only thing he knew to do.

He took him home.

Guy guided Roger to the guest bedroom. He lay him down on Eric's old bed and took Roger's shoes and socks off. He unbuttoned Roger's gray plaid flannel shirt and slipped it off, too. Roger's crying had diminished to a sort of sad, exhausted, steady leaking. Guy unbuttoned Roger's jeans, and unzipped the fly. He pulled the pants off. Roger wore no underwear. Guy couldn't help looking at the boy's body. Roger looked up at him.

"If you want to discipline me, you can," Roger whispered. "I deserve it."

Guy rubbed his fingertips across Roger's lovely chest, then followed the thin tantalizing line of hair that ran down his stomach. He felt his own dick becoming aroused.

Roger lifted his legs, looking directly at Guy. "I want you to," he said. "Do it. Don't even wear a condom."

With a single movement, Guy shucked his sweater, his undershirt still inside it, and climbed on the bed. Not even bothering to remove his pants, he simply opened his fly, freeing his now-hard cock. He positioned himself near the foot of the bed on his knees, holding the kid's ankles in his hands.

"Yeah," Roger said. "I want it. Let's do it. Go on, fuck me. Bareback me."

Oh, my God, thought Guy, seeing Roger's fierce, insistent urgency, thrusting sex on him. *This is exactly what I've been doing to Buck.* Suddenly there was absolutely nothing sexy about this. He didn't want to screw Roger. He wanted to heal him.

"I'm not going to do this," Guy said simply, rolling Roger over on his side. "Sweetheart, this is not what you need."

That truth pierced him, and Roger began to cry again. "I'm sorry. I'm so sorry."

"Shhh," Guy said lying down next to him. He wrapped his arms around Roger, spooning with him. "It's all right." Guy lay there holding him until Roger cried himself to sleep, and for the rest of the night.

STEALING ARTHUR

Thursday, February 15th

"Can you believe what is up for the Arthurs this year?" Patrick demanded the moment Guy answered his phone.

"I've been busy. Tell me," Guy responded.

"*Crouching Tiger, Hidden Dragon* and Steven Soderbergh. If you ask me — wait a minute. Busy? Too busy for the Arthurs? It's been two days! What, did you invite the bears over and install a sling?"

"I may have a new resident. Do you remember that young blond man at your Arthur party last year?"

"Darling, I drink specifically to forget most of my guests."

"Served drinks in his underwear?"

"Ah! Got him."

"Well, so do I. His boyfriend died in a wreck, and he's one himself. He's getting kicked out of his house on the 20th. Can't go to his parents' so he's got nowhere to go."

Patrick sighed in disbelief. "You are the biggest sucker in L.A. Guy, what is it about you that attracts these people?"

"I don't know but I'm going to let him rest here a couple of days. His boyfriend was Frank Powers."

"Oh, my God. I prepared him; we did the funeral."

"Yeah, well, I figure as many times as I've gotten off on him, from *Altar Bound* and *Serving Pvt. Ryan* alone, I owe his lover a couple of nights in the guestroom."

"What's he doing?"

"Crying mostly. It's weird, it's like he's glad about it or something."

"What are you doing?"

"Hiding my copies of *Altar Bound* and *Serving Pvt. Ryan*. I mean, how awkward would that be?"

"Ah, speaking of awkward and sex, how did your date go last night?"

Guy's mood darkened. "Did you see *Battlefield Earth*?"

"Oh, dear God, that horrible?"

"I told him I was okay if he was HIV-positive. Hell, I practically offered to marry him, but he said no. He said I wasn't ready! I don't even know what the hell that means. I've been going round and round with it for the last twenty-four hours and all I can tell you is that it's been one hell of a mindfuck." Guy stopped cold, then repeated, "Mindfuck."

"What?" asked Patrick.

"I just remembered something Rudy said to me when we were headed for the rodeo. Just before I met Buck."

"Which was?"

"He said, 'When the person is ready, the mindfuck will find him.'"

Saturday, February 17th

Roger came into the kitchen dressed in his jeans and gray flannel shirt to find Guy at the table, still in his full-length pink bathrobe, scanning the morning's paper for estate sales. "Thank you for letting me stay here," he said to his host, "but I think I should get back to the house and get my stuff together."

"You okay?" Guy asked, peering over the paper.

Roger nodded that he was. "A lot better. Still kinda shaky but I gotta move out."

"Okay, I'll take you in about half an hour?"

"That'd be great," Roger said. He hesitated a moment or two. "About the night you brought me here —"

"Forget about it," Guy told him gently.

Roger shook his head. "No, it made me see what I've been doing with myself. This sick cycle of abuse. When you looked at me that way, I saw that. Thank you, Sir."

"Please, I don't need anyone else calling me that. Let's just let all that go."

"Okay." He turned to leave as Guy returned to his paper, but turned back to add, "There's something else. I lied to you."

"Oh?"

"I could go back to my parents. Actually, it's what they want. But I got into trouble, bad trouble. And my stepfather got me out of it. I'm pretty sure he did something bad to do it. So I can't face him."

"Okay, so you can't stay in your current place and you can't go home. What are you gonna do?"

"I don't know. But I have three days."

Guy frowned at such a non-plan. "Well, you know my number," he said, returning to his listing of estate sales. "You've called it before."

After taking Roger back to his house in Culver City, Guy couldn't get him out of his head. *Gay, trying to be straight, only to fall in love with a man who's a porn star and high-end hustler. Damn,* he thought as he got home, *if this messed-up kid could completely give himself over to a man like that, I should be able to do that with Buck. Right?* He stood in the kitchen staring at the phone.

With other men the word "commitment" hadn't even been a part of Guy's vocabulary. With Buck, it didn't seem like prison, but promise. A promise of possibility. That was the word Patrick had used. "You have possibility, Guy," he had said.

He picked up the phone and dialed.

"I'm sorry about dinner on Wednesday," he told Buck. "I'm sorry I got angry and I'm sorry I pushed you so damn hard. I want to make it up to you. Please, can you come over tonight? I'm making sirloin tips in a red wine gravy with baby potatoes, fresh celery, and pearl onions."

"Huh?" Buck grunted.

Guy sighed. Who was he trying to kid? "Stew."

"Oh! Well, all right, then. Sure."

The dinner had gone well. Guy congratulated himself on keeping his mouth shut for most of the meal, and had managed a smooth transition from the table to the sofa in the den for *Jerry*

Maguire on DVD. By the time Tom Cruise told Renée Zellweger she completed him, Guy had maneuvered Buck into his arms to snuggle for the rest of the film. Once the movie was over, Guy turned the TV off with the remote, plunging the room into near darkness, save for some soft light spilling from over the kitchen stove. Buck gently twisted himself around so they were both facing each other while stretched out along the length of the sofa. Buck undid one of Guy's shirt buttons and slipped his small hand inside to feel Guy's chest. This finally gave Guy the courage to speak.

"I want you," he whispered. "I want you in my arms, in my bed, and in my life. I've never said that to anyone before, so it probably sounds pretty stupid. But I can't help it. You make everything so easy, but difficult, too, at the same time. And even with that, all I know is that I want to be with you." He traced Buck's eyes with his fingers. "I love you, Buck," he murmured. "You said I wasn't ready the other night. You were right. You made me really take a look at myself, and I'm a mess. I'm afraid of so much and angry. I don't know what's going on in your life. For all I know you're HIV-positive, or an ex-criminal, or a meth addict, or God knows what else, and frankly, all of that scares me to death. But right now the one thing that scares me the most is losing you. So I'm ready to take on whatever you've got."

Buck kissed him. "Sweetheart, you don't know what you're asking for." Buck opened one of his shirt buttons and placed Guy's hand over his heart. "Feel that." Buck's heart was thumping so hard and fast that Guy's reaction was to pull away in alarm, but Buck held his hand there. "You don't know how much I'm risking here, either."

Guy's adrenaline began to pump, making him all the more frightened. "Okay, so we're both taking a big chance," he said, his voice quavering. "I'm putting it on the line here." He swallowed. "You?"

In response, Buck opened Guy's shirt and began gently gnawing on his nipple. As he did so, he unfastened the rest of the buttons and pulled the shirt out of his pants. Guy pulled his arms out of it, wriggling to be free of it. He opened Buck's shirt and rubbed his hands over the small, lean body, the lightly hairy chest, the petit waist with the lightly furry stomach.

Buck deftly unbuckled Guy's belt, and pulled at the top of the button fly, popping it open all the way down. He kissed his way down Guy's chest and torso. His hand found Guy's hard cock and pulled it out of his boxers. He licked the clear liquid at the tip of Guy's dick, then swallowed it down to the root. Guy let out a moan and allowed Buck to do as he wanted.

After a while Guy realized he was close to ejaculating so he pulled Buck's head up for several minutes of deep kissing. He wanted to make this man feel wonderful. He wanted to give him the kind of pleasure Buck was giving him. He kissed Buck's neck and continued down to that tantalizing tuft of hair that had caught his attention so many months ago. He munched on the sparse chest hair and nipped at Buck's abdomen, causing him to spasm in pleasure. Guy's tongue swirled around the fur below Buck's navel, going ever farther south in sensuously slurping circles until it came into contact with Buck's jeans. Since he was wearing no belt, all Guy had to do was pull on the snap to open it.

Abruptly, Buck stood up from the sofa. He was breathing hard. "This is it," he said.

Guy sat up, surprised but concerned, too. "What do you mean? What's wrong?"

"Now I don't know if I'm ready," he said.

Guy stood and took him in his arms. "Shhh," he said to his trembling partner, "it's okay."

"I should have told you before."

"What?" Buck took Guy's hand and placed it over his crotch. There was practically nothing there. Guy smiled. "I don't care," he said tenderly. "Size doesn't matter."

"You don't get it, Guy," Buck said flatly. "I'm a transsexual. Female-to-male."

Guy froze. Then he relaxed and laughed. "You are so full of shit! Not with all this fur, you're not. C'mere, you," he said as he shoved his hand down the front of Buck's jeans. But there was nothing. Only the hair-covered curve of groin going down and back between Buck's legs. Guy gasped. He pushed his hand farther and felt the unmistakable sensation of his middle finger brushing against a vagina. He yanked his hand back with a guttural cry. He gaped at Buck in open-mouthed shock. "Fucking Jesus!" he said, backing away.

"Don't be like that, I'm still the same person!"

Guy could only babble fragments, unable even to put together a simple sentence. "But, but you, you don't . . ." Guy sputtered, pointing at Buck's chest.

"I had them removed. Look," Buck said turning on a lamp for better light. Guy saw the thin horizontal six-inch scars a couple of inches below each nipple.

"But, but then why —" was all he could say, pointing at Buck's crotch.

"Because I don't want penis construction surgery and I couldn't afford it if I did."

Guy was leaning against the wall shaking his head. "I can't, this doesn't make any, this can't, we — no! I'm a gay man!"

"So am I!"

"A gay man with a vagina!? Gay men like dicks! And balls! We have a thing about vaginas!"

"What were you in love with?" Buck demanded. "A person? Or a cock? You never even saw my dick. You were in love with me."

"You were a man — I thought — I expected you to have a cock. It's like buying a house, you look at it you expect it to have a bathroom."

"Well, somebody needs to figure out their shit," Buck said, angrily putting his shirt back on, "because love, real love, has damned little to do with plumbing."

"Gimme a damn break," Guy said defensively. "I'm just trying to make some sense about this."

"What's there to make? I'm a transsexual and you can't handle it, end of story."

"Well, give me a chance! Jesus. Okay, okay, you used to be woman, were you a gay woman?"

"I was a miserable woman. I thought I might be a lesbian. That's why I want to Desert Springs. It took me years to figure it out, but I was a gay man."

"Okay, hold it," Guy said, putting his shirt back on. "A gay man in a woman's body is called a straight woman."

"You don't have a fucking clue, Guy. Everything my brain was telling me was that I was a man, but when I looked at my body, it felt like a lie. And until I figured that out and was able to do something about it, life was miserable for me and everyone I met."

"So, what did you do about it?" Guy asked, intrigued.

"Found a psychiatrist and transitioned."

"How?"

"Therapy, hormones, I had my breasts removed. The therapy and hormones alone took every cent I had. Forget any help from my family."

"Then . . . how did you pay for the breasts?"

"I was a four-day champion on *Jeopardy!*," Buck said proudly. "Despite everything, you always said I was smart. Turned out I was."

Guy felt an icy chill. His eyes narrowed. "When did I say that?"

"You still haven't put it together, Guy?" Buck asked. "I didn't take the name Buck until I transitioned. Before that I was Bucky. When I was a woman, you knew me as Becky. Your wife."

Guy staggered backward against the wall. The room tilted like a fun house, it seemed to spin, making him nauseated. Time bent like rubber and giddy colors swirled madly. "No. No," he said, his mind grasping hopelessly for any kind of logic or reason. "No, no, no, no, no!" he shouted as he ran out of the room. He bolted through the living room and out the front door. He couldn't think. He needed air. And to get away. He desperately needed something to make sense, but it had all been wiped away. *Just keep going,* he told himself, increasing the pace to keep the panic at his heels from overwhelming him. An hour later he realized he was barefoot.

By the time he returned home, Buck was gone.

Sunday, February 18th

"That is the most unlikely, fucked-up thing I've ever heard," Patrick said in awe of Guy's story. "God, I love this town!"

"I don't know what to do," Guy said, still too upset to touch his breakfast pasta at Hugo's. "I don't know what to think. I don't even know what I want anymore. Everything I thought I knew is wrong."

"Maybe it's not wrong," Patrick offered, "just different. Terra incognita is always scary."

"He's called me, I mean she's called . . . shit, I don't even know what pronoun to use. Buck has called twice. I can't pick up the phone; I don't know what to say to her. Him. Shit, I'm falling apart. It's like I had this idea about what reality was and what I thought, and it just all blew up."

"You know," Patrick said, "if you were Parsifal, this is the kind of thing that would be considered a call to adventure."

"What the hell are you talking about?"

"When the hero's world is shaken to its core, that's when he has to take his journey. And the journey is how the hero finds himself."

"You want me to take a journey?" Guy asked.

"Like the character in Sarah's movie. Remember? The one she based on Parsifal? Oh! Which she sold, by the way, to a Japanese distributor. How cool is that! They're going to dub it and release it in Tokyo. I'm literally going to be big in Japan!"

"Hello! My crisis?"

"Sorry. I'm just saying this could be the beginning of a whole big new life adventure for you."

"Whoop-dee-fucking-do. And what am I supposed to find on this adventure?"

"The Holy Grail, of course, which is, essentially, yourself."

"Well, that sucks," Guy snorted. "I'm not wild about myself, never have been."

"Oh, but you will be when you meet the Grail King," Patrick assured him.

"And how will I know him when I meet him?"

"Because then you'll like yourself."

Guy looked at him cynically. "You learned this crap at some homo camp?"

"More or less. It was called the West Hollywood Public Library. If you weren't so busy being opinionated while knowing nothing, you might learn this stuff has been around for hundreds of years. There's a reason people keep going back to it, you know."

Guy laid his head on the table in defeat. "Okay, you're right, I apologize," he said into the table. "I don't know what I'm saying." He sat back up and took a deep breath to clear his head. "Does this Parsifal shit tell me what to think or do about Buck?"

"No, but what you do with Buck will tell you about yourself, Grasshopper. That's the journey."

Monday, February 19th

Just before leaving IMPAT, Bob Davis called his stepson's number. When the phone picked up at the other end, Bob was shocked to hear Roger crying in low guttural noises like a wounded animal. "Roger, are you all right?" Clearly Roger was not. He sobbed on and on. "Roger! Talk to me, are you hurt?" Bob begged.

But all he could make out was a final drawn out pathetic cry of, "Daddyyy!" before the call broke off.

Bob was frightened. He realized he didn't even know where his stepson lived. He rummaged frantically through his Rolodex. Nothing. Shit! Who could he call? His wife Betty wouldn't know. Fuck! Who, then? Diaz! He'd had Rudy Diaz take that car back there from the hospital. He quickly called his office assistant.

"Hello?"

"Diaz, you remember where you took my stepson's car when I had you pick it up from Hollywood Presbyterian Hospital? Back in August, I think?"

Rudy wasn't happy to be getting this call. It was 5:30 and he was driving himself and Eric home in their new used Corolla. "Yeah," he sighed. "I remember."

"I need you to take me over there right now."
"What, in my car, Mr. Davies?"
"Yes, it's an emergency! Where are you?"
"Now? Like, Wilshire and almost Fairfax."
"Turn around. I'll be waiting out front. And thanks."

Rudy flipped his phone shut, frowning. If they were picking him up out front in their modest little car, it really must be an emergency.

"What's that about?" Eric asked.

"Hell if I know," Rudy replied pulling into a McDonald's to turn around and head back to Beverly Hills. "But looks like our workday isn't over."

☆

"What are we watching on DVD tonight?" Patrick asked as Guy let him into his house. "*The Crying Game*?"

"Very funny," Guy said humorlessly. "At least Jaye Davidson had a dick. No, tonight it's *Life Is Beautiful*, and any time Roberto Benigni does something precious we have to take a drink."

"You realize we're risking alcohol poisoning?"

"Risking? I'm counting on it," Guy answered. His telephone rang.

Patrick shouted after him, "Maybe this is the same drinking game the Institute was playing when they voted Benigni the Arthur over Ian McKellen."

Guy appreciated Patrick for giving him the first smile he'd had all day as he picked up the phone. "Hello?" His smile vanished as he heard a familiar voice bawling on the other end of the line. "Who is this?" he asked as he struggled to place the voice.

But there was only weeping, until finally, a moan for help, "Guyyyy!"

He knew instantly. Guy quickly fumbled through the notes on the kitchen counter where Roger had left his address. "Roger, where are you? Are you at home?" There was a keening sound Guy decided was an affirmative. He found the address. "Stay there, Roger. I'm on the way."

✧

When Guy and Patrick arrived at Roger's house, they found Bob, Eric, and Rudy already there.

"What are you doing here?" Eric and Patrick asked each other at the same time.

Guy wondered the same thing, but remained focused, saying only, "Where is he?"

"In there," Rudy said, pointing into the living room.

At that moment, a worried Bob Davies came from the living room to see two new strangers in the house. Bob was the only person Guy didn't recognize. "Who are you?"

"Roger's father," Bob said. "You?"

"Friend. What's going on?" Bob explained how Roger was holed up in the living room closet, crying, and refusing to come out. "Can I see him?" Guy asked.

Bob led Guy into the chilly living room. Like the rest of the house it was empty of furniture and their footsteps echoed against the wooden floor. Guy heard Roger whimpering in the closet, the door barely ajar. Bob pulled the closet door open far enough to stick his head in. "Roger, there's a friend of yours here. Don't you want to come out and see him?"

"Huh-uh," Roger managed to say through his tears from inside the dark cubicle.

"Come on, Roger," Bob pleaded. "Put the ball down and come on out. Please."

"No," he moaned, sniffing back the snot. "I can't!"

Bob turned to Guy. "He's got a beachball that he won't give up and he won't stop crying. Is there anything, anything at all you can do?" he begged.

"I don't know," Guy admitted. He opened the closet door fully. There was Roger in the same jeans and gray plaid flannel shirt as the other day. He hadn't shaved and judging from the smell, he hadn't bathed either. He was sitting cross-legged on the floor, hunched over a medium-sized red, blue, and orange beachball which he was hugging, rocking back and forth, sadly sort of bouncing on it. "Hi, Roger," Guy said softly. "Hey, I thought you said you were gonna be okay."

Without looking up, Roger gave a painful shrug. "I was wrong," he whispered.

"Yeah, I see," Guy said. "Can I sit down with you?" There was no response, so Guy sat cross-legged on the floor in the doorway. "You know you can't stay in here forever, don't you?" Roger shrugged again and turned his head away. Guy reached out and rubbed Roger's shoulder. "Sweetheart, you're gonna have to come out sometime."

"No!" Roger said sharply, jerking his shoulder away from Guy's touch. "I'm staying in here."

"Okay. I'll stay here with you, then. Is that all right?" Nothing. "Can you give me your hand, Roger?" Again, no response, but at least the crying had abated. Guy again reached out to touch the beachball. "Can you give me the ball?"

"*No!*" Roger shouted, and he struggled to scramble farther away, angrily protecting the beachball. "This is mine! You keep away!"

"He won't give up that damned ball," Bob explained to Guy. "I've tried for half an hour."

Guy shifted position to sit back on his knees facing Roger. "I promise I'm not going to take your ball," he told Roger. "But I'd really like for you to talk to me. Can you help me understand why you're doing this?"

"This is all I have," Roger said simply, his fingers caressing the beachball. He laid his cheek against it and closed his eyes as quiet tears began to flow again. "This is everything."

"I don't understand, Roger," Guy said. "What is everything?"

"This," Roger said, crying softly. "Last summer Dave and I were going to the beach. Stuff happened. We never made it to there."

"That's just a memory, Roger. You don't have to hold on to that. You can let the ball go."

"No, I can't," Roger said, squeezing it tightly. "You don't understand." He lifted his head and for the first time looked directly at Guy. "Dave blew it up. This is his breath."

"Oh, honey," Guy whispered, reverently stroking the ball with the back of his fingers. "I can't imagine how painful this must be. But, but maybe it's also a gift."

Roger looked at him quizzically. "How?"

Guy had no idea. "It's . . . a kind of . . . terra incognita." He struggled with the concept. "What if this was a call to adventure? To a new part of your life?"

"How?" Roger repeated.

"I don't know," Guy admitted, shifting uncomfortably. "But what else could he have left you that would have been half so intimate? What else could he have left behind so beautiful, or painful, or priceless?" Guy let Roger take a minute or two to think about that. Surprising himself, it was starting to make sense to Guy. "You know, Roger, when we get a gift, especially a gift beyond value, I think it's important that we give a gift back."

Roger appeared very uncertain about that. "What could I possibly give him?"

"Well, first I think you should thank him," Guy said, working it through as he spoke. "Then celebrate him. And then let him go."

"I don't think I can do that," Roger demurred. "I'm too scared."

"That's okay," Guy told him, smiling kindly. "I brought friends. We can be your strength. We'll help you celebrate. And we'll help you let Dave go."

A short time later, Bob called Rudy, Eric, and Patrick into the living room. Guy was sitting next to Roger near the center of the room on the floor. The orange, red, and blue beachball was sitting a foot or so in front of him. The setting sun sent shafts of dappled orange light into the room.

Guy instructed everyone to sit on the floor in a circle. When they were in place, Guy explained how they were going to help. Patrick, Rudy, and Eric looked at each other in apprehension. Bob looked confused, but he was willing to go along with this person who seemed to be helping his stepson's crisis.

Guy turned to Roger. "Are you ready?"

"Yes."

There was grave silence in the room. Guy opened the plug on the inflation nozzle. There was a tiny whoosh of air escaping, but he immediately put his lips around the inch-long nozzle. Guy inhaled deliberately deep and long. When he was full, he pinched the nozzle closed to keep the rest of the air inside. He closed his eyes and ritualistically blew his lungful of Dave's breath into the center of the circle. After he had exhaled completely, he paused for a moment, and then passed the ball to Roger on his right.

Roger calmly took the beachball, pinching the nozzle as Guy released it to him. He brought it to his mouth, drew in a great breath, and pinched the nozzle closed. As Guy had done, he released Dave's breath to the center of the circle. A tear fell down his face. He passed the ball to his stepfather on his right.

Bob took his breath uneasily and exhaled into the center. He passed the ball to Rudy. Rudy did the same, passing the now only partially filled plastic ball to Eric. When Eric was done, he gave it to Patrick. From Patrick, back to Guy, and so on around a second time.

Bob noticed Roger watching it go around the circle of friends. Roger had tear tracks down his face, but he was smiling slightly, even though his mouth was quivering.

Patrick handed the almost empty ball to Guy. Guy didn't take a breath, but offered it to Roger saying, "I think there's only one more left."

Roger took it from Guy, and pulled as much air out of it as he could. It made a crinkling sound as the plastic folded in on itself. With the last breath that Dave had left him, Roger said simply, "I love you. Goodbye."

Tuesday, February 20th

Rudy and Eric had been profoundly affected by their experience with Roger and the others the previous night. After getting home they made love with an urgency and passion like when they were first together. They'd talked well into the morning about long-term plans, life insurance, wills, Eric's dream of purchasing a house together, Rudy's desire to raise children. They even made a commitment to go to the clinic together and get tested for HIV. Then they'd made love again. So this morning, when Bob Davies called Rudy into his office, Rudy hoped it wasn't for anything complicated because he was operating on only about an hour and a half's worth of sleep.

"Shut the door, Diaz," Bob said when Rudy entered the office. "Take a seat." Rudy did, on the loveseat. Bob rose from his desk and came to sit across from Rudy in one of the guest chairs. "I want to thank you for helping me out last night," he said. "It gave me a lot to think about. And I need to make some changes. Especially my, um, outside activities. When you started here, we had an agreement. But I think it's time we terminate that agreement."

"Are you firing me?" Rudy asked incredulously.

"God, no! You keep this operation running; everybody loves you. I'm saying I want to move our relationship into a different phase. One that's strictly professional."

"So, no more 'long drives out to Malibu' or 'special lunchtime office visits'?"

"You got it. But there's still a place for someone I can trust implicitly, so I'm making you my personal assistant, if you'd like it. You'll be working alongside my secretary, Doris, and it comes with a nice salary bump. The only problem is going to be finding someone to replace you on computer."

All of the plans from the previous night jumped into Rudy's mind. "How about if I train someone already here?" he asked. "How about if I trained Eric Burgess?"

"Who?"

"He was there last night. Works in the garage? Took care of things when Margaret Atherton died? He's my partner. In fact," Rudy said, suddenly awake, "if you gave us a computer, I could train him at home."

Guy stood beside his koi pond, skimmer in hand. He hadn't moved for almost ten minutes as he went over and over what had happened the night before. He couldn't imagine how Roger, in the space of only a few months, had fallen in love to the point of a kind of madness. Is that how love is? Guy wondered. It seemed terrible, like coming too close to a blast furnace or passing the event horizon of a black hole. It was an all-consuming, no-turning-back, leap into the Land of No Control Whatsoever. *If love didn't care about fuck films, why should it care about having a penis or a vagina? Or more importantly, a past?* Guy shifted his weight, wondering, *But how far can a person bend?*

"What time is it?" a groggy Roger called out from the sliding door to the patio.

"After lunch. How do you feel?"

"A lot better."

"That's why God made Valium. So how much do you know about computers?"

"Some."

"Well, get some coffee and something to eat," Guy said. "Then I'm gonna show you how to post stuff on eBay. You need to earn your keep if you're going to stay here."

After the experience at Roger's last night, Patrick, too, had had trouble sleeping. All this morning at work, he had been agitated and disturbed. Finally, he made a decision and left O'Leary & Finkelstein's in the middle of the afternoon. He drove to West Hollywood and found a rare parking space on the street. He walked the block and a half to the MCC church and entered. He sat in the back, nauseated from the terror, for half an hour or so. Finally, he knew he had to do this, so he gathered his courage and walked resolutely to the front of the meeting.

"My name is Patrick," he said, trembling before the group. "And I'm an alcoholic."

Thursday, March 1st
Twenty-five days before the Awards telecast

"Where are we going?" Ezra asked. They had been driving in the Angeles Crest Mountains for over an hour.

"I don't know yet," Michael replied, the large Baggie on his lap once again filled with what remained of his mother's ashes.

Ezra decided since this was Michael's birthday wish, he'd just give over to whatever Michael had in mind, and kept driving.

"Here," Michael said suddenly. "This feels right."

Ezra pulled to the side and parked his Neon in a turnout. "Okay, what now?"

"We walk." They got out of the car. Ezra followed Michael into the underbrush. Every so often Michael would stop, as if receiving instructions from space, and then change directions. They had trudged steeply downhill and were now headed uphill, breathing heavily from the exertion. Near the top of the crest they came upon a natural hollow. When he saw it, Michael smiled. "This is it."

There was a cleared area of white sand in the center. Michael dropped to his knees, inviting Ezra to do the same. He tore a hole in a corner of the plastic Baggie and began carefully sprinkling the ashes, which really looked more like gray-brown sand, in a neat circle. Then he pulled out his shred of the mandala Patrick had given him. Ezra recognized it immediately from the Gathering he'd attended.

"Mandala is Sanskrit for circle," Michael explained. "I looked it up at the library. And even though it's Buddhist, a circle's also a symbol for God who has no beginning and no end. So I'm making it into a Christian prayer. A prayer made of sand and my mother." His brow wrinkled in concentration as he delicately poured four crosses inside the circle. "And when it's done, it'll be blown away by the wind. Mother will be gone. And once again pure." He folded the scrap of mandala cloth, laying it in the very center of the circle. He poured a simple childlike valentine-shaped heart over it with the last of his mother's remains.

Michael leaned back on his knees. The two of them sat there in silence, broken only by the wind rustling through the surrounding brush, or the occasional piercing cry of a distant bird. At last Michael stood. "I think I'm done."

At that moment a gust of wind dipped into the hollow, blowing the sandy ashes up the side and off into the mountains. "There it goes!" Ezra cried. He grabbed Michael's hand and they both run up the side of the hollow, laughing. Standing at the top of the rim they were able to see the grains of sand carried away into the magnificence of the mountains. Michael put his arm around Ezra tentatively. He felt content and at peace.

That night Michael had the dream again. He was in a house that was floating, but not on blood this time. It was floating on the ocean. Clear, blue, and pure. The house pitched forward and the water came inside washing everything away. Michael had to fight to keep from being swept out into the open sea. He clawed at a doorway, hanging on for his life as he saw the water take all the old furniture, kitchen cabinets, carpeting, appliances, the medicine cabinet, everything. Then the water receded. There was a lurch as the house ran aground. Michael looked out a window. The house was on the shore of a beautiful pristine beach. He went to the front door, which had been ripped away by the force of the water. Standing in the doorway he felt the pleasant heat rising off the pinkish sand. There were people on a distant hill, waving, happy to see him.

And for the first time, he stepped out of the house.

Friday, March 2nd
Twenty-three days before the Awards telecast

"Everything's in here," Bob Davies said, sliding a report across his desk toward Big Ed. "I think you'll be satisfied."

"I sometimes don't like to read," Ed said. "Can you preview it for me?"

"Beyond getting your songs nominated," Bob told him with some pride, "I'm making progress at the other guilds and unions. Wining and dining key people, wooing the influential."

"Sucking up," Ed said nodding sagely. "That's good."

"On page 12 there's a list of people who are, shall we say, independent, resistant."

"Problems," Ed growled darkly.

"Possible problems. Where I know or have learned of vices and secrets, they are included in detail next to the names."

Ed grinned. This was a good team player. Ed was so happy as he left that he actually whistled a tune. Driving up Wilshire he sang along with the radio, his heart light at the thought of how his father was going to be truly proud of him at last.

The excitement was building for him. It was time to visit Hiro to kick things up a notch on his end of things.

Jimmy B came into Hiro Yamamoto's office and flinched at seeing Big Ed there. "You, uh, you wanted to see me?"

"Yes," Hiro said. "I've kept Mr. DeLello here apprised of how you've been creating a computer history of inappropriate websites Mr. Finkelstein has visited and downloaded."

"Kiddie porn," Big Ed said appreciatively to Jimmy B, smiling. "You'll go far."

Jimmy B managed only a small grunt. He reminded himself, *This is for Marcos.*

"The beauty of it is the partners would never report it," Hiro added. "The scandal would be too terrible. It was a wise choice."

"I'm glad you approve," Jimmy B said, trying to mask how trapped he felt.

"It's great," Big Ed assured him. "The thing is, Jimmy, now we need to bring it home. We need to make this whole thing blow up by the end of next week. We need a, whadja call it —?"

"Coup de grace," Hiro said.

"That's it. It's French for *shit hitting the fan*. Can you do that, Jimmy?"

Wednesday, March 7th
Eighteen days before the Awards telecast

Word of Finkelstein's call into the PrattswaterfordDouglas boardroom, the exchange of angry voices, vehement denials, and finally security guards escorting him from the property made for delirious, white-hot gossip. Hiro was curious to know how the news was filtering down. He approached his secretary. "Jenean, do you know what's going on?"

"Oh, Mr. Yamamoto!" she breathed, aghast in melodramatic horror. "It started yesterday around 4:30 when Mr. Finkelstein's secretary, Linda, opened a package addressed to him just like normal. And would you believe it? It was —" she looked around to make sure no one else would hear her say the vile words — "child pornography!" she whispered in indignation. "A whole box of it. Pictures, magazines, videos! She took it all straight to Mr. Wood's office."

Mr. Wood was the CEO. Hiro needed to know how it was received. "But this is Mel Finkelstein. Mr. Wood had to know it was someone playing a hoax."

"Yeah, that's what he thought, but he asked I.T. to check it out, you know, just to be sure. They found a whole history of visits to those kinds of websites — from his office computer!"

"No, I don't believe that. Wouldn't Mel be too smart to do that?"

Jenean shook her head tartly. "I think when you're that sick, it's a compulsion. I saw it on *48 Hours* and *20/20*, that kind can't help themselves. It's never the people you'd think. I tell you, Linda's just a wreck. She's got two kids and she is freaked."

Hiro made appropriately sad noises and withdrew back into his office. He paged Jimmy B.

Five minutes later Jimmy, looking worn and distraught, was at his office door. "Something wrong, Mr. Yamamoto?"

"Come in and shut the door, please." He watched as Jimmy obeyed.

"Mr. Finkelstein didn't deserve this," Jimmy said quietly, unable to look up. "I've been throwing up since yesterday. I feel like scum."

"No one will ever know."

"I'll know, okay?" Jimmy shot back at him. "God, there are three more packages on the way."

"You're very thorough. But I meant it as a question. No one will ever know, right?"

Jimmy B gave him an ironic look and laughed without humor. "Are you kidding? They put me in charge of the investigation. And it's strictly internal. So, no. You got what you wanted." His distaste was evident. "I'd like to go now."

Hiro snapped open his briefcase, turning it first so Jimmy wouldn't see the Arthur, as always, nestled inside. He removed an envelope and shut the briefcase. "This is for you," he said, proffering the envelope.

Jimmy narrowed his eyes. "What is it?"

"Five thousand dollars and a lesbian couple."

"What?"

"The names of two women. One American and her lover, Wendy, who is here illegally from South Africa. A situation much like yours and your illegal Guatemalan partner's. Contact them. If you marry her illegal partner and she marries yours, they become citizens. You can solve each other's problem."

Jimmy B blinked, struggling with distrust and fear, as to what he should do. All of it was overshadowed by his deep desire to end his lover's ordeal. Marcos could stay in the U.S. No more running and hiding. But like this? The nausea returned.

"Try not to let it bother you," Hiro told Jimmy. "It's just luck. Very bad for Finkelstein, but good for you."

Like a man receiving thirty pieces of silver, Jimmy took the envelope.

Thursday, March 8th
Seventeen days before the Awards telecast

"Hey, hon," Eric called out from the kitchen of their new apartment when he heard the front door open. "How's your pretty new niece?"

"She's fine," Rudy said darkly, slamming the door in the other room.

This brought Eric out of the kitchen. "Okay. What's up?"

"You know those guys who wait on the corner for jobs?"

"The day laborers?"

Rudy nodded. "*Jornaleros*. My brother, Mateo, he's been out of work for a while so he's been out there, too. He says there's some Anglo shit who'll pick up a guy for work, only he doesn't have work. He takes him to a hotel, ties him up, and rapes him."

"Oh, my God. They should go to the police!"

Rudy's laugh was ugly, mirthless. "Police? These are 'illegals,' Eric, they got no rights. INS will just send 'em back to Mexico. Families, too, if they can find them." Rudy paced around the living room, agitated and upset. "Whoever goes off in that black pickup of his, they're never seen again there. Maybe they show up somewhere else, but you can see the disgrace in them." He stopped his pacing. "But last week, an eighteen-year-old kid from Oaxaca killed himself over it."

"We can't just let this guy keep doing this. Isn't there anything anybody can do?"

It was the question that would keep Rudy awake all that night.

The next morning he called his brother with a plan.

Friday, March 9th
Sixteen days before the Awards telecast

Eric stuck his head into Rudy's new office. His partner had his back to the door.

"Look, you," Rudy barked into the headset receiver. "Tom Hanks is the host, I don't care if he wants the Taj Mahal back there. You find a way to fit it behind the Shrine close enough to the stage where he can make his changes or we'll contract with a company that can, got it?" He punched a button on his phone disconnecting the call.

"Ooh," Eric said. "Bad day?"

"Are you kidding?" Rudy grinned. "It's fantastic! All my life I've had the shit jobs, now I get to make other people's lives shit. Oh, damn," he said, adding a note to an already filled yellow pad. "That reminds me, gotta beef up Security. You know there's someone threatening to kidnap Russell Crowe?"

"Yeah, the suspects are every straight women and gay man in town. He was a hottie in *Gladiator*."

"Not as hot as you. What's up?"

"Guy and Patrick want to know if we want to go to Ojai with them tomorrow."

Rudy's demeanor darkened. "No. I can't. But why don't you go? There's some business I really need to finish here in L.A."

Saturday, March 10th
Fifteen days before the Awards telecast

Rudy was standing on the corner of Beverly and La Jolla with his brother Mateo and about fifteen other *jornaleros*. Mateo had handpicked five men he could trust for this job, and let Rudy explain the plan to them.

Rudy was wearing his tightest jeans and a ribbed form-fitting tank top. He made sure he was near the front of the men so when that fucker in the black pickup came by he could be clearly seen. But it was a slow morning for a Saturday. Waiting out here was boring, tense, and frustrating all at once. His adrenaline was pumping, but there was nothing he could do with it.

Then the black Ford F-250 slowed in front of the men. Petey leaned over toward the passenger window to inspect the meat and select a victim. "Uno," he said, and pointed at a kid barely twenty.

The unwitting kid started toward the truck. Mateo grabbed him by the belt, from behind. Rudy ran forward with the biggest grin he could muster and clambered into the bed of the truck. He wondered if the Anglo would accept him instead of the kid. The guy was glaring at Rudy through the back window.

"*¡Yo soy el uno!*" Rudy said, forcing a big, hearty laugh and nodding his head. "*¡Yo soy el uno, vámanos!*"

Petey looked at the kid he'd first wanted, then back at Rudy in his truck. *Well, ain't this Paco a pushy little wetback*, Petey thought as he scowled at this guy. *You wanna come with me?* he thought, *fine*. Petey hit the gas.

Rolling away, Rudy watched Mateo and the others scramble to get around the corner where the Corolla was parked. A moment later he saw it lurch into traffic. Rudy was trembling, but so far, so good. He just hoped like hell Mateo could keep up with the truck.

Everything depended on that.

Monday, March 12th
Thirteen days before the Awards telecast

"Armor-All on the tires, señor?"

"Sí," Big Ed told the sturdy Latino attendant at the WeHo Car Wash on Santa Monica. "And no spray wax, I know that's a ripoff." He got a check slip from the man and headed inside to pay. His cell phone rang.

"This is Ed."

"What the fuck happened to Petey?"

"Pop! How are you? How's Mom?"

"Fuck your mother. Petey's dead. Tell me you knew that."

"What? No!"

"In some fleabag motel tied to a bed with rope around his neck, *idiòta!*"

This was a huge problem. How was he going to collect debts? But something else was fishy. "Pop, how'd you know about it before I did?"

There was a hesitation on the other end. Then his father shouted back, "Because I pay attention to what I'm fucking doing which is more than I can say for you."

"And just what is it you're doing, Pop?"

Again that hesitation. Then, "Me and Petey were friendly, okay? He kept me abreast of how things were going with your Arthur scheme."

Big Ed was crushed. "He told you? Aw, Pop, I wanted it to be a surprise."

"Two things I don't like: surprises and bein' made a fool of. I suggest you get your shit together and know if the people working for you are alive or dead. Jesus, Eddie, try not to be a bigger embarrassment to me than you already are." He hung up on his son.

Ed tried to piece together what the hell was going on. Why was Petey telling Ed's father about his Arthur plans? And they were friendly? His father and a known gay guy?

Oh, fuck it, Ed thought. *When all this goes down he's going to change his tune.* He'd see just how smart his son was and finally be proud of him.

Tuesday, March 13th
Twelve days before the Awards telecast

"Good God, what is your problem?" Guy asked a frantically fidgety Patrick.

"It's my partner's son. He got himself fired," Patrick told Guy as he nervously fingered his tall glass of orange juice. "God knows what he did, it's all hush-hush so you know it's juicy. But the problem is Finkelstein gave him a job going over my books."

"At the mortuary? I thought they were silent partners," Guy said, sorting through a small box of antique netsuke he'd bought for twenty bucks.

"'Were' is the operative word," Patrick responded darkly, and chugged the juice. "Ugh," he said with a grimace. Sobriety had taught him orange juice was intolerable without vodka. He shouted to Roger who was in the kitchen cleaning. "Can you hit me with something a lot less healthy?"

"Diet Coke?" Roger suggested.

"Caffeine and aspartame," he muttered, his brittle façade at the breaking point. "The jitters and early Alzheimer's. Perfect."

"So you've got a new accountant on the payroll," Guy mused, "so what?"

"It's not just some junior bean counter, all right? He was VP at PrattswaterfordDouglas, for God's sake. One of the guys they schlep on at the Arthurs."

Guy was impressed. "Really?"

"Yes! So he's a very bitter, resentful man right now. And I think he's taking it out on my books."

"What do you care? You haven't done anything illegal." Guy paused and looked up at him. "Have you?"

In response, Patrick snapped over his shoulder toward the kitchen. "Are you coming with that fucking Coke, or what!"

"Oh, my God," Guy said, alarmed at Patrick's outburst. "Just how bad is it?"

"Sorry," Patrick said to Roger as he arrived with his Coke. "I can't talk about it. If I told you it might make you an accessory."

"'Nuff said," Guy declared, holding his hands up to show he wished to know no more. "So, that's it for Finkelstein at the Arthurs, huh?"

"Fuck him," his anxious friend sniffed. "We don't get to go, why should he?"

"Why, Patrick! All those years of petty, snotty toasts to the Arthur accountants, you were jealous!"

"Oh, like you weren't," Patrick shot back. "What self-respecting faggot wouldn't give his left nut to be at the Institute Awards? Well, other than Buck, of course, who never had any nuts."

"Patrick . . ." Guy warned with a threatening look.

"I'm just saying you want to be there as bad as I do, and you know it's true."

"Okay, I admit it," Guy said returning to his netsuke figures. "God, can you imagine actually being there, being part of it all? Sure, I've wanted it all my life, but let's face it, it ain't gonna happen. Which is just as well because I make regular and frequent use of my left nut."

"Didn't Daniel Day-Lewis win an Arthur for that?" Patrick asked.

"I think that was *My Left Foot.*"

Roger smiled and left Patrick and Guy talking in the den to go into Guy's office where he was staying these days. He picked up the phone and dialed.

"Dad? It's me. I've got a favor to ask."

Friday, March 16th
Nine days before the Awards telecast

"Why am I here again?" Patrick whispered to Guy across the remains of splendid dinner at Guy's house.

"Hell if I know. This is all Roger's doing," Guy whispered back as Roger brought two cups of after-dinner coffee to the table. Guy couldn't stand it any longer. "All right, already, you want to tell us what this is about?"

"I wondered when you were going to crack," Roger grinned. He leaned in and with a mysterious tone asked, "What is the one thing you've always wanted to do?"

"The Nazi kid in *Sound of Music,*" Guy said.

"Sorry," Roger informed him. "But I hope this is the next best thing." He stood at the head of the table to make his announcement. "Guy. Patrick. You are going to the Institute Awards."

"Get out!" Guy snorted in disbelief.

"No, it's for real. I called my stepfather at the Institute and arranged it. I got confirmation yesterday. I wanted to tell you both together. You are going to be seat-fillers for the Arthur telecast."

"Oh, my God!" Patrick squealed. He leaped to his feet and jumped up and down. "Oh, my God!" he screamed. "We're going to the fucking Arthurs!"

Guy was stunned. "How? What did —? Why?"

It was the first time Guy saw Roger laugh out loud. "Because I could, Guy. Because the other day you two were talking about how much you always wanted it." Roger became more serious. "But mainly because you let me know it was okay to be a sad fucked-up wreck," Roger told him. "And you didn't try to fix me, you just came out of nowhere when I needed a safe place."

Guy was speechless.

"Oh! And there's one more thing," Roger said, grabbing hold of Patrick to get his attention. "There are four positions to be filled," he added smiling broadly, "so choose carefully, but you can each pick one more person to fill seats with you."

"Oh, my God, just one?" Patrick asked, agog. "That gives me dozens of people to snub! Oh, do I love you!" He kissed Roger and hugged him. "Who are you gonna take, Guy?" he said releasing Roger.

"I don't know," Guy said wiping his eyes. "Maybe Eric."

Roger shook his head. "He's an employee so he's already seat-filling."

Oh!" Patrick exclaimed, smacking his hand against his forehead. "Of course! You have to take Buck!"

Guy glowered at him. "Not funny."

"Not joking. Take him, Guy."

"It's been a month, Patrick, he won't take my calls. I get the message."

Patrick's giddiness subsided as he considered that for a moment. "It doesn't matter. Find a way. Because, Guy, if you don't ask him, you're a fool."

☆

After the table had been cleared, the dishes washed, and Clint Eastwood's *Unforgiven* viewed, rewound, and ejected, Guy was ready to go to bed. "Good night, Roger," he said putting the video back on the shelf. "And thanks again for getting us into the Arthurs."

"It felt good to be able to do it. I feel like I've been such a fuckup for so long, it was good to finally be able to do something right. To give back something."

"Believe me," Guy said, surprised to find himself so emotional, "I got the better deal." Roger hugged him and Guy began to cry. "Oh, shit. I don't know what all this mushy stuff is about," he said wiping the tears away and collecting himself. "But do me a favor. Don't call yourself that. Loving Dave as hard as you did was no fuckup."

Roger kissed him on the cheek. "Thank you."

"No, thank you." And he gave Roger a sweet peck on the mouth. Roger held his gaze as Guy pulled back from his kiss. They stood there in the embrace, in the tension of eye-to-eye closeness, feeling each other's breath on their faces. Finally, Roger leaned in and kissed Guy full on the lips. Guy kissed him back, feeling Roger's warm mouth open to receive it. *Oh, this is not at all smart,* Guy thought.

But he wasn't about to stop.

Saturday, March 17th
Eight days before the Awards telecast

At the mortuary, Patrick looked in on Mel Finkelstein. "Morning! Get you anything?" His partner's disgraced son looked up from the 1989 accounting books with a sullen glower. That couldn't be good. "Something wrong?"

"Irregularity," he growled.

"Oh, honey," Patrick commiserated. "Would you like a bran muffin?"

"In the books," Finkelstein said through clenched teeth.

Patrick became defensive. "I told your father I was a mortician, not an accountant."

"I'm going to need to look at 1985 through last year."

"Fine. I'll have Lee get them for you." Retreating to the safety of his office Patrick wished to hell he could have a drink. Instead he called Lee.

"'Sup, boss?" she said as she entered.

"First of all, Finkelstein needs the books from '85 to present. Please see that he gets them. Second of all, how would you like to go to the Arthurs with me?" Patrick explained how the seat-filling job had come about.

"I'm sorry, Mr. O'Leary, I wish I could, but I can't. I'm going out of town that weekend. I'm getting married."

"You're dragging someone to Vermont?"

"Nope, closer. I'm taking my girlfriend Wendy to Vegas. We'll get married, and see us some Cirque du Soleil."

Patrick was having difficulty processing this. "Okay, I could be wrong, but I believe same-sex marriage is illegal, even in Vegas."

"That's why we're marrying us some men. Gay men. See, Wendy's from South Africa on an expired visa, but if she marries an American she can stay, no problem. We got hooked up with some guys with the same deal, only one's from Central America. I marry Guatemala boy, and she marries his American partner, and we all drink a big fuck-you toast to Immigration."

"And go see Cirque du Soleil."

"That's right," Lee laughed. "So I really appreciate you asking, boss, I do. But I can't go to the Arthurs. Anything else?" Patrick shook his head no. "Okay, I'll get those books to Finkelstein right away," Lee said walking toward the door.

"Get him a bran muffin, too." Lee looked at him quizzically. Patrick shrugged. "It couldn't hurt."

After hanging up from talking with Patrick, Suze was so excited and thrilled to be attending the Arthurs that she no longer minded having to work on a hectic Saturday. She was in because with only a week to go until the telecast, there were caterers looking for staff, limo companies desperate for drivers, delivery companies demanding messengers for gifts, studios frantically sending out their own fruit baskets and thousand-dollar tchotchkes to nominees and their production companies, and all of these positions needed to be staffed immediately.

The phone rang. "Star Temps," she chirped.

It was Midge, one of Suze's clients, the people who assemble the multi-thousand-dollar bags of swag that go to the stars at the telecast. "We've got 125 first-tier bags, 150 second-tier, and 197 third-tier gift bags that all have to be redone from scratch," Midge explained to Suze. "Those bastards at Bulgari are switching items on me, Fred Segal's pulling out of the third-tier but upping their first-tier, Perugina chocolate's behind on their Arthur edition, Petrossian's coming in with beluga but that can't happen until day-of, and there's some kind of pissing contest going on between Louis Vuitton and fucking Fendi. I need the guy, Suze, you gotta send me the guy."

"Absolutely, Midge. Which guy?"

"The guy! The one you sent us for the Golden Globes and People's Choice. The one who's a little nuts but he can count like a motherfucker."

"Thom?"

"Yes! Save my sanity as well as my doughy white ass and send him, *stat!*"

That afternoon Guy was looking for a parking place in an unfamiliar part of Hollywood below Sunset, an area packed with apartment buildings jostling for space among the few remaining bungalows. Once parked on Cherokee, he turned the motor off and took out his brand new phone. He dialed the number he'd called from his home phone a dozen times in the last month.

"Hello."

Guy pleaded quickly, "Please don't hang up, Buck, it's me."

"Aw, shit," Buck grunted.

"Come on, Buck, I got a cell phone just so your caller ID wouldn't recognize the number," he said, getting out of his car.

"Well, I've got it now so tell me what you want 'cause I'm not answering this number again."

"Come to the Arthur Awards with me."

"Bleachers on the red carpet?" Buck snorted. "Fuck that."

"No, inside. The real deal, sitting with the stars." Guy listened to Buck's very long silence anxiously.

"You're so full of shit."

"Yes, I am," Guy admitted striding toward the cluster of close bungalows. "I'm an asshole and a total idiot, but I promise I am not shitting you about this." He explained the deal to Buck, talking much faster than normal because he was afraid Buck would hang up and never take another call from him. "So, what do you think?" There was a silence he felt desperate to fill. He forced a dry laugh to say, "Hey, how many other dates offer to take you to the Institute Awards?"

Buck's doorbell rang. "Oh, shit, hang on." When Buck opened the door, Guy was standing there on his cell phone looking contrite.

Guy folded the phone shut and put it in his pocket. "Hi." He watched Buck frown and cross his arms. "It's good to see you."

"I'm not letting you in, Guy."

"Take a walk with me?" Guy asked. Buck hesitated. "For old times' sake?"

"I'm sorry, Buck," Guy said. "I'm so sorry for how I treated you."

They sat in De Longpre Park in the sun, near the commemorative statue to Rudolph Valentino.

"Oh, I know. I got over it," Buck told him.

"Then why wouldn't you take my calls?"

"'Cause you're still an angry man, Guy, even after all those years. Everything else was great, but I can't be with you angry. Not again. I'm tired of anger. Yours, mine, everybody's."

"What do you want me to do? Take an anger management class? I'll do it."

"Guy, you don't get it. Anger isn't the problem, it's the symptom."

Guy snorted in disdain. "What, did you grow chest hair and a psych degree?"

"Jesus, Guy, listen to yourself! And by the way, fuck you. This just proves my point. If I wasn't right you wouldn't be so damn angry and defensive about it."

Guy took several breaths, forcing himself to calm down. "Okay, okay. Sorry."

"I'm not just talking outta my ass here, all right? I've been there."

"Then just tell me," Guy implored, "if it's not anger, what the hell is it?"

"Forgiveness."

"Forgiveness? Fuck that! I don't have rights, I can't get married, straight people treat us like shit and get away with it? No. I'm not forgiving that. They should fucking come crawling to me for forgiveness."

"Not other people, Guy. Yourself."

"For what?" Guy demanded hotly. "Being gay? That's pure Desert Springs bullshit and those people should rot in hell. So don't hand me religious crap about sin, I've had enough of that for two screwed-up lifetimes."

"Fuck sin, fuck religion, and fuck God, okay?" Buck said in exasperation. "Everybody screws up! Everybody does stuff they wish they didn't! Think about it, Guy. Who was the person you treated the worst in your life? The one person you hurt so bad you never wanted to see her again?"

Guy looked at the ground. "You."

"But here I am."

It was true, and he couldn't understand it. "Why?"

Bucked looked at him tenderly. "Because all the rage was just too damned much work to carry around." Buck ran his hand along Guy's cheek. "If I can forgive you, why can't you forgive you?"

Guy had no answer. No words. No ideas. Just need. "I'll do anything to get you to come back," he whispered.

"Well, do ya know a good therapist?"

Tuesday, March 20th
Five days before the Awards telecast

"Over the years, Guy, you've sent me several clients," Dr. Larry said. "What is it that finally brings you to me?"

Guy frowned before answering. It made him cringe knowing how New-Agey it was going to make him sound. "I need to forgive myself."

"What do you feel you need forgiveness for?"

It seemed a simple question, but he'd been so angry all his life that there was no end to his regrets. Buck as Becky, his friends, his family, his life . . . It seemed impossible, insurmountable. He felt small and helpless. But he was also weary down to his bones, so infinitely tired of the effort. It was time to lay it down. He spoke one word.

"Everything."

Wednesday, March 21st
Four days before the Awards telecast

Alone in his office at the end of the day, Hiro personally sealed the envelopes containing the names of the Institute Award winners. In his restructuring of the department, it had been arranged that his and only his eyes would see the final Institute voting results. He, himself, had typed the winning names. The partners at PrattswaterfordDouglas were most pleased with this arrangement — especially after the unpleasantness with Finklestein — for Hiro Yamamoto was above reproach.

He locked the envelopes in his office safe and, clutching his briefcase with his own illicit Arthur, left for dinner with Noel and Big Ed. Afterward, they would call Las Vegas and place very large bets.

Thursday March 22nd
Three days before the Awards telecast

Everything had gone smoothly for Bob Davies until today. One of the bleachers outside the Shrine had collapsed injuring five workers and he'd spent the majority of the day dealing with hospitals, unions, and press.

Russell Crowe's people were demanding more Security. At three particularly inconvenient times the swaggering actor himself phoned Davies, the last time to ream him "a new arsehole." By the time the day was through, Davies was actually hoping somebody would kidnap this flaming ego. *Just so long as they did it before the telecast and not during it,* Davies thought to himself as he punched a number into his cell phone.

"Rudy here."

"Diaz, I'm adding you backstage Sunday. Just be alert, keep your eyes open, and for the love of God, keep anything from happening to Russell fucking Crowe, will you?"

Friday, March 23rd
Two days before the Awards telecast

Roger picked up the phone in his bedroom at his parents' house in Toluca Lake. His breathing was short and his hand was sweaty. He knew better, but —

"Roger!"

He jumped, slamming the phone down. Turning, he saw his stepdad in the hallway, smiling. "Damn, gave me a heart attack!"

"Aah, you got a guilty conscience," Bob laughed, coming into the room. "It's good to see you. What brings you by the house? Your friend with you?"

"No, Guy's getting a final fitting on his tux. I called mom to say hi, she asked me to dinner, so . . ." he trailed off and shrugged.

"You're looking a lot better," Bob said. "I'm glad you came."

Roger smiled. "Me, too, Dad. Thanks." His stepfather had an odd, soft expression on his face. "What's wrong?"

"Nothing. You called me Dad. You've done it a few times before, recently. I didn't say anything, but I like it."

"Okay, good."

Bob drew an emotional breath. This made up for all the Arthur bullshit he was dealing with. "Hey, your mother's made Argentine cuisine. Should be hard to mess up beef on swords, huh?" They both chuckled. "See you downstairs, son."

"Right. Dad."

Bob smiled with satisfaction and left.

Roger crossed to the door and closed it. He returned to the phone and dialed the number he knew he shouldn't.

"Yeah, I'd like to, um, I'd like to place a bet. A thousand apiece on Best Actor and Actress, Director, and Picture."

Saturday, March 24th
The day before the Awards telecast

"Thom!" Midge yelled from her desk at Creative Events.

Thom, who was halfway out the door at the end of a busy day, ran all the way back to her office. "Hi?"

"Yeah, hi. Honey, we all worked our asses off with the gift bags. But I need you back tomorrow. You're going back to the Shrine with me."

"Um, okay. Why?"

"Last-minute shit to add to the bags. Won't even get it in until tomorrow morning. Some of it's being messengered, I gotta go to fucking LAX to get some of it tonight, it's a train wreck. But I'm charging triple so we gotta keep it all straight, what goes where, who gets what, that's why I need you, baby."

"Okay. What time?"

"I'm telling everybody get here at ten. I got a call in to IMPAT for some backstage passes. That's you and me. We gotta be ready to roll when the passes get here. So get a good night's sleep and I'll see you in the morning, right, babe?"

"Okay."

Midge nodded her dismissal and picked up the phone. She punched in the number for those assholes at Swarovski. "Oh! And Thom!" she shouted after him. "Don't forget to take your meds!"

Sunday, March 25th
The Arthur telecast

The Shrine Auditorium is a production nightmare because it has no backstage area to speak of. For the Arthur show, a small, tight village of trailers, tents, cables, buffets, bars, lights, news uplinks, and equipment is jumbled together and assembled behind that overrated barn of a building. The entire contrived bustling "backstage" is surrounded by sixteen-foot high hurricane fencing with military-like checkpoints for entry. A little after three in the afternoon, Hiro led Noel and Big Ed to the back entrance that PrattswaterfordDouglas accountants and other lesser life forms were expected to use.

"Oh, my goodness, is that you, Mr. de Silva?" Hiro asked of the single security guard at this entrance.

The white-haired man in the blue uniform chuckled, shaking his hand. "It's me, all right. This is my eighteenth year with Arthur. How are you, Mr. uh, Prattswaterford?"

"That's right," Hiro said, displaying the ID badge around his neck for access. "Got the envelopes right in here," he added, patting his briefcase. "These are my guests."

"Okay," Mr. de Silva said after inspecting each person's badge. "Step through, please." The others entered with no problem, but the metal detector went off as Hiro passed through it.

"Oh, that would be this," Hiro said opening his briefcase to show his gleaming Arthur.

"Huh," remarked de Silva. "I expect to see Arthurs coming out, not coming in," he grinned. "You returning one of the missing ones from last year?" They all laughed and he waved them inside. "Can't have people waiting on the winning envelopes."

Suze, Eric, Buck, Patrick, and Guy along with two dozen other seat-fillers had been briefed and drilled in their seat-filling capacities by Clive, the imperious martinet ABC had insisted run this aspect of the show. At exactly 5:55 the seat-fillers were herded out of the cramped room they'd been stuck in and assembled in their ready-to-go lineup. They heard the telecast begin inside. After a confusing batch of clips, host Tom Hanks took the stage and the show got rolling. The sound of laughter from his monologue spilled into the lobby. "Listen to that!" Guy squealed in a whisper. "Isn't it just electric! That's the laughter of the most talented people on the planet!"

"And Björk," Patrick deadpanned.

"I can't believe I'm here!" Suze giggled like a six-year-old girl.

"I can't believe we're stuck in the lobby while it's all happening in there," Patrick complained, disappointed. He turned to Eric. "And you?"

"I can't believe how bad I need to peeeee!" Eric said.

Patrick craned his neck to check the front of the line. "I think Clive's got his head stuck inside the door," Patrick told him, "if not up his ass. Why not make a run for the bathroom? We're way back in the line anyway. Eric?" He looked around just in time to glimpse Eric dashing for the john down the short hallway on the other side of the lobby.

Security guard de Silva watched a painfully thin Latino man in a catering uniform approach his lonely backstage entrance pushing a large laundry cart loaded with wadded white table linen. Mr. de Silva felt sorry for these guys who were overworked and underpaid, but the man was trying to push it right past his metal detector.

"Whoa, whoa, whoa," de Silva said, hustling to stand in front of the laundry cart. "Gotta go through this," he told the man.

"¿Que?"

"*Aqui*," de Silva said pointing to the device. "Everybody go through detector of metal," he added in broken Spanish. "Seguridad, no weapon."

"Ah!" the thin man said, patting the rumpled linen. "No weapons." Suddenly he pulled out a government-issue semi-automatic M9 pistol with a silencer from the cart. "Just this." In one swift snake-like move he pressed the gun to de Silva's side and fired. The shot was calculated to enter between the ribs, tearing through both lungs, collapsing them so the victim couldn't scream or call for help during the very few minutes it would take to die of suffocation.

Not waiting for the guard to fall, the thin man pushed him into the laundry cart and covered him with more linen. He pulled a cell phone out of his pocket and dialed a number. "El Palo here," he spoke in Spanish. "Get in here now."

On his way back from the bathroom, Eric stopped at a water fountain next to a stairwell. He overheard a man in the stairwell speaking in urgent Spanish. Eric froze as he understood key phrases.

"... ready to take out Big Ed ... meet backstage ... don't care who he's with, we'll kill them all if we have to."

In horror, Eric peeked into the stairwell. It wasn't one but two massive Mexican men in obviously rented tuxedos on the next landing.

"... on our way," the first one said in Spanish, ending the call.

The other one spotted Eric and nudged the first. "Keep your voice down," he muttered, pointing at Eric.

The first one sneered. "You really think some preppie blond Anglo faggot is going to understand Spanish?" He called out to Eric in Spanish: "Hey boy, give me a hundred dollars and you can suck my juicy brown dick, you ugly, stupid son of a whore."

Eric smiled politely, trying to look embarrassed instead of scared. "Sorry," he said, "me no habla Spanish, por favor."

The thugs smirked as they rudely pushed past him. As they did, Eric saw the distinct heavy shape of a gun in the second one's pocket.

Eric raced back to the line of seat-fillers, which had advanced considerably in the short time he'd been gone. "Guy! Give me your cell phone!" As soon as Guy had it out, Eric grabbed it. He punched in Rudy's number.

☆

Backstage, Rudy was watching host Tom Hanks wrap up his opening monologue when he felt the phone in his tux pocket vibrate. "Diaz."

"Rudy, there's something going on! I heard two guys talking, they had guns! I'm not making this up and they were talking about killing someone. Backstage, they said!"

Rudy heard the fear in Eric's voice. "Slow down. What did you hear?"

Eric described the men he'd seen and told his lover, in Spanish, exactly what they had said.

"Big Ed?" Rudy wondered, frantically running down the list of nominees and presenters in his head. "You think they mean Ed Harris? He's up for *Pollack* but everybody loves him. Oh, wait! There's an Edward Zwick, a producer I think."

"Producers don't get killed, they get sued, even I know that. I think it's code, I think it's gotta be Russell Crowe! I mean, he's received the threats, right?"

"Holy shit. I thought they were only out to kidnap him."

"Whoever it is, whatever they're up to, these guys were serious."

"I hear you. Okay, thanks, babe."

"Rudy!"

"What?"

"Please be careful."

"I promise." Rudy slipped his cell phone back in his pocket with apprehension. This was just the thing Davies had feared. He knew there was already a detail specifically assigned to stay with the actor, so Rudy began searching the wings and backstage village for anyone hanging around who looked like they didn't belong.

⭐

Still in his catering uniform, El Palo met his bulky henchmen, Perez and Flores, at the now neglected entrance and quickly led them inside.

"Have you seen him?" Flores asked, hurrying to keep up with his boss striding through the maze of tents, trailers, and equipment.

"Not yet," El Palo said. "But I know he's here." He led his armed hulking flunkies into the milling crowd of backstage personnel, reporters, interns, assistants, technicians, and movie stars, looking for someone he had orders to kill.

⭐

In his urgent concentration, Rudy ran right into Tom Hanks as he and his assistant came out of his trailer hurrying toward the stage before the end of the station break. "Sorry," Rudy mumbled without stopping, his eyes scanning the bustling area for trouble. He continued on, looking for anyone who didn't have a laminated pass, or who resembled the descriptions Eric gave him. He saw a big guy leaning against a forklift, doing exactly nothing in the midst of others busily doing their jobs. He had dirty blond hair and was wearing a tux, but it was out of place on this guy. His back was to Rudy and it looked suspicious.

"Excuse me," Rudy said, approaching him. "Where are you supposed to be?"

The man turned around sullenly. "Right here."

He was familiar, but Rudy couldn't quite place him. "Don't you have something to do?"

The man shook his head, smugly pointing to his ID badge. "Union." That explained both the idleness and the tux. The Institute makes all backstage personnel wear tuxedos in case they get caught on camera. He squinted at Rudy. "Hey, dude, I think I know you. I ever let you blow me? If you're gay it's cool, I'll let you do it."

The name on his badge read Dan. "Oh, my God," Rudy said, remembering the encounter on Sarah's movie, "it's Dan the Man."

"Oh, yeah," Dan said, placing Rudy. "You were too good for a taste of this last time," he said, fondling his crotch with his left hand, the one with a wedding ring.

"I've got a job to do," Rudy told him in no uncertain terms. Just as he turned to leave, he saw two large Mexican men, both over six feet tall, following behind a thin man in a catering uniform. Eric hadn't said anything about a third guy. Was he the one they were talking to on the phone in the stairwell?

This did not look at all right because the catering guy was in charge of the ones in tuxedos. Cater Man must have seen someone around the corner because he suddenly altered his course. He scurried up the metal stairs at the door to a storage trailer. It was unlocked. He and the other two ducked inside. Rudy noticed the heavy shape of the gun in one of their jacket pockets. *How the hell did that get past Security?* Rudy thought angrily. *I swear, I'm gonna kill me a security guard.*

Rudy ran over to the trailer, wondering how to handle this. As he got there a group of three men practically ran into him.

"Very sorry," one of the two small Asian men said.

In fact it was two Asian men and an Anglo the size of one of the Mexicans in the trailer. Suspicious, Rudy demanded, "I need to see your badges, please."

"PrattswaterfordDouglas," the other small Asian man said, showing his ID badge. He gestured to the other two, also showing theirs. "And guests."

Rudy let them by, thinking *Jesus, even freaking accountants get an entourage in this town.* A backstage security guard passed and Rudy flashed his special IMPAT badge at her to prove his authority. "Watch that door," he instructed her, pointing at the trailer. "Make sure no one goes in or out." He then circled the trailer inspecting it. There were no other doors or windows. Rudy saw Cater Man peering out of the single tiny window in the door, only to duck away quickly. Rudy had to make sure he kept these guys trapped in there so they couldn't kill Russell Crowe, or worse, disrupt the telecast. He looked around, praying desperately for an idea. Tents. Cable. Boxes. Come on, come on. Loading pallets. Forklift. Folding chairs —

The forklift.

Rudy told the security guard to stay, and ran back to Dan the Man. "I need this forklift moved to over there," he told him. Dan the Man merely gave him a haughty smirk. "Do you hear me?" Rudy demanded. "I want you to drive it the hell over there with the lift pushed snug against the door now!"

"You want something, I want something." He reached up and took the keys out of the ignition to dangle in front of Rudy. "Let's talk about this," he said, again fondling his crotch.

"Oh, I'm not fucking believing this," Rudy said.

"No union person's gonna move this lift without my say so. And I'm not moving it unless I get a blow job out of it — nice and slow."

"Fuck you!" Rudy said, snatching the keys from him and climbing into the seat.

"No, none of that," Dan the Man laughed. "I'm straight." With a leering grin he watched Rudy start the engine, only to fumble with the gearshifts.

He couldn't figure them out. "Shit!" The controls looked hopeless to him, like the gear knobs for some 1920s version of a spaceship, or like some old truck, or even farm equipment. Farm! He grabbed the cell phone in his pocket. He pressed *69 to call back the phone Eric had last called him on.

"Hello?" It was Guy.

Damn. "Where's Eric?"

"He's seat-filling for Angelina Jolie, she's in the john."

Shit, oh, shit. He saw an ABC intern. "You!" he shouted at her. "Come here!" He put the phone back to his ear. "Guy, you have to make sure Eric stays in that seat for the next five minutes."

"But what if Angelina Jolie —"

"I don't care. I need Eric to stay exactly where he is until I can get to him. This is a matter of life and death, do you hear me? You do whatever you have to do, just keep her away from that seat!" He ended the call and took his lanyard with its IMPAT badge granting all access from around his neck. He gave it to the intern, telling her, "There's a blond Anglo man my age sitting third row, I think. He's right next to Billy Bob Thornton. Use this pass and get him back here as fast as you can. Run!"

Patrick, Suze, and Buck stared at the extremely serious look on Guy's face as he got off the phone.

"Well, what!?" Patrick demanded.

"Suze, you have got to go keep Angelina Jolie in the john," Guy said with deadly intensity.

"What?" she asked, stunned. "Why?"

"I have no idea," Guy admitted. "But Rudy swears it's a matter of life and death. Stalking, anonymous threat, God knows what's going on backstage but he wasn't kidding. Now go!" Suze remained frozen, her eyes wide in panic. "What's wrong?"

"I'm too nervous! I've never met a celebrity!"

"Working at Star Temps?" Patrick chided.

"Just their people," she snapped. "Their reps, not the real live stars. I can't do it, I can't face her. She won an Arthur last year for *Girl Interrupted*. That's all I can think of, is *Girl Interrupted*!"

"Think *Pushing Tin* and you'll be fine," Guy told her.

"But I don't know what I'm supposed to say. I'm, I'm — my mind's a blank! What should I do?"

"Tackle her!" Patrick said.

Buck and Guy glared at him. "Now you get butch?" Guy hissed.

"Well, I haven't had a lot of experience in a women's room, have I?" Patrick growled back.

"I have," Buck said, pushing his way between both of them and grabbing Suze by the shoulders. "Get in the next stall and ask for a tampon. God knows I've done it a million times. Or pretend your bra strap broke and beg her for a safety pin. Spill your purse. Just go do it!"

Suze nodded and hurried toward the ladies' room. Guy and Patrick were left staring at Buck.

"Guy," Patrick finally said, "your boyfriend the ex-wife rocks."

Suze entered the bathroom, her stomach nauseated and her heart pounding from the excitement and dread of meeting her first actual movie star. She cased the line of stalls. One pair of feet in strappy shoes in the far stall. Perfect. She entered the adjacent stall, locked the door, hiked up her dress and sat. She took a deep breath, both to calm her nerves and to ask Arthur-winning international film actress Angelina Jolie for a —

"Do you have a tampon?" Miss Jolie asked.

Thrown, Suze gulped air like a fish.

"Do you?" the actress repeated. "Have a tampon?"

Unsure, Suze looked through her tiny beaded clutch.

"Hello? You got a tampon or what?"

Suze, already nervous, was flummoxed by the demanding tone.

"Aw, hell," Angelina muttered. "I got Marlee fuckin' Matlin next door."

"I have a tampon."

"Oh. Well, thank God. This is a white Dolce & Gabbana pantsuit." A hand appeared under the door. "Gimme, gimme, gimme."

Suze wondered if she was like that with Billy Bob as she handed it over. If so, that wouldn't last long.

Suze knew Angelina would be coming out of the stall soon. She flushed and hurriedly smoothed down her gown so she could be out there to meet her. Stepping out of her stall, Suze urgently scanned the bathroom for something, anything, to keep Angelina Jolie in the can. She could splash water on her top. Steal her purse. Fake a seizure. But when the regal, cool, beautiful Angelina Jolie emerged from her stall, all Suze could do was stare.

"Is something wrong?" Miss Jolie asked.

"You're Angelina Jolie," Suze murmured, hating herself for being so dumbstruck and stupid. *Stall her, stall her!* she thought. The star smiled politely and washed her hands. "Could I have an autograph?"

Miss Jolie considered it, finished drying her hands, and replied, "Sure."

Suze fished a diminutive pen out of her small purse and handed it to Angelina along with a fresh paper towel. Miss Jolie wrote her name on the paper towel and offered the pen back to Suze. *Stall longer!* Suze grabbed another paper towel from the dispenser. "Could I have another one? For my mom?" Miss Jolie hesitated, but complied. "Okay, and, um, one for my very, very best friend in the world?" Miss Jolie's eyes narrowed at her. "He's dying of, of, um, rectal cancer." With a sigh, Miss Jolie signed a third paper towel. "Oh! And one more for —"

"Honey," Angelina said firmly, putting the pen down on the counter. "You gave me a tampon, not a kidney. The debt is paid." She turned to walk out.

"No, wait!" Suze said, blocking her way.

"What is your problem?"

Suze made a painful face, saying only, "Nerves." And she vomited.

All over Angelina Jolie's shoes.

Ezra had splurged on cable this month. He and Michael were curled up on his living-room sofa watching the live telecast when there was a wide-shot of the audience.

"Look!" Michael shouted, so excited he spilled popcorn. "There's Eric! Right near the front!"

"Oh, my gosh, it is," Ezra concurred. "And here comes Angelina Jolie."

"Why does she look so angry?" Michael wondered, settling back down. "You'd think she'd be happy to be there."

"Yeah," Ezra said, snuggling against him. "And why's she carrying her shoes?"

The intern made her way from backstage, through the long back hallways, into the auditorium near camera #3. She located Eric in Angelina Jolie's seat and instructed him to follow her just as the irritated actress returned with freshly rinsed and ruined Jimmy Choos. The intern led Eric backstage where Rudy and the security guard were watching the storage trailer. Eric could see the intense seriousness of the situation on Rudy's face.

"What's wrong?" he asked.

Rudy put his hands an Eric's shoulders to emphasize the gravity of things. "Sweetheart, I will explain everything later, but I need you to trust me on this."

"Okay. What?"

Rudy led Eric across the way to the forklift where Dan the Man was leaning and smirking. "In order to save Russell Crowe," Rudy said, "I have to suck this man's dick right now."

Eric goggled at him. "Are you shitting me? You dragged me backstage of the Arthurs for this? Which, by the way, has to be the most totally insane excuse to cheat on a person ever!" Rudy opened his mouth to explain, but Eric cut him off. "I was sitting next to Billie Bob Thornton! I was sitting in Angelina Jolie's butt warmth! Do you know what that means to a person from Missouri? And now I'm back here missing the Arthurs because you need to suck a stagehand's cock at this particular place and time?!"

"Okay, Mr. Missouri, shut the fuck up and listen. I've got your thugs holed up in that trailer and we need to keep 'em there, got it? To do that I need that forklift up against that door and this asshole won't give over the key unless I slob his knob, you with me? And even if I did — which I could do without ever telling you about, thank you — even if he gave me the key I can't move the damned forklift because, farm boy, it looks like a fucking tractor — from a farm. Now can you see why I called you back here?"

"Oh." Eric thought for a moment. "But wait. Why wouldn't he just move it for you after you sucked him off?"

"I'm sure he would but the problem is 1) he expects it to last a long time, and 2) we need those assholes shut up in there now and not later."

"And how do I know you really have those two big guys in there?"

"Go look."

Eric crept up to the trailer, and uneasily made his way up the metal stair unit. Just as he got near, one of the men stuck his face in the small window, startling Eric so badly he jumped, almost falling backward off the stairs. "That's them," Eric squeaked once he hurried back.

"Are you okay with this now?" Rudy asked.

"No, but I get it. Go on."

"Thanks, babe." Rudy turned to Dan, holding out his hand. Dan dropped the keys into it. Rudy gave them to Eric and with a jerk of his head to Dan, said only, "Let's get this over with."

Eric watched the skeevy blond head off into the maze of tents and trailers with his lover. *Can't dwell on that now*, he thought as he climbed into the seat of the forklift and started it. He shifted gears with familiar ease and drove the forklift across the concrete toward the storage trailer. In front of the door he lifted the metal stair unit on the lift prongs a foot off the ground and maneuvered the forklift to set it off to one side.

For the first time since he'd arrived in L.A. he was able to use the skills he'd always had. This was too much fun to end by simply parking the three ton machine against the trailer door and walking away. He looked around for things he could move.

Heavy things.

Trapped inside the trailer, El Palo surveyed what was available to them. The only stuff in there was patch cable, lights, and hardware to hang them. There was no other way out. In fact the only opening at all, besides the door, was an exhaust fan in a small vent near the ceiling opposite the door. It was about twelve inches square. He looked at Perez and Flores. "Open it."

The two men ripped the fan out with their combined strength. Using a flat piece of metal, Flores pried up the flashing around it, leaving a jagged one-foot square hole in the wall. Perez lifted El Palo up to where he could stick his head out. There was room behind the trailer but the drop was a good ten feet. El Palo pulled his head back and put his arms through the hole. He had to wriggle and squirm, but he managed to get his shoulders through. He pushed against the hole with his hands until his torso was out. He knew the next part was going to hurt. He gave a final push and fell to the concrete. When he hit, he landed on his right shoulder, dislocating it.

El Palo got to his feet painfully. "Perez!" he shout-whispered. He saw Perez's face. *Jesus, it filled the hole completely. There was no way they were getting out.* He'd just have to take care of business on his own.

"Toss me my gun."

Eric was surprised to see Rudy return in less than ten minutes. "That was quick," he remarked.

Rudy frowned with distaste. "Turns out Mr. Macho wanted to suck my dick while beating off. Took him maybe two minutes and I didn't even get hard."

Eric winced. "When we get home, you shower."

Rudy, though, was looking in amazement at the huge pile of metal and plywood crates all neatly and firmly stacked against the trailer door with the forklift neatly backed up against it. He broke into a grin. "My boyfriend rules!"

"Just call me Tractor Boy," Eric said proudly.

"Thanks, *mi niño*. I gotta get back to work and you need to get back out front." He gave him a peck on the mouth and headed toward the stage. "I'll see you after!"

Flush from his annual onstage appearance as the sole PrattswaterfordDouglas representative this year certifying the scrupulous veracity of the tallying of the Institute votes, Hiro came off the Arthur stage with a huge smile. He met Noel, who was holding his briefcase, with a kiss in the cramped wings. Ed was cruising Chow Yun Fat who was preparing for a piece honoring *Crouching Tiger, Hidden Dragon.*

Seeing a stage manager motioning for all non-stellar personnel to kindly-get-the-fuck-outta-there-now, Hiro told his group, "Let us find the Green Room tent."

Behind the Shrine it was beginning to get dark and the scoop lights had come on. Hiro led his party toward where the Green Room tent was usually set up — but it was not there this year. He approached a hunchbacked cater waiter in rumpled uniform who was looking around another corner.

"Where is the Green Room?" Hiro asked.

El Palo turned around, recognized Big Ed, and drew his gun. "It's this way," he said, gesturing to the nearest trailer.

"Oh, shit," mumbled Big Ed, who immediately knew who this was. He led his friends to the trailer and tried the door. It was unlocked.

"Inside, inside," El Palo ordered.

It was a star dressing room. There were mirrors with light bulbs around them at one end, and a makeup chair. Gift baskets of fruit, lavish floral arrangements, and platters of food covered nearby countertops, along with a TV monitor showing a live feed of the telecast. To one side was an ice chest with bottled water, diet sodas, wine, and champagne. At the other end were closets with sliding doors that were open revealing a tuxedo, extra white shirts, boxes of shoes, and other clothes. In the corner was an enormous bag stuffed with electronics, CDs, DVDs, boxes from Bulgari, Fred, Burke-Williams, Betsy Johnson, Armani, ABC, Jaguar, and more. Whoever belonged to this dressing room would be coming back any minute. Hiro prayed it would be soon.

El Palo had pulled the gun with his left hand because of his right shoulder, but it felt too awkward so he shifted it to his right hand. Keeping them at gunpoint, he patted them all down for weapons with his free hand. "Open the briefcase and step away," he ordered. Noel set it on the counter beside the sink and did as he was told. When El Palo saw the Arthur inside, he sneered. "Ah, yes," he said taking it out of the briefcase. "I'd like to thank the Institute," he said to them all in a grim parody of an acceptance speech, "for giving me the opportunity to kill one, two, maybe all three of you cocksucking *jotos*."

"Whoever sent you, El Palo, this is between you and me," Big Ed said, stepping forward. "You don't have to kill them or anybody else."

"That depends on you," he said, tossing the award onto the counter in disgust. Noel and Hiro flinched to see it bounce on the counter and skid into the mirror. "We know what you're doing here," El Palo continued. "And here is the deal. You give your Arthur rigging scheme over to us, or I have orders to kill you. And them."

Big Ed laughed. "You can't kill them, you dumb wetback. These guys are the one's making it happen!" While El Palo digested that, Ed began to get truly angry at the situation. Here he was, on the verge of setting up a major moneymaking operation, something that would finally win his father's approval, and some asshole sends this asshole to fuck it up. "You know, Palo," Big Ed said, "whoever's paying you this week must think you're pretty fucking stupid."

"Oh, yeah?"

"Yeah, 'cause, see, first of all, I'm not giving up jackshit. And second, if you kill me, you'll have about twenty-four hours to live before my father hunts your brown ass down and turns you into a little Mexican grease stain."

It was El Palo's turn to laugh. "Your father? Your father?" he cackled before turning deadly cold. "Who do you think sent me?!"

Big Ed reeled. He had to clutch the countertop to steady himself. It was too much to comprehend. But it explained how his Pop had known about Petey's death — Petey! Petey had sold him out to his father. But his own father? After all Ed had done to make him proud?

"Talking with your papi I learn some Italian," El Palo cooed. "*Effemminato. Busone. Leccacazzi*, which I understand is literally 'cock-licker.'" He enjoyed watching Big Ed's face, trembling and red. "No, I do not think he will hunt my brown ass, unlike you, *Finocchio*."

Big Ed seized the Arthur from the counter around the torso, and in one swift, enraged blow, drove the square base of it more than an inch into the side of El Palo's skull just above his ear. The force of impact propelled El Palo halfway across the trailer. When he hit the floor, Big Ed was on top of him, landing another bloody impact, crushing his cheekbone deep into his sinuses and sending three teeth across the room. The third slam came just above the hairline on his forehead, leaving a sharp dent in the smashed skull. Breathing hard and with blood spattered on his face, Big Ed, surveyed the broken corpse.

"Oh, shit," Noel whispered, cringing in the corner. "Oh, shit, oh, shit."

Big Ed rose to his feet and glanced at his reflection in a mirror. "Paper towels," he said, businesslike.

"What?" Hiro squeaked out.

"Get me some wet paper towels. Dry ones, too. Noel, help me get him in that corner." Hiro came with the paper towels. Big Ed washed his face and patted dry. The blood on his tux did not show because of the deep, black wool. The blood on his white tux shirt was another matter. He bent down to help Noel move the body.

The trailer door opened.

An olive-skinned woman wearing a dark-gray Dior business pantsuit entered carrying a clipboard, walkie-talkie, and a sharp attitude. She took in the scene without flinching. Big Ed dropped the body with a sickening thud. He grabbed the gun from the floor where El Palo had dropped it, and aimed it at the woman.

Her mouth drew tight. "Is that supposed to scare me?" she asked. "Because I've worked for Phil Specter."

"Who are you?" Big Ed demanded.

"That's a good question, only I should be asking you," she retorted with a clipped tone. "I am Gwyneth, Mr. Hanks's personal assistant."

"Don't scream," Ed warned her. "Don't call for Security."

"Do I look like I scream?" She glanced at her watch. "I have exactly seven and a half minutes to get this mess taken care of before station break and Mr. Hanks comes back here," she said looking around the trailer with angry disdain. She fixed them with a steely glare. "Are you here to harm Tom Hanks in any way?"

"No!" the men said in unison before erupting in a jumble of overlapping explanations. "This guy forced us in here —!" "We didn't mean to do it —!" "He tried to kill us —!"

"Not! My! Problem!" Gwyneth shouted over them, with a hand held up for silence.

Big Ed said, "Look, I don't think you understand, lady, we can't —"

"No!" she barked. "You don't understand, mister. I am a professional Hollywood assistant. You think I haven't dealt with worse messes than this? Two words, pal: Neverland Ranch." She surveyed the pool of blood around El Palo's head. "As long as that isn't my client, I don't care. But my client happens to be the host of the biggest live broadcast on the planet, and my job is to make damn sure this night goes perfectly for him, do you hear me? Perfectly! Now, put that gun away and make yourself useful." Gwyneth pulled her walkie-talkie from her beaded belt. "Bring the limo to the trailer," she ordered. "Yes, now." Turning to Noel she said, "You. Go next door to the Press Tent bar. Get a stack of towels." Noel scurried out the door. She shouted after him, "If they say anything, tell them Gwyneth sent you."

When Noel returned, he and Hiro frantically wiped spattered blood up with the towels as Gwyneth directed the cleanup operations expertly.

"Don't get any on you!" Big Ed said as he folded the thin, light body into doubled black plastic trash bags from under the sink. Gwyneth held the bags for him.

"You've done this before," she said with professional admiration. She tied off the bags neatly with a tight knot. She handed Big Ed a box cutter. "Hurry and cut the stained part of the carpet. Pull it up and put it in these other bags."

Ed cut the carpet and rolled it up. "This ain't your first time, either," he said with a similar admiration.

Their eyes met and held for the slightest moment. "You've got blood on your shirt," Gwyneth said. "Take it off and put one of those on," she added, pointing to the extras in the closet. "Hurry."

"Oh, my God, I found teeth," Hiro said on the verge of freaking out.

"Teeth, bone, bloody towels, it all goes in these bags," Gwyneth commanded.

Big Ed whipped his bloody tux shirt off, stuffing it into the towel-and-rug bags. He tried to put on the fresh shirt, but it was many sizes too small for him. Gwyneth took the box cutter and slit the shirt down the middle of the back from the tail to the collar. He was able to get it buttoned. "Just keep your jacket on," Gwyneth told him. "Two minutes everybody!" she announced just as the limo arrived outside the door. She spoke into her walkie-talkie, "Pop the trunk, please."

"Quickly! Quickly!" Hiro said wringing his hands as Noel and Big Ed took out the garbage bags.

"Is that everything?" Noel asked in a near panic himself.

"It had better be," Gwyneth said. She closed the trunk and patted it as a signal to the driver. The limo pulled away. "Did you cover the hole in the carpet with the flowers?" she asked the men.

"Shit!" Noel and Hiro said, scrambling back inside to do so. Ed and Gwyneth followed them to make sure it was done right. "That'll do," she announced. "By my watch we have —" she looked at it and her face fell, "— oh, hell."

Tom Hanks burst in, pulling at his tie, to change costume. "Gwyneth! I need my —" He surveyed this crowd of strangers. "Gwyneth, who are these people in my dressing room?"

"They're from ABC, Mr. Hanks," Gwyneth said coolly. "Just making sure everything is being taken care of."

"Oh," the star host said, mollified, now shucking off his jacket. "You want to do the world a favor?" he asked them, unbuttoning his shirt. "Get a restraining order on Debbie Allen. I mean, did you see that *Crouching Tiger* train wreck?" He peeled the shirt off, tossing it on the makeup chair. He held his arms out as Gwyneth toweled his sweaty body down, ending with his armpits. "And you might want to send a fruit basket to Chow Yun-Fat. He comes off after it and I think I heard Mike Myers ask if he remembered the egg rolls." Gwyneth stood holding a fresh shirt open for him to step into. "Unbelievable. I just hope nobody translates it for him." He buttoned his shirt looking at Hiro. "Were you at Will Smith's birthday last year? You look familiar."

"PrattswaterfordDouglas," Hiro said, smiling.

"Of course. That would be a big fat no on the Will Smith party." He gave up fumbling with his tie. "Gwyneth!" His assistant tied it perfectly in an instant. "Where am I going?"

"Stage left, introducing Julia Rogers. You have ninety seconds. Go."

"Got it," the host said putting his jacket back on and exiting.

As soon as he was gone Gwyneth turned sharply and pointed to an object by Noel's foot. "What is that?"

"Our Arthur!" he said scooping it up from the floor where it had been forgotten. "Ew! Blood."

Ed muttered to Gwyneth, somewhat shamefaced, "It's, um, how I killed him."

"Get it out of here."

"We can't," Hiro said, worried. "I threw the briefcase in a plastic bag."

"Why the hell did you do that?" Noel demanded.

"Ed flattened it in the fight and it had blood on it. What was I supposed to do?"

"Well, how are we supposed to get it out of here, Hiro? You can prance in here carrying an Arthur but you can't walk out with one in your hands unless two billion people saw you win it on live TV!"

"We can sneak it onto the table with the Arthurs they're giving out," Ed suggested.

"Like that wouldn't raise suspicion," Noel said, dripping sarcasm. "'Hey, everybody, the show's over but there's one extra left over! Let's investigate why'!"

"Then you tell me, bright guy," Ed retorted, "how are we gonna dump it?

Hiro was aghast. "You can't just dump an Institute Award!"

"The hell you say," Ed said, turning on him. "Fifty-five were dumped last year."

Hiro yanked the statue away from Noel. "You're not dumping mine!"

"You wanna go to jail? It's evidence!"

"No!" he yelled, hunching in a corner to protect it. "I'm not giving it up!"

"Hiro . . ." Big Ed said, advancing menacingly.

"If you don't let me keep this, I won't help with the vote count." That stopped Ed cold. "Yes," Hiro said making his stand. "Who else can you get in my position?"

"Fellas," Gwyneth interjected, "as scintillating as this is, I want you all the hell out of here. Now."

"Or what?" Ed asked sarcastically.

"Or I turn you over to Security. Now that he's made his costume change, I have thirteen minutes to get you out of my life and, trust me, I can do it in nine."

"Oh, yeah? Well, you also got three guys who'll finger you as an accessory."

Gwyneth bristled, but knew she was stuck. She looked at Hiro, the Arthur, and back to Big Ed. She clicked into crisis-solving mode.

"Sweetheart," she cooed to Hiro, "What if we got you another Arthur? A nice fresh one that hasn't killed someone? Would that do? Would you like that?"

"No," Hiro spat. "I don't trust you."

"Then trust me," Big Ed said holding his hand out. "You said it yourself, if I piss you off I'm fucked. Why would I do that?"

That made sense. Hiro grudgingly handed the statue to Big Ed.

"Great!" Ed said turning to Gwyneth. "Now what do we do?"

"I have to come up with that, too?" Gwyneth snapped.

"I thought you had a plan!"

"I did: swap Arthurs! You come up with the details."

"How are we supposed to just swap 'em?"

"I don't know! Cause a distraction."

"Even if we do that," Noel pointed out, "how do we carry the other one out?"

Gwyneth angrily shrugged him off, "That's not my problem."

"It is if you want us outta here," Ed reminded her.

Noel was at the breaking point. "How do we smuggle it out?" he pleaded.

"I don't know!"

The door opened. Thom stuck his head inside. "Gift bag additions," he announced meekly. There were four people not moving but staring at him making him extremely uncomfortable. "Um, last minute first-tier additions?" he murmured uneasily, shuffling uncertainly into the trailer to make his delivery. "There's a, uh, Sephora CitySkin Detox treatment and a Juicy Couture card and Valentino sunglasses . . ." he said setting items on the makeup counter by the door. "All 125 first-tier gift bags get them," he nervously explained. "Not the 150 second-tier or 197 third-tier bags, but these do. They're special. And also a Chloe bracelet bag and, uh, Perugina chocolate. That's all," he said setting a gold foil covered lifesize perfect replica of an Arthur in Perugina chocolate on the counter. "I'm gone now," he said, exiting hurriedly.

Hiro was the first to speak. "I've got an idea . . ."

"No shit!" said Big Ed.

"Get the foil off that chocolate," Gwyneth instructed Noel and Hiro. "Carefully," she added putting the real Arthur in a shoebox so she'd have the excuse of bringing Tom Hanks a change of shoes.

"What do we do with the chocolate?" Noel asked.

"For all I care, shove it up your ass," she said as she and Big Ed left the trailer.

Hiro leaned over to Noel and muttered, "We will not do that."

⋆

"Here's the system," Gwyneth explained as they strode swiftly toward the backstage area. "Presenters don't really present the awards, they just read the TelePrompTer. It's the Go-With girls."

"The what?" Ed asked, struggling to keep up with her.

"The models, the ones who 'go with' the presenter, that's who actually hands it off to the winner. So there's the envelope, the acceptance speech, everybody comes offstage, they go to the Press Tent for photos and all that, except for the Go-With girls. They stay to hand out the next award."

"Got it. We clobber a Go-With girl to make the switch."

"No," Gwyneth said emphatically, "we distract a Go-With girl. They're models, trust me, it'll be easy."

Onstage, Renée Zellweger described the Technical Achievement Awards ceremony held earlier in the week as Big Ed and Gwyneth got to the side of the stage where the Arthurs were kept. There was the Go-With girl standing there in lovely white chiffon — but without an award in her hands. What the hell?

"Sweetie," Gwyneth purred to her, "Shouldn't you be holding your Arthur?"

"Oh, no," the dazzlingly lovely model chirped. "Not until the very second they send me out there. Are you famous?"

"No," Gwyneth said tersely, ending the conversation. There would be no time to enact their plan.

"Suggestions? Comments?" Ed acidly whispered to Gwyneth.

"How about, 'We're fucked'?" she spat back.

A stagehand wheeled a full costume rack into the area, parking it right by the table with the Arthurs on it. It was as if God had smiled. Gwyneth and Ed glanced at each other with complete understanding. Gwyneth gave the shoebox to Ed and made her suddenly congenial way over to distract the armed security guard stationed at the other end of the table where the golden statues were in neat rows. He was a beefy Irishman with a red face and no-nonsense attitude. But this was Hollywood, where everyone has something to sell.

"I just know I've met you before," she said to him with silken coyness. "Hi, I'm Gwyneth, Tom Hanks's personal assistant?"

"Yeah, I've seen you 'round," he said, calculating her access. He knew opportunities like this had to be seized. "Would it be outta line," he whispered to her, "if I told you I have a script that'd be perfect for Mr. Hanks?"

"Not at all," Gwyneth smiled, without bothering to include her eyes. "Please, tell me everything about it."

While everyone backstage was watching the TV monitor to see their behind-the-scenes friends get their due, Big Ed slipped the Arthur out of the shoebox, setting the box on the floor. Holding the Arthur in his left hand, he stuck his right hand through the clothes rack, feeling for a free space to set his statue. He held his left hand out for balance.

"Oh, thank you," the Go-With girl said taking the award out of Ed's left hand.

Startled, Ed snatched it away from her. "That's mine!"

"No, it isn't," she pouted, grabbing it back. "You're not even famous."

Ed caught Gwyneth in his sight. She had turned the guard around to hug him so he wouldn't see this altercation with Ed. Daggers, machetes, javelins were shooting from her steely eyes at him. Big Ed realized what he was doing.

"Sorry," he said, releasing it. He watched the pretty model scurry off onto the stage after Sandra Bullock, who was presenting the award for Best Score. Their mission was halfway accomplished. All he had to do now was reach through the clothes rack and grab one of the other —

The clothes rack was gone.

Ed jerked his head around in horror to see a stagehand taking it around a corner to disappear into the dark shadows of the backstage world. People were busy again, no longer clustered around the TV monitor. While Billy Joel and Midori played selections from the Original Score nominees onstage, he racked his jumbled mind for a plan, any plan. He couldn't just swipe an Arthur now without a major distraction, but a chaos like that would draw the security guard into it. *Gwyneth,* he thought with a smile. He could count on her. All he needed now was the distraction.

Onstage, Sandra Bullock announced that Tan Dun had won for his score for *Crouching Tiger, Hidden Dragon.* After the acceptance speech, Sandra and Tan Dun, holding the murder-weapon Arthur, came off and were swept past everyone backstage including ... Renée Zellweger.

Since she hadn't actually presented an award, Renée Zellweger had not been whisked off to the Press Tent earlier. Big Ed considered her lingering there in her stunning soft lemon yellow strapless gown, bright ruby red lips, and long wavy blonde hair. She was loving being there, taking it all in with that one-day-all-this-will-be-mine look in her eyes. *Yeah, right,* Ed thought.

But she was perfect.

Ed kicked the shoebox along the floor, sliding it over to stop against Gwyneth's shoe. She knew better than to look down, God love her. Ed went up to Renée.

"Miss Zellweger, I just wanted to tell you," he said, getting just a touch too close, "you complete me."

Miss Zellweger contained her alarm admirably. "Oh. I do?"

"Absolutely. *Me, Myself & Irene, Nurse Betty, The Return of the Texas Chainsaw Massacre.* I've seen 'em all, like, ten times each. And *The Bachelor*? I wore out my VHS copy."

"That's ... thank you. I need to go now."

"No, wait, I wanted to show you something, something that proves how much I think of you." He turned his cummerbund around and unfastened his pants. Miss Zellweger began making little panic noises. "Right now it only says, like, REZWEG but when it gets hard you can read your whole —"

"Security!" she squeaked, covering her face. "Ugh! Pants! No!"

Gwyneth's security guard saw a star full-on freaking. "Get away from her!" he barked and rushed over. "What the fuck d'you think you're doing, pal?" He grabbed Big Ed's arm, jerking him away from Renée Zellweger.

"I was just tucking my shirttail in," Big Ed said in his smallest voice. He started to cry. "I'm sorry if I upset anybody," he blubbered. "I'd never want to hurt anyone. Especially Miss Zellweger."

"What the hell is going on here?" Rudy demanded, taking charge of the situation.

Gwyneth scurried over, the shoebox in her hands. "I'm so sorry about this," she said, taking Ed by the hand. "It's Mr. Hanks's nephew," she explained. Dropping to a whisper, she added ever so sadly, "He's developmentally challenged."

The security guard wasn't backing down. "He was about to attack Miss Zellweger. I'm calling for backup and having him arrested."

"No, don't," Miss Zellweger said, feeling deeply sorry for Tom Hanks's mentally deficient relative. "Really, it's all right."

"Get him back to the dressing room and keep him there," Rudy ordered.

"Right away," Gwyneth said, turning the sniffling Ed around and pushing him away from the gathering crowd.

The instant they turned the corner, Big Ed dropped the act to ask, "You got it?"

"Of course," Gwyneth replied. "You're not bad at this."

"You fuckin' rock. What were you scamming the guard about?"

"His crap script. Worst idea ever. Two hours of beating the shit out of Christ; it's a snuff film with Jesus. In some ancient language, for God's sake." She checked her watch. "Jesus Christ!"

"Yeah, you said."

"No, we've got to get the hell back, and fast!"

Gwyneth jerked the trailer door open and entered with a triumphant, "We got it!" Big Ed was right behind her. They both stopped at what they saw inside.

Noel and Hiro looked up from the few remaining pieces of broken Perugina like guilty children. They had chocolate all over their fingers and around their mouths.

"What?" Noel said. "You told us to get rid of it."

"I was thinking in the trash," Gwyneth said with disdain.

"Oh," the couple said in unison.

She threw a plastic jug of pop-up wet wipes from the counter at them. "Clean up!" she ordered, throwing a withering look at Big Ed.

"They're new to this," he said, taking a roll of paper towels to them. Big Ed glared at his cohorts. "You're embarrassing me!" he whispered at them.

Miffed, Hiro said, "Is that what you looked like backstage?"

Big Ed glanced in the mirror. His tux was all twisted, the shirt split down the back earlier was hanging out on both sides, and his hair was a wreck. "Don't start with me," Ed warned Hiro as he put himself back together. "If you didn't have to have your fucking Arthur we could've been outta here by now."

"I'll give you guys this," Gwyneth said, looking at the painstakingly removed golden remains of the chocolate Arthur. "You really got that foil off well."

"We are very meticulous," Hiro said pointedly for Big Ed's benefit.

Gwyneth took the real Institute Award she had swiped out of the shoebox. She pulled a bottle of eyelash glue from a bag under the counter. Working with Hiro, she dabbed drops of the glue on the Arthur, spreading it with a tiny makeup brush so the foil would adhere. Hiro applied the carefully preserved foil sections with delicate fingers and scrupulous attention. In less than ten minutes it was complete, and the quick-drying glue had set.

"It's a real Arthur pretending to be a fake Arthur by masquerading in a covering meant to make the fake Arthur look like a real one," mused Noel, admiring the results. "It's so *Victor/Victoria*."

"Okay," Gwyneth announced with a glance at her watch. "You've got your Arthur and its ticket out of here. It's time for your part of the deal. Leave. Now."

"Are we sure it's ready?" Hiro asked nervously.

Gwyneth picked it up and thrust it into his hands. "I'm ready, and that's what counts," she stated, herding them toward the door. "Just go. I want you all out of here before —"

Tom Hanks flung the door open and entered, immediately followed by an African-American entertainment reporter. Tom took one look and was instantly pissed off. Not only were these ABC and Prattswaterford nobodies still in his damned off-limits dressing room, they were helping themselves to his rightful swag? "Give me that!" he said, indignantly snatching it away from Hiro. "You think just because I wasn't here when it came I don't know I get one of these?"

"We saw the delivery guy," the reporter sniffed.

"Gwyneth!"

Ed, Noel, and Hiro looked at her in wide-eyed desperation. She hesitated only a moment. "I believe this is just a misunderstanding," Gwyneth spoke in warm, velvety tones, the very voice of peace and reason. "They weren't taking it, Mr. Hanks. They left right after your last change. Moments ago, however, they returned to bring that chocolate Arthur to you personally."

"Why?" the star demanded.

"Uh, because some were damaged," Big Ed said, the soul of network unctuousness. "We wanted to make sure you didn't get a crappy one."

Tom wasn't buying it. "And that's why they're here now?" he asked Gwyneth.

She made a slight frown and the tiniest "no" movement of her head. Big Ed, Hiro, and Noel tensed. Was she betraying them? The reporter smirked. This could be his exclusive backstage story.

Gwyneth leaned in close to Mr. Hanks ear. The reporter stuck his head in to catch the scoop. "They're star fuckers," she whispered. The three of them exchanged the disdainful looks of insiders understanding this particularly unsavory and unavoidable element of the entertainment milieu.

"Well, thank you very much," Mr. Hanks said with a plastic smile to the ABC nobodies. "But I need my dressing room and my privacy and I know you understand that. So thank you for coming and goodbye now." With his Arthur-free hand he held the door open for them.

"But . . . but . . ." Hiro sputtered, gazing desperately at his foil-covered Arthur.

"Goodbye, gentlemen," Gwyneth said.

And there was nothing they could do. Except leave. Empty-handed.

⭒

Immediately Tom Hanks took his jacket off, handing his personal Perugina to Mark Sparks, now Senior Reporter for *E! Entertainment News*. "No one, Gwyneth," Mr. Hanks said yanking his tie off. "No one else gets in here, understood?"

"You got it," Gwyneth agreed, helping him out of his tux shirt.

"You're doing a marvelous job as host this evening," Sparks gushed, thrilled to be watching Hollywood royalty getting his pits swabbed by an assistant. "What's next for Tom Hanks?"

Tom buttoned his fresh shirt and slipped into his jacket as Gwyneth held it for him. "I'm playing a hit man in a film called *Road to Perdition*."

Sparks had no idea what "perdition" meant, so he said, "That sounds wonderful!"

This reporter guy was sickening even by Hollywood standards. "Okay, that's it, gotta go. Here," Tom said, indicating the Arthur that Sparks was holding with "Perugina" on the base, "Think of it as a lovely parting gift. Gwyneth?"

"You've been terrific, really," Gwyneth said, escorting Sparks to the door. "We'll be in touch, okay?"

"I'm going to hold you to that!" Sparks said coyly, wagging a finger as he backed out the trailer door.

"Yeah," Gwyneth said, dropping all pretence, "Good luck with that."

The trailer door slammed shut on him, but Sparks understood. Tom Hanks needed time to focus on his important hosting duties, to center himself as an artist, or maybe take a crap. It didn't matter. Two-time Arthur winner Tom Hanks had just given him his Perugina chocolate Arthur. He put his chocolate in his bag, hitched it over his shoulder, and headed to the Press Tent to pester whatever star he could find.

Hiro, Noel, and Big Ed were drowning their sorrows at the bar next to the Press Tent while waiting for the Best Song category they had fixed. A largeish man sat next to Hiro and said, "Why the long face?"

"Lost my Arthur," Hiro said without bothering to look around.

"That's nothing. I mighta lost my career."

Hiro turned around to shut him up. It was John Travolta ordering a Scotch and water. Hiro backed down. Even what he'd lost would be hard to top *Battlefield Earth*.

Hiro and the rest of the people propping up the bar gave their attention to the TV monitor to watch Janet Jackson introduce Bob Dylan who sang, if you could call it that, the final tune nominated for Best Song. He performed the forgettable "Things Have Changed" from *Wonder Boys*. In extreme closeup, sporting a pencil-thin moustache, he looked as pale and old as cracked putty.

"Is it me," Travolta asked, giving voice to what everyone else was thinking, "or does he look like he should have been on that 'In Memoriam' reel?"

"I can't even tell what the words are," Noel marveled.

As Dylan finished, Janet Jackson came forward with the envelope containing the winner's name for Best Song. "Okay," Big Ed mumbled, "this is it." They all three knew the outcome, but were tense with anticipation as to what the reaction would be.

"And the Arthur for Best Song," Miss Jackson said, opening the envelope in her see-through Chanel, "goes to Bob Dylan for 'Things Have Changed.'"

That was the song, all right. All three of them looked around nervously, checking to see how people would respond to such an obvious travesty. Michael Douglas and Catherine Zeta-Jones were shown on screen applauding. There was Bob Dylan accepting it on stage.

The hideous truth of the Arthurs broke through for Hiro, and it nearly crushed him. The world is used to utter, meritless crap winning Institute Awards. Hell, people expect it. They celebrate it. Every flicker of respect and awe he had ever felt about the movies, about stars, about the Arthurs was gone like a puff of air blowing out a candle. He had put his life in danger, and his partner's life, for this?

And just as quickly, the epiphany hit him: I'm free.

All the sucking up, the collecting of memorabilia, even this scheme to win Arthurs was about nothing but grabbing after validation. What a useless, empty chase that was. How good it felt to be suddenly free of it. He wasn't sure what this new revelation meant for him, but he knew his grandmother was wrong. *There is no luck,* he thought. *There is only 'doing' or 'not doing.'* It was Zen. Or perhaps Yoda.

"Are you okay, honey?" Noel asked.

"I would like another drink," was all Hiro could say.

"We pulled it off, boys," Big Ed laughed triumphantly. "If they bought that piece-a-shit song as Arthur-worthy, they'll go for anything we give 'em."

After the Awards ceremony, Bob Davies made his rounds at the ritzy, self-consciously elegant President's Gala in a glorified tent behind the Shrine Auditorium. At least Russell Crowe had not been kidnapped, thank fucking Christ. He still had to congratulate winners and damn if half of 'em hadn't ditched this boondoggle for the more hip private parties around town. *Fifteen more minutes and I'm blowing this pop stand, too,* he thought. He grabbed champagne from a passing waiter and adjusted his smile.

"Congratulations on your win," he said to the owner of a freshly bestowed statue as he claimed a seat at the table. "I'm Bob Davies with the Institute."

"Tan Dun," said the winner smiling and shaking hands. *Crouching Tiger* director Ang Lee waved at Dun from four tables away. Dun asked Bob, "Take care of Arthur?"

"It's what I do," he said wryly, and watched Tan Dun run over to Ang Lee. Bob was grateful for a moment's peace alone. He took a deep sigh of relief. As he did he noticed a small chunk of bloody hair on the base of the award Tan Dun had left at the table. What the fuck do people do with these things? Bob thought. He flagged a passing waiter for another champagne so he wouldn't have to think about it further.

Four Los Angeles policemen marched the two goons Eric had helped Rudy trap in the trailer off to their squad cars. Rudy walked them to the back gate to see them all out. He'd report the matter to Davies in the morning. As their squad car doors were slamming shut, Rudy noticed a laundry cart off to the side, loaded with wadded white table linen — except for the tip of a shoe sticking out. He pulled back some tablecloths and gasped. Rudy spun around to call out to the cops who were already driving away. But the shout never came. Instead, Rudy tossed the tablecloths back over the body.

He made his decision. He opened his cell phone.

Bob Davies arrived at Elton John's party at the loud, multilevel Moomba in West Hollywood. As he entered, the host took the stage with a medley of his songs from *The Lion King*, just in case anyone had forgotten he, too, had an Arthur. Bob's phone rang. It was Rudy Diaz.

"What is it now?" Bob asked. His face went ashen. "Shot? No, no, you made the right call," he said, wishing he'd never answered his phone. "What should you do?" Horrified, Bob's mind was a blank. Across the room he spotted Big Ed. "Stay right there, I'll call you back."

Bob crossed the dance floor crowded with professionally beautiful people. He tugged urgently at Big Ed's sleeve.

"Bob!" Ed shouted happily. "Congratulations on everything going as planned."

"Did you kill anyone backstage?" Bob demanded through clenched teeth into Ed's ear.

Ed narrowed his eyes. "Define 'kill.'"

"Shoot someone! Did you shoot anybody?"

"Oh, shooting!" Ed relaxed. "No, not me."

"Well, somebody did and I've got a dead security guard backstage who cannot be there, do you understand?" Bob implored in a hoarse whisper. "What do I do?"

"You need a cleaner," Big Ed said, thinking who might be available. "Do you know a woman named Gwyneth?"

"Tom Hanks's assistant?"

"Tell her Big Ed sent you."

Bob whipped out his cell phone and ran through his numbers. He found Tom Hanks. The number would be his assistant's. He glanced up to say thanks and saw Hiro and Noel bringing Ed a drink. Bob thought, *What the hell . . . ?*

Hiro shrank, mortified to meet his IMPAT friend now. He cringed with guilt and shame. Then, with a start, Hiro thought, *But how does he know Big Ed? Unless . . .*

All Bob could think to say was a short, "Ah."

"So," acknowledged Hiro.

"Wow," Bob said, shaking his head as the connection sank in. "Why didn't we think of this, Hiro?"

"We did," Hiro said. "But we only joked about it."

"You know each other?" Ed asked, surprised. Bob, Noel, and Hiro nodded. Ed laughed. "Small world!"

"Yes," Bob agreed, "I suppose the underworld is."

Hiro opened his mouth to take offense, but with surprise, found he wasn't offended after all. His recent revelation of Hollywood as bullshit had not destroyed him. No longer held in thrall to the Industry, he could be fearless within it. By damn, there were movies to be made, and they would be the movies he wanted made.

Bob turned next to Noel. "And your part in this would be?"

"Investment."

Of course, thought Bob. It all came together beautifully. But he'd have to admire its elegance later. "Excuse me. I have a phone call to make." He left to find a quiet space to call his cleaner.

"Next year Bob will be adding other categories," Ed said, sipping on his drink. "With the group of us calling the shots on what gets financed, what gets made, who gets nominated, and especially who wins, in a couple of years we could own this town."

"*Chicago*," Hiro said.

"Actually I meant Hollywood," Big Ed replied.

"No," Hiro said, "I want us to make *Chicago*. I want to bring back musicals. I want to make *Phantom*. And *Dreamgirls*."

"Nobody does musicals," Noel told him. "Don't you think we should concentrate on regular movies?"

Hiro smiled slightly, feeling the fearlessness wash over him. "I think we should do," he said in measured tones, "what I want to do. And I want to see *Sweeney Todd* on the big screen."

"Yeah, that'll happen," Noel laughed. "Honey, this can't all be about you."

Hiro bristled. "It's not about me. Look at what's out there: *Road Trip, Nutty Professor 2, Scream 3*? This is bigger than us. We have an opportunity. We can make money, yes, but what we have is a chance to do something wonderful."

"Okay," Big Ed said, "like what?"

"I made a list while you were changing your shirt," Hiro said. "And on the top is *Chicago*. It's been bouncing around town for something like eight years, and it's time."

Noel shook his head, "At the moment, Madonna's attached."

Big Ed shrugged. "I know people who could pry her off. By the time they were done, she'd leave the fucking country."

"Reason enough right there," Noel muttered.

Hiro ignored his partner. "Who would you cast?"

"I dunno." Big Ed thought for a moment. "You know who looks great? That Renée Zellweger. You shoulda seen her when I started wailing on her backstage. And a good sport about it afterward. Anybody know if she can sing?"

Noel threw up his hands in surrender. "I'll ask around."

"Tomorrow," Ed said with a grin. "Right now, here's to us!"

"Yes," Noel agreed. "Gang to the stars."

"Not a gang," Hiro objected. "Better than a gang."

"Call it what it is then." Ed raised his glass. "To the Hollywood Mafia!"

Wednesday, March 28th

"You're already my hero for getting us into the Arthurs Sunday," Guy said to Roger as he unlocked the front door of his house after a dinner at nearby Morton's. "You didn't need to take us out tonight too."

"You sure you can afford that?" Buck asked as the tipsy trio tumbled inside. "I thought you were broke."

"Don't worry about it. I, uh, had an investment pay off," he said secretly pleased at having picked three out of four of the acting categories with the Vegas oddsmakers. *My luck is changing*, he thought, *It's time to try that again.*

They were still too wound up to go to bed, so Guy put on one of his favorite DVDs, *Cabaret*, and they all flopped on top of each other on the sofa, like puppies. Guy could feel Roger caressing his leg on one side, as Buck lazily stroked Guy's leg on the other side. Guy loved the sensation and relaxed into it. After a while he reached up with his right hand to find a gap between shirt buttons on Buck, and gently twirled the soft hair on Buck's chest. With his left hand he sensuously massaged Roger's scalp during the "Two Ladies" number.

"Hey, that's us," Roger commented.

"Who're you calling a lady?" Buck joked back.

"Shh!" Guy said. "No talking during a Kander & Ebb song."

Buck leaned slowly over to kiss Guy. He moved his hand inside Guy's shirt to play with his nipple. Roger's hand had found its way to Guy's inner thigh, his thumb gently rubbing against Guy's testicles. Guy became very nervous and felt a need to make a definite decision here. He shifted his weight toward Buck. Roger backed off, and soon Guy and Buck were kissing.

Guy felt Roger move off the sofa, believing that he was taking his cue to leave. But moments later there was Roger's warm, breathing presence very close to Guy's and Buck's faces. Confused, Buck stopped kissing Guy. The three of them held this unexpected nearness for several seconds. Sally Bowles, Max, and Cliff were in a similar breathless uncertain embrace on the screen.

Roger leaned forward, brushing his cheek against Buck's beard. He next brushed his lips across Guy's goatee. Coming up, he kissed Buck on the mouth, followed by a kiss for Guy. To Guy's surprise, Buck nuzzled Roger's nose and cheek, then moved down to kiss Guy. Roger followed his lead. Buck adjusted his head to make room for the three-way kiss. It was deep and long and passionate all around.

Locked in the kiss, Guy felt Buck unbuckling his pants and was aware of Roger's hand squeezing his tight crotch. *Where the hell did this come from?* he wondered, even as he began to imagine the possibilities.

Friday, March 30th

"When were you going to tell me your movie was opening next month in Japan, girl?" Mark Sparks asked his dear, close college friend Sarah over the phone.

Sarah was still jetlagged, having returned from Tokyo the night before. "I didn't know it was. They were talking November when I left, maybe even next year."

"I got a press release this morning. I'll show it to you if you'll have lunch and give me an exclusive."

Sarah laughed. "Mark, it's just a dinky little made-on-a-shoestring independent. No one here's even gonna see it."

"Someone hasn't read their *Variety*. Tochigi Films was bought by Time-Warner which owns Fine Line Features, girl. And Fine Line's slated it for limited late summer release —" he had to hold the phone away from his ear as Sarah screamed on the other end. When she was done, Mark asked, "I take it that's a yes?"

"Yes! No, wait! I don't know. Maybe I should wait and see who else . . . or get an agent first?"

"C'mon, girl, we started out together, you're my sistah!" He glanced around his senior reporter's cubicle for something to sweeten the deal. "Tell you what, make it noon at Newsroom and I'll bring you something really special."

"Oh, what the hell am I gonna do with that?" Sarah laughed on this beautiful day as Mark pulled the gleaming foil-wrapped statue out of his satchel.

"Tom Hanks himself gave it to me backstage at the Institute Awards last week," he informed her proudly. "Part of his very own swag bag." Off her duly impressed expression, he nodded, adding, "Yeah. We're tight. But you take it," he said sliding it across the table toward her. "It's chocolate, and I'm shooting for 7% body fat."

"Well, I'd like to thank the Institute," she said obligingly for his sake. "And *E! Entertainment* and especially Fine Line." But as she spoke she was pleased to realize she never really needed an Arthur. In fact, if somehow Mark Sparks had handed her the very one she had lost a year ago, she wouldn't care. She already carried her Institute Award where it counted — in her rapidly expanding ego. She put her gift aside to get down to delightful business. "Now, child, start telling me just how famous I'm gonna be!"

Saturday, March 31st

"I used to be in control all the time," Guy told Patrick over lattes at their neighborhood Starbucks. "Now it's like something inside let go and all this amazing stuff has been coming my way like tidal wave after tidal wave. I have no clue what's coming next. And you know what? It's great. I'm confused, I don't know what to think, and it's just fine!"

"Stop it right there," Patrick said, only then recovering from Guy's earlier statement. "Back up. You're having a three-way with another man, and a man who used to be a woman?"

"Parts of him still are," Guy grinned. Patrick made a face and Guy laughed out loud. "Believe me, I never saw any of this coming. It just happened."

"You selfish bastard. You go from having no one, to having two people?" Patrick narrowed his eyes to slits. "And for the record, exactly who sticks what where?"

"We stick whatever we want wherever it feels good," Guy answered pointedly, nipping that line of inquiry in the bud. Chastened, Patrick pouted, crossing his arms. "Don't be jealous, Patrick. You were the one who told me this was my journey."

"I just never thought your journey would be so heavily populated."

"Neither did I. So I want to know more about that Grail story, about that movie you did."

Patrick sat up straight. "Oh, my God, how did you know about that?"

"About what?"

"My movie. It's opening this summer."

Guy gasped in excitement. "I didn't know! Congratulations!"

"I just found out this morning. Sarah came over to the mortuary, told me all about it. Even gave me an Arthur for helping her make it. Tom Hanks gave it to her or something. But I'm going to be in limited release!"

Guy hugged his best friend. "That's great, Patrick, I'm so happy for you. But I'm not waiting until opening day to understand this Grail thing. So could you explain it?"

"Oh, really!" Patrick said archly. "I thought the Grail was a 'bunch of New Age crap.' But now you want to know? Why now?"

Guy sighed. "I wish I could tell you. There's just something in it that feels, I don't know, important, like I need to know it. It was important enough that Sarah made a movie about it, and I still don't get it."

Patrick looked at Guy with affection. It couldn't be explained, only understood. Nevertheless, he said, "It all boils down to the question 'Whom does the Grail serve?'"

"Okay. And what's the answer?"

"The answer is, 'The Grail serves the Grail King.'"

Guy considered that for a moment. "And where do I find this Grail King?"

Patrick gave him a sad smile. "He's closer than you think." He stood to leave. "Sorry, sweetie, but I need to get back to work. I have a bad feeling about things there."

Monday, April 2nd

After having worked both Saturday and Sunday, Patrick felt he could afford to arrive at O'Leary & Finkelstein's this morning a few minutes late. As soon as he entered the front door to find Lee waiting for him, he knew something was very, very wrong.

"It's the partners," she told him. "They're in your office." She gently took the bag holding his banana-nut muffin from him. "They want to see you."

The day had come. He felt a need to vomit. "Do I have time to go to the —?"

Lee shook her head sadly. "They want to see you now."

Patrick swallowed hard and walked to his office. He paused to smooth his pants and tie, and give his jacket a final tug. He took a deep breath. He stood tall.

He pulled the office door open and entered.

STEALING ARTHUR

Saturday, April 7th

Buck stepped into the office to kiss Roger goodbye. "Home by seven, I think."

"Grilled salmon sound okay?" Roger said, engrossed in his eBay postings.

"Sounds great," Buck called back, already halfway down the hall. He found Guy in the kitchen sorting this morning's early yard sale finds. "Scrape the grill, darlin'," Buck said, kissing him, "the boy's making salmon for us tonight."

"You got it, babe."

"Wanna invite Patrick?"

Guy shook his head. "I haven't heard from him in almost a week. Must be working like crazy."

After Buck had left and Guy had lined up the items he wanted Roger to process, Guy made himself a cup of Caffè Verona to cap off a perfect morning with his perfect little family. So many transitions, he thought, so many unexpected events. But since they had led to this, he was content — just so long as there weren't any more changes to deal with right at the moment.

The doorbell rang. When he opened the door, there was Patrick in highly unprofessional jeans and T-shirt. Shockingly, his head was completely shaved.

"Oh, shit," Guy said, staring open-mouthed. "What happened?"

"I got fired."

"Oh, my God. Come inside. Are you all right?"

"I can't come inside," Patrick said. "If I do, I'll break down and right now all I want is to get out of this town."

"How could they fire you?"

"Technically they bought me out. Finkelstein's son, the accountant? He dug up all those free funerals I gave. You know, to the guys who died of AIDS? Over the years it added up. Caskets, preparation, crematory services, yada-yada-yada. Turns out I gave, or in their words, stole over $875,000 from the company. So, in exchange for not pressing charges, I would allow them to purchase my half of the company for about thirty-five percent of what it's worth."

Guy wanted to protest the unfairness, the injustice, to argue for working something out, but there was a bigger fear that lurched in his gut. "So, what are you doing now? And please tell me you're just going on vacation."

"No, Guy," Patrick said quietly, emotion beginning to creep in at the edges of his resolve. "I'm leaving L.A. I've put everything in storage, given up my lease. Gave all my suits away. That's why I just couldn't return your calls."

"Oh, Patrick," Guy whispered. "I'm so sorry."

Patrick managed a kind of smile. "I'm not. It's funny. I'm terrified, and I don't know what I'm going to do, and I've got next to nothing, and it feels wonderful. I'm free, Guy. I never wanted that fucking house of death. I should have gotten out years ago but I was afraid of what my father would think. And the joke is the bastard's been dead almost a decade."

Guy was already mourning his friend. "When are you leaving?"

"Now. Right now. If I stay any longer I might not be able to do it."

"Where are you going?"

"I have no idea. But I feel like I'll know when I get there." Unable to hold it back any longer, he grimaced and then began to cry. "I love you, Guy."

Guy stepped forward to hug him. "I love you, too, Patrick." They held each other tightly for several minutes, taking turns sobbing now and then. "God, I'll miss you."

Patrick pulled away enough to look at his friend. "Well, I got you something to remember me by. Hang on." He went to his car in the driveway and reached inside for an item on the front seat. The car was packed with clothes and boxes. Wiping his eyes, Patrick returned. "This is for you." He gave Guy an 8x10 mirror with an ornate frame. Etched into the glass near the top of the mirror was a crown, like a beer ad.

"Well, it's a bit much for a tiara," Guy said, laughing through his tears, "but it's good enough for this queen." He hugged Patrick one last time and watched him get into his car and drive away.

Guy went back into the house. This time it was Roger's turn to hold Guy while he wept.

✫

"Wow," Rudy said, looking at Patrick's starkly smooth head. "Sexy!"

"Thanks," Patrick said with a smile. "I've always thought the same about you. Is Eric here?"

"He's out. Out . . . doing errands," Rudy told him. Actually Rudy and Eric had had another argument that morning about getting tested for HIV, and Eric had stormed out, taking the car to drive off his anger and fear. "Want to come in?"

"No, I'm leaving town, but I wanted to give him something before I did." He gave Rudy a heavy paper bag from Gelson's. He watched Rudy pull out the foil-covered Arthur. "It's only chocolate, but it came from this year's awards. It's to replace the one he lost, the one Guy and I gave him when he came to L.A. last year."

"I'll give it to him."

After hugging Rudy, Patrick smiled and started to leave, then turned back. "Oh, I wanted to tell you. Do you remember my dream, the one with the ax and I was stuck in mud like concrete? You said I had to chop off my feet?"

"Not really. Sorry."

"Well, I had it again last night. I looked down, only I had no feet. But it didn't matter, because I was flying. So, you were right."

Rudy struggled for something to say. "I'm sorry. I don't remember."

Patrick gave a happy little shrug. "Oh, well." They hugged again and Patrick walked to his car. He started the engine, and drove far, far away, flying from that City of Angels.

Saturday, June 9th
Two months later

Eric and Rudy drove into Hollywood without speaking. Eric found a space on Schrader, between Sunset and Hollywood and parked the car. They each got out of the Corolla and walked along the east side of the street, neither one saying a word. When they were across from the Jeffrey Goodman Special Care Clinic, they paused.

Eric and Rudy looked at each other. The months of debates, accusations, and anger had worn them down to where they could admit their fear of the virus. In a week they would know for sure.

Eric held out his hand. Rudy took it. Finally, together, they crossed the street.

Monday, June 11th

Housecleaning in the den with the television on, Guy took a moment to check his receding hairline in the mirror Patrick had given him. A mattress ad blared from the TV as he critiqued the newest tiny lines around his eyes, and the increase of gray hairs in his beard. Definitely not getting any younger.

"Climb into my bed!" the mattress storeowner shouted from the television, "I've got over twenty thousand to choose from!"

That was a pickup line if there ever was one. "Climb into my bed!" Guy repeated, smirking to think how ridiculous that would sound at Cuffs or the Faultline. Oh, hell, was that a zit starting on his nose? He looked closer into the mirror.

"Come see the king of mattresses," the announcer said.

"I am the king!" the owner proclaimed, tagging the ad.

"I am the king," Guy repeated unthinkingly. He stopped dead. His jaw dropped as he stared at his reflection in the mirror with the crown on his head. And he got it.

He understood what Patrick's last gift to him was.

"I am the king."

STEALING ARTHUR

Wednesday, June 13th

Dear Guy,

I'm sorry it's been so long, but when I left L.A. I needed to sever all ties. I'm working just outside of Helena, Montana, for two butch dyke lesbians whom I adore. They own the upscale organic garden store here called Helena Handbasket. The gals are great and the place is huge with gardening, landscaping service, a florist, and a gift shop that goes for days. I stopped in to see their amazing year-round Christmas section and never left. Unfortunately the only job they had at the time was in the greenhouse. The work is never-ending and I haven't even had time to think about drinking. It takes everything I have just to keep up with all there is to learn and do. But who knew I had a green thumb? I'm now manager of bulbs and perennials. I'm still burying things, only now they come up and bloom!

I'm also seeing one of the junior landscapers named Wally. He actually says things like "howdy" and "shucks" and calls the lesbians "ma'am." Two weeks into the job he made the moves on me in the potting shed. A month later he takes me home to meet his father Will. His father! — who says he thinks I'm "a right good'un." He even wants to take Wally and me camping next week. I'm terrified. Will says he's going to teach me fly-fishing. I feel like Woody Allen trapped in *A River Runs Through It*.

Please give my love to all. I miss you desperately. And I've never felt so alive.

Love,
Patrick

Friday, June 15th

Eric was making his mother's favorite, a tunnel-of-fudge cake, as a birthday surprise. She was scheduled to arrive at LAX at 12:09 the next day and he had plans to take her to high tea at the Beverly Wilshire with Rudy. At home afterward, they'd let her rest up that afternoon for her surprise birthday party that evening. While she napped, he and Rudy had separate appointments at 3:30 to learn the results of their HIV tests.

To keep from thinking about tomorrow, Eric concentrated on making the perfect birthday cake today. He scrutinized the recipe for exact measurements. Oh hell, he needed melted chocolate for the fudge and he'd forgotten to get the Hershey's when they went shopping yesterday. Rudy was out visiting his brother now and wouldn't be back with the car until late. Damn. What could he use?

He glanced around the tiny kitchen. On top of the fridge was the Arthur with "Perugina" on the base. Oh, what the hell, he thought taking it down. Made with such fine chocolate, this would make a nice surprise even better.

He peeled back the gold foil.

The End

Acknowledgments

Special thanks to the guys at *Instinct* magazine who let me serialize the earliest incarnation of this story over eleven issues back in the early days — especially to publisher J.R. Pratts and senior editor Parker Ray for saying yes when I thought I was crazy for even pitching it.

Deep gratitude goes to those who so generously contributed their special knowledge, expertise, and loving support to this project: James Bowling, Rosie Reeves, Jim Zangara, Jeffery Jones, Harold, Trevor, and Mickey.

Super-big burly bear hugs to those who read early drafts and gave me invaluable feedback: Matthew Alexander, Robert L. Goodman, and Bryan Burch.

And finally, I thank everyone who ever told me a story.

About the Author

Joel Perry is the author of *Funny That Way; That's Why They're in Cages, People!; Going Down: The Instinct Guide to Oral Sex;* and *The Q Guide to Oscar Parties and Other Award Shows.* He grew up hairy, heavy, and homo in North Carolina. He has been an actor, writer, comedian, producer, and spiritual director. After twenty-eight years in Los Angeles, Joel has returned to his hometown of Wilmington, N.C., where he lives with his husband and two cats that are so adorably cute you just want to vomit.

Bear Bones Books
An imprint of Lethe Press

NOVELS
BearCity: The Novel, novelization by Lawrence Ferber,
based on the screenplay by Doug Langway & Lawrence Ferber
Bear Like Me, by Jonathan Cohen
Cub, by Jeff Mann
Fog, by Jeff Mann
The House of Wolves, by Robert B. McDiarmid
The Limits of Pleasure, by Daniel M. Jaffe
Purgatory, by Jeff Mann
Salvation, by Jeff Mann
Stealing Arthur, by Joel Perry
To See What He Could See, by Michael Thomas Ford
Woof, by Dylan Thomas Good

SHORT FICTION COLLECTIONS
A History of Barbed Wire, by Jeff Mann
Night Duty, and Other Stories, written and illustrated by Nicolas Mann
Spring of the Stag God, by J.C. Herneson, illustrated by Kupopo
Summer of the Stag God, by J.C. Herneson, illustrated by Kiyoshi Nohara and Fedini
Waking Up Bear, and Other Stories, by Jay Neal

FICTION AND POETRY COLLECTIONS
Bear Lust: Hot & Hairy Fiction, edited by R. Jackson
Bearotica: Hot & Hairy Fiction, edited by R. Jackson
Bears in the Wild: Hot & Hairy Fiction, edited by R. Jackson
The Bears of Winter: Hot & Hairy Fiction, edited by Jerry L. Wheeler
Hibernation, and Other Poems by Bear Bards, edited by Ron J. Suresha
Tales from the Den: Wild & Weird Stories for Bears, edited by R. Jackson

NONFICTION
Bears on Bears: Interviews & Discussions, revised edition, by Ron J. Suresha
Binding the God: Ursine Essays from the Mountain South, by Jeff Mann
Edge: Travels of an Appalachian Leather Bear, by Jeff Mann

CPSIA information can be obtained at www.ICGtesting.com
Printed in the USA
BVOW07s1630110115
382682BV00001B/6/P